LANDS BEYOND THE SEA

About the author

Tamara McKinley was born in Australia and
returns there every year to do her research for
her novels, which are coloured with the red,
green and gold of her beloved homeland.

www.tamaramckinley.co.uk

TAMARA McKINLEY

Lands Beyond the Sea

HODDER

Copyright © 2007 by Tamara McKinley

First published in Great Britain in 2007 by Hodder & Stoughton
A division of Hodder Headline

This paperback edition published in 2007

The right of Tamara McKinley to be identified as the
Author of the Work has been asserted by her in accordance
with the Copyright, Designs and Patents Act 1988.

A Hodder paperback

1

A CIP catalogue record for this title is available from the British Library

ISBN 978 0 340 92467 9

Typeset in Plantin Light by Hewer Text UK Ltd, Edinburgh
Printed and bound by Clays Ltd, St Ives plc

Hodder Headline's policy is to use papers that are natural, renewable
and recyclable products and made from wood grown in sustainable forests.
The logging and manufacturing processes are expected to conform
to the environmental regulations of the country of origin.

Hodder & Stoughton Ltd
A division of Hodder Headline
338 Euston Road
London NW1 3BH

For Eric John Ivory,
in loving memory of a man I called Father.

ACKNOWLEDGEMENTS

This book would not have been possible without the help, support and advice from the many people who were generous enough to share their expertise with me.

Wilfred Gordon is a Nugalwarra Traditional owner and Elder who took me on an amazing journey into the North Queensland bush and shared his knowledge of Dreamtime traditions, bush tucker and the history of his own family. His friendly company and the stories he told were an inspiration, and I pray that his work with the younger generations of his people flourishes, for without men like him, the Aboriginal youth of Australia will remain anchorless. Dr Andrew Griffiths, MA MD FRCP, for his vast knowledge of hereditary skin markings and much more besides. I also give my thanks to his wife, Elizabeth, for the good company and wonderful dinner.

To Ashley and Debbie at the Panorama Hotel in West Looe, who led me to Mousehole. Thank you for your superb hospitality and a friendship that I'm sure will endure.

To the team at Hodder, especially Sara Kinsella, whose enthusiasm and belief in this story has made it all happen. Thank you for your endless good humour and support.

Heartfelt thanks also go to my agent, Teresa Chris, who never stopped believing in me even when the going got rough.

And last but never least, I thank Tina, Val and Ann, for their friendship and girly lunches, which are always so important after emerging bleary-eyed from my office.

Past land bridges

▓ Pleistocene landmass 30,000 years ago

☐ Present landmass

scale in nautical miles
400   800   1200

TIMELINE

1500–1700 Indonesian Trepang fishermen visit
northern Australia.

1606 Dutchman Willem Jansz explores the
western coast of Cape York Peninsular and
clashes with the natives.

1623 Jan Carstenz has several armed encounters
with Aborigines on the northern coast.

1688 William Dampier becomes the first
Englishman to explore and map parts of
Australia.

August 1768 James Cook and the *Endeavour* depart
England for Tahiti, anchoring in April 1769.

October 1769 Cook anchors in Poverty Bay on the
eastern side of New Zealand's North
Island. The crew have their first contact
with the Maoris, who prove unfriendly.

November 1769 Cook begins to chart North and South
Island, New Zealand, extreme weather
conditions severely hampering progress.

April 1770 Cook leaves New Zealand intending to reach
Van Diemen's Land (Tasmania). Storms
force the *Endeavour* to anchor at Botany Bay.

May–August 1770	The *Endeavour* is seriously damaged whilst trapped on the Great Barrier Reef. Attempted repairs to the *Endeavour* and the search for a safe passage through the reef take place at a shallow river estuary now named Cooktown. It is here that the crew are influenced by the survival techniques of the native Aborigines until a route is discovered to take them back into open water.
July 1771	The *Endeavour* anchors in England following the loss of a number of crew from disease and consumption; men included were Sydney Parkinson and Robert Molyneaux.
1786	The British government choose Botany Bay as a penal colony.
1788	Aborigines watch as Captain Arthur Phillip and the First Fleet (11 ships carrying 778 convicts, 191 marines and 10 officers, both military and civil) arrive in Botany Bay, before sailing on to Port Jackson. Only 717 convicts survive, and following fleets also suffer due to overcrowding, disease and starvation.
	Frenchman La Pérouse and two more ships arrive in Botany Bay.
	Resistance and conflict between the British and French navies and the native Aborigines begins.
1788–89	Smallpox decimates the Aboriginal population of Port Jackson, Botany Bay and

Broken Bay, and spreads inland and along the coast.

1790 Second Fleet of six ships arrive in Port Jackson. 278 convicts dead. Supply ship founders on ice, leaving the colony starving.

1791 Third Fleet of eleven ships arrives in Port Jackson. 2,000 convicts on board, including first Irish Catholic convicts. 194 men and 4 women dead.

The New South Wales Corps is formed by the British government to police the colony.

1791–2 Time-expired convicts are granted land around Parramatta whilst colonist holdings spread rapidly to the areas of Prospect Hill, Kissing Point, Northern Boundary, the Ponds and the Field of Mars.

1798 Aborigines dispossessed of land around Georges River flats and Bankstown.

1799 Two Aboriginal boys are killed by five Hawkesbury settlers who are later pardoned by the Acting Governor King. This incident is indicative of a long period of conflict between the Aborigines and the Western settlers; a period later known as the Black War.

FOREWORD

This is a work of fiction and should not be regarded as anything more, but I have done my best to stick to the historical facts concerning the discovery of Australia and its subsequent history. The fictional characters are witnesses to the painful birth of the Southern Colony, and they move alongside the true pioneers who made Australia what it is today. The Cadwallader and Collinson families are fictional, and any resemblance they may bear to anyone living or dead is purely coincidental.

William Cowdry was the chief gaoler on the hulk *Dunkirk*.

Captain Cook, Joseph Banks, Solander and the young botanic artist Sydney Parkinson are true figures of history. The one-armed cook on board the *Endeavour* existed, and Banks indeed took three greyhounds on board – one of which caught a small wallaby during their sojourn in Cooktown.

Arthur Phillip was the first governor of Australia, and the Reverend Richard Johnson was the first minister.

The horrors of the Second Fleet are well recorded. Donald Trial, master of the *Neptune*, was charged with his chief mate of murder at the Old Bailey in 1792. They were both acquitted.

I travelled among unknown men
In lands beyond the sea.

Wordsworth, 1770–1850

PROLOGUE: VEILS OF MORNING

Kakadu, 50,000 years ago

Her name was Djuwe, she was thirteen and she was beautiful. Djanay watched as she laughed with the other young women, noting the delicate curve of her back and the promise of her buttocks as she strolled away, the reed basket held provocatively against her hip. He'd wanted her from the moment he'd set eyes on her.

As if aware of his scrutiny, Djuwe glanced over her shoulder, her amber gaze meeting his, the challenge unmistakable. With a flash of her eyes and a smile, she turned and was soon lost in the dappled shadows of the trees.

Djanay rolled over in the long grass and stifled a groan of frustration. He could never have her, for such a union would be against their sacred law, their *mardayin*, and to break it meant banishment, even death. So why did she taunt him? He closed his eyes. Because, he knew, she had power over him – and was not afraid to use it.

'Get up, lazy boy.'

A sharp kick in the ribs startled him and he glared up at his half-brother. 'I'm not lazy,' he retorted, clambering hastily to his feet. Malangi was many seasons older, more than twenty years, with silver glinting in his hair, the initiation scars etched deeply in his lean torso. An experienced hunter and respected Elder, he was not a man to cross.

'You sleep in the sun like the old women,' Malangi snapped. 'There's food to be hunted before our journey.'

Djanay nodded, unwilling to meet his gaze; Malangi might

read in his eyes his yearning for his brother's young wife. He strode away, his emotions in turmoil, all too aware of Malangi's stare following him, like a well-aimed spear at his naked back.

The sun was high, the shadows of the surrounding trees reflected in the lagoon. Djanay turned towards the bush and the towering peaks of the red cliffs that plunged towards the snaking river. He began to climb, sweat washing away his longing for the unattainable. He was typical of his clan, tall and slight, ebony flesh imprinted with tribal markings. Naked but for a thin rush belt and a necklace of kangaroo teeth, his eyes were amber, his hair a tangled halo of black curls that fell about his round face. His nose was broad, pierced by the bone of a bird, the lips curved in youthful fullness above the first few wisps of beard. At fourteen he was newly initiated into manhood and was expected to gain the respect his father and brother had earned as hunters.

He swiftly reached the smooth, flat stone that jutted from the face of the cliff and afforded him a magnificent view of the great forests, the thrusting mountains and the glint of water far below.

This was the land given into his clan's care by the Ancestor Spirits. It was sacred, with reminders of the Creation Spirits in every rock and boulder, in each twist of the river and whisper of wind. Like the rest of his clan, Djanay would be its custodian until his bones turned to dust. Mother Earth was provider, comforter and tutor, and it was important he learnt to harmonise with the seasons, and the ebb and flow of the creatures that walked with him, for each depended on the other and their spirituality must be guarded at all cost.

The Kunwinjku people had come to this place when Djanay's Ancestor Spirits lived in the Dreamtime – a time before all man's knowledge, a time when the Spirits had shown themselves and guided the clan into this land of promise.

They had been led by the great Elder Bininuwuy, who had long passed on to live with the Spirit People in the sky, but the journey lived on in the story-telling of the Elders and in the pictures painted on the walls of the cave behind him.

All was silent high on the cliffs, and Djanay could feel the weight of his ancestors' expectations as he flexed his muscles. It was a heavy burden to obey the laws when every fibre of him ached to be with Djuwe. He thought of the girl who'd been promised to him since he was five years old. Aladjingu was of the Ngandyandyi tribe, who lived further to the north-east, and was the daughter of his mother's uncle. They had met only fleetingly, but after the *corroboree* she would become his wife. She didn't set his loins on fire as Djuwe did.

With a sigh he padded into the sacred cave hoping to find solace. It was forbidden for women and uninitiated boys to enter it, but Djanay had gone through the ceremony with honour as the flesh was cut from his manhood and the sharpened stone traced the sacred lines into his chest and arms. He was now familiar with the secret rites performed here, and experienced in the dangers of surviving alone in the great wilderness called Kakadu.

Standing before the ochre wall-paintings, he followed the tale that the Ancient Ones had left behind.

The first picture was of a vast land the Elders called Gondwana. It showed his people living there alongside other tribes, and the bitterly cold white rain that froze the earth and made it difficult to hunt. The second showed Gondwana breaking away, shallow water separating it from a greater mass filled with trees and animals. The third showed the members of many tribes crossing that water in canoes and on foot, and a fourth followed their trek across the broad expanse of land where Djanay now lived.

There had been wars between the tribes with many deaths. Females had been kidnapped, warriors slain; there had also been marriages and alliances as even more tribes made the journey south. Soon the hunting became difficult, communication between the clans almost impossible because of tribal friction and the many different languages and dialects. Eventually they had dispersed to all corners of this vast new land, leaving the Kunwinjku people in charge of Kakadu.

Djanay wondered what lay beyond the hunting grounds he knew so well, but he had accepted that he would never find out. There were unmarked boundary lines – song lines – around the Kunwinjku territory that were crossed by permission of the Elders, which was granted only during a *corroboree*. If he were to go without their leave, he would die.

After he had muttered the time-honoured blessings over the sacred bones of past Elders, he began the long, rocky descent. It was time to hunt.

The ducks had proved easy prey. The delicious aroma of baking goanna and wallaby rose with the smoke of the campfire and his stomach rumbled as he presented the twenty birds to his mother.

'You did well, Djanay.' Garnday's face wrinkled into a grin as she settled the suckling baby more firmly in the crook of her arm.

Djanay squared his shoulders and tried not to look too pleased at her praise, but he couldn't resist a swift glance at Djuwe to see if she had noticed his cleverness.

She was bent over the berries she was preparing, but her sidelong peep through her hair told him she was aware of him.

'Your father waits for you,' muttered Garnday, her gaze keen. 'You would do well to hurry.'

Djanay realised he must be careful: his mother's eyes missed nothing. He joined the other initiated boys at a respectful distance from the Elders, who were lounging beneath the trees with the usual collection of dogs. The yellow-coated *dalkans* provided warmth in winter, food in times of famine, and guarded them against danger; although far from tame, they seemed to have an affinity with the men of the bush.

Djanay's father sat cross-legged with the other Elders, his grey hair and wizened features testament to his great age and wisdom. Djanay still felt awkward in the presence of such worthy men. Without them, there would be no initiation ceremonies, no telling of the Dreamtime and no cohesion in the lives of the spiritual and law-abiding Kunwinjku.

He scanned the encampment and felt content. The women and girls were chattering like birds as they cooked the evening feast and shooed away the inquisitive dogs. Babies clung to their mothers' breasts, and some of the small children played on the ground with a captured lizard. His mouth twitched with amusement. His mother was giving orders as usual, even though she was only a second wife and therefore in no position to do so.

He looked at his father's first wife, the mother of Malangi. She was old, frail and wrinkled. Soon it would be her time to hear the singing of the Spirit People and follow them to the stars. Perhaps Garnday sensed this and was testing her authority. She should do it with subtlety, he thought, for the senior wife was respected and wielded great influence over their husband.

Garnday's mind was working furiously on what she should do about Djanay. He was foolish to have such hot eyes for Djuwe, and sooner or later blood would be spilt: Malangi was a jealous husband. Djanay was a man now, and expected to abide by the *mardayin*. She'd been so proud of him, and had had such high expectations of this most beloved of sons, for his imminent marriage to Aladjingu would bring him closer to the ruling Elders. One day, if all went well, she hoped to see him as leader of their tribe – Malangi was already thirty-five and would be long dead when Djanay came of age. Now her ambitions were turning to dust – and it was all the fault of Djuwe, the interloper, the bearer of troubles.

Her eyes narrowed as she watched the girl. Djuwe had been promised to Malangi from babyhood. She was the daughter of an Iwadja Elder, and although the age difference was great, that wasn't unusual. The alliance between the two tribes was important, for they shared hunting grounds and stood shoulder to shoulder when invading tribes attacked.

Garnday suddenly saw that the old woman was watching her and, with a shiver of foreboding, knew that Djanay was in grave danger. It was only a matter of time before he took the girl into the bush, and the old woman would be swift to punish him. Despite her great age, she too had ambitions, and wanted to see Malangi lead the tribe.

The two women glared at each other. There was little love lost between them, and Garnday knew that her own youth and capacity to give their husband many living sons was resented. Yet, as the junior wife, she had to show respect, had to learn the older woman's special secrets for survival, bow to her wishes and care for her in old age. She squared her shoulders, swept back the cloud of dark hair in a gesture of defiance and hurried back to the fire.

Djuwe had been with them for ten full moons, and still showed no sign of being with child. Garnday eyed her with loathing. She suspected she'd been eating the mixture of leaves and berries that would purge her of new life.

All the women did it because it was impossible to suckle more than one child and remain a useful member of the clan. Should a woman give life to twins, one was slain immediately, for during the dry seasons they often had to take long journeys across arid plains in search of water when only the strong could survive.

'She has no reason to remain childless,' she muttered,

'unless she's barren – and I doubt that.' She saw the girl shoot a provocative glance at Djanay. 'No – she has another motive.'

The ritual of the evening meal brought her back to the present and the division of the food. The men and initiated boys were served first with the choicest meat. The young women fed their children and then themselves, leaving the elderly to hunt among the ashes for the remnants. This custom did not show lack of respect: soon the aged would be sung to the Land of the Spirits, the food wasted on them. It was better to feed the hunters and gatherers, then give strength to the next generation.

As Garnday ate the sizzling meat, she watched Djuwe surreptitiously. The girl was laughing with the other young women, lips glowing with the grease of the birds, eyes darting repeatedly to Djanay. She was beautiful, she admitted grudgingly, but Malangi was already suspicious, watching her every move. Trouble was imminent, unless Garnday could prevent it.

The meal was finally over. The fire was stoked to give light, warmth and keep predators at bay, and the story-teller's soft voice related the Dreamtime legend of why the owl hunted at night. Families lay together beneath the pelts of wallaby and wombat on the soft red earth, and soon the encampment was silent but for snores or the occasional whimper of a restless baby.

Garnday nestled into the curve of her husband's bony body, the two little boys and her baby snuggled against her belly, the dogs curled close by. The older woman huddled at their husband's back, her arm snaking across his waist as if to underline her claim of seniority.

Garnday knew she wouldn't sleep easily tonight. Djanay was with the other unmarried boys on the far side of the camp, and although she could see his prone figure in the firelight, she could tell he was not yet asleep. Malangi and his three wives lay some distance away, and Garnday noted how Djuwe had placed herself on the outer perimeter of the tangle of women and children around him. There was a stillness in the air that boded ill and made Garnday's heart beat faster. She lay watchful and tense as the moon-shadows danced beneath the trees.

Djanay's belly was full, but he couldn't sleep. He moved stealthily away into the deeper shadows, for he could no longer bear to see Djuwe lying with her husband, and needed to escape his mother's watchful gaze.

His bare feet made little sound as he headed for the solitude of the riverbank where the water swirled in eddies as it caught on rocks and tumbled over ledges. Djanay squatted on a boulder, still warm from the day's heat, and stared down at his reflection. He saw a man at the peak of his virility, yet he'd never been with a woman. Tribal law forbade it until marriage. He knew Djuwe could never be his, yet the excitement she promised made it impossible for him to think straight. He dipped his hands into the water and drank deeply, hoping the *wanjina*, the water spirit, would help him.

The whisper came out of the darkness: 'Djanay?'

Startled, he looked up. His determination fled.

He rose to his feet, entranced by the way the moonlight played over her beautiful body. The touch of her hand sent fire through him and he followed her wordlessly into the bush.

They stood facing each other, their breath the only sound between them. Djuwe's fingers traced a line of heat from his temple to his lips, then down his chest to his belly and beyond. She smiled up at him through her lashes, the dimple appearing fleetingly as she moved closer and whispered, 'At last.'

Djanay could hardly breathe. Tentatively he touched her breasts, marvelling at how they filled the palms of his hands, at how the dark nipples stiffened as he ran his thumbs over them.

Djuwe's hand moved over his belly and down to the aching, throbbing pulse of his manhood. 'Quick!' she gasped. 'Before we're discovered.'

At last he gave vent to the pent-up desire he'd held back since the first moment he'd seen her.

Spent, they lay on the ground, limbs entwined, sweat slicking their skin as they waited for their breathing to steady. But the forbidden fruit had been tasted and as their hands explored one another again, the need returned ever more urgently.

They were so engrossed in their love-making they didn't notice the silent, watchful figure that eventually moved away and was lost among the shadows.

It was not yet dawn, and Garnday's eyes were heavy as she suckled the baby and sent the two other boys to fetch wood. Her husband still slept, but the old woman was already stirring the embers of the fire. Garnday yawned and scratched her head, picking out the ticks and lice with practised skill, then pinching them dead. She'd managed to stay awake long enough to hear the old woman's snores, but when she'd woken at dead of night, a glance had told her she was too late to prevent the inevitable.

Her only solace was that the old woman had remained asleep, and Malangi had snored on, oblivious to his youngest wife's adultery. Garnday knew she had to talk to her son before someone noticed what was happening. He had to grasp the danger he was in – she would speak to him when the rest of the clan was occupied elsewhere.

She squatted by the fire, picked up the smooth pounding stone, and began the tedious process of grinding seeds and herbs into flour, which she mixed with water and kneaded into patties to cook in the embers. This unleavened bread was a staple of their diet, and they would eat it with meat and fish before sunrise, and again at nightfall, if they'd been blessed with good hunting.

Djuwe approached the fire with a rush basket of freshly caught fish, which she let slide into a silvery shoal beside Garnday. 'I am a good fisher,' she said. 'I catch big fish.'

The triumph in her eyes bordered on insolence, her words double-edged, and Garnday's palm itched to slap the pert face. She bit the inside of her lip and remained silent as she wrapped each fish in leaves and herbs and set them beside the baking bread. She would bide her time but, sooner or later, Djuwe would know the strength of her anger.

Not that she blamed the girl entirely. Djanay was foolish, headstrong and weak – but, then, he was a man and couldn't help it. For all their hunting prowess and boastful talk, men could not survive without women: they had their needs, and therein lay their weakness.

The sun had only just breached the horizon and the night chill still glittered in the long grass. There was an air of excitement as plans were discussed, and as soon as everyone had stuffed their bellies to bursting, the fire was doused and the men gathered up their spears, boomerangs, *woomeras* and shields.

The senior wife began her yearly ritual of collecting emu eggs. To her barked orders, Garnday and the other women carried them carefully to the river. The meat of the *ngurrurdu* was tough and held little goodness, but the unhatched eggs, whose contents had long since evaporated, made excellent water-carriers. A sharpened stone had pierced a neat hole in each, and after the shells were filled, the holes were plugged with wads of knotted grass.

'We have enough,' the old woman declared. 'Share them out. They must not be used except in an emergency,' she rasped. 'There are other sources of water in the desert.'

Hitching the baby on to her hip, Garnday settled eggs and

child more comfortably, leant on her sturdy digging-stick, and waited for the Elders to sing to the Spirits before they began the journey. There had been no chance to speak to Djanay – it would have to wait.

A flock of tiny, brightly coloured birds swooped over the encampment in a great cloud, dipping now and again towards the water before finally settling in the trees. It was a good omen. The birds had returned home – and so would they.

With the necessary songs and rituals over, the Elders stamped their feet, raised their shields and gave a great cry of triumph. It was time to go.

Once the clan had left the long, cool shadows of the cliffs, they entered a land of great contrast. The earth was as red as blood, the trees stunted and wilting, and the heat rippled across the parched ground. Eruptions had formed cavernous gorges and soaring, rocky peaks of red and black; giant anthills stood sentinel as, slowly, the clan travelled south. The sky was the clearest blue, darkened on the horizon by a pillar of grey. This was the Spirit of the Hollow Mountain belching fire and smoke as a warning to trespassers, but Garnday knew they would not cross the angry spirit's land, for their path lay to the south, to the heart of the Dreaming and the sacred mounds of Uluru and Kata Tjuta.

Sweltering days were followed by freezing nights, and the trek south had lasted a complete cycle of the moon before Garnday found an opportunity to speak to her son – Djanay had been avoiding her.

They had reached the searing heart of their great island, and the earth was softer here, lifting as dust as they made their way to the traditional campsite. Scattered around them lay enormous boulders, each as round and smooth as an egg. This was Karlwekarlwe, and these were the eggs of the Rainbow Serpent, left here during the Dreamtime.

It was a sacred place with a special aura that kept voices hushed and children close to their mothers, for evil spirits lived among the eggs. They took the form of humans who lured away children. The lost children were never seen again unless the special songs were sung – and sometimes even they didn't work, for once the spirits had taken the little ones, they were loath to give them up.

Garnday joined in as the women chanted to the Rainbow Serpent. The medicine-woman rattled her magic gourd and the men banged their shields with their spears to chase away any evil spirits. Finally the site was declared safe.

The men had caught a couple of snakes and a big fat lizard during the day's trek, which were thrown on to the fire. Garnday hunted out the broad fleshy leaves of the plants that grew in the shadows of the Serpent's eggs. The leaves contained water and sap, and when crushed would provide a healing balm for insect bites, cuts and grazes. But she had a far more pressing reason to leave the fire: she had seen Djanay wander into the darkness.

'We must speak,' she began.

'I have nothing to say to you,' he retorted. 'Leave me alone.'

'I have eyes,' she snapped, her voice low, for others might be listening. 'I know what you and Djuwe are doing.'

He wouldn't meet her gaze. 'You know nothing,' he muttered.

She grabbed his chin, forcing him to look at her. 'I know,' she said, 'and it must stop. Now. Malangi is watching her, and he will kill you both.'

He looked down at her. 'Tend your children, Mother. I am a man now.'

He was about to turn away but she grasped his arm. 'As a man you know the penalties for breaking the sacred *mardayin*. Djuwe brings only trouble.'

Djanay's thoughts were unreadable. He pulled free of her and in two strides was lost in the darkness.

Garnday's lip trembled and she felt the rush of tears. Angrily she brushed them away, gathered up the precious leaves and looked back to the glow of the fire. Her son was lost to her. 'What to do?' she moaned. She closed her eyes and prayed to the Rainbow Serpent for help, but in her heart she knew that even that Great Spirit couldn't fight her son's lust, or the wiles of a wanton girl.

Once the evening meal was over and the ritual story finished, Garnday settled her children close to her husband. Her heart was heavy, and she knew she would sleep little tonight despite her weariness, for Djuwe was again on the perimeter of her family group, and Djanay's excitement was almost tangible. She pulled the kangaroo pelt over her sleeping children and encouraged the *dalkans* to share their warmth. Satisfied that they were safe, she slipped into the darkness.

The spring moon was almost a third of the way on her night's journey when Djuwe sat up and shed the animal pelt.

Garnday tensed, her gaze flying to Djanay. He feigned sleep, but she could see the gleam of the dying fire in his half-open eyes.

With a glance at her sleeping husband, Djuwe stretched and yawned. Carefully disentangling herself from the group, she padded softly into the scrub.

Garnday froze.

Malangi was sitting up, watching his wife.

Garnday glanced across at Djanay, her heart drumming. He still feigned sleep.

Malangi pulled the kangaroo skin over his shoulders, his expression grim as he glared at Djanay, then beyond the circle of fire.

Garnday held her breath.

Djanay was stirring, easing back the wombat pelt, rising on an elbow, poised to follow the girl.

Malangi stiffened, alert to the movement.

Garnday wanted to cry out, to warn him, but Djanay's fate was no longer in her hands.

Malangi's hard stare settled on his brother and, as if he was aware of it, Djanay froze.

For endless moments he remained propped on his elbow. Then he shifted as if trying to find a more comfortable spot, and rolled back beneath the pelt.

Garnday breathed a sigh of relief, but her heart was pounding and her mouth was dry. That had been too close. She moved silently from her watching place. She had to find the girl and make her understand how dangerous it was now that Malangi's suspicions had been roused.

The eggs were eerie silhouettes against the night sky. Their size and majesty almost unnerved her as she crept along the ancient, star-lit tracks. Her pulse was racing and when a lizard skittered from beneath her feet, she had to stifle a cry of alarm.

A soft noise that had no place in the night sounds made her falter. She stopped and listened, but it didn't come again. She shook her head, steeling herself to move on, but the tension was so great that every sigh of the wind made her flinch.

She rounded the voluptuous curve of a giant egg and froze.

'Go away,' hissed the senior wife. 'This is not for you to witness.'

Garnday stumbled past the sacred rock and approached the crumpled figure on the ground. 'What have you done?' she whispered.

The old woman weighed the heavy rock in her hand as she looked down at Djuwe. There was surprisingly little blood, considering the gaping hole in the girl's skull. 'She broke the law,' she said. 'She had to be punished.'

Garnday looked at the body with horrified fascination. Her

stomach churned and her mouth tasted bitter, but somehow she mastered herself. 'It's for the husband to punish,' she breathed.

The other woman tucked the rock into the pouch of wallaby pelts at her waist. 'Help me get rid of her.'

Garnday took a step backwards. The killing of another of the tribe was against the law – and to do such a thing on sacred ground would anger the Spirits and bring their wrath upon them all. This was the work of a mad woman and she wanted no part of it.

The senior wife's clawed hand fastened round her arm. Her breath was foul when she leant close. 'She broke the law with your son. She brought disgrace to my son and to our family. Better she is removed before the Elders hear of it. Better for you if you do as I say.'

There was no mistaking the menace, but Garnday was more afraid of the Spirits. 'But what you've done is worse,' she hissed back. She tried to release the vice-like grip on her arm, but the old woman was surprisingly strong. 'Why didn't you leave her to Malangi? He knew that something was happening between them. He has been watching her all night and is probably on his way to find her now.'

'Then we must hurry.' The old woman released her. 'We are the mothers of sons,' she murmured. 'It is our duty to defend their honour – no matter what they do.' Her wrinkled face and faded eyes were a death-mask. 'Your son is to be married soon and you have others to follow him. I have only one and he is destined to lead the tribe. This girl would have destroyed all of it. Will you help me?'

It was not a request. There was no escape. 'But where can we hide her?'

'I know a place. Come quickly.'

Garnday grabbed the girl's feet as the older woman took the arms and led the way. Garnday realised she had special

knowledge of this sacred place, for a deep fissure in the rock
led to a secret, narrow cavern.

'Hurry!' hissed the old woman, as Garnday hesitated. 'My
work isn't finished. We have little time.'

Garnday obeyed, and soon they were carrying their burden
down a long tunnel. The echoes of their breathing sang in the
walls, and she thought she could feel the eyes of the evil spirits
watching her as they went further into the cave.

'This is far enough.'

The darkness was complete. Garnday dropped her burden
and took a hesitant step back. Her nerve was at breaking-
point, the walls of the cave closing in.

The old woman's voice echoed in the blackness. 'There's a
deep hole here.' Her bony hand clutched Garnday's arm,
pulling her forward until her toes were at the edge of the
unseen abyss.

Garnday trembled at the danger, but she knew she had to
obey if she was ever to leave this terrible place.

On the older woman's command they swung Djuwe out
into the void, and listened as her body thudded, like ripened
fruit, against unseen walls, loosening rocks and pebbles. There
was something obscene about that screamless drop, and the
time it took for the corpse to hit the bottom.

The old woman threw the heavy rock after her. 'There,' she
muttered. 'It's done.'

Garnday raced back down the tunnel. She scrambled into
the cave and, heedless of the cuts and scrapes of the sharp
stones and clinging, spiky plants, shoved her way through
the fissure and out into the open. Slithering down the steep
curve of the egg, she fell to the ground and clawed gratefully at the soft red earth, gulping in the cold, sweet night
air.

The tumble of pebbles heralded the older woman's descent,
and Garnday heard a sharp intake of breath and a low keen of

pain as she collapsed on the ground beside her. 'What is it?' she demanded. 'Are you hurt?'

She was waved away imperiously. 'It's nothing. Go back to the others.'

Garnday didn't need encouragement. She ran towards the welcoming glimmer of light still coming from the fire and crept beneath the kangaroo skins. As she lay there shivering, she sensed rather than felt the older woman's return. She moved like a shadow. No wonder she'd managed to spy on the lovers.

'She's gone! My baby's gone!' The terrible scream ripped through the silence.

Garnday sprang up, heart pounding, clutching her startled children. Everyone woke, the men rising immediately, spears poised.

The young woman's face was streaked with tears as she tore at her hair. 'She's disappeared. My little girl's been taken by the Spirits.'

'How long ago?'

'When I woke she was gone!' the mother wailed.

Malangi strode into the circle. 'My wife is also gone,' he proclaimed. 'I have been searching for her most of the night.' He glanced at Djanay. 'Perhaps the Spirits have her too.'

Djanay's eyes were wild. 'She's too old for the Spirits,' he blustered. 'They take only children.'

There was a murmur of agreement, broken only by the wail of the bereft mother. 'We're wasting time!' she shrieked. 'We must find them!'

The senior wife pushed her way to the centre of the group. 'Search the stones and the hidden ways,' she ordered. 'If they are not found we will sing to bring them back.'

Garnday looked sharply at her. Surely she wouldn't take a child to cover her evil-doing. And if she had, what had she done with her?

'Come! What are you waiting for, Garnday?'

Garnday watched her hobble away, favouring her right hip. Perhaps that was her punishment from the Spirits for the evil she had brought – injury meant death if she could no longer keep up with the clan.

As the sun rose higher the women gathered into a dancing circle and began to sing. They had to appease the Spirits of Karlwekarlwe if they were to see their lost ones again.

Malangi's face was like stone as he stared into the flames. Djanay's eyes were red, but he had strength enough to hide the extent of his emotion. Garnday turned her attention to the songs. The punishment that the Spirits would mete out to her would be far worse if the child was also lost.

The words they sang were ancient, handed down from mother to daughter since the Dreamtime. One by one the women left the circle and walked among the sacred stones, calling to the Spirits to release the lost ones. All eyes turned in hope as each returned, and the song faltered when she was seen to be alone.

The singing grew more fervent as the sun beat down and there was still no sign of the child or the young wife. Garnday returned to the circle, and watched as the old woman took her turn. She was gone a long time, and a frisson of expectation rippled through the circle. She appeared finally, but her arms were empty. Garnday eyed her with suspicion. She could have sworn she'd seen triumph in her face. But how could that be when she'd returned without the child?

A single trembling wail rent the air.

There was instant silence, and they turned as one towards the sound, hoping beyond hope to hear it again. And there it was, strong, angry and determined.

The mother screamed and raced towards it, the other women following closely. The little girl was lying on a rock shelf, unharmed but hungry and afraid. There were shrieks of joy as the mother snatched her up, and no one thought to look back at the two women who had not joined the stampede.

In that single moment Garnday understood the cunning and strength of the senior wife and knew that she and Djanay were in mortal danger.

The celebrations were joyous, but necessarily short, for all were sharply aware that the Spirits had not returned Djuwe. The rituals must be held immediately if her spirit was to be set free into the Great Beyond.

Garnday hugged her children as she watched Malangi smear his body with cold ashes from the fire, and begin the long, repetitive song for the dead. What were his thoughts? She couldn't tell. Usually the widower would mourn for twelve moons, leaving his wives and children in the care of relatives while he roamed the land, but because of the *corroboree*, Malangi's solitary expedition would be postponed.

Garnday slipped away to look for Djanay. She found him eventually in the lengthening shadows.

'Why did they take her?'

Garnday knew she must reply with wisdom. 'She angered the Spirits.'

He nodded as he stared out on to the plains. 'Then they should have taken me too, not the child.'

She squatted at his feet. 'They chose to return the little one,' she said quietly. 'It is not for us to question their reasons but to give thanks for their timely warning.'

There was a long silence as Djanay absorbed her words. 'You tried to warn me, but I was too proud to listen. Now Djuwe is lost.' He turned to her and she saw the terrible fear in his eyes. 'We broke the sacred *mardayin* – what will happen to me?'

'There will be punishment,' she said carefully, 'but it seems that the Spirits have been appeased for now.'

He looked over her head towards the singing. 'What shall I do, Mother?'

There were many dangers and too many secrets: Garnday had to choose her words wisely. 'You will forget Djuwe,' she said, with a firmness that belied her own fear. 'Mourn her with the rest of us and continue the trek to Uluru and your marriage ceremony.'

'How can I, knowing the terrible punishment the Spirits have forced on Djuwe?'

'Because you are a man with responsibility to your family, your clan and your intended wife. The Spirits will be watching you, Djanay. You must tread carefully for they have been angered.'

'They're watching me?' He glanced around fearfully.

Garnday pressed her point: 'Always. That is why you and Aladjingu must not return to the Kunwinjku people once you are married,' she said. Ignoring his gasp of horror, she hurried on: 'You must travel towards the north wind and make your place with the Ngandyandyi. They are related to Aladjingu's mother's uncle and you will be welcomed.'

'But my place is with the Kunwinjku,' he said. 'I am a son of the clan leader, and destined for the Council of Elders.'

'The Spirits are vengeful,' she told him. 'But they are also just. If you accept the banishment, and the loss of your true place among our people, they will be satisfied.'

Djanay was silent, and Garnday could see the nervous energy within him in the way he paced, fidgeted and gnawed his thumbnail. When he turned to face her, he looked defeated. 'Then I have no choice.'

She shook her head.

His shoulders slumped. 'I listen to your wisdom, Mother.'

He bowed his head, and she was tempted to reach out and touch the wild black curls, yet she knew he was past the age for a mother's caress, needing only her strength to get him through this time. At least she had guaranteed his safety from the vengeful Malangi and his witch of a mother – for he would pose no threat once he'd left the clan.

After ten journeys of the Sun Goddess across the sky they reached their destination. The ancient mound of Uluru rose majestically out of the surrounding forests, its curves, folds and pitted sides shadowed in the setting sun. An aura of power emanated from the steep red slopes and sprawling grandeur of this most spiritual of places, and the clan watched in awe as the setting sun burnished the ochre-brown to gold and orange, then through deeper, darker shades of red to charcoal. They had returned to their spiritual home and now they must pay their respects to the guardians of Uluru, the Anangu people.

This was the most important *corroboree* of the year, attended by every man, woman and child who could make the long journey. The fires burned as the sun disappeared, and a host of different dialects and languages drifted with the smoke – yet the excitement was shared, and past irritations or enmities were forgotten as they prepared for the ceremonies.

The Kunwinjku set up camp and began to trade spear-heads and stone tools for boomerangs, bull-roarers, ceremonial masks and headdresses. As night drew in, the Elders and initiated boys painted themselves with ochre and clay, and donned the masks and headdresses in readiness for the first ritual, which would be held at the base of Uluru. F/2140962.

Then came a distant, vibrating hum of a dozen or more bull-roarers. The flat, ornate slivers of wood were being whirled through the air on lengths of fine plaited hair. The volume of sound ebbed and flowed, increasing like the noise of a mighty wind at one moment and at the next diminishing into a moan, like the voices of departed spirits. The ceremonies were about to begin.

Garnday watched Djanay stride off, proud t

accepted her wisdom and begun to prepare for his marriage. She turned back to the fire, glancing across at the old woman. The days following Djuwe's death had not been kind to her. The injury to her hip meant she had fallen further and further behind as they had crossed the desert. Garnday had seen the effort it had cost her to continue.

Their eyes locked, and Garnday read the fear in the other woman's and understood it. Malangi's mother knew that the Spirits were calling her, and that her final punishment was at hand. Yet a fierce determination had set her aged mouth in a thin line and the fiery brightness of fear had become a gleam of defiance, for she knew she had power over Garnday and was not yet ready to relinquish it.

The *corroboree* lasted for fifteen journeys of the sun across the sky. With much singing and dancing the ancient rituals were carried out, alliances made, future marriages arranged and great feasts consumed. The story-tellers enthralled their audience with different interpretations of the Dreamtime, and the artists recorded the event on the hallowed walls of Uluru.

The wedding of Djanay and Aladjingu, a union of two powerful tribes, was to be held at midnight on the last night. Aladjingu's people were camped at the proper distance from Djanay's, and just before sunset a huge fire was built. Then the soft, pulsating hum of the bull-roarers sent out their mesmerising call.

As midnight approached, the uncles began to chant the declaration, announcing to the gathering that there was to be a marriage ceremony. The procession started with each member of both tribes carrying a fire-stick. They moved in a line to form a spear-head, and as they came together, the fire-sticks joined and the flames rose high into the clear, still air.

Djanay's nerves were on edge as he and Aladjingu approached their uncles. Malangi was standing to one side, his face grim beneath the white clay and ash of mourning. One word from him would bring the ceremony to a terrible end, and Djanay didn't dare to meet his eye.

'Children,' called the senior uncle. 'The fire is symbolic of the severity of the *mardayin*. You must neither abuse nor make light of the privilege of becoming husband and wife, father and mother. It is the will of the Great Spirit that you honour and respect the bond of marriage. As fire consumes, so will the law of your fathers destroy all who dishonour the marriage bond.'

Djanay trembled as a great shout went up, and hundreds of spears clattered against shields as the fire-sticks were thrown into the flames and everyone danced and sang. The vows he'd taken tonight were a terrible reminder of how close he'd come to feeling the wrath of the Ancestor Spirits. He looked down at Aladjingu, the powerful words of their marriage vows ringing in his ears.

The girl looked back shyly and took his hand. 'Husband,' she murmured, 'together we will travel towards the north wind, and one day you will lead my people wisely, for I have heard the whispers of the Ancestors.'

Djanay realised he had been blessed with a wife who held the same ancient wisdom as his mother. 'Wife,' he replied, 'together we will be strong.'

The great meeting of the tribes was over and they dispersed. The Kunwinjku started their long trek north, but it soon became apparent that the senior wife could no longer match the pace. The clan slowed for her to catch up, and rested indulgently for a day by a water-hole for her to regain her strength. But it was soon agreed she had become an impediment: she leant so heavily on her husband that the pace was a crawl.

On the fourth day, when it was expected that they would leave her behind, Garnday came to her husband's side. 'Let me help you,' she said quietly, taking the old woman's weight on her arm.

But as dusk fell, they had fallen far behind the rest of the clan with little hope of rejoining them. With a sigh, her husband helped Garnday to settle his dying wife on the ground beneath a tree. 'It is the last night,' he said mournfully.

Garnday picked up one of the smaller water-filled emu eggs and presented this last offering to the senior wife, as was the custom. 'We must leave now,' she said quietly. 'I bring you farewell, Kabbarli.'

The old woman accepted the respectful title, 'grandmother', and took the offering, but her eyes were shadowed with death.

Their husband touched the aged forehead. His tears fell into the deep crevices and wrinkles of his face as he bade farewell to the woman he'd married more than thirty years before. Then he turned to walk swiftly after the others. He did not look back.

Garnday leant on her digging-stick, and reflected on the time they had spent together and the things they had done. Then she strode off to assume her rightful place as senior wife.

Djanay and Aladjingu settled in the north-east. The land was lush with grass that encouraged the grazing animals, and trees gave shelter from the heat. Fish could be caught in the sparkling ocean and oysters prised from its depths. It was good hunting country, and as Djanay and his wife watched their family grow and prosper, he accepted that he'd been given another chance.

The strength and wisdom he'd gained from his youthful experiences made him a popular Elder, and when the time came for him to lead the Ngandyandyi, he proved to be one of the wisest. And in the centuries that passed after his death, his legend lived on in the cave paintings that lay hidden in an area that was eventually known as Cooktown.

* * *

When the great drought came once more, Garnday was almost forty, but the Spirits spoke to her in dreams, and she led her depleted tribe in a great trek south to the lush hunting grounds, plentiful rivers and crashing seas of Kamay and Warang and lived in the strict but simple way that hadn't changed since the Dreamtime.

However, as the world grew hungry for new land and riches, the nature of the clan's life was about to die. Kamay would soon be at the heart of the white man's invasion and its name would become notorious throughout the world as Botany Bay.

PART ONE

The Unknown South Land

I

Cornwall, June 1768

Jonathan Cadwallader, Earl of Kernow, suppressed a yawn and tried not to fidget. Luncheon had finished some time ago, and Uncle Josiah seemed determined to talk all afternoon; but the sun was shining, Susan would be waiting for him and he was desperate to be with her.

'Do sit still, Jonathan,' admonished his mother, with a cluck of impatience.

'Leave the boy be, Clarissa,' rumbled Josiah Wimbourne. 'Seventeen's a restless age, and I suspect he wants to escape to the great outdoors, not listen to an old fossil like me expound on the advantages to Britain of winning the Seven Years' War.'

'Seventeen is old enough to mind his manners, brother,' Lady Cadwallader retorted. She snapped open her lace fan to emphasise her displeasure. 'If his father were still alive, he'd be appalled. Jonathan seems to have learnt nothing from his time with you in London.'

Jonathan caught his uncle's eye and suppressed a grin. They both knew this wasn't true, but to distract his mother, Jonathan encouraged his uncle to continue. 'So what are the advantages, Uncle?' he asked, as he took in the customary carelessness of the older man's attire.

Josiah's eyes twinkled as he scratched his head, dislodging the scruffy wig until it settled askew over one ear. He was a bluff man, who spoke as he found, suffered no fools, and cared little for his appearance. At almost forty-five he remained steadfastly unmarried. Not that he didn't like women, he had often explained to his exasperated sister, he just didn't understand them and preferred the sober company of books and scholars.

'Unlike earlier wars, this was a global conflict, fought not only in Europe but in America, India and the Caribbean islands. Britain's victory means that the strategic balance of power lies heavily in her favour.'

Jonathan affectionately eyed the old-fashioned, threadbare frock-coat that strained over the paunch and draped almost to the sturdy calves. 'I know France has lost most of her North American possessions and considerable territory in India to Britain, but what of Spain?'

'We have emerged with unparalleled naval superiority over our old enemies,' rumbled Josiah, as he clasped his hands behind his back and stuck out his stomach. 'Our victory is so complete that we can turn our attention to the Pacific and Spain's claims there.' He rocked back and forth in his buckled shoes, eyes bright with excitement, wig now in danger of falling over his brow. 'The lure of the Great Southland and the riches of India and the South Seas are magnets to explorers, buccaneers and those seeking glory. These are exciting times, my boy.'

Jonathan had only recently turned seventeen, but he had always been infinitely curious about the world in which he lived, an ever-expanding world in this age of exploration and invention. Although he'd spent the past four years in the gloomy halls and dour surroundings of a London school, he was Cornish born, and his formative years in that county had instilled in him a passion for the sea and the desire to climb aboard a great sailing ship and discover what lay beyond the horizon. How he envied those buccaneers – and wished he could join them.

The legend of *Terra Australis Incognita*, and the rumours of an almost uncharted southern continent of staggering riches, had whetted every adventurous schoolboy's appetite since Marco Polo's expedition. Portugal, Holland, Spain, France and England had taken to the sea in search of empire, trade and plunder, but it was the Spanish and Dutch who had begun slowly to establish the existence of such a land. 'According to those who have navigated the western shores, it's an inhospitable place,' he said.

'That opinion was certainly confirmed by the unfortunate English crew of the *Triall*, which was wrecked on the reef off the Monte Bello Islands in 1622. More than sixty years passed before William Dampier set foot in New Holland and survived to write about it.'

Jonathan smiled. 'He wasn't impressed either, so why do I imagine there's adventure to be had in searching for the mysterious New Holland?'

Josiah ignored his sister's look of reproach and spent some moments lighting his clay pipe. His ruddy face was alight with interest: there was nothing he liked better than lively discourse with his beloved nephew. 'Scholars and geographers argue that New Holland lies in the same latitudes as regions renowned for their fertility and mineral wealth. Why should it be any different? Mariners have seen only a small portion of what appears to be a vast continent. Who is to say that that is representative of what lies further inland?'

'The Dutch East India Company wasn't interested in establishing a colony there, despite Jean Purry's advice,' Jonathan reminded him.

Josiah sucked at his pipe until he'd worked up a good fug, and stoically ignored his sister's frantic fan-waving. 'Purry was no explorer,' he said. 'His advice came from intelligent reading of geography and climate. Besides, the East India Company had already colonised South Africa, which is, of course, a useful stopping-point on the trade route to Indonesia and Batavia.'

Jonathan rose from his chair and tugged at his embroidered waistcoat. In his imagination, he was already on the high seas. 'I wish I was free to explore the southern waters.'

'You have responsibilities here,' intoned his mother. There were high spots of colour on her powdered, imperious face that had nothing to do with the artful use of rouge or the fire's heat. 'With your title comes responsibility, Jonathan, and I cannot be expected to carry the burden of the estate any longer.'

It was a familiar argument, but it held little force: the estate was well managed by an efficient manager, Braddock, and a host of others, and despite her willowy figure and delicate features, Clarissa Cadwallader kept her hands firmly on the reins of her household. 'Surely it would be good for me to explore the world outside the estate, Mama?' he said quietly, as he glanced at his pocket watch. Susan would be wondering where he'd got to. 'With education and travel comes maturity, and I'm sure both would enhance my capabilities here.'

Her patrician nose seemed to narrow and the pale eyes lacked warmth as they regarded him. 'Your time in London should have been enough,' she said finally. 'But it appears you still lack the wisdom to understand the constraints of your blood-line.' Her chest rose and fell beneath the froth of lace. 'And the impropriety of consorting with the lower orders.'

Jonathan reddened. His love for Susan Penhalligan was another source of contention between them, and it seemed there was to be no softening in his mother's attitude. He was about to retort when his uncle broke in.

'Dear sister,' he boomed, 'you are too harsh. The boy's young, and has wild oats to sow. His penchant for fisher-girls will wane.' He must have noted her flush of distaste for he hurried on: 'Anyway,' he blustered, 'the estate will come to no harm if the lad is permitted to escape for a while.'

Jonathan's interest was piqued. He'd long suspected his

uncle's flying visit had been prompted by an ulterior motive, and now he knew the older man was up to something.

Clarissa's lips thinned and her severely plucked brows rose beneath the elaborate wig. '*Escape?* Why should he need to escape?'

Josiah shuffled his feet, cleared his throat and dared to look her in the eye once more. 'I have a proposition, my dear,' he began, with a glance at Jonathan. 'Although I cannot offer the excitement and adventure of searching for the elusive Terra Australis, I can promise the opportunity of a lifetime.'

Jonathan tensed, his imagination taking him far from the stifling room and his mother's annoyance.

'You speak in riddles,' she said crossly.

'As a respected astronomer and member of the Royal Society, I have been asked to join the expedition to Tahiti to plot the transit of Venus over the face of the moon. I should like Jonathan to accompany me.'

Jonathan could hardly breathe. Tahiti! And the chance to sail the seas unencumbered by the strictures of life in England would be the fulfilment of all his dreams. He watched his mother's face, willing her to give her consent.

'Is it to be an educational expedition?'

'Certainly,' replied Josiah, refusing to meet her eye.

'Will it be dangerous?'

The tension was almost unbearable, and Jonathan had to perch on the window-seat to still the trembling in his limbs as his uncle explained the nature of the trip. The importance of a lunar eclipse would mean nothing to his mother, but if anyone could persuade her to let him go, Josiah was the man.

'You wish for the boy to gain a mature understanding of his place in the world, Clarissa,' Josiah said. 'As his uncle and guardian, I will see that he comes to no harm.' He tapped out his pipe into the hearth. 'You have permitted me to control his education and care for him over several years. Allow me to continue a little longer and return him to you fit and ready to take up his duties.'

Jonathan could almost read his mother's thoughts. As a young widow, Clarissa had found the raising of a son beyond her. She had handed him to nursemaids until he was old enough to go to Josiah in London, and was so grateful for her brother's help that she found it difficult to refuse him anything. There was also the perceived complication of Jonathan's love for Susan Penhalligan. She was torn between the desire to pass on the running of the estate to her son and the likelihood that time and distance might put an end to a romance she found inappropriate.

Her gaze met Jonathan's across the room. Clarissa Cadwallader had supplied the late earl with an heir, and considered her duty done. She did not love her son: to her, he was merely assurance that the blood-line and title would endure, and that he would take over the vast estate when he'd reached his majority.

Clarissa selected a sweetmeat from the silver tray that sat on the table next to her. With the delicacy of a high-born lady, she nibbled the edges, then dabbed her lips with a napkin before she spoke again. 'I can see the advantages, brother, but the expense of such a journey . . .' The earl's death had revealed his numerous gambling debts from which the estate was only now recovering.

'It will be met by me, sister,' Josiah stated. 'I take it we have your approval?'

Jonathan stood up, his pulse pounding in his ears. He watched his mother select another sweetmeat and nibble it. His impatience was so great that he wanted to stride across the room and snatch it from her, but it seemed that she was aware of her central role in the little drama, and determined to play it for as long as possible.

She finished the confection and nodded. 'But on his return

he is to take full responsibility for the estate and find a suitable wife, who will bring with her a generous dowry.'

Her meaning was all too clear, but Jonathan refused to rise to the bait. He would fight that battle when he returned from this adventure. Susan was his love – his only love – and nothing his mother could say or do would change that.

'That's settled, then.' Josiah gathered Jonathan into a bear-hug that almost squeezed the life out of him.

Jonathan caught sight of his mother over his uncle's sturdy shoulder, but she was intent on the confectionary. 'When do we leave?' he gasped.

'As soon as the Royal Society has settled on a leader for the expedition,' replied Josiah. 'But we must away to London tomorrow to prepare. There is a great deal to do.' He released his nephew and stood back, his expression quizzical yet understanding as he looked into Jonathan's face. 'Go, my boy,' he said quietly. 'We will talk this evening.'

'His sort don't marry the likes of you, and you're a fool to think otherwise.'

Susan Penhalligan left the steep, cobbled lane and began the long climb from Mousehole village, through the tall grass to the top of the cliffs. Her mother's words rang in her ears, and although she tried to ignore them, they wouldn't go away. 'She doesn't understand,' she panted, as she negotiated the steepest part of the track. 'Nobody does. But one day we'll prove them wrong.'

She reached the summit and stood still, allowing the wind to whip her hair from her face and tug at her skirts as she waited for her breathing to slow. There wasn't far to go now, and Jonathan would be waiting. She took a deep, appreciative gulp of the salt-laden air. It was so clean and fresh up here, away from the stink of fish, and she never tired of escaping the cramped cottage and busy quayside to be renewed by the silence and the majesty of the vista before her.

Mousehole lay far below, a cluster of tiny cottages huddled beneath the cliffs, sheltered from the sea by a stone quay and a narrow beach. The fishing-boats rode at anchor in the shallow waters of the harbour, the nets hung out to dry, the lobster-pots stacked and ready for Monday morning. The smoke-house and herring barrels were abandoned on this day of rest but, come morning, the quay would be alive with the cries of the fishermen and women as they struggled to make a living.

Susan pulled the ragged shawl more firmly round her shoulders and tucked the ends into her waistband as she set off, barefoot, across the hills. Her bodice was a little tight, and her skirt only just reached her ankles, but they were her Sunday best and she'd taken special care in washing and mending them. There was little enough money to go round as it was, so a new set of clothing would have to wait, even though at sixteen she had grown out of everything she owned. But it didn't matter. Nothing mattered today, except her meeting with Jonathan.

The cave was their special place, and they had been going there since they were children. It lay at the base of the dark cliffs, out of sight behind tumbled rocks. The only way to reach it was down a treacherously steep slope, but familiarity lent wings to her bare feet as she scrabbled and slid down the little-used path.

Susan paused for a moment to dust off her clothes and bring some order to her hair. There was no sign of Jonathan's horse, so she had time to prepare for his arrival. She picked her way over and round the rocks and pools, then entered the chill darkness of the cave. The tide was out, and wouldn't turn for another hour, so it would be safe.

The cave stretched back into the heart of the cliff, the ceiling as high as that of a church, the walls solid, covered with lichen and stained the dark red and ochre of the minerals mined around Newlyn and Mousehole. Susan lit the candle she'd brought with her and fixed it in a pool of wax to a handy ledge, then settled down to wait.

Pulse racing, Jonathan hobbled the horse and slithered down the cliff path towards the cave. There she was, her slender figure silhouetted against the darkness of the cave, fair hair framing her heart-shaped face and spilling over her shoulders to tumble almost to her narrow waist. How beautiful she was.

'I thought I'd never get away,' he said breathlessly, 'but I have so much to tell you, I hardly know where to start.'

'Then it will do little harm to keep it to yourself for a while,' she murmured, as she looked up at him and smiled. 'You haven't kissed me yet.'

He took her hands and gazed into eyes that seemed to encompass the ever-changing moods of the sea. From the deepest green to the most limpid blue, they spoke to him in a way no words ever could. He drew her close until he could feel the beat of her heart against his ribs, and as she lifted her face to him he captured her lips in a kiss that he hoped would demonstrate the depth of his love.

It was some while before they drew apart to catch their breath and stare in wonder at each other, hardly daring to believe the strength of their feelings. 'How can anyone say this wasn't meant to be?' he asked softly.

Susan pressed her cheek into his palm as he caressed her face. 'They know nothing.' Her eyes darkened to deepest blue and a dimple appeared in her cheek as she grinned. 'But let's not spoil today by thinking about them.' She slid her fingers into his dark hair. 'Kiss me again, Jon.'

He crushed her to him and kissed her deeply, longing to make love to her, yet knowing that to do so would be wrong. She was not some cheap doxy, but the girl he hoped to marry one day. Their love was perfect, and for it to remain so they would have to gain the approval of their parents. But they would overcome petty prejudice and prove to the world that they were meant to be together for always.

Susan sat beside him on the flat rock at the cave entrance as he told her about the voyage to Tahiti. She had never heard of the place, but understood that it was on the other side of the world, would take a long time to reach – and that the journey might bring danger, perhaps even death. She watched his face as he spoke, saw his excitement, and realised that no matter how much he loved her, she would never hold him until he'd had his fill of adventure. Life with her in Cornwall would seem tame after such a journey, and she feared she would lose him.

He seemed to sense her disquiet, for he held her close and kissed her. 'I'll come back for you, Susan,' he murmured. 'I promise.'

She leant into him, wanting to believe him. His words had been honestly spoken, she knew, but would they carry the same sincerity once he'd tasted the thrills he'd always craved? She drew back and studied him. With his black hair and dark blue eyes he was handsome, despite the small teardrop birthmark that reddened the flesh on his temple. Jonathan had told her that one in every generation of the Cadwalladers bore this mark somewhere upon their person and that he barely noticed it. To her, it was another precious part of the man she loved and now she planted a kiss on it.

She looked into his eyes and remembered the small boy who'd come down to her cottage with a housemaid to play with her among the lobster-pots and nets. She could see again the eleven-year-old shedding his stiff, formal clothes to wade into the sea with the rest of the villagers when the great shoals of pilchard had been spotted coming into shore. And she remembered that special morning a year ago when they had realised they were more than friends, and that their childish affection had grown into something far stronger.

'When will you leave?'

'I have to return to London tomorrow,' he replied, his arm tightening round her waist. 'There are preparations to make.' He tilted her chin with his finger and looked into her eyes. 'But I've taught you to read and write so we can still communicate – at least until we set sail.'

She nodded, unable now to speak. Her reading and writing were still in infancy, and his letters would be poor compensation for not seeing him.

The tide had turned and the sea was rushing up the beach and splashing against the rocks. The sun was low in the sky, gilding the rocks and the water with a golden glow. It was time to leave the cave and return to their different lives. Jonathan swung up into the saddle and held out his hand. 'Ride with me.'

She put her foot on his dusty boot, her hand in his, and was lifted into the saddle behind him. Clasping her arms round his waist, she fought her tears. She would hold this memory in her heart until his return.

2

Jonathan hung over the side of the ship, and could barely
contain himself as he watched the bustle on the docks and the
embarking of the other passengers, with their luggage, vast
boxes and cases of instruments. He recognised the botanist
Joseph Banks and the naturalist Daniel Solander. He still
couldn't quite believe he was there, yet the noise below him
and the creak of the timbers beneath his feet told him he was.

They had sailed from Deptford on 30 July and had arrived
in Plymouth thirteen days later to pick up the rest of the party
of scientists who would plot the transit of Venus across the
sun. After a glance at the ornate pocket watch he'd carried
since his father's death, he tucked his neat tricorne hat beneath
his arm and wondered how much longer the boarding process
would take. The ship had been in Plymouth for almost five
days, and there seemed no end to the constant stream of things
coming aboard.

He lifted his face to the sun and closed his eyes, breathing in
the tang of the sea as the gulls screamed overhead. Patience
was all very well, but it was difficult to calm the thud of his
heart or control his fidgeting feet. As he opened his eyes, he
gazed over the green hills of southern England and couldn't
help wondering when he would see Cornwall and Susan again.

There hadn't been time to return to Cornwall since that day
at the cave, and Susan wasn't yet confident enough to send
him a letter of more than a few words. How she would love to
be here, he thought. He pushed all thoughts of her to the back

of his mind. His love would stand the test of time, he was certain, but although he would miss her, there was little to be done but put his energies into this adventure. He turned his back on the bustle below and took in his surroundings.

She was hardly the most imposing of ships, and Jonathan had felt a pang of disappointment when he'd first seen her at Deptford. However, he had pestered the officers for information about her, quizzed his uncle, explored her from stem to stern, and had concluded that she was infinitely suitable for the task ahead.

The *Earl of Pembroke* had been purchased by the Admiralty for the expedition. She was an east-coast collier, small and sturdy, built in Whitby and refitted in the Deptford naval dockyards with additional light planking, accommodation for the prestigious passengers and a new name – *Endeavour*.

'She'll do us well enough.'

The gruff voice broke into his thoughts and Jonathan turned to his uncle. 'I was just thinking so,' he replied, as he took in his uncle's attire.

Jonathan's breeches and shirt were white, his buckled shoes polished and his neckcloth pristine above the neatly buttoned ornate waistcoat. His thick dark hair was tied back, and he'd gladly dispensed with his wig in favour of feeling the wind on his scalp. He hid a smile as his uncle tugged at the powdered horsehair that threatened to make him look ridiculous. More used to studying the solar system or poring over books in his vast library, Josiah had few social graces. Yet that hadn't hindered his progress in his chosen career, or diminished the high regard in which he was held as a leading member of the Royal Society.

Josiah gave up the struggle and rammed the troublesome wig deep into the capacious pocket of his coat. He cast a belligerent eye towards the tall, brown-haired man who was overseeing the loading of provisions. 'Let us hope our newly commissioned lieutenant proves as reliable as his ship,' he remarked.

Jonathan knew better than to reply. There had been fierce debate among the members of the Royal Society over the Admiralty's determination to appoint Lieutenant James Cook as commander of the expedition, and his uncle still held the view that Augustus Dalrymple was the only man experienced enough to lead such a venture.

'It's a disgrace,' he rumbled now, pulling at the hem of his long waistcoat and popping open another button. 'The Royal Society sponsored this voyage, yet the Admiralty will not allow us Dalrymple. Why Cook? The man's a nobody. What does the son of a Yorkshire farmer know about astronomy – or the sea, for that matter?'

Jonathan knew his uncle didn't expect an answer – and would never accept the Admiralty's choice of Cook over Dalrymple, regardless of how long they debated the point. Dalrymple had taken umbrage and had refused to join the expedition once the Admiralty's decision was deemed final, thereby ending the debate as far as Jonathan was concerned.

From his own research, he'd learnt that, although Cook had no important connections and had come from lowly origins, his ability at sea had brought him fame during the recent Seven Years' War. He had charted the St Lawrence river in Canada, and piloted Wolfe's successful expedition to capture Québec from the French, so he was evidently an experienced and competent mariner.

Jonathan stood beside his uncle and watched as the quietly spoken lieutenant directed his crew and passengers with an air of command that suggested complete belief in his own capabilities. James Cook would make a fine commander, he decided, but he wished things would move more rapidly and that they could be under way before they missed the tide yet again.

Waymbuurr (Cooktown, Australia), December 1768

The crescent of sand lay between the sheltering arms of two rocky cliffs, which were heavily wooded with the same lush pandanus palms and ferns that ran the width of the bay and fringed the northern coastline. Beyond were the hunting grounds, the lush grass areas cleared regularly with fire-sticks, the flames encouraging new growth so that the animals returned every year to graze. The trees were more slender there, with pale bark and silvery leaves, but in their branches nested not only the birds but the koalas and possums that were so good to eat. This was the home of the Ngandyandyi tribe, and had been in their guardianship since the ancient ancestors had roamed the earth.

Anabarru squatted at the water's edge, waiting for the tide to ebb so that she could collect the shellfish that clung to the rocks. She was naked but for a slender belt of plaited hair, a string of shells round her neck and a delicate bone piercing her nose. At fifteen she was initiated into womanhood and her ebony skin was decorated with the deep scars and lacerations of the ceremonies. Her marriage to the Elder's son Watpipa two years before meant that her children would be direct descendants of the great ancestor Djanay, whose time of wise and successful leadership was drawn on the walls of the sacred caves.

She was content with her life, as she watched the Sun Goddess's fiery chariot complete its journey across the sky, and looking forward to the evening feast. The sweep of beach was as deserted as the water, the tranquillity and timeless beauty of her surroundings untouched by invaders. Her family lived in peace now that a truce had been called with the Lizard people who lived on land adjoining their borders; the lighter-skinned fishermen and shell-gatherers, who had come once to these shores from the far north in their strange seacraft, had not been seen for generations. There had been rumours at the *corroborees* of ghostly men appearing in the north and the far south-west, of great canoes with white wings wrecked on the rocks, but as no living man or woman could say that they had truly seen them, they were accepted as myth.

Anabarru stared out to the horizon, her thoughts drifting as the ripples lapped the sand at her feet. But as the sun sank behind the trees and the birds swarmed before roosting for the night, she shivered. It wasn't because she was cold, more that she felt uneasy – which was unusual and she wasn't sure what to make of it.

She looked down the beach, then over her shoulder, peering into the gathering gloom of the lush rainforest. No one was in sight, but there were nearly always children playing on the sand or men spear-fishing from their bark canoes. She straightened, turned her back to the sea and squinted into the setting sun. The shadows were deep beneath the trees, but she could see no movement, no sign of her family.

When the sound of chattering and laughter drifted out to her from beyond the trees she accepted she was being foolish. Soothed by the knowledge that her family were close by, she picked up her daughter and settled her on her hip. Birranulu was a year old, and her smile warmed Anabarru as she clung to her. Anabarru kissed her and waded into the water. It was cool and refreshing against her skin, and the child laughed with delight as the waves splashed her legs and crept up to her belly.

As the sun streaked the sky with the orange and red of fire, Anabarru brought Birranulu back to the sand and gave her some shells to play with while she hunted for shellfish. Carrying a stone cutting-tool, and with a plaited grass dilly bag hanging from her wrist, she waded into the pools that the ebbing tide had left between the rocks and began to prise off the shiny black mussels. Soon, she thought, as she filled the dilly bag, it will be the season of the oysters, and I shall collect the little white stones to make a necklace for Birranulu.

Anabarru returned to the beach and began to sing softly to her now sleepy child. As she reached down to pick up the baby, a hand was clamped over her mouth and she was lifted from the sand.

She tried to scream, but the hand was too firmly over her mouth, an arm too tightly round her body. As her abductor ran across the sand and into the bush, she struggled, lashing out with her hands and feet, pulling his hair, gouging at his eyes. But his strength was too great, his intent too determined, and Anabarru had to fight not only the man but the paralysis of terror.

He carried her into the darkening shadows of the trees, where Anabarru knew that if only she could scream she would be heard. For they were still close to her family – still within range of their spears. She fought him as he wove round the trees and the ferns that grew taller than a man. Then she heard the wail of her baby, and it gave her hope. Perhaps now Watpipa would be alerted and come to her rescue.

As Birranulu's cries echoed through the trees Anabarru increased her efforts to escape, trying to unbalance her kidnapper by kicking out at passing trees and grabbing their branches. Her screams were smothered by his hand, and her ears rang with their hollow sound in her throat as she tried desperately to breathe through the restricting fingers.

Suddenly the hand lifted. Before she could gather breath to cry out there was a blinding punch to her head and the world went black.

Anabarru watched him through her eyelashes as he raped her again. The feel and stench of him made her flesh crawl, but she knew that to fight him would earn her yet another beating – perhaps even death. Despite the terror, and the knowledge of what he was, she lay submissively beneath him, her mind working furiously on escape.

She could see that he was one of the Lizard people from the tribal initiation scars on his face and body, and because he seemed confident that he could do as he liked with her, she guessed they had reached his tribal lands. She battled to contain her terror. The Lizard people were known to eat human flesh, and if she didn't escape she would die when he had had enough of her.

She clenched her teeth and thought of her family. Watpipa was the best tracker in the clan – surely he couldn't be too far away. But would he break the sacred laws and enter Lizard territory? She had to hope that he would – had to hope that she was important enough to him.

Her gaze slid away from the man above her, and through half-closed eyelids, she tried to make out her surroundings. They were deep within a cave, she realised. The sun cast only fingers of light at the entrance, but they glistened strangely on the rock walls as if the sun were trapped in their very fabric – yet the light was enough to reveal the paintings on the low ceiling, the litter of bones and ash on the stone floor.

She looked away hastily. She couldn't count on Watpipa. She had to make her own escape. She also had to remain calm or she would die here among the remains of the dead and the evil spirits who lived here. Anabarru looked into the face of her tormentor as he plunged into her, hurting her. She knew that her only means of escape was his death. But first she had to find a weapon.

She began to search with her fingers. She shuddered as they touched decaying meat. Broken twigs and desiccated leaves littered the cave floor, but they were not killing weapons, and she despaired. Then her fingers touched something hard, rough and cold.

She felt the quickening rhythm of his lust as her fingers

closed over the rock. He would soon be finished. She had to be swift.

The rock filled her palm. She clutched it and, with a deep breath, gathered her strength. Then, with one mighty blow, she smashed it against his temple.

He grunted, froze inside her, eyes rolling in shock.

Anabarru's heart was racing and the sweat almost blinded her as she saw that she had only stunned him. She took an even firmer grip on the rock and hit him again – dread giving her the strength of a man. The blow punched through flesh and bone, leaving a hole the size of a fist in the side of his head.

She held her breath as he remained on top of her for what seemed an eternity. She was about to hit him again when he sagged, his weight collapsing, crushing her. His foul breath was expelled into her face and then he was still.

Anabarru shoved him off and squirmed away, the rock still raised ready to strike. She backed away from him, seeking the comfort of the solid walls and the darkness. Her body ached and her stomach finally rebelled, yet her eyes never left him as she watched for signs of life. She had to be sure that he wouldn't come after her, for she was too weak to outrun him.

It was a long time before she plucked up the courage to approach him and prod him with her foot. He didn't stir, didn't open his eyes. Blood had leaked from the wound in his head, and had run down his ugly, scarred face to pool on the cave floor.

With the rock in her hand, she stumbled out of the cave and into the blinding heat of day. Slithering and sliding down the stony outcrop, she gained the valley floor and collapsed in the grass. Her head felt as if it was filled with feathers and her mouth was parched. She'd had no water since the previous day, and her ears still rang from the beating he'd inflicted. She looked down at her legs, still shaking from the effects of what had happened in the cave, and saw drying blood. The rest of her body was splattered with it too, and she shuddered as she understood that it had come from him.

Anabarru groaned. She ached all over, and wanted to curl up and go to sleep. But she was still in the land of the Lizard people – still in danger – and knew she had to escape. She clutched the rock that had become a symbol of her freedom and limped through the grass until she reached the relative safety of the trees.

It was easy to track his passage through them, and after following the trail for miles through the thick undergrowth, she sank to her knees beside a stream and drank. Then she picked a broad, flat leaf from a nearby bush and cleaned herself, wincing as the healing sap flowed into the cuts and grazes. The thought that she might be carrying his seed made her feel sick, and once she'd treated her wounds and rid herself of his smell, she hunted for the special plants that would bring the blood of the moon and kill any new life inside her.

It had taken longer than she'd expected, and the knowledge that she might be discovered kept her alert for any alien sounds in the bush. She kept her face turned eastward and continued to hobble towards her own lands and the family who camped in the path of the rising sun.

She didn't notice the glint of yellow that sparked in the rock and veined its rough surface. Even if she had, she wouldn't have known what it was, or appreciated its worth. To Anabarru it was the rock that had saved her life – not a vast nugget of the gold that would bring destruction to future generations of her people.

At long last she staggered out of the trees and reached the safety of her tribal hunting grounds. The long grass was sweetly cool from the night dew, but as the sun rose she felt its heat hammer down on her until her head buzzed and her vision blurred. She was still far from the camp, and could go no further. Still clutching the rock, she crawled into the shelter of an overhanging bush and closed her eyes. She would rest awhile.

When she opened her eyes she was surrounded by familiar faces. Cool water and healing leaves soothed the cuts and bruises, and soft words consoled her. 'How did I get here?' she whispered.

'Watpipa was leading the hunting party. He found you and carried you home two full moons ago.' The senior wife continued to massage her limbs. 'Sleep now.'

Time lost all meaning as she drifted in and out of welcoming darkness, but eventually she became aware of a change in the voices surrounding her. Gone were the soft, soothing sounds and in their place came sharp discussion. She opened her eyes and sat up.

'Where is Birranulu?' she demanded.

'She is with the other women,' she was told by the senior wife.

'I must see her.'

The senior wife ordered the other women to leave. Then she shook her head. 'Now you are well you must leave the camp and have no contact with the child or Watpipa until you have been purified.'

Anabarru looked at her in puzzlement. Then the ugly truth dawned. 'I'm carrying the Lizard's seed.'

'You must leave today.'

The two women stared at each other for a long, silent moment of understanding. Then Anabarru nodded. It was the tribal way. Until she had rid herself of the alien seed she would taint them all. Slowly and painfully she rose to her feet.

'I will come to help you in the birthing cave when your time comes,' said the older woman. 'You know what must be done before you can return to us?'

Anabarru nodded again, but the knowledge that she was

banished through no fault of her own, and that she would have to spend many moons outside the safety of the camp and away from her family, made her want to beg to be allowed to stay. But she knew her words would not be heard. The sacred *mardayin* was immutable.

She watched the old woman leave the shelter of branches and grasses that had been erected to keep her from sight of the tribe and knew she would not see her again until the pains started. She looked down at the rock that had saved her life and placed it in the large dilly bag the old woman had left for her. Fish and berries had been gathered to ease her first few days of solitude, and for that she was grateful. She was still weak, and doubted she had the strength to hunt and fish.

The sun was high above the trees, its light casting dappled shadows on the forest floor, its heat shimmering on the gum leaves. Anabarru could hear the distant sounds of the camp, which lay beyond the trees and out of sight. With a heavy heart, she picked up her short digging-stick and slender spear, and began her journey into banishment.

3

Tahiti, April 1769

They had been at sea for almost nine months, and although there had been sickness, Cook's strict rule that citrus fruit and vinegar were to be taken regularly meant that no one had suffered from the dreaded scurvy.

Jonathan had revelled in the stormy waters off Cape Horn, and he'd been one of only a few passengers who'd braved the plunging decks and icy spray to watch the hazy outline of land slip by on their starboard side. His uncle Josiah had not fared as well: he'd spent most of the voyage lying in his cabin, too ill to move. Their arrival in the calm, turquoise waters off Tahiti had seen his health improve, and as fresh supplies of fresh fruit, clean water, fish and meat were brought on board, he was soon on his feet and as bluff as ever.

Tahiti was a revelation to Jonathan. He could never have imagined that such a place existed. As the *Endeavour* was escorted towards land by a pod of dolphins, he saw palm trees bowing low over the pale sand, and birds of every colour flitting among them. From the shores there appeared dozens of bronze-skinned natives, who waded into the water and swam towards the *Endeavour* as she dropped anchor. They were joined by exotically decorated narrow canoes, paddled rapidly by smiling, well-set men who wore little more than grass skirts.

A festive mood took over the ship, with shouts from the crew who had scaled the rigging for a better view. The passengers hurried to the railings, calling and waving to the natives, who waved back. Jonathan gaped as they climbed the ropes and gained the deck: the women were bare-breasted and shameless in their near-nakedness.

He blushed to the roots of his hair as a golden-skinned beauty slipped a wreath of exotic flowers round his neck. Her skin glistened from her swim and her long black hair fell beyond her waist to the tiny grass skirt that hugged her slender hips. She smiled up at him with almond-shaped eyes, the lashes dewed with water diamonds, her breasts almost brushing his shirt front. 'Thank you,' he stammered, unsure where to look.

'Come me,' she said, and flashed him a shy smile. She put a hand on his arm.

'Oh, no, you don't, lad,' said Josiah, who unhanded the girl and dragged him away. 'More trouble than they're worth,' he muttered.

'But she's beautiful.' Jonathan was unable to take his eyes off her as she smiled at him over her shoulder.

'Indeed she is,' his uncle agreed, 'but probably full of pox. Leave well alone, lad. That's my advice.'

Jonathan blushed again. He was watching the enticing sway of her hips in the grass skirt and the undulation of her magnificent breasts as she walked among the passengers, artfully avoiding the exploring, snatching hands of the sailors. It had been a long time since he'd experienced the pleasures of a girl, and he felt the familiar stirring in his groin. Surely one so young and beautiful couldn't be poxed.

A heavy hand fell on his shoulder and his uncle chuckled. 'We're a long way from home, lad, and a young man has his needs, but you'd be wise to forgo the pleasures of this island, no matter how tempting. Every boat gets the same welcome, and the men are all too willing to sell their wives and daughters for a tot of rum.'

Jonathan stood beside his uncle and watched as the natives

teemed over the side of the ship with their offerings of flowers and fruit. Their language was incomprehensible, a sort of pidgin English as loud and cheerful as the squawks of the birds. The men were sleek, with muscled arms and oiled bodies. The majority of the women were young and desirable, with their long black hair and almost naked bodies – the sailors were shoving and pushing now to get closer to them.

'Cook will have his work cut out,' Josiah muttered. 'The crew will have scavenged the ship's iron before he knows it.'

Jonathan tore his gaze from the girls and looked at his uncle, puzzled. 'Why should they do that?'

'To pay for favours,' Josiah replied, as he waved away the offer of coconuts from a girl with skin the colour of honey and black eyes. 'Nuts, bolts, nails and latches can buy a woman here, and if Cook doesn't watch out, we'll be in the same dire straits as Wallis was two years ago. The *Dolphin* was virtually wrecked, and they nearly failed to sail home.'

Jonathan heard what his uncle had said, but it was hard to ignore the girl who was smiling at him, her hair draped seductively over her breasts so that only the dark nipple peeped out at him. She was exotic, beautiful and tempting – but Josiah was right: she was not for him. He disentangled himself gently from her clutches and watched her walk away, his thoughts on Susan and the promises they had made. Far from home and the girl he loved, he was determined not to betray her.

During the following ten days, Lianni pursued him, her persistence wearing him down until he could think of nothing else. When he finally surrendered to her he hated himself for his weakness. Susan was his love, but Lianni had cast a spell over him that he found impossible to fight.

Over the following three months Jonathan battled with his conscience, but it was all too easy to find an excuse to slip away from the rest of the party and be with Lianni. In London his dalliances had been furtive – a fumbling tumble, a swift release with girls as ignorant as he. But in Tahiti he was far from the restrictions of Georgian England, and coupling was accepted as part of life and openly encouraged. It was a gift willingly given, and although Jonathan felt guilty for his weakness, Lianni saw no shame in it.

Her skin was as soft as silk, perfumed with oils from the tropical flowers that grew in profusion on the island. Her long hair stroked his belly as she moved over him, their sweat mingling as their limbs entwined and their pulses raced. Thoughts of home and Susan were swept away in the velvety soft nights. The stars were bright in the black sky and the wind sighed in the palm trees, scenting the air. As he lay with her in the shade of the trees, during long, sleepy afternoons, or in the caressing warmth of the turquoise sea, he still could not quite believe it wasn't a dream.

He wasn't so naïve to think he was the first to lie with her or that he would be the last. Neither was he so blinded by lust that he couldn't see that this paradise, these gentle, simple people and their way of life, had been compromised by the advent of ships and sailors who came to replenish their water supply and cavort with the women. The Tahitians lived in poor grass huts, life expectancy was short and disease rife. Despite the beauty of their surroundings and the richness of the seas around them, they lived in as great squalor as the slum-dwellers of London.

August 1769

The *Endeavour* was due to sail in two days' time, and Jonathan was under strict instructions to be on board by eleven the next morning. Now he led Lianni to the waterfall deep in the palm forest where they could be alone. They made love beneath the trees and swam in the icy water of the rocky pool as parrots and finches flew around them. He was sad to be leaving her behind, never to see her again, and held her close through the warm night.

At dawn, they made love and swam for the last time in the pool. As he sat on a rock and dried himself with his shirt, he watched as she emerged from the water like a mermaid. His gaze devoured her as she tucked a flower behind her ear and combed her hair. He was etching her into his memory so that he would never forget her.

She smiled at him as he drew her to his side and stroked the lustrous black hair that shone blue in the sunlight. 'I don't want to leave,' he murmured. 'You and this place have bewitched me.'

'Me come you,' she replied. 'Tupaia, he come. Him priest. Cook like.'

He took her in his arms. 'Cook will not allow it.' He fell silent, knowing it was a poor excuse, but their time together was at an end. 'Tupaia is only coming because he can interpret for us when we explore your other islands,' he explained.

She laid her head on his shoulder. 'You come back?' she whispered.

He kissed the smooth brow and the closed eyelids, fringed with long dark lashes. 'I don't know.'

She was still in his arms and he wondered what she was thinking. Then she opened her eyes and gazed at him with searing intensity. 'You not come back,' she said quietly. 'Men on ship never come back.'

Jonathan knew she was right. He held her tightly, wishing he could offer her more, knowing it was impossible. They lay entwined as the sun rose and speared the glade with its beams. The ring of the ship's bell pierced the silence, and Jonathan's spirits fell. It was time to go. He disentangled himself reluctantly, then dressed in the damp shirt and his grubby breeches. He reached into his pocket and pulled out the fob watch his father had always worn. It had been specially commissioned almost half a century before, and was a prized and valuable possession, but it was all he could give her.

The gold glinted in the sunlight, but it was no match for the fiery diamond that nestled at the centre of the finely etched initials *C.C.* He carefully pressed the rim so that the casing opened and revealed the watch nestled inside. The white enamel and black Roman numerals were starkly simple in such exotic surroundings, and the precise movements of the gold workings glittered. A tiny key was fitted into a specially designed niche; it was used to wind the intricate mechanism. Each element of this masterpiece of craftsmanship was stamped with a hallmark.

'I asked Sydney Parkinson, the ship's artist, to do this for me,' he explained, and showed her the exquisite miniatures that had been fitted to both sides of the outer casing. One bore a head-and-shoulders portrait of him and the other one of her. Each was signed by the artist and dated.

She looked at them in amazement. 'Is you.' She pointed to his portrait with a slender brown finger.

He nodded and grinned. 'And that's you, Lianni.'

Her eyes sparkled as she studied the miniature portrait of himself. 'Me?' Her face was alight with pride. 'I am beautiful, no?'

'You are,' he said, closing the watch and nestling it in her palm. 'This is my gift. Take care of it, my sweet girl, and remember me every time you look at it.'

She hugged it to her breast. 'Is mine?' At his nod she clutched it tighter and a single tear rolled down her cheek. 'You go on ship, but you not leave.'

Jonathan kissed her for the last time, warned her never to let the watch get wet or lose the key, then pushed his way through the bushes to the beach and the row-boat that would take him to the ship.

★   ★   ★

Lianni followed soon after and stood in the shadows of the trees at the edge of the beach. She watched the men row the small boat out to the ship, saw Jonathan climb the rope-ladder and disappear. She looked down at his gift and clutched it to her heart as the first stirring of life fluttered inside her. Because of his gift, her child would always know the face of its father.

Later that morning Jonathan emerged from the cabin and went on deck. He'd long ago discarded the heavy outer garments in favour of working only in his breeches and shirt during the heat of the day. His sleeves were rolled up to reveal muscled, tanned arms, and his hair hung loose about his face. He'd turned eighteen shortly after they'd arrived in Tahiti, and he felt strong and invigorated from the labour of helping to build the fort at Port Venus.

The sun beat down on his head and dazzled him, but he no longer sought shelter from it – indeed, he revelled in it after London's smog and filth. The three months in Tahiti had swept away the pallor and pretensions the city had forced upon him. It had also enhanced his thirst for exploration and adventure. His one regret was Lianni. She had bewitched him, but he'd been living in a fool's paradise, and he wished with all his heart that he could hold Susan close. She was his true love, and he needed to tell her so.

He leant against the side of the ship and stared at the shore, his thoughts full of her and the future they had planned, despite their parents' disapproval.

'I wonder what our lieutenant wants,' muttered Josiah, as he came to stand beside his nephew. He dabbed his sweating red face with a handkerchief and pulled his hat further over his eyes. 'Fancy calling a meeting on deck at this time of the morning. This heat is appalling. How can you bear it?'

Jonathan regarded his uncle with a mixture of affection and

exasperation. 'Why don't you take off your coat, Uncle?' he coaxed. 'You'll roast alive.'

The old man glared at him from beneath the wide brim of his old-fashioned hat, his gaze taking in his nephew's casual attire. 'It's not seemly for a man of my age to wander about like a native,' he responded. 'If your mother could see you now, she'd faint with horror. You look nothing more than a damn gypsy.'

'At least I'm comfortable,' Jonathan replied cheerfully.

'Hmmph.'

Speculation about the purpose of the meeting had been rife among the passengers and crew ever since it was announced, so there was much debate and an air of expectancy as the ship's bell rang out the hour. Cook appeared on the poop and an excited murmur ran through the assembled passengers as they caught sight of the regal native at his side.

'He's only introducing the native priest to the rest of 'em,' muttered Josiah, 'and we already know why he's here.'

'I have orders from His Majesty's Government, which until now I have not been able to reveal. The reason will soon become apparent.' Cook paused as another murmur went through the crowd. 'I have asked the Tahitian priest Tupaia to accompany us on the next leg of our voyage to act as interpreter. After charting the many other islands in this region, as planned, we will sail south to forty degrees latitude to resolve the issue of a great southern continent.'

A stunned silence greeted this announcement, and Jonathan and his uncle exchanged a wide-eyed look of disbelief.

'If we find no landmass, we will sail west and into the eastern side of the land recorded by Tasman, and try to determine whether it is an extension of the polar land Le Maire identified or whether it is separate.'

Jonathan could barely contain his excitement and grinned at his uncle, then returned his attention to Cook.

'Those of you who do not wish to remain on board will be offered passage back to England on the *Seagull*, which is due here in about a week's time. I have asked my first officer to compile a list of those remaining in Tahiti, and I request that you are ready to disembark before sunrise tomorrow.' Cook was a man of few words. Now he turned his back on his stunned audience and closeted himself with the Tahitian priest in his cabin.

'So that's why Dalrymple wasn't chosen to lead the expedition,' said Josiah. 'His views are too well known, his papers on the southern land too widely read. The Admiralty and the King didn't want the French and Spanish to suspect the real reason for our venture.'

Jonathan grasped his uncle's arm. 'The orbit of Venus across the sun gave them the excuse, and they took it. Oh, Uncle, think. We might be about to discover a whole new continent.'

Josiah's thick eyebrows came together in a frown. 'I don't know,' he murmured. 'Your mother put me in charge of your safety, and so far you've proved a handful, gadding about with that native girl and dressing like a ragamuffin. The good Lord only knows what might happen further south, and the voyage may be fraught with danger.'

'But we *must* go,' Jonathan said. 'Don't you see, Uncle? This is our chance to discover whether or not the legend of the great southern continent is truth or myth. You can't deny us this, surely?'

Josiah mumbled, grumbled and fidgeted with his handkerchief. 'Your mother will not thank me if any harm should come to you, boy,' he said, 'and I'm too old for adventures – especially in a little tub like this.' He flapped a hand scornfully at the *Endeavour*'s masts.

'Since when have you been afraid of doing something out of the ordinary – of flouting authority, breaking rules and speaking your mind? As for this little tub, she's seen us safe so far, and Cook has proved an expert commander.'

At his nephew's hectoring tone a deep flush darkened Josiah's neck and face.

Jonathan saw that he had overstepped the mark of civility. 'Think of the respect we'll earn in England if we find this southern land,' he coaxed. 'The discoverers will be fêted – perhaps even rewarded by the King.'

Josiah mopped his face and stared into the distance, but Jonathan could see the thoughtful gleam in his eyes and pressed his advantage. 'This may be history in the making, Uncle. The discoverers will be asked to write papers on the subject and give lectures all over England – perhaps in Europe too. And what about the astronomy of the southern lands? Wouldn't you like to see it for yourself?'

Josiah gave a deep sigh and rammed his hands into his pockets. 'As you seem determined to have your way, I suppose I must agree to accompany you. But if I die of seasickness or end up in a savage's cooking pot, you'll have to explain to your mother.'

Jonathan's shout of victory rose to the crow's nest and startled the other passengers. He gathered the old curmudgeon to his chest in a hug. 'You won't regret it,' he promised.

'Hmmph,' was the reply, as Josiah's hat fell off. He caught it just before it fell into the sea. 'Steady on, lad. Decorum decorum.'

'Decorum be damned!' shouted Jonathan, grabbing the hat and sending it spinning out across the water. 'Here's to adventure, and the finding of the great southern continent.'

Waymbuurr, September 1769

The land had been recently fire-sticked so the earth was still black in places, the silver bark on the trees peeling and charred. Yet life was already returning in the tender green shoots and bursting buds, and Anabarru knew that soon it would encourage the grazing beasts back to her lands. There would be good hunting when the rains returned.

Her bare feet made little sound as she crossed the parched ground and headed for the hills, which rose like a woman's breasts above the forest floor. The heat was intense, the sky clear of cloud as the sibilant call of countless insects accompanied her. Birds flitted in the trees and spiders spun deadly webs between branches to catch the unwary. But Anabarru's practised eye and inbred knowledge of her surroundings meant she was aware of the dangers – had lived with them in solitude for many moons as she hunted, fished and grew stronger, more accustomed to fending for herself. Now her time had come to be rid of her burden and freed to return home.

She hurried on as the land sloped up towards the twin peaks and above the forest. The pains were stronger now, and she must hurry. As the sun began to cast shadows behind her and glare into her eyes she paused to catch her breath, endure the pain and check her position. The voluptuous hills were so close now that she could make out every tree that grew on them, and from her high vantage-point, she could look out over the tops of the tallest to see the sweep of land stretching to every horizon, the glitter of water far below where the other women would be fishing.

Tapping the ground with her digging-stick, she heard the hollow response and knew that she was almost there. She walked carefully over the smooth mound of rock and headed for the narrow gap between two sentinel stones that had been carved over the centuries by wind and rain. Her toes grabbed at the loose earth as her hands clasped the sturdy plants that grew on the sides of the rocks and she slithered down the steep slope until she reached the plateau above the forest floor.

The senior wife was waiting; the knowledge of many years had brought her in time. A small fire had been lit and smoke drifted from the mouth of the cave as she sang the ritual songs and honed the stone cutting-tool against a rock.

Anabarru squatted on the ledge and murmured the ancient prayers to the ancestors, asking them to help her through the coming ordeal. Then she glanced out over the forest, walked across the ledge and went into the birthing cave.

It was a sacred place that only women could enter – no man, however important, was permitted to know what happened here, and the rituals and ceremonies surrounding the birth of a child must never be revealed outside it.

It was shaped like a gaping mouth in the rocky hillside and between its craggy lips she had a magnificent view of the twin hills and the forest below her. Special bushes had been planted by the ledge, their berries and leaves used to ease the birth pangs. The floor was littered with the ashes of many fires, and the small bones of animals and fish that had provided food during the long hours of vigil. At the throat of the cave were the ochre paintings the women had made to tell their stories. Most had faded or been painted over, lichen growing across them, the rock crumbling in places where rain had come in.

The senior wife beckoned to her and, after a cursory examination, nodded approval. 'It is almost time. Take these. They will help.'

Anabarru placed her talisman rock at the back of the cave and noted how the sun sparked on it as she sat on the warm stone floor and ate the fruit. It had remained with her through-out her exile, but now she was relieved that she could leave it behind. It was a reminder of the events that had brought her to this cave, and once she was cleansed, she would have no further use for it.

As the pains grew stronger and the child began to push its way out, the senior wife took control.

Anabarru was almost smothered by the smoking fire, and the berries no longer seemed to dull the pain as she sweated and strained to rid her body of the Lizard child. It seemed reluctant to leave her. Then, in a rush of blood and water, it was born.

The older woman grasped the delicate neck and twisted hard before the infant could cry out and give life to its spirit. It was done.

Anabarru lay still as the cord was cut and tied. One final push and the afterbirth slipped from her. It was put on to the smoking fire to be burnt before it was buried with the child. She closed her eyes as the ritual prayers were said and the washing ceremony took place. She felt no regret, no pity for her dead child: this was their way, and had been since time began. Now she could return to her family.

Off New Zealand, October 1769

Nick, the ship's boy, sighted the prominent headland, which Cook named Young Nick's Head in his honour. Two days later they lay at anchor in a place Cook eventually called Poverty Bay, for it was impossible to find anything useful there to provision the ship. They had arrived in Tasman's Staaten Land – North New Zealand.

Jonathan and the rest of the passengers remained on board as Cook, his officers, the toughest of his sailors and the Tahitian interpreter went ashore. Josiah handed Jonathan the telescope. 'My eyes aren't good, lad. Tell me what you see.'

Jonathan peered through the brass instrument and kept up a running commentary as Cook and his companions were met by fearsome dark-skinned warriors, whose bodies and faces were heavily tattooed and whose welcome was far from friendly. They stood on the shore chanting and stamping their feet, making strange, rather daunting signals with their arms and hands, tongues sticking out, eyes staring. They carried spears and clubs, and there was no doubt that they were little more than savages.

'I don't like the look of this,' muttered Jonathan. 'Why's that fool showing off his sword to them?'

There wasn't time for his uncle to reply, for the Maori had snatched the sword and was making off with it down the beach. The officer drew his pistol and fired. The sound echoed in the deserted bay and there was great consternation and fear among the Maoris as their brother dropped dead.

Cook and the others retreated swiftly to the little boat where the sailors were already digging in the oars. Confused and frightened by this mysterious method of dealing death, the Maoris huddled on the shore. Then, as they saw that the murderer was getting away, they rose as one and, with a mighty roar of rage, threw their spears.

The sailors dug harder with their long oars and one or two spears thudded into the wooden sides of the boat, but they were soon out of range and the rest fell harmlessly into the water.

Jonathan rushed to the side of the ship and helped the men aboard as the Maoris jumped into their long canoes and advanced at surprising speed. Cook strode to the helm, shouted orders and, within moments, the sails were billowing and the anchor had been raised.

Jonathan stood on the deck, the wind in his hair, the sharp tang of the sea spray on his face as the *Endeavour* ploughed through the heavy waters. He wanted to laugh with the sheer joy of it all – this was the adventure he had dreamt about as a boy when he had watched the ships sail past that tiny harbour in Cornwall.

4

Mousehole, April 1770

Susan Penhalligan stood with the others on the narrow quay-side and stared out to sea. The wind tore at her hair, plastered her long skirts to her legs and made her clutch the woollen shawl closely round her shoulders. The cold that numbed her had little to do with the chill of the wind – it went deeper than that and clawed at her insides like a hand from the grave.

The sea crashed relentlessly against the grey wall that curved out in a sturdy arm from the quay. It sent spray high into the sky where it was whipped by the wind into icy needles that battered her face and soaked her to the skin. She thrust her chin into the meagre warmth of the shawl, dug her cold bare toes into the cobbles and leant into the gale in an effort to remain standing against the onslaught. Only four of the ten boats had returned, and as night approached hope was fading with the dismal light.

Every stone cottage in Mousehole was empty, but a lantern burnt in each window to guide the men home. Susan glanced at her mother and saw that, despite her stoicism, Maud Penhalligan was almost mad with worry. Her eyes hardly blinked as she peered into the storm-lashed night, her hands clasping thirteen-year-old Billy, the youngest of her six sons, as if by holding him close she could also embrace her other boys to keep them and their father safe.

Susan slipped her hand round her mother's narrow waist, but there was no easing her. She was focused on the raging sea, desperate for a sighting of the little boat that was surely battling home. With a tremulous sigh Susan glanced at the gaunt faces around her. Her brothers' wives and sweethearts gripped each other's hands, and Billy stood like a statue in his mother's arms. A broken leg had meant he had not sailed with them, and the anguish in his eyes told of his relief and guilt – he had always hated the sea.

Her gaze trawled the quay, seeing all the familiar faces, sharing their fear and knowing how hard it was to keep spirits high and hope alive. Old men sucked at their pipes, their eyes faded, their faces lined and weathered by many years at sea. All were silent. This was not the time for talk or speculation, not even to give thanks for those men who had returned – not until the last boat had been accounted for.

Susan shivered and turned away. She ran through the rain, her feet splashing in the puddles that lay between the broken cobbles until she reached the cottage. She closed the door behind her, leant back against the wood and tried to take strength from its solid familiarity. She had been born in this house and knew no other. The way of life in the tiny fishing community was tough, but it was healthier than that of the tin miners, who burrowed beneath the earth and rarely saw the light of day; few lived beyond middle age because of the dust in their lungs, but old fishermen lived on to tell their tales of the sea as they helped mend the nets and encouraged the next generation to follow in their footsteps. Their cottages were warm, there was always food on the table and illness was rare.

Yet there were dangers in both kinds of work. Pits caved in and men suffocated or were crushed because the mine-owners were concerned only with profit. Fishermen were at the mercy of the weather, and during her short life, Susan had witnessed the loss of men and boats in just such a storm as the one that raged outside. 'Dear God,' she muttered, on a sob, 'keep them safe. Bring them home.'

The wind battered the stout walls and howled down the

chimney, sending a choking grey cloud of smoke into the room. Susan listened to the silence within the cottage and shivered again. It was as if the four walls were holding their breath, waiting for news of those who lived there.

Determined to keep these thoughts at bay, she blinked away her tears and hurried across the flagstone floor to the range. The only light came from the lantern at the window and the grate, but the flickering shadows were welcoming and for a moment she felt comforted. Yet the gloom refused to leave her, and she felt a surge of panic as she thought of what might happen to her family if the men didn't come home. How could they afford the rent? Would Lady Cadwallader give them notice to leave? She'd been known to do such things before when tragedy struck. If only Jonathan was here – he'd see they weren't turned out on to the streets.

'You mustn't think of Jonathan,' she muttered. 'He can't help. No one can.' Not wanting to speculate on what Fate might bring, she placed the big kettle on the heat. As she waited for the water to boil, she gathered up dry shawls, pushed her feet into her worn clogs and snatched up a blanket. This wasn't the first night the villagers had mounted vigil on the quay, and it wouldn't be the last. Susan knew that if they were to survive this terrible night they must keep as warm and dry as they could.

Having warmed the ale, she poured it into a large earthenware bottle, laced it with a spoonful of honey and pushed in the stopper. They would need strength for whatever lay ahead. With a shawl wrapped tightly round her head, she hooked the blanket and spare shawls under her arm, gathered tin mugs and picked up the heavy bottle. The wind tore through the cottage and slammed the door behind her as she ducked her head and hurried back to the quay, the clatter of her clogs smothered by the boom of the waves against the sea wall.

'I've brought ale,' she shouted, above the banshee wail of the wind.

Maud was unable to smile, but there was gratitude in her red-rimmed eyes as she took the mug between frozen, work-worn fingers so that the fragrant steam could warm her face.

Susan placed the blanket over her mother's sodden hair, then wrapped the spare shawl round Billy's head and poured warm ale for the others. It was apparent that there was no news, for their faces were pinched, their eyes dull with dread. 'Why don't you go indoors, Mother?' she shouted, close to her ear, on her return.

Maud shook her head.

Susan glanced at her youngest brother and felt a twist of anguish. Billy was fighting inner demons, trying so hard to be a man yet harbouring the fears of a child whose world was about to collapse around him. She had few words to comfort him, so she put her arms round him and, despite his reluctance, drew him to her. She felt a fierce love for him and held on to him as passionately as her mother had. It was only when he squirmed away from her that she realised he was too old to be treated in such a way. She watched him move away, then she huddled in a nearby doorway to watch the harbour.

The same four boats lay on their sides high up on the leeside of the beach and away from the heavy waves that thundered through the narrow opening in the harbour wall to drag relentlessly at the shingle. It was pitch black away from the feeble light of the lanterns, and the howl of the wind drowned the women's quiet weeping. She felt a flash of anger, born of frustration and helplessness. She longed to haul one of those boats off the shingle and set out in search of them, yet she knew there was nothing to be gained by such a reckless action. She could only wait.

Dawn struggled through heavy clouds, the watery shafts of a frail sun silvering the restless ocean that heaved, swelled and broke less wildly now against the grey harbour wall. Susan had slept fitfully through the last of the night, lurching from hope to despair when news had come of two more boats reaching the harbour, of eight men spared, but none were Penhalligans.

Sick with fear and weariness, she rose from the fireside settle and left the house. The rain had stopped, and although the wind buffeted her as she walked down to the quayside, it was no longer so cold. The sun gleamed on the wet cobbles, gulls squabbled, and the sea hissed on the shingle. There were no boats in the harbour, for the men had taken them out at first light to search for survivors.

Susan's mouth was dry and her heart pounded as she caught sight of the solitary figure sitting on the low wall that ran in front of the cottages and formed part of the quay. Maud had returned home just before dawn to change into dry clothes, but her face had been ashen and a hacking cough tore through her chest. Despite Susan's pleading, she'd refused to remain indoors.

'Where are the others?' Susan asked, of her brothers' wives and sweethearts, concern for her mother making her voice sharper than she had intended.

'I sent them home to their own mothers,' Maud said. 'They'll be back soon.'

'And Billy?'

'Gone out with the men to search.'

With a broken leg, and his fear of the sea, Billy was showing great courage for one so young. Susan could only pray that he would return home safely.

The day wore on and as, one by one, the remnants of Mousehole's fishing fleet returned from their fruitless search, the silence grew more profound.

The storm hit again that night, and in the still, bitter dawn that followed, the women gathered their children and turned their backs on the sea. Hope had died with their men. It was time to grieve.

The Tasman Sea, May 1770

In three months' time they would have been at sea for two years and Jonathan would celebrate his nineteenth birthday. He lay on his uncomfortable bunk and listened to his uncle snore. The poor man had suffered since they had left New Zealand, and Jonathan was concerned. The ship's doctor had done his best, but Josiah Wimbourne was no sailor, and the slightest sway and dip of the *Endeavour* had him green at the gills and flat on his back.

If the weather didn't let up soon, the old man would die, for he had barely eaten and could only take an occasional sip of water or brandy. At the thought of losing the man who had been almost a father to him, Jonathan felt cold. He should never have insisted they continue after Tahiti. The weather had been appalling: they had been blown repeatedly off course, and apart from a couple of months at anchor in a sheltered North New Zealand bay, they had battled against the wind and the waves ever since. It was extraordinary weather for such southerly waters, where they had been led to expect light winds and a flat sea. Even the sailors were exhausted by the constant battle to keep afloat.

With a deep sigh, Jonathan stood up and looked at the cramped space. Boxes and cases needed during the trip were stored in every corner. He felt restless after the inactivity of the past few months, while the stench of sickness and the claustrophobic atmosphere of the tiny cabin were making his head ache. He needed fresh air and exercise.

He snatched up a heavy coat and left the cabin. As he closed the door quietly behind him the wind and rain assailed him, tearing at his clothes and whipping his hair. He made unsteady progress along the deserted deck, almost revelling in the needle-sharp attack of the rain. Anything was better than sitting in the cabin, and the rain was washing away the stench of sickness that clung to them all, these days.

After many windswept months of charting New Zealand, they had anchored for a second time in a sheltered bay, restocked the ship and left its shores eighteen days ago. The bad weather had followed them, with the wind still blowing, the sea running high. They were sailing west, heading for Van Diemen's Land and the coast of New Holland. From there, they would go north for the East Indies and England. The adventure was almost over.

The *Endeavour* bucked and plunged, and the sailors struggled to haul in the mainsail, letting the foresail, mizzen staysail and balanced mizzen take the strain as the spray lashed the deck and the rain soaked them to the skin. Jonathan braced himself against the rail, his feet planted on the deck so that he could ride with the roll of the ship. The stormy waters reminded him of Cornwall and how the sea raced into the harbours and thundered against the cliffs. But there were no cliffs here, no sight of land at all, and the fear returned as it had when they had so nearly been grounded by a great ledge of rock off New Zealand. They were a long way from civilisation – a long way from home – and the sheer size and power of the ocean made him realise how small they all were, and how vulnerable.

He'd begun to wonder how he would settle down to normal life on his return to England. It would seem mundane after this trip. He couldn't envisage living in Cornwall and running the estate any more than he could see himself furthering his education in London or taking his place in the House of Lords when he attained his majority.

The tameness of working on the estate accounts didn't appeal to him, and he knew that this journey would be the first of many. He'd been lured by the freedom of travel and, regardless of what was expected of him as the Earl of Kernow, he planned to marry Susan. Together they would begin a new life far from the stultifying ways of England.

The memory of her smile, of her long hair blowing in the wind and her beautiful blue eyes made him long to see her again. The life of an explorer need not be lonely, and his Susan had always been curious as to what lay beyond the horizon. He vowed that the promises he had made in Mousehole would not be broken.

He lowered his head as the rain hammered at his face. He was no longer a child, and neither was Susan – and therein lay the truth. It was time to take their chance of a good life together and fly in the face of convention. He sighed deeply, knowing the trouble it would cause. Why must life be so complicated?

Turning his back on the waters, he made his way carefully along the deck to the small stateroom that had been furnished for the officers and passengers. With comfortable chairs and a well-stocked library, it smelt of leather, brandy and pipe-smoke, and had become a favourite haunt of those who had not succumbed to seasickness, to wile away the long hours of inactivity. Jonathan peered through the window and saw that there were only two occupants. The rough seas were taking their toll.

He went in and closed the door behind him. Straight away he was assailed by the reek of damp dog. The three grey-hounds were sprawled on the floor, moving only to scratch or bite at worrisome fleas. Their master, Joseph Banks, the wealthy botanist, was pontificating as usual and ignored him, but Sydney Parkinson flashed him a grin.

Jonathan grinned back. 'Hello, Syd. Rough day – even for dogs.'

Sydney tried to keep a straight face. They had agreed that Banks was tiresome in his condemnation of Lieutenant Cook while his dogs stank to high heaven and were a constant nuisance. Not that Sydney would say so within earshot of Banks, his mentor and benefactor: he was too canny an Edinburgh man for that.

Sydney was a Quaker, and although he was five years older than Jonathan, the two young men had become firm friends during the voyage. He was a gifted artist and had caught the eye of Joseph Banks, who had made it possible for him to be on board the *Endeavour* as assistant to the official artist Alexander Buchan. That unfortunate man had died before they had even reached Tahiti, so now Sydney was constantly busy with botanical drawings and natural-history specimens. It was a heavy responsibility and brought with it a tremendous workload for one so young. He often sat up all night to complete a drawing.

Jonathan poured a glass of brandy, stepped round Banks's greyhounds, which were taking up most of the floor, and settled into a chair with a book. Yet it was difficult to concentrate as Banks droned on. He was tempted to interject, to contradict the man, for he was all hot air and displayed the pompous self-righteousness of someone accustomed to having his way. But Jonathan knew his views would not be appreciated and that a shouting-match would result.

The change in atmosphere on the *Endeavour* had become apparent when they were navigating the southernmost tip of New Zealand. Banks had been insistent that Cook should navigate the deep fjords on the western coast. Cook had known the danger of being in a sailing ship on a west coast with a west wind blowing. To enter a narrow confine in which turning would be difficult, if not impossible, would have been foolish to say the least. The nature of the fjord indicated a rocky bottom, which would offer poor purchase for an anchor, and Cook had – quite rightly, to Jonathan's mind – refused to jeopardise his ship.

Banks's pride had been dented, and although he remained coldly polite in his dealings with Cook, he never missed an opportunity to remark that the commander lacked the nerve to explore such a tempting series of waterways. The other passengers were reluctant to be drawn into the argument and refused to take sides. But Cook seemed undisturbed by the sniping – in fact, he ignored it, just as he had Banks's order.

Jonathan finished his brandy and closed the book. Even the fustiness of his cabin was more tempting than listening to Banks talk nonsense. He caught his friend's eye and winked in sympathy. Poor Sydney, he thought, as he stepped over the damned dogs and headed for the door. Banks had him cornered.

Mousehole, May 1770

The granite church of St Pol de Leon was less than a mile inland and sat high on the hill above the village, surrounded by wind-bowed trees, standing stones and tiny granite cottages. The Celtic cross built into the churchyard wall was more than a thousand years old. Gulls screamed as they circled in a sky almost clear of clouds, and far below in the distance, the sea sparkled benignly in the sunlight, its power harnessed now that the storm had passed.

The remnants of the fishing fleet rocked at anchor in the harbour, the nets and creels stacked ready in the bows. The village was silent and sombre for the inhabitants of the cottages had wound their way up the path they trod every Sunday to hear Ezra Collinson commit to God the souls of the lost.

He had arrived to take over the parish a year ago. He was a single man of indeterminate age, but most of his flock were of the opinion that he was approaching thirty, and therefore in need of a wife. His dark hair and eyes should have made him handsome, but his nose was too long, and his lugubrious

expression rarely softened into a smile. Lean of body and long-limbed, he'd become a familiar sight in his black coat as he tramped the hills and shores. A rousing orator in church, he seemed driven in his calling and had little time for social intercourse, except when Lady Cadwallader commanded his presence at the manor.

With the words of their minister in their ears, the congregation shuffled away from the hard pews, clogs clattering on the cold stone floor, to make for the door and the steep trek down the valley to the village. They had tried to find something uplifting in the sermon, but the kingdom of heaven seemed far from the reality of life without their sons and husbands. It was as if God had deserted them, and all the faith in the world wouldn't bring their men home or ease their lives.

'It's not right we've no bodies to bury,' wheezed Maud, as they left the gloomy interior and stepped out into the sunshine. 'How can we mourn when we have no proof they be gone?'

Susan signalled to the others to start back without them, and took Maud's elbow as the racking cough almost bent her mother double. They had had this conversation before and still her mother wouldn't accept that her men were dead. 'It's been more than a week,' she murmured, in the Cornish language they still used among themselves. 'Miracles don't happen to folk like us.'

Maud wiped her mouth on a scrap of cloth and sank gratefully on to a tussock of rough grass, her rusty-black skirt billowing. 'I know,' she gasped. 'But I can't seem to get it into my head they be really gone. That I'll never see them again.' The shadow of her plain black bonnet veiled her face as she burst into tears.

'You will see them in the kingdom of heaven.' Ezra Collinson had approached unseen from the church doorway. He put a hand on Maud's shoulder, his pale face creased with concern. 'Have faith, sister.'

Maud looked up at him, blue eyes damp. Her face was ashen but for the bright spots of colour the fever had put into her cheeks. 'Keeping faith isn't easy, Mr Collinson,' she said, in heavily accented English. 'It don't pay the rent or feed the family. It certainly don't soothe the pain.'

'Earthly burdens have to be carried in the sure knowledge that we've earned our place at God's right hand,' replied the minister, his pale, delicate fingers clutching at the edges of his long black coat just as they did when he preached. 'God is merely testing our faith.'

Susan had had enough of his clap-trap. She'd never taken to the man, or understood his ability to ignore the poverty and desperation of his parish at times like these. 'We have burdens enough, Mr Collinson,' she snapped. 'If God was as loving as you say, then why did He take our men? Why test us at all?'

The sallow cheeks reddened as the dark eyes shifted to avoid her furious glare. 'He had His reasons,' was the reply. 'It is not for us to question them.' With another pat on Maud's shoulder, he left them and strode across the churchyard towards his house, coat-tails flapping, stoutly shod feet unhindered by the rocks that pushed up through the grass.

'You shouldn't speak to the minister like that,' scolded Maud, as she struggled to her feet and adjusted her skirt and bonnet.

'What does he know about burdens when he lives in that house and has a servant and housekeeper to run around after him?' hissed Susan. 'He's never done a day's labour in his life, yet he preaches about burdens and suffering as if he understands what they are. Look at his hands – as soft as her ladyship's.'

Maud grasped her arm and leant heavily on it as she caught her breath. Her grief had sapped her energy and made her old, yet she was barely past forty, her dark brown hair remarkably

untouched with grey. 'He's a good man, Susan,' she puffed. 'You'd do well to remember that later.'

Susan frowned as she adjusted the shawl over her wind-swept hair, and eased her ribcage beneath the tight bodice. She had already let out the seams, so there was little more she could do except try not to breathe too deeply. 'Why?'

A fit of coughing shuddered through Maud's narrow frame, making it impossible for her to reply. The night's vigil on the quay had taken its toll on a constitution weakened by hard labour at the gutting tables and herring barrels. When she was able to speak, her words dripped like icy water down Susan's spine.

'He'll be coming to the house to ask for your hand within the month.'

Susan couldn't believe she'd heard her mother correctly, yet there was a determined light in Maud's eyes that said she had. 'You've a fever,' she said, with a nervous laugh. 'You don't know what you're saying.'

Maud tightened her grip on Susan's arm and forced her to walk through the long grass towards the path that would take them down to the village. 'He spoke to your father ten days ago,' she said, voice breaking at the mention of her husband. 'We talked it over and I was going to tell you when your father . . . your father and the boys . . .'

They remembered that last morning when their men had left early to catch the pilchards that had been sighted far off the point.

'I won't marry him.' Susan stood squarely on the grass that swayed and rustled round the leaning granite headstones. She folded her arms as her skirt brushed pollen from the wild-flowers. 'Nothing on this earth would make me.'

For a long moment Maud looked into her face. 'You always were a headstrong girl,' she said, 'but you'd be wise to consider him.' Before Susan could reply, she tugged her daughter's arm and they resumed their journey.

Susan stared out over the sea and down to the tiny white houses that clustered in the lee of the steep valley. She couldn't possibly marry Ezra Collinson. She'd rather die. The thought of that solemn face, the soft white hands that she suspected were cold and clammy, made her feel sick. How could her parents have contemplated such a match for her when they knew she loved Jonathan?

'Ezra Collinson has connections,' Maud said eventually. 'He's the youngest son of the Earl of Glamorgan, and although he won't inherit the family fortune, he has a healthy income from a trust set up by his grandmother, as well as his minister's stipend. You'd be set up for life, girl, and never have to work on the nets or salting tubs again.'

'You seem well informed, Mother, but it won't do any good,' she retorted. 'He could have treasure chests stuffed with gold and I still wouldn't want him.' She took the shawl from her head and let her hair blow in the wind coming off the sea. There were tears in her eyes, but she was damned if she would let her mother know the extent to which she raged against the prospect of having to marry such a humourless man. If only her father had lived long enough to discuss it with her – he would never have forced her into such a union. And if only Jonathan hadn't gone away to sea. The thought of marriage to anyone else – let alone Ezra Collinson – left her shaking with anger, even fear. She would lose Jonathan for ever.

'Since when does a girl like you turn down such an offer?' Maud came to a halt, her skirt scuffing the path, her bonnet ribbons fluttering beneath her chin. 'You should be married with a home of your own by now, but instead you're sighing for Jonathan Cadwallader, the young wastrel.'

'He's not a wastrel,' Susan protested.

Maud pursed her lips. 'He's gone, Susan, and even if he does come back, he won't be free. Lady Cadwallader's found a suitable wife for him. She's the daughter of a titled family in London.'

Susan's heart constricted at the thought of Jonathan married to someone else – she had indeed been waiting for his return and the fulfilment of the promises they had made on his last visit home. 'Since when has her ladyship confided in you?' Her tone was laced with pain and disbelief.

Maud grimaced. 'She hasn't. Our paths crossed one day shortly after his lordship left on that expedition with his uncle. She said she was glad that her son would be away for at least two years. It would give both of you time to come to your senses, and she hoped you'd find a husband among the men of the village.' Maud was overtaken by another coughing fit. 'We are agreed that your friendship with him isn't proper now you're both grown-up. People like them don't marry people like us – I've told you so often enough.'

Susan could imagine the haughty dowager sitting in her carriage in her finery, talking down to her mother, Maud bobbing a curtsy and simpering. It was true, what her mother said: there was a whole world of difference between her and Jonathan, but that had never mattered to them – the proof was in his promise to marry her.

She lifted her chin defiantly. 'Lady Cadwallader should mind her own business,' she hissed. 'My finding a husband has nothing to do with her, and if Jonathan was here he'd agree with me.' She lifted the hem of her skirt out of the dust as they began to walk again.

Maud seemed to be tiring and her footsteps were less confident as they negotiated the last, steepest section of the cliff path. 'His lordship's a long way away,' she sighed, 'and his future's arranged from the minute he returns. I'm sure he meant any promise he might have made, but he could never marry you.' The air rattled in her bony chest. 'Her ladyship was only being wise, my dear, and for once I agree with her.'

'Just because she owns all the land round here and we pay

her tithes and rent, it doesn't mean she can poke her nose into our lives.'

Maud's smile was sad. 'She can if it concerns her one and only son,' she said softly. 'He's all she has.'

'His lordship died a long time ago,' retorted her daughter.

Maud ignored her and carried on as if she needed to say everything before they reached the cottage. Perhaps she imagined her time was running out. 'Her ladyship spoke to me again about six weeks ago. She mentioned Ezra Collinson's interest in you and, believe me, Susan, I was as shocked as you that he should wish to court the daughter of a fisherman.'

Susan felt a chill run through her as she saw the glint of pride in her mother's eyes. Now she understood. She stopped walking and faced her. 'Her ladyship knew just the right strings to pull, didn't she?' Her voice was low, anger simmering beneath the surface.

'I don't know what you mean,' muttered Maud.

'Some may reckon Ezra Collinson a catch. He's of good breeding and education, and has his own money. Her ladyship knew you couldn't resist the thought of your only daughter marrying such a man. And you certainly couldn't resist boasting about his connections.'

Maud flushed. 'I only want what's best for you,' she said. 'Just think, Susan, you'd be mistress of your own household – the minister's wife, someone the whole village would look up to.'

'Her ladyship wants me married before Jonathan comes back,' Susan replied coldly, 'and you want to have one up on all the other old tabbies at the salting bins. Well, I won't have him, and that's that.'

'I knew you'd be difficult. I thought that if perhaps I tried to . . . But it's too late.'

Susan felt the colour drain from her face. 'Why?'

'I hinted you'd view Mr Collinson's proposal favourably,' Maud replied, in a small voice.

'Well, he'll be disappointed.'

Maud shook her head, her bonnet tipping over her eyes. 'You don't understand,' she croaked. 'Her ladyship has promised . . . and I've promised . . .' Words failed her and she looked away.

Susan stared at her in horror. 'What have you promised?'

'That you will agree to marry Mr Collinson.' Maud squared her shoulders and looked back into her daughter's furious face. Now her words came thick and fast: 'Her ladyship sent for me the day after your father . . . She promised that when you marry she'll sign papers that'll let our family live rent free in the cottage always.'

Susan's legs wouldn't hold her up any longer. She sank on to the grassy bank and hugged her knees. 'How could you do such a thing?' she gasped. 'You're my mother! You should be protecting me, not selling me as if I was the day's catch.'

Maud seemed to have regained some of her formidable strength as her shadow fell over Susan. Her voice was firm and brooked no argument. 'I had no choice. If you don't marry Mr Collinson we'll be thrown out of this cottage. We have no boat, no man to look after us. Where would we go? What would happen to you, Billy and me?' Her voice rose with every word. 'Should we go and live out on the moors like those poor souls who scratch a living sifting through the muck at the pit-heads? Should I see my only living son sent down the mine so he can die of the lung fever before he's thirty?'

'We'd find a way,' muttered Susan, through numb lips.

'How?' her mother shouted. 'Without a boat we'll have no fish to sell, and work's hard enough to find as it is, with so many widows now.' The energy left her as swiftly as it had come, and she seemed to shrivel in her despair.

Susan could barely see her mother through her own tears. She rose slowly to her feet, gathered Maud in her arms and

held her. Maud was right. She had no alternative. She was
trapped.

The Great Barrier Reef, June 1770

It was a clear moonlit night, with only a light breeze to fill the
sails as the *Endeavour* ploughed slowly along the coastline.
They'd had first sight of land some weeks ago, and with the
weather improving, Josiah had at last found his sea-legs. He
was ensconced in a chair on deck, swaddled in blankets, which
were in danger of being set alight by his pipe, his drawn face
and sunken eyes testament to his erstwhile suffering. He
watched the sailors heaving casts to measure the depth of
the water. 'Tricky business with so many islands about and an
uncharted coastline,' he muttered. 'Cook's taking a huge risk
in trying to navigate these waters in the dark.'

Jonathan, who was enjoying some brandy and an after-
dinner cigar, was contemplating the magnificent sky. The
stars were quite a sight beyond the billowing sails and he
couldn't get over how bright and clear the constellations were
in the south. 'He's managed well enough so far,' he murmured. 'And you have to admit, Uncle, the scenery on this
coastline is extraordinary. Just look at those islands.'

Josiah pulled a face. 'Once the initial pleasure is over, one
realises that one island is much like another, and none offers
more than a few palm trees and a sandy beach.'

Sydney Parkinson had emerged from his cabin and over-
heard Josiah's comment. He flopped into the chair beside
Jonathan. 'Rather more than just a few palm trees, sir. We
discovered thousands of new species of plant and wildlife in
Botany Bay alone. It will take me years to catalogue and draw
them all.'

Josiah regarded the young Scot. 'Plants aren't much use
when there's no fresh water, food or wood,' he grumbled. 'You

need only look at the natives to see that life is barely sustainable here.'

Sydney chewed his lip, his delicate features lit by the lantern behind him. 'They may appear wretched,' he said, 'but it seems to me they are content. The earth and the sea sustain them, the climate is clement, and as they have no need of the superfluous trappings we Europeans deem so important, they are happy in their ignorance.'

'They're savages,' rumbled Josiah, 'poor, skinny, ignorant wretches who've barely evolved from earliest man, and are eking out an existence in a barren, God-forsaken land to who knows what purpose? So much for the great southern land that was to provide King and country with gold and riches beyond our dreams. It doesn't exist.'

'I agree that it might not appeal to those who seek their fortune,' said Sydney, 'but it excites the imagination, don't you think?'

Jonathan threw the last of his cigar overboard. 'It certainly does,' he said, rising to his feet. 'I want to know what lies beyond the shores, and what manner of country this is. I want to explore as much as possible, for this must indeed be a vast place if the old maps are anything to go by.'

Sydney nodded. 'I've seen those maps too. If it is indeed all one continent, perhaps the stories of a great southland are not to be dismissed.'

'Savages and tropical fever,' grumbled Josiah. 'Mark my words, lads, you won't find much more than that.'

'There are savages on board, sir,' Sydney protested. 'Remember what happened to Mr Orton.'

'The man is a sot,' snapped Josiah. 'If he'd been sober, it wouldn't have happened.'

'Nevertheless, sir,' Sydney pressed, 'no man deserves to be stripped of his clothes and have his ears docked. It's the act of a barbarian, and I cannot feel safe until the perpetrator is caught.'

'Cook has already suspended Midshipman Magra from duty.' Josiah wrapped the blanket more firmly round his wasted body and shivered, although the evening was warm. 'It seems he has his man, so you can rest easy.'

Jonathan hadn't been listening to this exchange. His mind was still working on what Sydney had said about this land exciting the imagination. He paced the deck as he envisaged a life of discovery and exploration. He'd longed to go further inland at Botany Bay, and been frustrated that he was unable to talk to the natives there – even Tupaia hadn't understood their language. Jonathan had been sure they would have learnt much more if they could have found a way to communicate. 'You're right, Sydney,' he said, breaking into the conversation. 'We've only seen this eastern coastline, and no man has penetrated further inland. What an adventure it would be to survey the interior and discover what lies beyond those forests.'

Both men stared at him, taking a moment to gather their thoughts before they returned to the previous conversation. 'You have an overactive imagination, my boy,' said Josiah. 'This enterprise should have been adventure enough for you. Now it is time to put aside childish dreams and think of your position in life and the responsibilities that come with the estate. There won't be time for exploring after you return home.' He waved away Jonathan's attempt to continue the argument. 'I'm for bed,' he said, struggling out of the chair. 'It's almost eleven, not the hour for debate.'

Jonathan saw that there was no point in voicing his ambitions further, yet he knew his dream would live on and one day he would fulfil it, with or without his family's blessing. He grasped his uncle's arm to help him, reminded once again of how frail he'd become as the older man clung to him and swayed on his feet.

The ship came to a sudden grinding, shuddering halt and they were both sent crashing to the deck.

'What the blazes?' Josiah grasped Jonathan and, with Sydney's help, managed to get back on his feet.

'We've hit rocks,' his nephew told him, as chaos broke out and the sailors ran round them, their bare feet thudding on the planks as Cook and his officers yelled commands.

'We'll drown.' Sydney was paler than ever now, his delicate hands grasping at his throat as though he was already in the water.

'Pull yourself together, Syd,' Jonathan said. 'This is no time for hysteria, and Cook's going to need every hand on deck if we're not to sink.'

The sails were taken in and the small boats hoisted into the water so the sailors could measure the depths round them and gauge the damage. Their cries drifted up in the light breeze.

'Four fathoms here, Captain.'

'Only three here, sir.'

'Down to one fathom, sir.'

'Coral ledge!'

Jonathan held Josiah's arm as the other passengers streamed from their cabins. Sydney, he realised, wasn't the only passenger who seemed convinced they were about to sink or be taken captive by savages. There was a great deal of speculation and doom-mongering, and even the usually calm Banks said he found the situation somewhat alarming. Yet as Jonathan watched the sailors he felt oddly calm. It was not his fate to die here, even though the tide was high and the reef must have struck below the ship's water-line.

Cook took charge. 'We must lighten her. Throw overboard anything of weight – guns, iron, stone ballast, casks, hoops, staves, oil jars, decayed stores.'

Jonathan, the rest of the passengers and the crew worked through the night. Josiah was still weak, and soon tired, but he refused to return to his cabin to rest. Placing a chair next to the hold, he sat down and helped form a link in a chain of men who passed things up from the hold and along the line to the side of the ship where they were dropped in the sea.

Jonathan grasped that Sydney might panic, and therefore should be kept occupied. With little concern for his friend's artistic hands, he made him help lift the six carriage guns and heave them over the side. They were soon sweating and filthy, but at five in the morning their work wasn't complete. The *Endeavour* remained wedged on the coral.

Empty casks and even fresh-water barrels were tossed over the side. Iron was ripped from the deck and heavy furniture wrestled from the staterooms and officers' quarters to be cast into the sea. The little boats were tied together and filled with the heavy cases of scientific instruments that were too precious to discard, followed by the plant samples, books and maps. The pigs squealed as they were tossed into the water to sink or swim, and the goats that had provided meat and milk bleated as they went over the side. The ducks paddled off happily, but the chickens flew up into the rigging.

Their efforts through the night appeared to be rewarded, for the ship wasn't taking on water, and the sea remained calm. Jonathan reckoned they'd disposed of at least fifty tons, but even that wasn't enough to refloat the *Endeavour*.

It was now eleven in the morning and everyone was exhausted, but Cook ordered them to lighten the ship by any means they could think of: it was imperative that they floated free before high tide.

Josiah reluctantly gathered up the books in the library while the shelves were dismantled. Barrels of rum and beer were brought up from the hold and the sailors watched grimly as they floated away. Jonathan went to his cabin, jettisoned his heavy suitcases and trunks, then ripped out the bunks and other furniture. In the galley the one-armed cook was removing heavy pots, pans, sacks of flour and vegetables, and yelling at his men to unbolt the table and dismantle the great stones that formed the three ovens of which he'd been proud.

They were working against the tide, and as it rose, the ship took on water. Two of the pumps were working flat out in the hold, but as noon approached, the *Endeavour* heeled alarmingly to starboard.

'Man all four pumps,' commanded Cook. It was now five o'clock in the afternoon, and the tide was rising again.

Jonathan dragged Sydney with him into the bowels of the ship and, with three other men, tried to work the fourth pump. But something was wrong. It wouldn't budge, even after Jonathan had put his considerable strength to the handle. He kicked it in frustration, using every profanity he knew, but still it wouldn't move – and they were running out of time. The tide was rising, the ship was righting herself and the leak was gaining on the three remaining pumps. Sydney's prophecy was looking more likely with every passing minute, and for the first time in his life, Jonathan knew fear.

Night had fallen and everyone was bedraggled and exhausted, dredging up every last shred of energy to man the pumps. The ship had righted, but the leak was threatening to overcome them.

Jonathan's muscles ached and his hands were blistered, while sweat soaked his shirt and stung his eyes. It was dark and musty, deep in the *Endeavour*, and water was slapping at his calves. Despite his determination to remain calm the fear returned. They were seven leagues from shore, too far to swim after toiling for nearly twenty-four hours. Perhaps he was indeed fated to drown in the star-studded night of this southern ocean.

Nine o'clock came and went. Their situation was still grave. If they remained trapped on the reef the ship would keel over and break up. If they floated off, the water would rush in and they would sink.

'I have no choice but to heave her off,' said Cook, as he stood by the pumps. 'It's a risk, but one that must be taken if we are to have any chance. I need as many hands as can be spared from the pumps to work the capstan and windlass.'

Jonathan eyed Sydney, who was soaked with sweat, his hands bloody from his efforts. 'Keep pumping,' he said quietly. 'Cook seems to know what he's doing.'

The *Endeavour* was finally floated off the reef and into deep water just after ten o'clock that night. More than three feet of water stood in the hold as the fore-topmast and foreyard sails were raised and the ship was warped to the south-east and land. Jonathan and Sydney climbed wearily on to the deck for a rest as some of the sailors were taken to one side to work on a lower studding sail or shovel out the animal pens – a bizarre activity at a time like this. 'What are they doing?' asked Jonathan, of the grizzled sailor who'd been working beside him on the pumps.

'Preparing to fother the ship,' came the rasped reply. He was sweating profusely, and the veins stood out on his neck and sturdy arms. 'Making a plug for the 'oles.'

'How can they do that with a bit of sail?'

The sailor spat a gobbet of phlegm over the side and looked at him as if he should know better than to ask. 'We untwist and unpick the old ropes, mix 'em with wool, chop it up into little bits and stick it over the sail. Then we chucks chicken and pig shit and any other kind we can find at it. Horse is best, but we ain't got none, so them dogs is useful for something at last. Then we 'aul it under the ship's bottom with ropes.'

'What if you don't know where the hole is?'

The rheumy eyes regarded him with disdain. 'We 'aul the bloody thing from one end to the other until we finds it, o' course.'

'And then?' The sailor was tiring of his questions – but Jonathan had to understand what was happening.

The sailor spat again. 'Then the wool and such is washed off and floats into the 'ole and plugs it up enough to let us get to shore.'

'Ingenious,' muttered Jonathan.

'You want to 'ope it works, sir. Otherwise you and me'll be pumping till kingdom come.'

Sydney slumped to the deck, his face grey. Jonathan passed him the small silver flask of brandy, which they shared to the last drop.

'Stop all pumps but one,' came the order, after what felt like hours of nervous waiting. 'The fothering has worked well enough for us to get ashore.'

The mood on the ship lightened. Passengers and crew sprawled on deck as two of the little boats went out to scout the coastline for a safe harbour in which they would make the repairs.

Jonathan staggered away from the object of torture he'd been working on for so many hours and emerged into the fresh air to slump with his back to the denuded stateroom, feet splayed before him on the deck. He was bankrupt of strength, too tired to eat, sleep or talk. Sydney collapsed beside him, arms and legs trembling from the unaccustomed effort, chest heaving.

Josiah had managed to keep his chair, which he carried over to them. He sat down. 'Well done, boys,' he said, as he mopped his sweating brow. 'Knew Cook wouldn't let us down.'

Jonathan eyed him with affection. He'd known nothing of the sort, but at least the threat of shipwreck so far from home had brought colour to his cheeks and restored him to his bombastic self.

Tahiti, June 1770

The island was silent in the heat of the day for there were no ships at anchor in the bay and only one outrigger canoe lay on the shore. The beach was deserted but for wading birds, and at the heart of the village beneath the shade of the palms nothing moved but lazy plumes of smoke from burnt-out huts. Where once there had been women cooking and children playing, the central clearing was silent and deserted, with only the remnants of old cooking vessels and coconut husks left behind. The smell of death hung over the deserted village.

The sickness had come to the island a few weeks ago, carried by sailors from one of the big ships that had anchored in the bay. At first there had been only mild concern, for since the coming of ships and sailors, there was always sickness on the island and the witch-doctor had seemed to have it under control.

Then people had begun to die. The very young, the old and weak went first. Then the stronger men and women were struck down, which cut a devastating swathe through the population. Some survived the pestilence, but they were few and random. Panic set in, for their wisest, most revered leader, Tupaia, was still away, and the witch-doctor's medicine no longer worked. Those unaffected by the fever left, their belongings packed into their outriggers as they paddled away to other islands in the hope of escaping death. They left behind the dying, and the few who wanted to look after them.

Lianni's teeth chattered as the fever tore through her and soaked the brightly coloured sarong and plaited grass mat beneath her. She lay on the floor of the palm-leaf hut, curled beneath a thin blanket, her knees to her chest in an effort to quell the tremors that shook her wasted body. The red spots that had appeared some time before itched and burned, but no amount of cooling water or scratching could relieve them and she was in torment.

A long time ago, a man had come from the ship with a black bag, had held her wrist, looked into her eyes and mouth, and inspected the spots. He'd said it was measles, and that she would soon be better. But Lianni didn't feel better and now she was terrified, not only for herself but for her baby. This sickness had already killed her mother, two of her sisters and an uncle. Now the sound of weeping drifted in from a nearby hut, reminding her that nearly every family on the island had lost someone to it.

She huddled beneath the blanket, eyes aching, head pounding as wave upon wave of heat seemed to burn her up from inside, yet her teeth chattered and her body shook as if she was standing in the coldest water at the mercy of a bitter wind.

'Lianni, drink this. It will cool you.'

Gentle arms lifted her head from the floor and through the haze of fever she could see it was her father's sister, Tahani, who had fallen ill early on but had miraculously survived. She felt the cool, sweet coconut milk dribble into her mouth, but it hurt to swallow and she soon gave up trying. 'Where is Tahamma?' she whispered.

'He's well and safe, Lianni. Your papa took him and the other young ones to another island, to our brother's house. There is no sickness there.'

Lianni barely heard what her aunt was saying, and certainly couldn't understand why her precious baby wasn't lying with her as usual. Her mind was fogged, her thoughts muddled. 'I want to see him.' Her voice was a sigh, the words barely audible above the raucous cries of the birds in the surrounding forest. 'I must hold him just once more.'

Tahani put her arms round her, rocking her as she had done when she was small. 'It's not safe, Lianni,' she murmured, as she smoothed back the sweat-dampened hair. 'He's too small to fight this thing, and I have no way to send a message to the other island.'

Lianni closed her eyes, soothed by her aunt's embrace. Tahani was right, she realised, as the fog of confusion cleared momentarily. Tahamma was only a few months old, and although he was a sturdy baby, with chubby arms and legs and a rounded belly, she knew of other children who had been just as sturdy but had succumbed anyway. At least he would be safe on another island.

Her eyes flickered open and she became agitated as she remembered what had worried her for the past few days. She struggled away from her aunt and, ignoring her pleas to lie down and rest, crawled from the mat and scrabbled in the earth at the back of the hut. Her fingers caught in the rough cloth and she drew up the parcel, dusting it off as she held it close. She crawled back to her aunt and collapsed on the blanket, all energy spent, the spark of life dimming.

'Give this to Tahamma when he reaches manhood,' she whispered, handing the parcel to her aunt. 'Guard it with your life. It is his inheritance.'

Tahani turned back the cloth and her eyes widened. She took out the pocket watch and lifted it so that the sun shone on the bright stone at the centre and glinted on the gold. 'Where did you steal this?' she breathed.

'I'm not a thief,' gasped Lianni. 'Tahamma's father gave it to me before he left with Tupaia.'

Tahani opened the casing and stared at the two miniature portraits. Her expression softened as she saw that Lianni had spoken the truth.

Lianni rolled on to her side and, with surprising strength, clamped her hand on her aunt's arm. 'Promise you will keep it for him, Tahani. Promise you will never sell it, no matter how bad things become.'

Tahani nodded. 'I promise,' she replied. 'But I will have to keep it from my husband. A thing like this would buy much rum and tobacco.' She closed the casing and wrapped it in the cloth again.

'Hide it,' Lianni whispered. 'Guard it with your life.'

Tahani clutched the parcel to her chest as tears rolled down her face. 'With my life,' she murmured.

Lianni closed her eyes. It was done. Her little son would never remember his mother's loving embrace, but he would know the faces of his parents and recognise the red teardrop on his skin as having come from his father. Slowly she released her hold on life, and as her last breath left her in a sigh, she sank into the welcoming void of darkness where there was no fever, no pain and no earthly cares.

5

Mousehole, June 1770

The house stood beyond the church and out of sight of the granite and greenstone quarries that neatly bisected the village. It was ugly, with little to recommend it. Built of the local granite, its windows overlooked the windswept grass of the headland and the bleak churchyard in which so many fishermen and sailors were buried. The enormous rooms echoed with every step, and draughts whistled under the doors and round the windows. It was meagrely furnished, so Ezra had taken to using two rooms downstairs and the smallest bedroom, which looked out towards the moors. A woman came up from the village each day to cook and clean, and Higgins, his manservant, lived in a room off the enormous kitchen – the only really warm room in the house because the range remained lit even at the height of summer.

Ezra slowed his pace as he approached, and although he was still buoyed by the rousing Sunday sermon he had given that morning, his spirits tumbled at the thought of what he must do this evening. Even though he'd waited several weeks, the timing was still wrong, his proposal inappropriate after the loss they had suffered. He had tried to change the arrangements, but Maud Penhalligan had been strangely adamant that they should remain the same. He was committed to make a fool of himself.

Not that he didn't find Susan Penhalligan attractive – far from it – but she had made her dislike plain, and he was dreading her scorn. If only he hadn't confided in the dowager.

If only she hadn't bullied him into this ill-fated proposal. But things had gone too far for him to back out now, and Maud was expecting him at seven.

With a deep sigh he turned his back on the house to look out over the grassy headland towards the sea. A naturally shy man outside his church, he had always found it difficult to communicate with his parishioners, and he knew he often gave the impression that he was cold and distant. He was not: he became awkward when faced with their poverty and stoic acceptance of tragedy. It hid the heart-wrenching pity he felt for them and the frustration that he could offer no real solace or help. He knew he would always be an outsider, a stranger with soft hands, stilted manners and wealthy connections, a curiosity foisted upon them by the Church, but he longed for their belief in the message he brought them.

Ezra was stirred from his thoughts when he caught sight of two women making their way down the steep path to the village. His pulse raced and his mouth dried as he realised it was Susan and her mother in a heated exchange. He had little doubt it was about himself, and felt a sickening jolt at the thought of what Susan might be saying.

Did she despise him? Was she telling her mother she would never contemplate such a match? Could she not see beyond his awkwardness to the depth of his feeling for her? But, then, why should she? He'd maintained a correct distance between them, aware of protocol and his position in the community. His demeanour had remained polite, perhaps chilly, even though he'd longed to look into her eyes and talk to her privately. But the gossips would have pounced, and Susan had enough burdens to bear without that.

He knew he should have walked away, but he couldn't take his eyes off her. She had taken the old shawl off her head, and now her glorious hair was streaming in the wind. She was as untamed as Cornwall itself, as tough as the grass that clung to the rocks and as desirable as the most precious gem. She was magnificent in her rage, her bosom rising and falling beneath the tight bodice, her chin held high. He wished he could see her eyes – surely they flashed sapphire in her sun-kissed face?

He saw the women embrace and continue their journey. He watched until they were out of sight and then, with a deep sigh, turned back towards the lonely, echoing house. To possess that fire, to hold that voluptuous body in his arms and kiss the desirable lips was a dream. She would never be his, and although she was only a fisher-girl, he felt unworthy of her. His spirits plummeted further at the thought of facing her tonight.

Ezra stepped into the gloomy hall and closed the door behind him. He stood there for a long moment, listening to the silence in the house. It would always be so for a man such as himself. Another might have founded a real home here – it had been made for a large family. The sound of children's voices and the light, quick footsteps of their mother would chase away the gloom and bring much-needed life and warmth to the echoing rooms.

Yet God had chosen him because his solitary destiny had been laid down at the moment of his birth. As the third and much younger son, he had always known he had been an unwelcome surprise to his middle-aged parents. They had had little expectation of him and, indeed, had almost forgotten he existed, leaving him for long periods with the servants to care for him until he was packed off to school.

His mother despaired at his lack of social graces and his father had made it clear he was destined for either the Church or the army. His grandmother had been the only one to show him affection. Her loving arms and soft kisses had helped heal the wounds of rejection, and when she had died it was as if his world had ended.

Her legacy had rescued him from penury and the threat of military service, and once he had heard the preaching of John

Wesley, he had known that he had found what he'd been searching for. At last he felt he belonged.

He had been chosen for God's ministry on earth, to preach His gospel and bring His flock to Paradise. The family of Christ was all he had needed – until he had seen Susan on that day almost a year ago, standing on the headland, gazing out to sea. The sight of her had taken his breath away, and he had searched for her among the parishioners, and down on the quay, feasting his eyes on her. God moved in mysterious ways. Perhaps her rejection tonight would only reinforce his belief that he was destined to do the Lord's work alone, that the message he had to give could only be delivered through abstinence and humility.

With Ezra's proposal imminent, Susan was working like a fury. Her hands were raw with cold as she gutted the herrings and packed them into barrels, but she had barely noticed: her thoughts kept returning to her mother's betrayal. Now she was back in the cottage, surrounded by the noise of too many people in too small a place, and all she wanted to do was escape.

'It's almost time,' said Maud, as the hooters sounded at the quarries. 'You'd better go and get ready.'

Susan ran her reddened hands over the coarse fabric of her skirt and apron. 'I'm ready enough,' she replied.

Maud eyed the stained skirt, the grubby bodice and bare feet. 'No daughter of mine is receiving a gentleman like that,' she rasped. 'At least wash the fish scales off your hands and change your skirt.'

'It's honest work and I'm not ashamed of it.'

Maud's hand closed tightly round her arm, and her voice was low: 'If I could change it I would, but it's too late. And you've no call to go punishing the minister – I'm sure he has no inkling of her ladyship's blackmail.' She glanced over her shoulder at the others who now lived with them. 'Neither does anyone else, so be warned.'

'Then perhaps he should be told,' said Susan. 'It might shame her into changing her mind.'

Maud looked pained. Once her mind is made up, there's no changing it. Please, Susan, think of what this marriage will mean to Billy and me, and to your brothers' widows.'

Susan bit her lip and looked at the remnants of her family. Her young sister-in-laws had gathered in Maud's kitchen, garnering warmth and comfort from the fire as they talked and wept, knitted and tried to come to terms with their loss. Two were already homeless, and one was expecting a baby soon. They had moved in with Maud, and now the tiny cottage was crammed.

Maud's two grandchildren were too young to be aware of the crisis, but not so Susan's younger brother, Billy. He was standing in the doorway, watching his friends kick a tin can over the cobbles. His leg was splinted and tightly bandaged and he leant heavily against the door jamb. It would be a long while before the break healed well enough for him to go back to sea – and even then there was no guarantee that there would be room for him on the few boats left from the fleet.

The bitterness rose in her throat and tears threatened as she thought of her lost brothers and her beloved father. How cruel Fate was, and how she hated the dowager for her lack of compassion. They had had no time to mourn properly, but their lives had been thrown into confusion by her high-handed actions. If Jonathan was at home it would never have happened.

She looked into her mother's eyes, saw shadows in them and in the lines that were etched in her face. Her hair was the only reminder of her true age, for she was as bent and bowed as an old woman with the burden she carried on her shoulders. The spirit and determination she'd shown all her life had been knocked out of her, and with a sick heart, Susan accepted that she was the only one who could repair some of the damage. 'I'll put on a clean skirt,' she murmured.

'That's my girl.' Maud's expression lightened.

Susan hurried up the wooden stairs to the bedroom she now shared with her sisters-in-law. It was a tiny space under the roof, with mattresses placed on the floor and a window that let in barely any light. Their clothes hung from nails in the heavy beams, and the only piece of furniture was a rickety table that held a bowl and jug for washing. She stripped off her clothes and used the bar of lye soap to scrub away the fish scales and the stink of pilchard until her skin glowed.

As she struggled into the only clean clothes she possessed, she thrust away the knowledge that what she was doing was wrong. She combed the tangles from her hair and blanked out the image of the minister as she tied it back with a strip of black ribbon. It didn't matter – none of it mattered now that she had lost Jonathan. The sacrifice would be worth it if only to see her mother well again and her family settled in the cottage – but she would make sure her ladyship kept her side of the bargain: there would be no marriage until Susan had seen her signature on the cottage deeds.

Ezra stared at his reflection in the pier glass. His hair shone and he was freshly shaven. The white of his neckcloth gleamed in the dull light coming through the deeply recessed window, and the cut of his breeches and jacket sat well on his lean figure. Yet he despaired: he still looked like a country parson – a scarecrow of a man with a nose that jutted from his face like a beak and bony wrists that protruded from his cuffs. He turned from the mirror and planted his hat over his hair. Vanity was a sin, but even if he had been blessed with better looks, Susan still wouldn't have wanted him.

He picked up the velvet box from the bed and opened it.

The diamond ring had been part of his inheritance from his grandmother. It wasn't valuable, the stone was quite small, but the old lady had worn it every day, and because of that it was precious to him. The gold smouldered in the dying rays of the sun, the chip of diamond sparking fire and hope. He snapped the box shut and put it into his pocket. He couldn't prevaricate any longer. The quarry hooters had sounded some time ago, and Susan would be waiting for him.

As usual Higgins was nowhere to be seen, and the cleaning woman had left. He gave a sigh of relief as he closed the front door behind him. The fewer people to witness his humiliation the better.

Ezra's heart was in his mouth as he made his way along the cobbles. He rarely came down to the quay, for the superstitious fishermen regarded it as a bad omen if they saw him as they prepared for sea, and he was sure that every window hid watching eyes and ears tuned to the clip of his buckled shoes. Did they all know the reason for his visit this evening? Maud Penhalligan had assured him that she would keep it to herself, but could she be trusted? Was his shame already public knowledge?

He reached the door. Before he could change his mind and flee back to the house on the clifftop, he rapped on the salt-seared wood.

The door opened. Maud bobbed a curtsy and pushed past him. 'I've made sure you won't be interrupted, sir,' she babbled. 'Go in. Susan's waiting for you.' With that she hurried off, the rasp of her clogs on the cobbles echoing in the still evening.

Ezra stood there, legs trembling, his nerve almost failing him.

'Please, Mr Collinson, come in.'

He felt the colour crawl up his neck to flood his face. Susan emerged from the darkness within the cottage and stood before him, plainly dressed, hair gleaming, eyes the deepest blue he'd ever seen. She had never looked lovelier, and he was lost for words.

'I don't think you want to hold this conversation on the doorstep, Mr Collinson – not unless you don't mind the whole village listening in.' She spoke to him in English, with only a hint of the Cornish burr.

He ducked his head and entered the single downstairs room.

Susan closed the door, plunging them into the flickering light of the lanterns and the glow from the stove. She indicated that he should sit on the settle, and he waited until she'd placed herself opposite him. They stared at one another, neither sure how to proceed.

Ezra wondered what she saw as she regarded him so solemnly. His spirits leapt when she smiled at him, and he finally found the courage to speak. 'Miss Penhalligan' – he cleared his throat – 'I have already spoken to your mother, and she has indicated to me that you might not be averse to my calling upon you.'

Susan inclined her head, but remained silent.

Ezra cleared his throat again and fumbled in his pocket. Drawing out the velvet box, he clasped it in his palm. 'This must have come as a surprise to you,' he began, 'but I have admired you for months, and now that I'm here, I'm almost afraid to speak.'

Susan moved restlessly in the chair, her gaze challenging, her expression coolly formal.

Ezra threw caution to the wind and dropped to his knees before her. His words rushed out of him in a storm of passion. 'Miss Penhalligan – Susan. I love you with all my heart, and although I must appear far too old and dull for one such as you, take pity on me. Beneath this rather stern façade beats the heart of a man who adores you, who yearns to love and cherish you and do all in his power to make you happy.'

Susan had been about to enlighten him on how her ladyship had blackmailed her and how she felt nothing but contempt for his part in the woman's evil-doing, but his words and actions silenced her. She was astounded by his passion, by the sheer desperation in his proposal. She had had no idea of how strongly he felt – had barely noticed him except in church. Now here he was, on his knees at her feet, his dark eyes pleading with her to hear him out. It was extraordinary – and humbling.

Her expression softened as she looked at him closely for the first time. His eyes were fine, and he was quite handsome now that his face was flushed and his mouth less stern. Perhaps he hid his feelings because he was afraid of being hurt. She felt a wave of pity for them both. She could never love him – could never help but compare him to Jonathan – and he was entitled to much more than she could give him. Her mouth dried as she tried to imagine being locked in such a one-sided marriage. Perhaps Ezra had enough passion for both of them.

'I'm honoured you feel so strongly, Mr Collinson,' she murmured, 'and your declaration has indeed come as a surprise.' She smiled to take the sting from her words. 'But I am in mourning and I don't—'

'I know you are grieving,' he cut in, 'and that this was not the time for me to speak to you.' His hands trembled as he opened the box and held it out to her. 'But when the mourning period is over, will you do me the great honour of becoming my wife?'

Her chest rose and fell within the constraints of her tight bodice as she looked first at the ring, then back at him. She could see the pleading in his eyes as the silence stretched between them, and knew that he was innocent of the dowager's conniving. He'd bared his soul, laid his pride at her feet in the hope that she could return his love. Her heart ached for him, for his vulnerability, and for the betrayal of his trust she was about to commit.

'Yes.' It was almost a sigh.

He stared back at her, clearly not daring to believe what he'd heard. Then joy flooded his face as she touched his hand in confirmation. He fumbled with the ring, almost dropping it on the stone floor before he managed to get it on to her finger. It was a perfect fit.

If only Susan could have felt a tiny fraction of Ezra's joy perhaps she wouldn't have been so desolate.

6

Endeavour River (Cooktown), June 1770

It had taken four days to limp from the reef into the mouth of the river Cook had named after his ship. When anchor was dropped into the sand and an inspection was made of the hull, they discovered just how lucky they had been. Although the fothering had partially plugged some of the jagged holes, the coral had saved them. The largest gash was jammed with a huge wedge that made it watertight. Without it, the *Endeavour* would have sunk with all hands.

Anabarru and the other women cowered with their children in the shadows of the forest as the Elders held an urgent meeting. The strange-looking canoe with the big wings had been seen some time ago, and its slow, but steady progress up the river had been watched and reported on by runners. There was great consternation. Did this frightening vessel bring an enemy to kill them? Or the Ancestor Spirits to punish them? Had they angered the Spirits in some way – and, if so, whose fault was it?

The Elders were in heated argument, their voices rising as they shook their fists and shouted in an effort to be heard. The younger men suspected enemies from the north and favoured battle. They were already preparing their spears and painting their bodies with ochre clay. The older and wiser counselled calm and dignity: they should wait to see what the craft had brought to their lands. Several respected voices insisted repeatedly that it was the Ancestor Spirits who had come so they must prepare for the end of the world.

Anabarru hugged her baby son and gathered her daughter to her side. She was terrified for them and for herself. She didn't want to die – didn't want the world to end before she could see her children grown. She watched as her husband, Watpipa, stood up and walked into the centre of the circle of Elders. He had become much respected over the past seasons and, like his illustrious ancestor Djanay, was a leader of the Council. Djanay's spirit lived in him, for he was a wise and charismatic man who silenced the angry voices and cooled the heat of their debate.

'We must remember the stories of the Ancient Ones,' he said quietly, into the silence. 'They have told us of the canoes with the wings of seabirds and the men who sailed them. Those men were hunting only the special shells and our people remained in peace with them. The Ancestor Spirits do not come as men but as a light in the sky or in the breath of a great wind.' He looked at each Elder in turn. 'We will know when the end of the world is near for the Spirits will send a sign to warn us – and they have not done so.'

'The canoe is a sign,' interrupted a younger man.

Watpipa's expression hardened as muttered agreement ran round the circle. 'You speak so because you wish to bring bloodshed and terror to our people. If the Spirits were angered they would shake the earth and send fire from the skies, not a canoe made by men.'

'So what shall we do?' asked the senior Elder. 'The canoe is beached in the river. Already our sacred lands have been violated.'

'We are hunters,' said Watpipa. 'We are taught during initiation that we must move with the silence of a snake, be as still as an anthill and as cunning as the possum. We must learn the ways of the animals and plants around us, read their signs and know all about them so that we can survive. It is the same with this canoe. Once we know and understand what it brings, we can decide whether or not it poses a threat.'

Anabarru's sigh feathered through her baby's hair as the Elders agreed to follow his advice. The end of the world hadn't come and the Spirit Ancestors had not been angered. Yet she couldn't dismiss the thought that she might not yet have fully appeased the Sacred Ones so had brought these troubles to the tribe; her actions had introduced an evil spirit among her people.

She rose to her feet, the baby on her hip, Birranulu clutching her hand. The child was a toddler now, but she was a shy, nervous little girl who rarely left her mother's side. Anabarru wondered if she remembered that terrible day on the beach. It was sharply etched in her own mind. Even now she was often woken at night by the bad dreams that had her trembling in fear.

As she stood in the shadow of the trees to watch the men gather their spears and move towards the forests that ran down to the riverbank, she knew what she had to do. She hurried across to Watpipa's mother. The old woman had gathered the children round her as their mothers went off to find the fat barramundi that lay in the shallows far upstream. She had just begun the Dreamtime story of Otchout, the father of all the great cod, and the children were entranced.

Anabarru smiled her thanks as she left her two children with her, gathered up her dilly bag, digging-stick and short spear, then hurried after the others. But once out of sight of the camp she took a different path: her destination was far away, in the middle of the bush. The journey was a reminder of the one she'd made long ago when the cleansing ceremony had taken place. When she reached the mouth of the birthing cave and had muttered the time-honoured prayers, she shivered in apprehension. Then she entered and squatted in a patch of sunlight. She hugged her knees as she followed her own story, painted in ochre on the sacred wall. It was all there. The abduction, the killing of her rapist, the birth and death of the child she had not been permitted to keep.

She felt little emotion as she looked at the crude paintings, for although her time of exile had been one of fear and danger she had come through it to be cleansed and welcomed back into the tribe. The death of the infant had been a necessary part of the cleansing. The purity of the tribe's blood had to be maintained, and the product of rape by a Lizard man could not be allowed to survive.

Anabarru wiped a trickle of sweat from her eyes and stared out over the land. On that long-ago day she had left the birthing cave as soon as the rituals were complete. She smiled as she thought of how passionately Watpipa had taken her that first night. He had been insatiable, and she had clung to him, relishing the feel of his body and the strength of his sheltering arms. Her belly had soon swelled with their son, a sure sign that the Spirits had once again looked favourably upon her.

She drew back from her memories and looked out at the sun. It was dipping fast behind the twin hills. She must hurry.

Her gaze fell on the lump of rock with which she had killed her abductor. She had placed it there many moons ago, but the strange colour that glittered in it had made her feel uneasy as she had suffered the birth pangs and given life to her new son. Other women had spoken of the same unease, of how they had found their eyes drawn to it, of their relief at leaving the cave.

Now she saw that its presence was an evil reminder of what had happened. There was malevolence in its essence, which seemed to permeate this most sacred place, and she had put it there. Her theft from the land of the Lizard people was bringing bad luck to them all, for how else could the arrival of the strange canoes be explained? She had to return it.

She stood, took a deep breath for courage, grasped it and

put it in her dilly bag. Then she gathered up her digging-stick and short spear, left the cave and plotted her way west.

As the sun continued to dip and the heat lessened, Anabarru reached the boundaries of the Ngandyandyi people's tribal lands. She climbed a tall tree, perched on a stout branch and took the rock from her dilly bag. Without glancing at it, she flung it as hard and as far as she could into Lizard people country. It was done.

'We're still being watched,' murmured Sydney, as he and Jonathan collected the boxes of specimens and books of drawings from the small boat to return them to Sydney's denuded cabin.

'They've been there for two days.' He eased his back and wiped the sweat from his brow. It was excessively hot, and even the water in the sandy river was as warm as a bath. 'But they're more curious than savage. Probably never seen white men before and can't make out what we are.'

'They're carrying spears,' muttered Sydney. 'I shouldn't be at all surprised if they don't kill us all while we sleep.'

Jonathan slapped his friend on the back and laughed at his gloomy countenance. 'Your optimism knows no bounds, Syd. For goodness' sake, cheer up or you'll have me forever looking over my shoulder.' He glanced towards the tree-line. 'If they were going to kill us, they'd have done it by now, but it seems we're merely providing their entertainment, not filling their cooking pots.'

They carried on working, but Jonathan could tell from his friend's expression that he was uneasy. As the last box was stowed safely in the cabin, he left Sydney to his work and returned to the sandy riverbank to watch the activity around the ship.

The *Endeavour* had been hauled high up the sandbank so that work could begin on the repairs. Even he could see that it would be some time before the ship was seaworthy but at least there was plenty of stout timber to be had here. As for escaping this hot, sandy, tropical estuary, that depended upon finding a way through the great barrier of coral that seemed to follow the coastline all the way to the north. Cook would need all his wit if they were to sail unscathed to deep water and the ocean.

Josiah interrupted his thoughts by stamping through the sand to collapse beside him. He still wore his thick coat, but had discarded the waistcoat and wig in deference to the debilitating heat. 'Cook and Tupaia plan to try to communicate with the natives,' he growled, as he glowered towards the trees. 'They've been watching us since we entered the estuary.'

Jonathan nodded. 'The natives were friendly enough in Botany Bay. I can't see that it will be any different here.'

Josiah pulled his hat low over his eyes as he regarded the shifting black shadows among the trees. 'Reminds me of when I was a boy,' he murmured.

Jonathan looked at him in puzzlement.

'The gamekeeper would put out feed for the deer in early spring,' he explained. 'The stags always came out of the forest first. They'd sniff the air, show off their antlers and keep guard.' He nodded towards the watching native men with their spears. 'As they do.' He gave a gruff cough of laughter. 'The does were next, hesitant, wary, emerging slowly from the forest, poised to flee at the slightest sound. They were followed by the fawns, in a rush of legs and flicking tails.' He dabbed his eyes with his handkerchief. 'It was a sight I never tired of.'

Jonathan could see why his uncle had chosen the analogy: over the past two days the native men had been joined by their women, and now he could see the darting shadows of children peeping out from behind their parents and high in the trees. He smiled: he had discerned naked curiosity in the little faces as they stared in awe at the *Endeavour* and the men who worked on her. They appeared to be lively little devils, with the same wild hair, big eyes and skinny limbs of their counterparts in Botany Bay.

He'd studied books on the subject, and been fascinated to see how different they were from the black men of Africa. These natives were slighter in build and shorter of stature, and instead of the tightly curled black nap of the Africans, their hair was sometimes straight and lank, short and curly, or like a halo of tangles about their heads.

He and Josiah got to their feet as Cook, Tupaia and three of the ship's officers emerged from the *Endeavour* and began slowly to approach the tree-line. The time had come to make first contact, and they would know soon enough if they were welcome.

The passengers and crew stopped what they were doing and, with hands on guns and cutlasses, grouped into a phalanx in front of the ship. Banks's dogs were straining at their leashes, whining and yapping, tongues lolling as they scented sport.

'I hope he keeps the damn things tethered,' muttered Josiah. 'One bite of a native's ankle and we could all be massacred.'

Anabarru and the other women could contain their curiosity no longer. They had crept out earlier that morning to join their men and look at the strange thing on the shore. They were soon followed by their children who, despite dire warnings, ran about until they were reprimanded by the Elders.

Anabarru held the baby, but Birranulu for once refused to take her hand and darted back and forth between the trees. She wasn't alone: all the children were curious – and unafraid – even when the *dalkans* were brought out on ropes. They were peculiar-looking dingoes, long-legged and thin, with pointed noses and floppy ears, their fur a strange grey. And they made an odd noise, too, not like the soft chuff of the native dogs, and pawed the air as if they wished to leap at the watchers' throats.

Anabarru peered out from the trees as Watpipa and the other Elders shifted in the shadows. The canoe was enormous, and as the hot wind buffeted the strings that were tied to the leafless trees, it was as if a giant snake was coiled ready to strike. She watched the men clambering around the canoe and up into the folded wings, and shivered in fright at their ghostly faces. The great craft was being used by the spirits of the dead. Perhaps this was a sign from the ancestors that the end of the world was at hand. Perhaps the evil lingered even though she had returned the stone.

She looked around for her daughter, but the child had cast off her shyness and was chattering excitedly to her friends from a perch in a nearby tree as they pointed and exclaimed at the strange goings-on. The children had no fear, and Anabarru wondered why. Hugging the baby close, she was about to drag Birranulu from the tree when the agitated voices of the men stopped her. The Elders had grouped tightly together, their shields and spears held in readiness. She glanced out towards the beach and saw why. A group of ghosts was walking towards them.

Anabarru was torn. She wanted to back away and melt with the other women into the trees, but Birranulu was perched on a branch, out of reach, and she couldn't leave her. She looked to her husband for guidance, but he and the other Elders were standing firm, focused on the men who approached them. As an Elder's wife she was expected to lead by example. If her husband was not afraid, she had no choice but to stand beside him – or, at least, some way behind him.

A fevered, low-pitched debate flew among the Elders as the strangers drew near. Anabarru hovered uncertainly behind Watpipa, the baby on her hip, her eyes on the faces of the ghostly men. Her eyes alighted on the shorter man who led them, for he wore no strange skins on his body and no headdress. Her curiosity was piqued, for this was no ghost.

His skin was dark, but not as dark as hers, and his hair was black and long, almost to his waist. He was naked but for the grasses he'd woven into some kind of covering that girdled his hips and fell to his bare feet. He was broad and sleek, the muscles of his chest and arms gleaming in the sun as if he'd rubbed himself with animal fat.

Watpipa and the other Elders stepped as one from the trees into the glaring sunlight. They stood proud and tense, their shields and spears held in readiness for attack. 'Who are you and what do you want?' demanded Watpipa. 'You break tribal laws by trespassing on our sacred land.'

Anabarru listened as the dark-skinned man said something, but his words were strange and she did not understand him. Then it was the turn of a very tall man with long brown hair and an odd headdress, but she couldn't understand him either. The men from the canoe eventually sat down in the sand and, with a series of hand gestures and smiles, invited the Elders to join them.

As the sun beat down the tension increased. Anabarru could hear the babble of debate among the Elders and knew they were wary of the strangers despite their apparent friendliness. Her eyes widened in fear as Watpipa led the Elders out of the protective trees and approached the group who sat on the sand.

Anabarru felt the tension ease as she watched her husband and the others lower their spears and squat in the sand. Watpipa was unafraid. It would be safe to creep a little closer and eavesdrop on the men's conversation.

She, the other women and children began to emerge warily from the trees. They came to a halt, terrified, as more men approached the group on the sand. Anabarru watched carefully, ready to flee, but it seemed they meant no harm, for their hands were empty and they were still smiling. She clutched the baby tightly to her side as she took a few steps further into the sunlight.

The man with the *dalkans* drew nearer and she hesitated, uncertain of his intention, or the ferocity of these strange animals. Her fear was swept away as they sat at his command and panted in the heat, their eyes bright with mischief, tongues lolling.

It was too much for the children: they swarmed out of the bush and formed an excited, chattering ring round the man and his dogs. Anabarru shouted a warning as Birranulu put out her hand and stroked the head of one. The fear was charged with anger, for the child had been told not to approach an unfamiliar dog: although there were always puppies about the place, the fully grown animals could be dangerous.

Her fear was misplaced, for it licked the child's hand and soon children and dogs were cavorting about the beach in play. Anabarru squatted in the sand as some of the men from the canoe joined the children and began to kick a round red object about, encouraging the younger boys to join in. It was all very strange, and she was unsure what to make of it. It resembled a *corroboree* yet it was like none she had attended.

She looked at the circle of men and saw them smiling at one another. Hands were being clasped and bright cloth and strings of pretty stones laid out in the sand as offerings of friendship. It seemed they had agreed a peace pact. Anabarru sighed with relief. She had done the right thing by getting rid of the rock: the evil spirits it had carried were not with these men but far away in the land of the Lizard people where they could do her tribe no harm.

7

Waymbuurr, June–August 1770

Jonathan stood outside the circle and watched the faces of the natives as Cook and the Tahitian priest tried to make themselves understood. They had been there several days now, and so far the only communication they had achieved with the black men had been through facial grimaces, arm-waving and mime. It was frustrating, but at least the natives' initial fear seemed to have dissipated, the ice broken by the children's delight in having new playmates.

He caught the eye of the young man who seemed to be a leader of the small band and grinned. They had studied one another surreptitiously over the past few days, exchanging smiles and nods.

The man grinned back and shrugged. It seemed he, too, was weary of the talk. He stood up, his lean figure silhouetted against the dark backdrop of the forest, slapped his chest and proudly lifted his chin: 'Watpipa.'

Jonathan supposed it was his name. Touching his own chest, he returned the compliment. 'Jon,' he said, realising the black man might struggle to get his tongue around 'Jonathan'.

Watpipa grinned, showing fine teeth. 'Jon.' He laughed, babbled something unintelligible, then gestured to Jonathan to follow him.

After a swift glance at the others, Jonathan left the beach. His spirits soared. This was what he had been waiting for. Perhaps now he would discover the secrets of this intriguing place and its people.

Watpipa set a fine pace, weaving in and out of the trees, his bare feet hardened to the sharp pine needles and razor coral that littered the forest floor. Jonathan was already sweating, and as they moved further into the surrounding trees he felt the bite of mosquitoes. He slapped them away, determined to show no weakness in front of the other man.

Watpipa led him to a fast-flowing river, squatted beside it and scooped the water into his mouth. Jonathan followed suit, and never had water tasted so good. They didn't linger, and as they continued their journey through the trees Watpipa plucked some broad green leaves from a bush and indicated that Jonathan should crush them and rub the sap over his skin. The relief from the bites was almost instant, and Jonathan's step lightened as they left the shelter of the bush and stepped out into blistering sunlight.

They had come to a vast plain of grassland that stretched to the horizon. The sky was clear and incredibly blue, the grass yellow and rustling, flowing back and forth in the soft, warm breeze like a huge inland sea. He was about to remark on it when the black man put a hand on his arm and pulled him roughly to the ground.

Startled and alarmed, Jonathan lay beside him in the long grass and followed the pointing finger. He had to stifle a gasp. He'd never seen such a strange creature before. With huge back legs and tiny front paws, it was the colour of the ochre earth and stood higher than a man.

'Kangaroo,' whispered Watpipa, as he rose slowly to a crouch and drew a bowed length of wood from the grass belt at his waist. He froze, eyes narrowed. Then, with infinite care, he advanced on the creature, his feet making no sound as he placed one in front of the other. The arm was drawn back. The weapon spun through the air and caught the beast on the side of the head with a resounding thud, which felled it immediately. Watpipa turned to Jonathan, face creased in delight. 'Kangaroo!' he shouted.

Jonathan realised he'd been holding his breath and expelled it. 'Well done,' he breathed. 'What a shot.' He patted the other man's shoulder.

Watpipa stilled, his smile now uncertain, but he must have read the delight in Jonathan's face, for he grinned again and gave Jonathan a hearty slap on the back.

Jonathan realised that the kangaroo was merely stunned when Watpipa drew a sharpened stone from the sheath at his waist and slit its throat. He picked up the other weapon and balanced it in his hand. Made of dark timber, it had been decorated with signs and symbols, and was quite heavy. 'What do you call this?' he asked, as he handed it back.

'Boomerang,' Watpipa replied. He took up a stance and threw it once more.

Jonathan watched it spin away with a scything hiss, then gasped in amazement as it came back and Watpipa caught it. 'What a marvel,' he exclaimed. 'Can I try?'

The boomerang proved far trickier than Jonathan had thought. It seemed determined to embed itself in the ground, or fly off and sink out of sight in the grass. Try as he might the damned thing wouldn't come back. Presently he gave up – the heat was too debilitating for him to run across the grassland to retrieve it.

Watpipa's face was alight with good humour. Perhaps he was amused by Jonathan's bungling efforts. He hauled the dead beast across his shoulders and began the journey back to the beach.

Jonathan walked beside him, taking in the unusual trees, ferns and grasses. Green ants crawled over branches and leaves and Watpipa gathered up a handful, squeezed the life out of them and popped them into his mouth as if they were sweetmeats. He offered some to Jonathan, who, afraid to give offence, took them, closed his eyes and chewed. To his surprise they were pleasantly sweet.

As they continued on their way he heard the cackling laugh that had intrigued them all when they made camp on the beach. He looked up into the trees and saw a small brown bird that resembled a kingfisher, but for its lack of colour, and stopped to watch it.

'Kookaburra,' said Watpipa. He threw back his head and imitated its call, making it laugh again.

When they reached the beach, Watpipa threw the kangaroo on to the sand.

'It's his gift to us,' Jonathan told the amazed onlookers, 'and he's shown me where to find water.' He smiled at Watpipa. 'Thank you.'

Watpipa nodded back, then glanced in scorn at the coloured beads and trinkets the others tried to give him, called to his wife and children, and disappeared into the bush.

That night, Jonathan lay awake in the tent he shared with Sydney and his uncle and relived his journey into the interior. The others might be impatient to leave, but he prayed fervently that it would take a long time to repair the *Endeavour*, for if Watpipa grew to trust him, a whole new world might open up to him and the adventure would be complete.

It was late the next morning when Watpipa returned, and Jonathan was waiting for him. They left the beach and headed for the trees. This time they took a different path and followed the river upstream. Soon they were walking through grass as high as his hip. Anthills stood sentinel on the dark red earth, their height ranging from a few inches to more than six feet, their girth too wide to measure with human arms.

Jonathan breathed in the hot, humid air and gazed back at the forest they had left behind and the blue hills that rose far in the distance. This truly was an ancient paradise, untouched since time immemorial. He looked at Watpipa, who was searching for game, and hoped that their arrival on the *Endeavour* would not bring about change, for Watpipa and his people were true primitives. They lived in harmony with this land as naked hunter-gatherers. They grew no crops, farmed no animals and, if left alone by the outside world, would continue to do so for ever.

They caught fat barramundi that day – or, at least, Watpipa did. He tried to teach Jonathan how to lie on his belly in the shadows, hands in the water, wait until a fish was within his grasp, then scoop it out. He laughed uproariously every time Jonathan missed. Jonathan laughed with him, aware of how foolish he must seem, but having the time of his life.

When Watpipa had prepared a hot stone over a fire-pit, he began to gut one of the fish. Jonathan reached into his pocket and gave him his own small penknife. It was all he had that Watpipa might find of some use.

Watpipa looked at it long and hard, turning it this way and that, fascinated with the way the sun caught the metal blade and gleamed on the ivory handle.

Jonathan showed him how swiftly and neatly it would cut through the fish, and Watpipa snatched it back so he could try it for himself. When the fish was cooking in a blanket of leaves on the hot stone, the knife was tucked away with the primitive cutting-stone and the two men sat in harmonious silence. It was the start of a friendship they would remember all of their lives.

As the weeks passed, Jonathan made regular forays into the bush with Watpipa, and the tribe accepted the passengers and crew of the *Endeavour* as welcome guests. They showed them the best trees to cut for their repairs to the ship, guided them to fresh water and edible berries, and entertained them at night with singing and dancing.

The women of the clan had been kept away from the men of the *Endeavour*, and guarded jealously. Thankfully none of the sailors had approached them, perhaps intimidated by the tribal markings and sharp spears of their men. This was not Tahiti: there would be no licentiousness and their survival depended on good relations.

Jonathan was entranced by Anabarru and her children, and frustrated by his inability to communicate properly with them. Their language twisted his tongue and he'd managed to learn only a few words. The women seemed equal to their men except when it came to boomerang-hunting and making decisions. They appeared to have their own code of conduct, their own mysterious taboos, and family ties were strong. They had their own hierarchy, the young looking after the elderly, who cared for the children while their mothers foraged and fished. The whole tribe had a vast knowledge and deep understanding of their land, and although it was a primitive life, it gave them all they needed. In a way, Jonathan envied them.

Not every day could be spent with Watpipa, for there were tasks to be performed. A camp had been set up at the edge of the tree-line, canvases stretched between branches to give shelter. Work on the repairs was going well, but there was still the problem of how they would escape this tropical beach. Jonathan accepted an invitation from Banks, Sydney and Solander to go out in one of the small boats to inspect the reef.

The great wall of coral rose almost perpendicularly out of the fathomless ocean. It was always covered at high tide, but the teeming life of the brightly coloured fish and molluscs could be viewed easily from the boat, for the water was as clear and blue as the sky.

Sydney's face was alight with joy. 'This is an artist's paradise, Jon. I hardly know where to start – there's so much to paint, and so little time to capture it.'

'No doubt you'll manage,' replied Jonathan. 'But remember to sleep and eat, Syd. You can't paint all day and night and survive on fresh air.'

'Ah, but what air, what beauty.' He took a deep breath. 'This is nothing like Scotland.'

'I should hope not,' Jonathan said. He'd marvelled at the colourful coral and fascinating marine life, but he wished he was in Watpipa's flimsy bark canoe, hunting the giant turtles that swam so lazily in the warm waters, and whose flesh was so delicious to eat.

He grinned as Sydney waxed lyrical on the botanic wonders of this isolated corner of the world. Jonathan knew little about plants and cared less, and certainly couldn't dredge up any of his friend's enthusiasm for the shape of a leaf or the colour of bark. It was the devil's own job to persuade Sydney to stop painting and join him in a drink during the heat of noon.

Sydney had relented as the thermometer climbed and it became impossible to work any longer. He and Jonathan shared one of the bottles of rum that had floated back to them on the tide and they sat beneath a canvas awning and watched the fun on the beach.

For the first few days Josiah had marched about getting in everybody's way until he discovered that his appalling singing captivated the native children. In a very short time he'd had them singing nursery rhymes in English as their mothers and grandmothers looked on in wonder. Now he was trying to teach them the rules of cricket.

Jonathan roared with laughter as Josiah tried to organise his recruits, who seemed far more interested in running round him in circles and plucking at his shirt-tails. His uncle had discarded his coat and was barefoot and bare-headed, his face growing more puce by the minute. Jonathan had never seen him so relaxed and carefree, and it warmed his soul to watch him grow stronger every day.

When the sun had lost some of its power and a cool breeze drifted over the sand, Cook announced that he was going to climb the tall hill back among the trees to gain some idea of their position and see if he could plot a way through the reef. Jonathan had had enough of sitting about so he joined the expedition.

It was a steep hill that seemed to go on for ever. Sweating copiously, and out of breath, calf muscles stiff and sore, he finally reached the summit. He hadn't been prepared for the sight before him, and as he stood there, gazing in awe, he couldn't share Cook's despair. It was low tide, and there were numerous sandbanks and shoals all along the coast, but far out to the horizon he could see a glorious sweep of the deepest blue and the clearest green.

'We're prisoners here until passage can be found through,' said Cook, as he surveyed the view through his telescope. 'I shall send Bob Molyneaux out to reconnoitre, and keep sending him until we find a way.'

Molyneaux went out every day, and everyone but Jonathan became exasperated at the fruitless search for escape from their beautiful but isolated coral gaol.

Cook finally climbed the masthead and looked down upon the reef at low tide. Then he took a small boat out to an island, which he reckoned was the outermost reef of coral. To Jonathan's dismay he returned to the shore declaring that he had found a way through. 'It will be a tricky enterprise, but we cannot afford to remain here any longer and risk being caught in winter storms.'

Jonathan's fellow passengers were delighted with this news. They had grown tired of the heat and the brief but heavy downpours that brought everything to a halt and made the humidity rise. They were ready to go home.

'Thank goodness,' sighed Sydney. 'I thought we would never see Britain again.'

'I thought you were happy,' Jonathan said, surprised.

'I've enjoyed finding so many wonderful specimens, but I'm a Scotsman. I need to feel the cold wind on my face and have the smell of heather in my nostrils.' He frowned at the turquoise sea. 'I'm happier knowing we can escape to civilisation.'

The night before they sailed Watpipa and the Elders issued an invitation. There was to be a feast in their honour, with much singing and dancing. Jonathan's heart was heavy as he sat for the last time at the campfire, and he tried to etch the faces, scents and sights on his memory to carry home.

Watpipa, Anabarru and their tribe had provided a meal fit for a king. There was roasted goanna and wallaby, pigeon and turtle, and delicious unleavened bread full of herbs. When everyone was sated, Watpipa signalled it was time to dance. The movements bore little resemblance to the erotic swaying of hips by the Tahitians, or the stylised prancing of the London aristocracy: this dance imitated the birds and animals of the bush – it was wild but contained, as if each step was important, each flutter of the hand and facial grimace conveying the beasts' spiritual essence.

The music was provided by the clacking of wooden sticks and the deep, rhythmic drone of a long, hollow wooden instrument, heavily decorated with swirls and crude outlines of animals. 'Didgeridoo,' said Watpipa, handing it over to Jonathan.

It was surprisingly heavy and unwieldy, but after a nod of encouragement from his friend, he tried hard to get a note out of it. He managed something that sounded like the bellow of a cow, and handed it back, shame-faced, as the natives' gentle laughter rang in his ears.

Watpipa returned it to him and signalled that it was a gift, and Anabarru presented him with a necklace of shells. Jonathan bowed his head and she placed it round his neck, then ran back to her children, giggling.

Eventually the evening was over and the two men faced one another, knowing they would probably never meet again. Jonathan put out his hand and Watpipa grasped it. For a long moment they silently acknowledged their friendship, then Jonathan turned away and headed for the ship.

Dawn had just lightened the sky as Jonathan stood on the deck and watched the sailors prepare to raise the sails and follow the pinnace – the ship's small boat – through the labyrinth of coral.

He would miss this glorious place, the people, the climate and the mysteries of the natives' lives.

'A sad day,' muttered Josiah. He waved to the children on the sandbank. 'I shall miss the little blighters.'

'They certainly put a spring in your step, Uncle. Perhaps you should consider marriage when you return home. You're a natural father.'

'Hmmph. Children are only good company when they belong to someone else. You can send them back when you've had enough of them.'

They fell silent as the ship slowly began the long journey down the estuary to the mouth of the river, and Jonathan leant as far out as he could to keep sight of Watpipa and his family.

The *Endeavour* passed along the narrow passage into the sea, the crew taking soundings all the way as they reached the coral wall and headed for the northern end of what Cook had dubbed Lizard Island. Passing carefully through the labyrinth of reefs, they were out of sight of land by the following day.

'She's taking on water at an alarming rate,' muttered Jonathan, to his uncle. 'The pumps are useless and the sails are rotting. We'll be lucky to reach Batavia.'

It took the *Endeavour* eight anxious days to escape to open sea and begin the long journey north to Batavia. Not one man had been lost to scurvy during the long voyage but the journey home was plagued by sickness and death, for Batavia was rife with disease. During the three months they had to remain there for the *Endeavour* to be completely overhauled, the surgeon was the first to die, soon followed by Tupaia and his serving boy. Forty more fell ill and the whole crew was weakened as the sickness took its toll. The effects lingered with them well into the Atlantic and as they sailed to the Cape of Good Hope, the one-armed cook, ten sailors, three marines and the tough old sail-maker died, along with Astronomer Green, Midshipman Monkhouse and Sydney Parkinson.

Jonathan risked his own health to sit with his friend and listen to his fevered rambling. He took Sydney's death hard – they had made many plans for the future after they had arrived in England. As Jonathan stood weakly to attention on the deck and watched Sydney's body committed to the deep, he realised that the world had lost a talented botanic artist and he a good friend.

Four more died at the Cape of Good Hope, then three more, including Molyneaux, who'd rowed so gallantly day after day in search of a passage through the reef.

To Jonathan's surprise, Josiah shook off the tropical fever quickly and, despite the heavy seas around the Cape, seemed to have found his sea-legs. He walked the deck each day, encouraging others to follow his example, and as Jonathan recovered, the older man insisted that he join him.

Jonathan soon returned to good health and enjoyed his exercise on deck: he was on his way home, to England and Susan. He couldn't wait to see her again and make her his wife.

One day as they strolled the deck Josiah said, 'Cook has charted the east coast from Botany Bay to Cape York and taken possession of all its islands, bays, harbours and rivers in the name of King George. But I have to agree with him – our expedition will have only marginal relevance in the global context of empire.'

Jonathan dragged his thoughts from Susan. 'It will become hugely relevant once the interior is explored,' he argued. 'There is a great deal of the country you didn't see, and I would stake any money you like on the chances of there being many riches there.'

Josiah snorted. 'The annexation of Australia is designed to deny our enemies a new territory that might, at some future time, prove worth having,' he replied. He looked at his nephew, brows beetling. 'Although what possible use it would be to anyone is highly debatable.'

Tahiti, August 1770

Tahani had returned to the island with the other survivors. It had taken many weeks to clear the encampment of the reminders of what had happened, and even after the new huts had been built and normality restored, she thought she could hear the voices of the dead whispering in the trees. They didn't frighten her for she believed that Lianni was beside her son in spirit, watching him grow healthy and strong.

There were two ships in the bay, and trading had been brisk for rum, iron and the medicines that would cure the diseases the foreigners had brought with them. The heavy rains had come and gone, and sweetness hung in the air from the colourful flowers that swarmed in profusion among the trees.

Tahani returned from the beach, the reed basket heavy against her hip with the silvery fish she'd caught. She was humming softly, her mind busy with plans for Tahamma. He was a sturdy child, and although he was only several months old, there was a bright curiosity in his eyes and an almost imperious nobility in the way he observed his surroundings. He'd quickly responded to voices, colour and the flit of the birds, and chuckled happily when she sang to him. She smiled and hitched the basket more firmly against her hip. Only Tahamma seemed to appreciate her singing – her own children and grandchildren covered their ears.

She left the basket at the door of the hut and stooped to enter the cool darkness. Tahamma had been sleeping when she'd gone fishing, but now he would be ready for his milk.

'Where have you been?' The surly voice came from the deepest shadows in the corner.

Tahani's spirits plunged. Her husband, Pruhana, had been drinking rum again. 'Fishing,' she replied quietly. She was about to turn to the baby, who was gurgling in his rush basket, when her husband's voice stilled her.

'Where did you find this?' He held out the watch to her.

'Lianni,' she whispered. 'It belonged to Lianni.'

He twisted the watch back and forth so it caught the sunlight, his eyes glinting with greed. 'She has no use for it now.'

Tahani made a grab for it, but he held it out of her reach. 'It's mine,' she said firmly. 'Lianni gave it to me to keep for Tahamma.'

'What does a baby want with such things?' Pruhana sneered. He struggled to his feet, swaying, as he attempted to focus his eyes. He was a big man, broad of shoulder and girth, who could move surprisingly quickly when he was sober. He had a volatile temper that manifested itself when he drank rum, and Tahani knew she had to use all her wiles if she was to escape his fist and regain possession of the watch.

'It's his inheritance,' she replied, with as much calm as she could muster. 'I promised Lianni just before she died that—' He hit her so hard that she was across the hut and on the floor before she knew what had happened.

'It's mine now,' shouted her husband. 'Mine! Do you hear me, woman?'

Tahamma was crying and Tahani was reeling from the blow, but she staggered to her feet and flew at her husband, fingers clawed. 'It's not,' she yelled, as she went for his eyes. She beat her small fists against his broad chest and kicked his shins. 'I made a sacred promise to Lianni,' she gasped. 'It's *not* yours.'

Pruhana fended her off as if she were a swarm of flies. He grasped a fistful of her hair and pulled hard, making her neck arch until she had to drop to her knees. 'You shouldn't hide things from me, Tahani,' he slurred. 'Promises don't fill your belly or give me rum.' He shoved her away from him. 'The sailors will pay me well for this.'

Tahani knew that if he left the hut with the watch she would never see it again. She scrabbled in the dirt, found a cooking pot and, without thought for the consequences, hit him over the head.

Pruhana's feet remained planted on the ground. He turned, the fire of rage alight in his eyes as he advanced towards her.

Tahani screamed as she backed against the grass wall and found she was trapped. He began to beat her, and she cowered on the floor as his fists and feet pummelled her. Her screams died and the world became a dark abyss of pain.

Suddenly it was over. She looked up fearfully and wept with relief when she saw that her brothers had come to her rescue. The burly Pruhana was no match for the two sets of strong arms that held him.

She scrambled to her feet, and despite the swelling over her eyes and the cut at the side of her mouth, her first thoughts were for Tahamma. As she picked him up from the rush basket, she told her brothers of her promise to Lianni, and Pruhana's theft of the watch.

The brothers tore it from her husband's grip and handed it back to her. They hauled him outside and tied him to a tree to await his punishment. Wife-beating and stealing were bad enough, but to break a sacred oath was worse. A meeting of the Headmen would decide what to do with him, but at the very least he would be banished to another island.

Tahani sat in her hut with the baby, stilling his crying as tears ran down her bruised face. She held the watch close to her breast. The gold didn't shine so boldly now, and there was a dent in the casing, but her promise had been kept. Yet she knew she had made an enemy of her husband, and that Tahamma's inheritance would be in danger for as long as Pruhana drew breath.

8

Almost a year had passed since Ezra's proposal, and Susan knew she couldn't put off the wedding any longer. The period of mourning was over, her mother had recovered her vitality and the dowager was impatient. Jonathan had been away for almost three years, and Susan had received no word from him. There was nothing for it but to marry Ezra and make the best of it.

She paused in her work on the quay, and thought about the bleak house that would soon be her home. Its position seemed to emphasise the isolation she would feel when she lived there. Marriage to Ezra would distance her from her family, and the way of life into which she had been born.

Preparations for her new life were under way and her English had improved. Ezra was also teaching her how to use the bewildering number of knives, forks, spoons and glasses at a dinner table. It seemed the upper classes were more concerned with the ritual of eating than with the food – but, then, they had never gone hungry. She had had to learn, too, about table napkins and how to speak to servants – which made her feel awkward, for Mrs Pascoe and Mr Higgins had made clear that they disapproved of the marriage. Ezra had been kindness itself, his gentle patience making the lessons fun, but she dreaded the day she would have to take tea with her ladyship – and it would happen, for Ezra's mother was the dowager's distant cousin.

Her thoughts were broken by a sharp elbow in her ribs.

'Thinking about your wedding night, girl? Reckon the minister will have you on your knees in no time – my old man likes that.' With a great shout of laughter her friend Molly nudged her again and nearly knocked her off the stool. 'They say you can tell the size of his rod from the size of his feet,' she spluttered. 'You'd better prepare yourself, girl. That Mr Collinson's shoes are like boats.'

Susan blushed and laughed. She was used to Molly's sense of humour: her coarse jokes made the work at the salting barrels a little less grim. 'You're jealous, Moll. I've seen your old man's shoes and they'd fit a boy.'

They fell about, holding their aching sides, and Susan was glad of the excuse to let off steam. Things had been too serious for too long. They eventually wiped their eyes and carried on salting pilchards, then packing them into barrels for export to Spain. Molly was her closest friend, and their childhood had been spent in mischief. She had married eight months ago, and was already heavily pregnant. She was a sturdily built girl, with a ruddy face, blue eyes and a cheerful disposition.

'You ready for Saturday, then?' said Molly, in a low voice. The old biddies had sharp ears and even sharper tongues.

'As ready as I'll ever be,' Susan replied, avoiding Molly's penetrating gaze.

'You don't love him, so why marry him? There's men here that'd have you tomorrow if you gave them a fair chance.'

Susan hadn't fully confided in Molly, who had a mouth the size of a whale's. 'I'm marrying Ezra because he asked me, and I want to,' she said firmly. 'My life's about to change, Moll, and I'm just nervous, that's all.'

Molly's rosy cheeks were blown out in a sigh. 'The minister's wife,' she breathed. 'Who'd have thought it? I bet you never told him about that time we got caught in the drying sheds with those two lads, or when you got drunk on ale at that wedding, and your father had to carry you home over his shoulder like a sack of coal.'

'Of course not, and you're not to say anything either.' She grinned. 'I'm about to be an important person in the village, a minister's wife who will live in the big house on the hill. You'll have to be careful how you talk to me from now on, my girl.' She burst out laughing but stopped when she saw that her friend was looking at her with sad eyes.

'I reckon you and me won't see much of one another once you're married,' Molly said. 'You won't be working the nets or salting fish any more – it wouldn't be fitting for a minister's wife.' She gave a long sigh. 'You won't want to know us down here, and we certainly wouldn't feel easy visiting you up there.'

'I'm not going to ignore you just because I'm married to Ezra,' Susan protested, 'and you know you'll be made welcome in my house.' She put her hand on Molly's and tried to smile, but she knew her friend spoke the truth. Once she'd married Ezra she would be far removed from life on the quay and the stench of fish. She would have to learn to be a lady, and act accordingly.

'At least you won't have fish scales in your drawers no more,' said Molly. But the joke fell flat. They gazed at one another for a long moment, then turned back to their barrels and worked on in silence.

Billy Penhalligan waited in the long grass and watched the beach. It was a still night, the moon hidden by the thick cloud that had come in with the darkness. He'd been there for some time – there was no knowing when the boat would arrive – and his stomach was growling. At fourteen he was growing fast, and a hunk of stale bread and hard cheese did little to stave off the hunger that always gnawed at him.

He rolled over in the grass and stretched, easing cramped muscles as he surveyed the coastal path for any sign that he was being watched. The Revenue men could be lurking anywhere in the darkness, watching and waiting for the Retallicks to come ashore. Billy grinned. That was all part of the excitement, and as he hadn't been caught in the six months he'd been involved with the brothers, he relished the thrill it gave him.

Satisfied that he was alone, he took a swig of rum from the pouch that hung at his belt, and returned to his surveillance.

His eyelids were drooping with weariness when he heard a sound. He lifted his head and peered into the darkness. There it was again. The soft splash of water and creak of oars could be heard over the waves that broke on the shore. The Retallicks were back.

He grabbed the lantern, slithered through the grass and scampered down the rocks to the beach. He lit the lamp, then swung it back and forth to guide them in. The sharp call of an owl told him he'd been seen, and he answered in the same fashion. Moments later he was wading into the sea, grasping the rope and helping to haul the boat up the shingle.

'Well done, lad,' whispered Ben Retallick. 'You sure you weren't followed?'

Billy nodded as the big, bearded man grasped his shoulder. Ben Retallick was a good deal older and broader than he was, and rather daunting, but to Billy he was a hero. 'We have to be quick. The cloud's clearing.'

The big man looked up at the sky and whispered instructions. Billy helped unload the casks of brandy, the bolts of silk, the boxes of tobacco and sweetmeats, and carried them to the cave that ran deep into the cliffs above the high-water mark. They would remain there until he returned the following night with a horse and cart and took them into Newlyn to the Beggars' Roost tavern. From there they would be sold to the highest bidder, and Billy would take his share of the proceeds.

The cloud cover was almost gone as the final box was stowed away. 'I'll leave the horse and cart in the usual place,' mumbled Ben, as he stepped back into the boat. 'Take this for now as a bonus, and don't let me down.'

Billy looked into the stern face, saw the twinkle in the dark eyes and knew he had the older man's approval. 'You can count on me,' he whispered.

Ben Retallick joined his brother in the boat and Billy watched as they rowed round the point and into the darkness. He looked down at what he'd been given. Two gold pieces gleamed in the moonlight. Not bad for a couple of nights' work. Smuggling was not only exciting, but profitable. If it kept up he would never again have to climb into a fishing-boat.

'That boy will be the death of me,' snapped Maud, as she prepared the evening meal. 'He's with the Retallicks, I'm sure, and you know what that means.' She stirred the fish broth with rather more vigour than it needed. 'He's always been one for mischief, but this time he'll be arrested, I know it.'

Susan remembered how Billy had always been the ringleader when it came to pinching apples, rapping on doors and running away, or fighting with the other boys. They had hoped he'd grow out of it, but it seemed not. 'I'll have a word with him, but he won't listen to anyone these days.' Susan paused as she put the bread on the table. 'The money he brings in is a Godsend, though.'

'I know.' Maud sighed. 'What with so many mouths to feed, and work almost impossible to find, we'd be hard pressed to put food on the table without it.' She pushed the hair out of her eyes.

She left the range to make a grab for her youngest grandson, who was running about naked, yelling, as he avoided all attempts by his mother to get him into the washtub that stood by the back door. It was Friday, bath night, and Maud was losing the battle to bring order to the chaos in preparation for tomorrow.

Susan took over the pots and pans and listened as her mother catalogued Billy's failings. He had never wanted to be a fisherman, and had dreaded going to sea. Fate had kept him at home on the day of the storm and had led him into the clutches of the Retallicks. He had discovered the excitement to be had in selling smuggled goods, and seemed to thrive on it. Poor Mother, she thought. As if she didn't have enough to contend with, Billy was now in constant danger of arrest.

Her thoughts turned to her brothers' widows. Two still lived with them along with their children, and had finally found work in the fish oil press. The money was poor, but it was better than nothing. The youngest had gone back to her parents in St Mawes, and was working in the rope factory there. It was rumoured she was courting the son of an innkeeper. And within a few short hours Susan would leave this cottage for the last time.

She fingered the ring Ezra had given her and which she wore on a strip of leather round her neck to protect it from the fish and salt. Her spirits sank as she thought of her bridegroom, and wished he would show the passion he had when he had proposed to her, instead of the stilted and proper manner he'd adopted once they were engaged.

He was almost fawning in his willingness to please her, and she'd learnt quickly that she could take charge of their relationship if she wished. But she believed that a man should be assertive and strong – and a wife should have her way through quiet understanding of how his mind worked, not by trying to rule him.

Despite her growing affection for Ezra, the thought of the intimacy necessary in marriage made her dread her wedding night. How could she forget the shared kisses with Jonathan, the strength and warmth of his hands on her body, and the urgency to feel his flesh against hers?

'You're burning that soup,' muttered Maud, as she took the wooden spoon and shoved her out of the way.

Susan realised she was of no help to anyone, and left the cottage, drawing the shawl round her shoulders as the evening breeze chilled her arms. At the end of the sea wall, with the sharp tang of salt rising from the spray, she looked out beyond the tiny Isle of St Clement to a sea that rippled like molten silver beneath the rising moon. Jonathan was out there somewhere, and she wondered if he was thinking of her. Had time and distance erased her from his memory, or was he yearning to make her his bride? Tears blurred her vision as she realised she would never know.

Tahiti, June 1771

Tahani knew Pruhana would be smouldering with resentment. His banishment nine months ago to Huahine Island meant he'd live alone, shunned by his neighbours and the entire community. He'd be forced to eke out a living by trading the few pearls she knew he had for rum – but he was no longer a young man and couldn't dive deep or for long enough to reach the richer oyster beds that lay further from the shore.

She had made contingency plans after his banishment, for she knew he would try to get back to Tahiti and have his revenge. The craving for rum was a powerful demon, and by now it would be clawing at his belly, fuelling his resentment. He was sly enough to escape and come looking for the watch.

Tahani moved restlessly on the mat, unable to sleep. The watch was safely hidden in her brothers' hut, but if Pruhana came to find it, she would be in mortal danger. She rose from the ground, wrapped a sarong round herself, stood in the doorway and looked out at the night. The sky was jewelled with stars, the moon's reflection floating on the water that lapped on the deserted beach. The scent of flowers was heavy in the air, and the village was silent, for it was late and everyone was asleep. She glanced at the precious child who slept in the corner. Perhaps she should take him to her brothers' hut. They would understand her fears and make her welcome.

She turned from the doorway and sat on the sleeping mat. She was being foolish, jumping at shadows, she thought crossly. Pruhana wouldn't dare break the laws, for the punishment was death, and he was too cowardly to risk his neck. She lay down and closed her eyes, determined not to think of him.

She woke to the sound of breathing. Stealthy footsteps were approaching her, and she could smell his sweat. Paralysed with terror, she feigned sleep, but through half-closed eyelids she recognised her husband and saw the flash of a blade in his hand.

Before she could scream, the knife plunged into her back. She slumped on the floor, her only thought for the sleeping child. She prayed that Pruhana wouldn't kill him too when he discovered the watch wasn't in the hut.

9

The morning dawned with bright sunshine and a clear sky. Ezra threw open the bedroom window and breathed in the summer air as he lifted his face to the sun. He felt reborn, imbued with joy for the future, for this was his wedding day.

The house was buzzing with a dozen voices as Lady Cadwallader's servants prepared the wedding breakfast, dusted, polished and moved the new furniture. Life had returned to this dour old house because of Susan. There was the scent of beeswax, roasting meats and baking bread, and the sound of scurrying feet, laughter and bright chatter.

He turned from the window and eyed the room. It, too, was changed. The vast four-poster was a gift from Lady Cadwallader, and the heavy curtains and canopy were of the finest blood-red silk, lavishly embroidered and tasselled. It was fit for a queen. The roses Ezra had picked at sunrise still had dew on them, and filled several vases, sending their fragrance sweetly into the room. A linen press had been brought all the way from Truro, its lower drawer now filled with sheets and blankets, scented with lavender. The other drawers had been lined with pretty paper, awaiting Susan's dresses, nightgowns and undergarments.

Higgins had laid out Ezra's clothes on the bed, but he had dismissed the man earlier, wanting to be alone for these last few hours to ready himself for the day ahead in quiet contemplation. The only dark cloud on this special day was the absence of his family. His brother Gilbert hadn't replied to the invitation, but he was in the army and the mail was unreliable. His parents were in London for the season, as was his eldest brother, James. They had sent letters of stilted congratulation and regret that previous engagements made it impossible for them to attend, with expensive gifts: a dinner service, and several large pieces of silver.

Ezra suspected they would want nothing to do with him after his marriage to a fisher-girl, and that their over-generous gifts were merely to assuage their guilt at having disowned him.

He finished dressing and carefully pinned the perfect white camellia to his coat. It had been plucked from a bush in the manor's garden the previous day and kept in water overnight. He looked at his reflection in the pier glass and smiled. For the first time in his life he was almost handsome.

The deeds had been explained to Maud by her ladyship's lawyer, and were brought to the cottage at first light by the estate steward. He had watched as Maud carefully added her signature below that of the dowager, then witnessed it with a flourish. He'd left immediately after he had deposited a large parcel on the kitchen table.

Susan glared at the man's back as he hurried away, then turned to the parcel. 'Aren't you going to open it?' squeaked Maud.

She picked up the card and slowly deciphered the spidery scrawl. Ezra had been helping her with her reading, but it still didn't come easily to her. 'It's a gift from her ladyship,' she said flatly. 'No doubt I'm supposed to be grateful.'

'Susan,' said her mother, her reddened hand enveloping her daughter's, 'what's done is done, and Ezra's a good man. He'll make a fine husband, if you let him.'

Susan sighed deeply. 'I know. But he deserves better.'

Maud ignored her and began to tear open the parcel. As the

paper fell away they gasped in awe, for there on the scrubbed kitchen table lay a dress of the finest ivory silk. It seemed to glow in the pale light coming through the window, the embroidery and delicate stitching on the bodice enhanced with seed pearls and glass bugling that glittered and winked in the gloom.

Susan picked it up, almost afraid to handle it. The bodice was low-cut and dipped to a point below the waist. Puffed sleeves were drawn in at the elbow to drop in a waterfall of frothy lace to the wrist. The underskirt was embroidered at the hem with flowers and leaves, and the same design ornamented the front panels of the overskirt, cut away to reveal the decoration beneath. It was the most beautiful thing she'd ever seen, even though it was a cast-off from a woman she hated.

'There's more,' said Maud, pulling out petticoats, dainty heeled slippers and fine silk stockings. 'Oh, Susan.' Tears were coursing down her sallow cheeks. 'You'll look like a princess.'

Susan clamped her mouth on a bitter retort. Lady Cadwallader had known she could never resist such a dress. It would serve her right if Susan ignored it and wore the dress she and her mother had been sewing for weeks – or, better still, if she went to church in her working clothes. But she would hurt only Ezra if she did such a thing. No, she would show the old bitch just what a fine lady she could be, and she would do her best to be a good wife to Ezra and make something of herself now that she had the chance.

She snatched the dress and hurried up the steep stairs to the room she shared with her sisters-in-law.

Ezra shook hands with the members of the Church Board as they arrived. He greeted the minister who'd come from Penzance to conduct the ceremony and explained that he would stand alone – for without his brother Gilbert by his side, he wanted no best man.

The guests were arriving, some in traps or gigs, most on foot or horseback. His parishioners, coming from Newlyn, the hamlets of Sheffield and Tredavoe as well as Mousehole, formed the core of the congregation – a wedding was an occasion to catch up with gossip – but there were one or two dignitaries from the local council, the owners of a few businesses in the area and several elderly ladies. The dowager arrived in a coach with a footman to help her alight and, after an imperious nod to Ezra, disappeared into the church.

Ezra was not a man who made friends easily, and most of the people there were mere acquaintances, but the mood was cheerful, the sun shining and the bright bonnets and pretty dresses of the women suggested somehow that the day would progress smoothly. Yet Ezra was nervous as he glanced at the steep path that led down to the village. What if Susan had changed her mind? His growing panic was halted by a heavy hand on his shoulder.

'What's all this about no best man, Ezra? I thought that was my job.'

Ezra spun round. 'Gilbert,' he gasped, almost lost in a bearhug. 'What a surprise.'

Gilbert released him and grinned. They were of similar height and features, with the same black hair, but that was where the likeness ended. Gilbert had been with the army in India for ten years and his skin was the colour of mahogany. He cut a dashing figure in his bright red jacket and cockaded hat, the broad shoulders and finely muscled legs testament to rigorous exercise, the vast moustache to his vanity. 'I couldn't allow my little brother to be married on his own, could I?'

'Absolutely not,' Ezra agreed. 'But why didn't you write and tell me you were coming?'

'Army life, dear boy. Never know where one's about to be sent from one day to the next, and the post is unreliable at the best of times. Came home for a spot of leave and the parents couldn't wait to tell me of your plans.' He raised an eyebrow and twirled his moustache. 'You're a dark horse, Ezra.'

'If you've come to make fun of me, you may as well leave now,' Ezra said quietly. His joy at seeing his brother was ebbing.

A meaty hand slapped him on the shoulder as Gilbert roared with laughter. 'Our parents forbade me to come, and James's refined wife almost fainted when I told everyone I intended to stand by you as your second.' His twinkling dark eyes gazed into Ezra's as he smiled. 'But you know me, old boy. I was never a man to listen to witless females.' He paused, and his expression grew earnest. 'I might not have been a good brother to you, Ezra, but I shall change that now. You've been roughly treated by our parents. We younger siblings should stick together.'

Ezra's heart was full as he embraced his brother, and thanked God for this most precious gift.

The moment was broken by the sound of fiddles, drums and some rather discordant singing. 'What a jolly procession. Is the bride on her way, do you think?'

Ezra looked towards the path, filled once more with joy. He felt as if he'd swallowed the sun. 'She is indeed. We'd better go inside.' He fumbled in his pocket. 'You'll need this.'

Gilbert took the plain gold ring in his large fingers. 'Grandmama's, if I'm not mistaken,' he said quietly. 'You were always her favourite.'

'At least someone loved me,' said Ezra. 'No one else seemed to know I existed.'

'Well, you have me now. Come on, or the bride will be upon us before we have taken our places.'

Lady Cadwallader was already ensconced in her gated pew at the front of the church. Ezra hesitated in the doorway, unable to take his eyes off the extraordinary profusion of feathers and stuffed birds that were pinned to her elaborate wig.

'I see the old tabby's here,' whispered Gilbert. '*Noblesse oblige.*'

Ezra nudged his arm. 'Quiet! She'll hear you.'

Gilbert twirled his moustache and lifted his chin. 'The lady already knows what I think of her,' he replied loudly, making heads swivel.

A whisper of speculation ran through the congregation as the two men entered the church. All eyes followed their progress down the aisle, with much fluttering from the younger women. Gilbert certainly cut a splendid figure, thought Ezra, as they took their places in front of the altar, but this was his day, his and Susan's, so he must not be distracted.

A commotion at the back of the church heralded the arrival of the bridal procession, and the villagers hushed their children. The organist waited until all were still, then the first notes soared to the rafters and the congregation stood to welcome the bride.

Susan's hands were trembling as she smoothed her skirt. It had been the devil's own task to walk up that damned path and keep the hem out of the dirt, but no harm had been done. She kicked off her clogs and stepped into the delicate slippers, then took the posy of wildflowers from her mother.

'Are you ready for this, Susan?' Billy was very smart in his father's suit, even though it was a little large.

Susan's stomach were churning and she was finding it hard to breathe. This was how she'd always dreamt of her wedding day, with a beautiful dress, flowers and a church filled with friends and family. But the dress was part of the price she'd had to pay to keep her family safe, her father wasn't here to lead her down the aisle, and her groom was a man she didn't love.

She looked over her shoulder in a final vain search for Jonathan's ship, but the horizon was empty. She had to accept that he would never again be part of her life, and that their promises would never be fulfilled.

'Susan?' Billy's face was concerned.

'I'm as ready as I'll ever be,' she murmured.

'I say,' exclaimed Gilbert, as Susan began to walk down the aisle, 'she's quite a catch, your little fisher-girl. You old dog, Ezra, who'd have thought it?'

Ezra didn't bother to reply: he was entranced by the girl approaching him. Her hair had been smoothed back from her brow and pinned high on the crown of her head to fall in glossy coils that tumbled over her shoulders. She looked exquisite in Lady Cadwallader's gown as she glided along the dark grey stone slabs. Susan Penhalligan was a queen among women.

Susan looked into Ezra's face as she made her vows before God. The love shone from his eyes and he seemed to grow in stature and confidence as he slipped the ring on to her finger. She saw how his hand trembled, and stilled it with her own, realising suddenly that he needed her, that in marrying him she could chase away his shyness and loneliness and make him whole. It didn't matter that she couldn't love him. He loved enough for both of them.

The English Channel, 13 July 1771

Jonathan stood on the deck, drinking in the sight of England. He was almost home – almost within sight and sound of Susan – and once the *Endeavour* had docked, he would race to her side and fulfil his promise.

PART TWO

The Road to Botany Bay

10

Newlyn, Cornwall, January 1782

Life was good for Billy Penhalligan, and this year it would get even better, he thought. His rooms above the Beggars' Roost were warm and comfortable, he had money to spend and his clothes were of the finest cloth. Smuggling was highly profitable, and Billy had a talent for finding customers and distributing the goods the Retallicks brought from France. As the years had passed and the Retallicks had come to trust him, he'd taken over as banker and middle-man. Now he was twenty-five, and rich beyond his dreams. His only regret was that he rarely saw his mother or sister.

He settled the girl more comfortably on his knee and drank from the pewter tankard. She was willing, the alehouse was crammed and noisy, and his belly was pleasantly full of the dinner he'd just eaten.

'Revenue men!'

The silence was instant as everyone turned towards the urchin in the doorway.

'They're already at the corner and coming this way!'

Billy was on his feet, the barmaid dumped unceremoniously on the floor as he ran behind the bar and grabbed the landlord. 'Have my horse taken to Tinners Field,' he said quietly, as he pressed a gold coin into the man's hand. He didn't wait for a reply and hurried up the narrow stairs to his rooms.

The wooden wall panels concealed a secret doorway that led to a dark chamber and a rope-ladder. A carpet-bag lay packed there, ready for just such an emergency. It contained his money, account books and a change of clothes. He closed the panel behind him, grabbed the bag and climbed the rope-ladder, which he drew up behind him when he'd gained the attic space. He paused to catch his breath and allow his eyes to grow accustomed to the gloom. The shouts of men and the clatter of horses' hoofs drifted up to him from the street. He didn't have much time.

The attic ran in a low tunnel above the line of houses. He crouched and hurried across the mouldering rafters praying they would hold his weight. The smell of vermin was strong in the fusty air, and dusty cobwebs stuck to his face and hair, but he scarcely noticed. Having reached the last house, he paused to listen. There was no sound from below.

He swung down from the attic and landed softly on the floor of a deserted room. The wheelwright had obviously decided it would be better to remain at the alehouse while Billy made his escape. He would be well rewarded when all the fuss had died down.

Billy raced down the narrow stairs and into the workshop and living quarters. The shouts were louder now, the sound of approaching horses making his pulse leap.

The hatch was well hidden behind a stack of unplaned wood, and Billy crawled through it and down into a labyrinth of tunnels designed to confuse the ignorant. He knew the way well, for these tunnels had been in use over many years, and he'd had to come down many a time. He began to run as fast as he could beneath the streets and houses of Newlyn.

He emerged to a moon veiled by scudding clouds, the wind sharp from the sea. Tinners Field lay at the eastern end of the town, and if he'd had either time or inclination, he could have looked across the headland and seen the flickering lights of Mousehole.

The grass was already damp and he lay there for a moment to catch his breath and look out for any sign of the Revenue men. The crumbling stone chimney of the played-out tin mine was a darker silhouette against the feeble, irregular gleam of the moon. Nothing stirred but the grass in the wind. He gave a low whistle.

The horse whinnied and trotted towards him out of the darkness. Billy climbed on to its back, secured the bag to the saddle and, with a soft dig in the ribs, coaxed it forward.

'You there! Stop, in the name of the King!'

The shout came from the shadows of the old chimney, and was accompanied by the emergence of several riders.

Billy froze, then yanked the reins to turn his horse. His spirits plunged as he saw yet more men on the skyline. The only way open to him was the cliff. He was cornered. He swore as he twisted the horse round and rammed his heels into its sides. Startled, the animal lurched into a gallop.

'Halt or we fire!'

Billy leant forward in the saddle, urging the beast to greater speed. There was a gap between the riders in front of him. If he could get through it he had a chance of escape, for his horse was swift, and he knew the country like the back of his hand.

The men behind were gaining and the ones in front were up to something.

Billy narrowed his eyes and peered into the darkness as his horse hurtled across the grass towards the line of armed men. A hay-wagon was being pulled into his path. He had no option but to gallop straight into that line and risk being shot. He lay low on the animal's neck, making himself as small a target as possible. He could see their pistols now, and the gleam of their eyes.

'Fire at will!'

Something thudded into his shoulder, and Billy knew he'd been hit. The horse flinched beneath him and, with a terrible scream, crumpled to the ground. Billy was thrown from the saddle, his boot caught in the stirrup. He looked up, dazed and in pain, at the men who gathered round him.

'We meet at last, Billy. It is my pleasure to inform you that I am arresting you for crimes against the Crown. It is to be hoped you will receive a long sentence.'

Billy dredged up the last of his bravado as the horse was dragged off him and he was pulled painfully to his feet. 'Very well,' he drawled. 'But it's taken you eleven years to catch me, and you've killed a good horse.'

Bodmin Assizes, April 1782

The trial took place three months later and lasted a few hours. The evidence was damning and there was no chance of reprieve. Billy stood in the dock with Ben Retallick and a host of others. His shoulder still hurt from when the so-called surgeon had dug out the bullet. Ben had paid for medicine and clean bandages, so at least the threat of blood-poisoning had been reduced, but he still fretted that his arm would remain useless.

The traitor turned out to have been the wheelwright, who had told all he knew in exchange for a pardon, but now he would be forced to move away from Newlyn and the close-knit fishing community, which relied heavily on the smugglers.

As he listened to the lawyers drone on in the stuffy court-room, he eyed the baying crowd who had come to watch. It was a rabble, and the court officials could barely be heard above the shouts and cat-calling.

Her stillness marked her out, and as their eyes met he felt ashamed. Susan had come to support him, but she was a witness to his shame, an innocent victim of the disgrace he had brought to his family. He had hoped they would remain in ignorance of his plight, but the gossip had reached them within days of his arrest. He tried to return her smile, but his heart wasn't in it. He just thanked God their mother hadn't come too.

'Benjamin Retallick. You will be hanged by your neck until you are dead. Take him down.'

Shocked beyond words, Billy could only look at the man he'd admired for so many years and grasp his hand before he was dragged away. Dear God, were they going to hang them all? He looked at the judge, the sweat cold on his back as sentences were passed on the other men. They ranged from seven years' hard labour and transportation to hanging. For once in his life Billy prayed.

'William Penhalligan. You will serve fourteen years' hard labour, and await transportation on the *Chatham* hulk.'

Transportation? Good God in heaven, he wouldn't survive that. His stomach heaved and all his childhood nightmares returned as he imagined the horrors of the endless sea journey in the holds. The noose would have been kinder. 'No,' he stuttered, struggling against the warder. 'Not transportation. Please don't send me—'

'Silence.' The judge crashed his gavel. 'Take him away.'

'Please, sir. Don't do this. Transportation will kill him.'

Billy shot a glance at his sister, who was now on her feet, her face almost bereft of colour.

'Silence, madam,' the judge roared.

Billy saw her tears and was almost grateful to the gaoler for shoving him out so he didn't have to bear her distress.

The holding cells were infested with vermin and fleas. The straw was filthy, the slop buckets overflowing. Women were crying, children bawled and men fought over a bottle of liquor that someone had smuggled in. He looked for Ben and the others, but was told they'd been taken to another prison to await execution.

'Penhalligan! Get over here.'

He pushed his way through the seething mass of stinking humanity and approached the gaoler. 'What now?' he muttered. If the man expected money for extra food or blankets he'd be disappointed: the Revenue men had stripped him of everything but the clothes on his back.

'Visitor,' the man said, with a leer, as he opened the locked gate.

Billy's shoes slipped on the slimy cobbles as he passed through to the open courtyard of the prison where those more fortunately endowed could pay for a modicum of freedom within the granite walls. 'Susan,' he said. 'This is no place for you.'

'You're my brother,' she said, her voice catching. She threw her arms round him and burst into tears. 'I tried to change his mind, but . . . Oh, Billy, I can't bear to think of you transported.'

He tried his best to contain himself, but the sight of his distraught sister was too much for him. 'I'll be all right,' he murmured. 'They'll probably keep me on the hulk now that they can't send us to the Americas.' It was poor consolation and he didn't believe a word of it.

'Do you think so?' She drew back from him and gazed up into his face.

He saw the hope in her eyes and couldn't bear to distress her further. 'I'm sure,' he said, the firmness belying his fear. 'Now, dry your eyes, and show me what you've got in that basket.'

She blew her nose, lifted the hem of her dainty dress out of the mire and drew him to a quiet corner where they were out of earshot of the other prisoners. 'I've paid the warder enough so we won't be disturbed,' she said, as she unfurled a blanket and spread it on the straw.

Billy's heart ached as he watched her unpack the hamper. She was trying to be brave, but she knew his fear of the sea, and understood that for him transportation meant death or insanity. He forced the dread to the back of his mind as he listened to her news from home.

Few would have guessed she was thirty, but there was barely a reminder of the girl who had worked on the quay in the elegant figure opposite him. Her hair had been smoothed back from her forehead and fell in ringlets at either side of her face, and her bonnet and dress were of the best quality. He noted the clarity of her eyes and the creaminess of her skin, and saw that time and circumstance had been kind to her. Her figure was still slight, although she had had five children, and her waistline was only marginally thicker than it had been on her wedding day.

'You've done well, Susan,' he said softly. 'I always said that life with Ezra would turn you into a fine lady.'

'It hasn't been easy,' she said, as she handed him a golden pasty, 'with all the lessons in etiquette I had to endure before I was permitted to associate with the parish's more genteel citizens.' She grinned, giving him a glimpse of the hoyden he remembered. 'I can't tell you how many times I wanted to break away from it and race barefoot over the cobbles to join in the rush when the shoals of pilchard were sighted.' She sighed. 'I even envied you for a while, free to come and go as you pleased, without a care in the world. But you've had to pay a terrible price and I wish . . . I wish . . .'

Billy realised she was close to tears again, and didn't reply. Nothing he could say would console either of them, and she needed to compose herself. He bit into the pasty and savoured the taste of proper food. The slops doled out in prison were disgusting but had to be forced down to sustain life. And if he survived transportation and the hulk, another fourteen years of filth lay ahead. He ignored these thoughts and concentrated on his sister.

'Does Ezra make you happy?' he asked, as he finished the pasty and began another.

Susan nodded. 'He's a good man, and I am content.'

He looked into her face and saw that she spoke the truth. 'Have you grown to love him, then?'

Her laugh was light. 'I confess I never thought I would, Billy, but Ezra has earned my respect and affection and we rub along well. He is a good husband, and I have grown to love his gentle ways and the deep commitment he has to his parishioners and the church. We also have the shared love for our children to bind us closer.'

'But he'll never set you afire as Jonathan did?'

Susan busied herself by cutting the cake she'd brought. 'That,' she said firmly, 'is none of your business, Billy Penhalligan.' She handed him a slice and became businesslike. 'I have some money for you, not much but it's all I could scrape up. There are medicines and clean bandages in this bundle, and a change of clothes.' She wrinkled her nose as she eyed the ragged remains of his filthy clothes. 'I've also put in some soap and lavender water.'

There was a lump in his throat as he tried to thank her. He'd seen her tears as she'd noted how far he'd fallen and felt ashamed.

She waved away his thanks, handed him the bundle, and began to pack away the hamper. The warder was approaching – their time together was almost up. 'You've given us money in the past, and helped more than you could ever know. Now it's our turn to help you.'

She kept her attention on the hamper, but Billy could see the effort it took her not to cry.

'I can't believe they'll transport you, Billy, and I can't bear to think of you trapped . . .' The words hung in the air. 'I've made enquiries. The *Chatham* hulk is in Plymouth so I'll be able to visit you.'

'No.' He got to his feet and winced as the movement sent a jolt of pain through his shoulder. 'I forbid it. This place is bad enough, but I've seen the hulks. They're no place for any woman, least of all my sister.'

'You can't stop me,' she said.

'I'll refuse to see you.'

Susan gave a trembling sigh. 'You always were headstrong, Billy.' Her face was a picture of anguish. 'I understand why you don't want us to see you,' she said thickly, 'but we need to know you're safe.'

'It will be too painful,' he replied, as he took her hands. 'Bad enough you came today – the shame in the years to come will finish me if you witness it.'

She nodded. 'Very well,' she murmured. 'I will arrange for someone to deliver food and clothes whenever I can.' She touched his dirty, stubbled chin with her cool hand. 'I must go,' she said quietly, tears glistening on her lashes. 'God speed, Billy. Remember that we love you and will help whenever we can.'

When she hugged him, he smelt the freshness of her hair and the lavender water on her skin, felt the wiry strength in her slim body that seemed to encompass the essence of home. Fourteen years was a long time to serve, but he vowed that, should he survive, he would make it up to her.

Mousehole, April 1786

Susan stared at her reflection in the hand mirror and wondered where the years had gone. It was four years since she'd seen Billy. All her requests to visit him had been denied, and although they'd sent parcels, there had been no word from him.

She put down the mirror and made a determined effort to put Billy's troubles to the back of her mind: it was her daughter's fourteenth birthday today and she had a party to host. She stood up, brushing the creases from her skirt, relishing the feel of the lavender cotton beneath her fingers. It was a new dress, made especially for today, and she knew it looked well on her, enhancing the blue of her eyes and the narrowness of her waist. As she slipped her feet into the matching slippers, and picked up her fan, she heard voices below in the walled garden and stepped over to the window to look out. The family were gathering and she should hurry down to them, but for a moment she preferred to be up here in quiet contemplation.

From her vantage-point high above, she could see Ezra in deep conversation with his brother Gilbert, who had arrived from London with his wife, Ann. It had come as a shock when they had married three years ago, not least to Ann, for she had confided in Susan that she had always considered herself a rather ordinary woman, destined for spinsterhood, until at the advanced age of thirty-one she had caught the eye of the dashing General Collinson.

Susan smiled. Ann's marriage to Gilbert had been the making of them both, and although their union might have come too late for children, Gilbert took a great deal of looking after. From her correspondence, Susan knew Ann regretted the lack of little ones, but found it exciting to follow Gilbert all over the British Empire.

She turned her attention to Maud, ensconced in a bath chair on the lawn, issuing orders to the housekeeper. Her weakened constitution had finally taken its toll and she could no longer walk, but her frail, bird-like appearance masked a will of iron that kept the children in awe of her. A game of croquet was in progress and a gaggle of girls sat beneath the tree, flashing smiles and flirting eyes at the young officers Gilbert had brought with him. Some of the boys were larking about, and received a stern reprimand from Maud.

Susan breathed a deep sigh of relief. The weather had held, even though it was only early April, and tea was laid on tables covered with snowy white cloths, which undulated in the spring breeze that came up from the sea. The rectory was no longer a house of gloom but alive with colour, noise and the flit of pretty dresses and scarlet uniforms.

As she watched the shifting kaleidoscope beneath her, Ezra seemed to become aware of her presence and looked up to the window. His smile told of his happiness, and she felt warmed by it. Their fifteen years of marriage had indeed brought her a contentment that had deepened over the years as she helped him about the parish, and although Billy had been astute enough to know she could never love her husband with the same passion she'd had for Jonathan, she was determined he should never learn of this failing in her.

She caught sight of her daughter, flirting outrageously with the young lieutenant as they played croquet. Emma had come into the world fourteen years ago, her angry cries accompanied by flying fists and kicking legs – a precursor of the temper tantrums she threw during childhood and the boundless energy she showed in her work at the school Ezra had set up in the village.

She searched for Ernest, and felt the familiar pang of loss. He and his twin had been born two months early, and Thomas had not survived a week. Ernest was the most placid of her children, and she often wondered if he missed the twin he'd never known. At thirteen, his roguish good looks and shy smile already cut a swathe through the local female population when he returned home from work on the farm at Land's End. He hoped one day to have his own land, and Susan knew the life would suit him, for he was not academic and liked nothing better than to be outside in all weathers, looking after his stock.

She watched him as he stood chatting to a couple of girls. He was tall for his age, his figure promising broad-shouldered manhood, and his light hair glistened gold in the sun as he bent to hear something one of the girls was saying.

Susan was surprised he was there: usually he was absorbed in his work, and often forgot important occasions. Perhaps the lure of female company had concentrated his mind.

Her gaze roamed further and settled on twelve-year-old Florence, who was organising the tables and chairs. She had been born exactly nine months after she was conceived, and was efficient in everything she did. She was a neat little body and more than a match for her grandmother when it came to a sharp tongue and a keen eye for detail, which was disconcerting, considering her youth.

Susan gave a wry shake of her head as she watched her. The child might be a younger version of Maud, but with the advantages provided by Ezra's income, she would never live in a fisherman's cottage or go hungry and cold in the winter. Susan suspected that, when the time came, Florence would find a wealthy husband – she had already shown a liking for the finer things in life.

A familiar pang tugged at her. Florence was a strange child. Even as a baby she'd had a particular way of staring at her that she'd found painful. It was as if Florence was measuring her, and found her wanting, and despite all her efforts, Susan realised the girl needed little from her. Ezra was the one who could still her crying – the one she would turn to when hurt or disgruntled.

She left the window after searching the garden for George. He was out of sight, but she fancied she could hear him. With a cluck of disapproval, she left the bedroom and hurried downstairs. The boy was far too boisterous and, at eleven, should have been more concerned with his school reports than running wild about the place and getting into mischief. The manager at the quarry had already been up to the house to complain about him and some of the other boys, and there had been further trouble from the fishermen when they had hidden the nets and lobster-pots down a disused mineshaft. Ezra had reluctantly beaten him with a cane from the school, but it hadn't done much good, and Susan fretted: his behaviour was all too reminiscent of Billy's when he'd been that age.

Billy was still incarcerated in a hulk at Plymouth, with another ten years to serve. The War of Independence had kept him from being transported to the Americas and, in a way, she was glad, for it kept him within reach and off the high seas.

She and Ezra had ignored his demand that they stay away, and although they had not been allowed to see him, they had been appalled at the conditions in which he was living. She had

had many sleepless nights, but had to accept that Billy had broken the law, had known the risks and was being made to pay for his crime. There was little she could do but pray that he would survive.

'Hello, my love,' murmured Ezra, as she emerged from the house. He greeted her with a soft kiss on her flushed cheek. 'You're lovely as usual, but I sense you're a little distracted.'

Susan shook off the dark thoughts of Billy and smiled fleetingly. 'Have you seen George?'

'I've sent him to his room for half an hour,' replied Ezra, with a sigh that didn't disguise the quirk of amusement about his lips. 'He pulled Florence's hair and earned himself a clip round the ear.'

Susan grinned. 'Our daughter can throw a punch worthy of a fisher-girl,' she replied, 'which serves him right.'

Jonathan knew it wasn't wise, but after so many years away from Mousehole he had to see her. The shock of learning that Susan had married Ezra Collinson a few days before he'd landed in England had left him reeling. His mother, of course, had been delighted.

Was Susan happy? Not that he could have done anything about it, he admitted ruefully. Their lives had moved on, yet her happiness mattered to him and he regretted the long years he had spent away from Cornwall. He should have made more effort to come down, but he hadn't been able to face her now that she was married to another. He'd thrown himself into London life, and had pursued his thirst for exploration on the seas, which left little time for introspection and Cornwall. After his mother's death two years ago, Braddock had proved capable of seeing to estate business in his absence.

He helped his wife into the carriage and ignored her pained expression as he settled on the driving seat, caught up the reins and set the horse into an easy trot.

Emily sat frostily behind him, her mouth a thin line in her thin face, her gloved hand welded to the handle of her parasol. 'I don't see why we have to call on the minister,' she snapped.

'He happens to be a distant cousin,' he retorted over his shoulder, 'and I'll thank you, madam, to be civil.' He kept his eyes on the track in front of him and his temper in check. It was pleasant to think of Susan and speculate on how she might have changed – and how he would feel when he saw her again, for he had never forgotten that last day in the cave.

Unfortunately, he could not ignore his wife's presence for she continued to snipe, and it became increasingly difficult to rein in his impatience. Emily had been foisted upon him in 1772, soon after his return to England. He was at a low ebb, heartbroken at what he saw as Susan's betrayal, and his mother had taken full advantage of it. Before he knew it, the arrangements had gone too far for him to back out.

The estate had never recovered after his father's gambling debts had been paid, and an injection of capital was needed if the family was to retain its high profile in society. At the tender age of twenty-one, Jonathan had found himself tied irrevocably to a harridan.

Emily was the plain daughter of a wealthy earl and was sharp-tongued even in her youth, which explained the generous dowry she had brought to the marriage, and the lack of other suitors. Bedding her was no pleasure for either of them, and when their son, Edward, was born, Emily considered she had done her duty and, to Jonathan's relief, banished her husband from her bedroom.

Over the years her sour countenance haunted him, and he'd sometimes sought comfort with other women. He'd felt guilty at first, since she'd been as much a pawn in his mother's scheming as he. But she seemed determined to hate him, and he'd accepted there would be no reconciliation.

It was a marriage made in hell, as far as he was concerned,

and he'd spent the past fourteen years sailing the high seas rather than spend a minute more than he had to in his London home or on the benches at the House of Lords. If it hadn't been for his son he would have left England for good.

The high-stepping horse made easy work of the rough tracks and steep hills, and soon the house was in sight. Jonathan slowed the animal to a walk and took the opportunity to watch the ebb and flow of the party through the iron gates of the garden. His gaze trawled the faces and came to rest on the pretty woman in the lilac dress. His pulse began to race. He would have recognised her anywhere.

Her hair had been tied back with a ribbon that matched her lavender dress, and her figure was trim, belying her age. He watched her animated face as he drew up outside the front door. Susan had always been beautiful, but now she was even more so, he thought. She seemed so alive, so full of energy – it was as if the sun and the wind of Cornwall were embodied in her slight frame, and that at any minute she would simply fly away.

'When you've finished daydreaming, I'd appreciate your hand to get down,' snapped Emily.

Jonathan was thrust from his reverie and hastily helped his wife to alight. He looked at her pinched face and dull grey clothes and couldn't help but contrast her with the lively Susan who could still make his heart beat faster. His spirits plunged. He shouldn't have come.

Susan was laughing with Emma at Ernest's antics as he tried to teach croquet to a couple of pretty young girls, when Ezra's hand cupped her elbow. 'We have visitors, my dear,' he said quietly.

She turned and her smile wavered. Her heart leapt and thudded painfully against her ribs as she saw him approach. He'd barely changed from the boy she'd loved and dreamt about for so many years. His black hair was only lightly salted with silver at the temples, his face was handsome, and his figure that of a man who was supremely fit. But it was his eyes that mesmerised her and brought back the memories, for they were as blue as the Cornish sea and fixed on her.

'Susan?' Ezra's grip tightened on her elbow.

She blinked and pulled herself together, aware of others watching and that she had to maintain a cool detachment despite the pounding of her pulse. 'It's a surprise to see them,' she murmured. 'I didn't know they had been invited.'

'I'd heard they were here and sent the invitation at the last minute. I hope you don't mind?'

There was no time to reply for Jonathan and his sour-faced wife were upon them. Susan executed a curtsy. 'How very kind of you to come.'

Emily nodded imperiously, mouth turned down, eyes like gimlets as she regarded Susan, who could feel the colour rising in her face as the woman's glare of disapproval said more than words. She was sixteen again, a fisher-girl working on the quay, not the minister's respected wife.

Jonathan shook hands with Ezra and her colour heightened as he took her hand and kissed the air above her fingers. Their eyes met and the rest of the world melted away. Susan swayed towards him. 'Jonathan,' she murmured.

Gilbert shattered the moment. 'Ezra,' he boomed, as he clamped a hand on his brother's shoulder. 'It's time for the champagne I brought from London, and for me to announce my news.'

Susan tore her gaze from Jonathan as she felt Ann slip a hand round her waist and propel her gently from the group.

'You look quite flushed, my dear,' she said. 'Come, let me pour you some lemonade. It will cool you.'

Susan trailed beside her, dazed. Jonathan had returned, and her feelings for him were as strong as ever. It was in the drum of her heart and the tingle of her skin – she hadn't felt so alive for years.

'I'm surprised to see the earl here,' said Ann, as she poured lemonade from the jug into a crystal glass. 'He's so rarely in this country, and it must be years since he was in Cornwall.'

Susan forced her thoughts into some coherence. 'Ezra invited them.' She couldn't resist darting a glance at Jonathan, who was helping his wife to a seat in the shade.

'How foolish of him,' Ann replied, as she handed her the glass.

Susan started. 'Whatever do you mean?' she stammered.

Ann tucked her hand into the crook of her arm and led her to two chairs that were set apart from the others beneath a tree. When they were settled and their skirts arranged decorously, she said, 'I've heard the rumours. You and Jonathan Cadwallader have a history, albeit an ancient one, but I don't think it's ever wise to return to the past, or to pine for what might have been. It only disappoints.'

Susan blushed. 'We were children,' she said softly. 'I'm perfectly content with Ezra.'

Ann patted her hand. 'As long as you remember that, my dear,' she replied.

Susan didn't miss the gentle admonishment, and noticed how Ann drew back her shoulders and stiffened her spine as she watched the subject of their conversation join the game of croquet. She was positively bristling with dislike – which was unusual in such a sweet-natured woman – and Susan experienced a twinge of unease.

Ann took a sip of lemonade before she spoke again. 'Jonathan Cadwallader has quite a reputation with women, and in some quarters is regarded as an adventurer,' she said flatly. 'He might be dashing and wealthy, his discretion immaculate, but he's the cause of many a broken heart. No wonder his poor wife looks so bitter.'

Susan dismissed this as idle gossip, caught Jonathan's eye and blushed as he flashed her a smile. She wished she could walk and talk with him alone. How she longed for the party to be over so she could think of a way to meet him.

'My dear,' murmured Ann, with a soft nudge.

Susan realised she was expecting a reaction to her opinion. She was about to advise her not to listen to gossip when Gilbert bellowed, 'My lord, ladies, officers and gentlemen.'

Ann snapped open her fan and waved it. 'My husband seems to think he's still on a parade-ground,' she whispered.

Susan giggled with relief at having escaped from Ann's well-meant interference.

'But he does cut a dashing figure, don't you think?' her sister-in-law went on. 'One would hardly believe he's forty-eight.'

'Marriage to you agrees with him,' observed Susan.

Ann blushed and fanned her face.

Gilbert's voice rang out: 'Today is a day of celebration, not only for the birthday of my niece, Emma, but for the news I bear from London.'

'He does so enjoy the sound of his own voice,' remarked Ann, comfortably, 'but I do wish he'd get on with it.' She noticed Susan's look of enquiry and patted her hand. 'You'll find out soon enough,' she promised.

'Following the unfortunate events of the American War of Independence, and the subsequent hostilities from France and Spain, our prime minister, William Pitt, has recognised that our continued presence in the East is our only hope for British recovery.'

'Oh, dear Lord,' Ann sighed, 'he's off. We'll be here for hours.'

Susan barely heard a word either of them said, for she was gazing at Jonathan.

'But there are other concerns, which must be addressed if Britain is to regain her naval power,' Gilbert roared. 'The provision of hemp is vital to this sea-faring nation, and our supply of this commodity has been sorely depleted by Queen Catherine of Russia, who has seen fit to purchase all available supplies from the Baltic.' He paused to catch his breath and smooth his flowing moustache. 'The founding of a colony in New South Wales offers a solution. It will not only provide a source of flax and timber but will secure the military and strategic objectives of precluding French settlement and a prime naval base in wartime.'

There was a murmur among the gathering and a rustle of impatience. He hurried on: 'This brave venture will also alleviate the problem of what to do with the hundreds of convicts awaiting transportation who would have been sent previously to the Americas.'

That harnessed Susan's attention and her thoughts turned to Billy.

'Lord Sydney, who holds the seals at the Home Office, announced this week that His Majesty has agreed on Botany Bay as a suitable place to establish a convict colony. He has instructed the Admiralty to provide vessels for seven hundred and fifty felons and such provisions, necessities and implements for agriculture as might be needed in the new land. The First Fleet will leave in the spring of 1787.'

Susan's heart was hammering. Would Billy finally be transported? Was he about to be sent to the far side of the world to a land of uncharted and savage character to live and die as a bonded prisoner with none of his family around him? She glanced at Maud, who had paled beneath her bonnet and their eyes met in silent anguish.

'Make no mistake about it, ladies and gentlemen. This new colony is to be founded *by* convicts, not *for* convicts – they are merely a means to an end. Arthur Phillip is to be appointed Captain General and Governor in Chief of New South Wales, from Cape York to latitude forty-three degrees thirty-nine minutes south and westward as far as the one hundred and thirty-fifth degree of east longitude, including all islands adjacent in the Pacific Ocean.'

Most of the party had no idea what he was talking about, for news took time to travel this far west, and the talk of longitude and latitude was as incomprehensible as ancient Greek.

Susan sat beside Ann, her thoughts in a whirl.

Gilbert still hadn't finished: 'To assist Governor Phillip in his administration there will be a strong military force, and I'm delighted to announce that I have been promoted to Field Marshal and will take up my post as judge advocate of the military court on arrival with the First Fleet.'

A polite round of applause followed, and Susan turned to Ann, fear for her brother making her voice tremble. 'What will this mean for Billy?'

Ann patted her hand. 'I don't know, Susan, but Gilbert will make enquiries, and if he is to be sent, we will watch over him.'

'You're not going too?'

'Of course,' she replied. 'My place is at my husband's side, as any good wife's should be.'

Susan heard the uncharacteristically barbed remark. 'But what will you do in that God-forsaken place? Surely it won't be safe?'

Ann watched her husband graciously receive congratulations from the people who crowded round him. 'It won't be God-forsaken, Susan,' she replied. 'We will have the Reverend Richard Johnson as chaplain to the colony, there will be other wives and many children, and more ministers will come with the Second and Third Fleets.'

Susan looked at her in admiration. They were the same age, yet there was a world of difference between them. 'You're so brave, Ann. I don't know that I would have the courage to go so far to an unknown land.'

Ann's eyes were alight with excitement. 'It's a thrilling venture, my dear, and one day, when the colony is settled, you and Ezra might wish to join us. There will be a great deal of work for a minister such as Ezra.'

Susan shuddered. 'I'll never leave Cornwall.' Her gaze drifted to Jonathan, and she found he was watching her.

'Life has a habit of changing the most fervent beliefs,' Ann murmured.

But Susan didn't hear her. Jonathan had moved away from the cluster round Gilbert, and was making his way towards the walled garden. With a glance over his shoulder he met her eye, then strolled out of sight.

'I must congratulate Gilbert on his speech,' said Ann. 'Will you come too?'

Susan shook her head. 'I must see to George. It's time he was allowed to rejoin the party.'

She hurried towards the house before Ann could question her further, and once George had been shooed downstairs, she wove through the vegetable plot and slipped through the side door into the overgrown walled garden. She wouldn't be missed for a while, and she had to see him – had to ask all the questions that had plagued her over the years, and try to come to terms with his sudden appearance.

He was waiting for her in the shade of an old plum tree. 'Susan. It's been so long.'

It would have been the easiest thing in the world to throw herself into his arms, but something in his expression stopped her. 'Too long,' she said quietly, her gaze devouring him. 'Why didn't you come back for me as you promised?'

'I did,' he protested. 'But when I got here my mother told me you'd married Ezra Collinson. You only had to wait another eight damn days and I'd have been with you. I was wrong to trust your promises.'

'How dare you?' The longing to hold him was replaced by anger. 'I waited three years without a word from you that you'd meant what you'd said.'

'I could hardly have posted a letter in the middle of the Tasman Sea,' he retorted. 'You should have had faith in me.'

'Three years,' she repeated, 'when it should have been two – what did you expect of me, Jonathan? To sit and wait while you were playing sailor?'

'Of course not,' he said. 'But three years is nothing when we could have spent the rest of our lives together.' He took a step towards her. 'I intended to marry you, Susan, but you couldn't wait. And why Collinson of all people?' He took a deep breath, evidently battling to keep his temper. 'I trusted you, and you broke my heart.'

'It couldn't have pained you much,' she retorted, unwilling to acknowledge the anguish in his eyes. 'You were married to Emily within a year.'

He ran his fingers through his hair and Susan could see the battle going on inside him as he told her about his mother's meddling and his arranged marriage. 'I had little choice,' he said. 'She was plotting to marry me off even before I left for Tahiti and had made it plain she expected me to agree to her plans the minute I returned. That was why I was determined to marry you before I found myself attached to someone I didn't love. But your union with Collinson ruined everything, and without you, I didn't care what happened to me.' He was still angry as he looked down at her. 'I'm sure you'll be delighted to know it is not a happy match.'

She could see his unhappiness and, having met Emily, understood it. 'I'm sorry, Jon,' she murmured. 'It seems we are both victims of your mother's plotting.' She went on to tell him about the loss of her father and brothers and the reason for her own marriage.

Jonathan balled his fists as the colour drained from his face. He let out his fury and frustration in a deep groan. 'Dear God, I'm so sorry I wasn't here to protect you.'

She stepped back from him, remembering the hours she'd

spent gazing out to sea, the prayers she'd made that he would come back in time, and her final acceptance on the church steps that he was lost to her. At length she looked up at him, all anger spent, heart heavy with sadness that Fate had dealt them such a cruel blow. 'Why *did* you stay away so long?'

'We went much further south and were caught in a series of bad storms.' He told her of the long voyages round New Zealand, the search for and discovery of Australia, the nightmare of Batavia and the journey home. 'There were no other ships to take our letters – I had no way to send you a message. But I thought of you constantly, Susan. You never left my heart.'

She wanted to cry but tears couldn't salve the hurt that had been caused. 'Oh, Jonathan, your coral reef trapped you as surely as it did me. Now it's too late for either of us.'

He took her hands and she didn't resist. 'Seeing you today proved to me that I have never stopped loving you,' he said softly. 'You feel the same, I can tell.'

The sounds of the party faded. She wanted to kiss him, to feel his arms round her again – yet she knew that she must resist. She had to be strong. 'Yes,' she admitted softly. 'But this must be an end to it.'

'But why, if we love one another?' He pulled her closer, face drawn with pain.

'Because I have a duty to Ezra and my children. I don't wish them to be hurt – and because . . . because it's too late.'

He lifted her hands to his lips. 'Can we at least be friends?'

She heard the longing in his voice and wanted to comfort him, but any sign of weakness now would mean the end of her good intentions. 'Friends always,' she murmured.

The Dunkirk *hulk, Plymouth, May 1786*

Billy could see the reflection in the still, dark waters that reached almost to his waist, and wondered for a moment who it was. The young man he remembered bore no resemblance to the one he was staring at and, perplexed, he ran his roughened hands over his straggling beard and long hair. Billy Penhalligan had always been well groomed and upright, proud of his good looks and the fine clothes that moon-raking had brought him. This creature was unkempt, wore filthy rags, and his eyes were those of a man who had looked upon the world and seen the darkest evil. They were lifeless orbs in the haggard face of a man far older than twenty-nine.

'Move yer arse, Cornish, or I'll 'ave yer flogged again.'

Billy emerged from his thoughts and picked up the heavy hammer. Wielding it high, he slammed it down on the piling, wishing it was the guard's head he was driving into the mud. The man was forever on his back, and seemed to like nothing better than to deliver a flogging.

'Only another twenty to go and then you can 'ave a rest.' Alfred Mullins gave a sharp bark of humourless laughter and moved on.

Billy kept swinging the hammer and cast a glance at the warder's retreating back. 'I'd love to teach him a lesson,' he growled to Stan, working beside him.

Stanley Irwin was a Norfolk man, sent from the Assizes with a death sentence commuted to transportation. He had a wife and child on board the *Dunkirk* hulk, both gained during his time in Norwich Castle gaol. His health was failing, and he'd suffered too many floggings to retain his once belligerent stance. 'Chance'd be a fine thing,' he mumbled. 'Best keep your head down, Bill. Serve your sentence and get out.'

Billy kept working, his thoughts racing. With another ten years to go, there were times when he wished he'd been hanged with the others outside Bodmin gaol. A smile tweaked his lips. The only brightness in his life was provided by Nell, a young London whore who'd come aboard a few weeks ago. With red hair and a temperament to match, she had latched on to him and they had recognised they were kindred spirits. Nell was a fighter, would never give up while she had breath, and her energy and determination kept him sane. He had yet to lie with her, but the time would come, he was sure of that.

He stood back from the piling, measured it to make sure it was at the correct height, and splashed through the water to the next. He looked over at the *Dunkirk* and grimaced. The old naval frigate lay embedded in the Plymouth mud, her timbers rotting, the stink from the convict holds drifting across the water. It had been his home for the last twelve months after the *Chatham* had fallen to pieces and sunk. If it hadn't been for the war in the Americas he'd have been long gone, probably working the cotton fields on some plantation as an indentured servant. There would have been the chance of escape there, of earning remission, but here there was only misery, each day dragging, each night spent half awake, alert for attacks and the rats that crawled over him. Thank God for Nell, with her raucous laughter, dubious jokes and endless energy.

The light was failing. Soon they would be herded into the small boats and taken back to the hulk. Billy breathed in the warm, salty air, and flexed his still-powerful back and shoulders. He was tired and every muscle ached, but he wasn't looking forward to the fetid stench of the convict quarters and the shrieking of the whores as they plied their trade in exchange for extra food from the sailors. All he wanted was to return to Mousehole and home – to the smell of baking fish and bread, the soft burr of the Cornish dialect. He felt a pang of regret for the freedom he'd squandered in his pursuit of riches.

'Stand back.' The shout came down the line and the warder shoved each man with his wooden baton. 'Visitors approaching. I got me eye on you, Penhalligan. One move and I'll 'ave you in irons.'

Billy stepped back until he could lean against the piling he'd just driven into the estuary mud. He'd become inured to the sightseers who would hire boats, paddle out to see the convicts, turn up their noses at the stench and gawp. The women were the worst, with their handkerchiefs pressed to their noses while their eyes were hot as they raked the half-naked bodies of the men. They giggled and exclaimed behind their fans as if the objects of their admiration were deaf or even dead.

He hawked phlegm and spat into the water as he glared at the little boat that was fast approaching. The occupants should try one night out here: they'd soon discover that the men they jeered at could turn savage in moments, given half a chance.

The boat had come up the estuary and was now close to the end of the pier the men were building. The man who seemed to be in charge was in conversation with Mr Cowdry, the chief gaoler.

'William Penhalligan?'

Billy was thrust from his dark thoughts and his head went up. 'Yes?'

'Visitor for you. Get up here.'

Mullins gave him a shove, which nearly knocked him off his feet. 'Move yerself!'

Billy dragged his bare feet through the mud, which clung and sucked at his legs. He kept his mouth shut as he waded through the water into the shallows.

'Ah, there you are, Penhalligan. Look lively now. Important visitor for you.'

Billy glowered at Cowdry, who was standing on the pier like a stuffed pouter pigeon, then turned to his visitor. He frowned. The man was dressed in full army uniform, which could only mean trouble. He dug his toes into the mud and dipped his chin.

'Billy, I'm here on behalf of your family.' There was a pause in which Billy raised his head and looked him in the eye. 'I'm Field Marshal Collinson of His Majesty's Dragoon Guards.'

'What's happened to them?' Billy was about to take a step towards the officer when Mullins dug him in the ribs with his baton and told him to stand to attention.

'No need for that,' growled the field marshal, with a fierce glare. Mullins glowered but held his silence. 'Your family is well. Come, Billy, we can talk more privately ashore.' Without waiting for a response, Gilbert Collinson dismissed the guard, stepped out of the boat and on to the pier, then headed for the grass bank that lined the shore.

Billy hoisted up the baggy trousers that were in danger of falling from his wasted hips, and dragged the remains of his shirt across his chest. Joining the field marshal, he was all too aware of the contrast between them and made sure he remained downwind of the patrician nose. The shame of his circumstances burned within him, but he regarded the man with defiance. 'What have you to do with my family?' he asked, as soon as they were alone.

'I'm related to your sister's husband,' Collinson said quickly. 'I don't have much time, so listen carefully.' He glanced across at the watching warders. 'I'm reliably informed you are on the list to be transported to the convict colony of New South Wales.'

Billy frowned. He'd never heard of such a place, but the thought of transportation made him dizzy with dread.

Gilbert enlightened him, and as he listened, Billy's spirits plummeted even further. Yet he was determined not to let the man know how the news had affected him. He gave a wry smile. 'And I was thinking you'd got me a reprieve.'

'I'm afraid not, with all the counts against you.' His dark eyes were twinkling. 'But I can offer you easier, cleaner work than this once we reach Botany Bay. Your skills of requisition and deployment will be needed as we build our new colony, and I want a man like you to keep an eye on my interests.'

Billy almost smiled, despite the sickness twisting in his gut. 'Set a thief to catch a thief, eh?'

Gilbert nodded. 'Quite so,' he agreed. 'And if you behave yourself, I'll make sure you get the appropriate parcel of land on your emancipation.'

'Land?'

'His Majesty's Governor will issue parcels of land to the military, freemen and convicts who prove themselves worthy of it. It will be your chance to begin again and to redeem yourself for your past misdemeanours.'

'But it won't bring me home,' muttered Billy. He doubted he'd even reach Botany Bay, let alone survive to return to England.

'In years to come that might be possible, but I wouldn't set your hopes too high.' Gilbert sighed. 'Your deeds have brought this upon you, Billy, but now you have come under my jurisdiction you have a chance to make something of your life. Your mother misses you, of course, and so does Susan. They wanted to come with me today, but I knew it would only distress them.' He glanced at Mullins and then at the *Dunkirk* hulk.

'How is Mother?' It had been years since he'd seen her, and Billy swallowed hard, determined to keep himself under control.

'She's in robust health,' Gilbert said. 'Busy with her grandchildren and interfering in everyone's business as usual.'

Billy nodded. He remembered his mother's bossy ways and boundless energy even in the darkest times. He was glad she hadn't changed. He pumped the man for information of Susan and her family, and was amazed at how life had moved on in his absence. He left the final, most important question until last. 'When do we leave?'

'Next spring.'

'Another year in this hell-hole.' He glanced at Mullins. 'Any chance of a change of scene?'

Gilbert shook his head. 'The judge was adamant, even though I leant on him pretty hard.' He began to lead the way back to the boat. 'I have some things for you. I hope you manage to keep them.'

Billy's eyes widened at the sight of the parcel of food and the bundle of clothing Gilbert placed in his arms. Then the field marshal dropped a handful of silver into his palm. 'A man can be murdered for a quarter of this.'

'I've already spoken to William Cowdry on your behalf. You can give the money to him and he will use it to provide you with extra rations. You can trust him. He's an honest fellow.'

Billy glanced across at the chief gaoler. Cowdry was about as trustworthy as the rest of them. 'I'll take the risk and keep it myself,' he muttered, as he tied the coins tightly into the corner of his ragged shirt.

'I wish I could do more.'

Billy shrugged as he held the bundles tight to his chest, high above the water. 'Thank you, sir,' he said, 'but if you could send my love to Mother and tell her not to fret, that will be enough.' His face broke into a defiant grin. 'They haven't found a way to cow Billy Penhalligan yet, and I doubt they ever will.'

Gilbert's gaze was steady and appraising. 'I believe you may be right.' He thrust out his hand. 'I look forward to seeing you in Botany Bay.'

II

Mousehole, May 1786

April had been surprisingly warm, but May was stormy, keeping the fishing-boats in the tiny harbour and the men at their strip-farming. An epidemic of influenza had cut a swathe through the most vulnerable, and Susan had been busy with parish duties. She had learnt a great deal since her marriage to Ezra, and now she understood his seemingly stoic detachment as they did what they could to ease suffering. He had taught her there could be no displays of pity or disgust, or even anger at the conditions in which the poor had to survive: pity helped no one, but practical advice and quiet efficiency eased burdens.

She was lying in bed that May night, listening to the rain pounding on the windows as the wind howled round the chimneys. The house seemed to be holding its breath as the storm whipped up the sea and waves thundered against the cliffs. It was not a night to be out, and she nestled beneath the blankets, thankful for their warmth and comfort. Yet she found she couldn't sleep. Jonathan would soon return to Cornwall.

Closing her eyes, she conjured up his face, the way he moved and spoke. Their short exchange in the walled garden had been filled with emotion, and despite her good intentions, she'd known that if they met again she would not be able to resist him.

She tried to blank out the sound of the storm and Ezra's snoring. Jonathan hadn't written as she'd thought he might, but that hadn't stopped her eagerly awaiting news of his return. It had come this morning as she'd tended the estate steward's wife. The poor woman had lost another baby and, although deeply distressed, she'd been determined to return to the big house to prepare it for Jonathan and Emily's arrival. After that Susan had found it hard to concentrate, and had left the gatehouse as soon as was decent.

Ezra muttered in his sleep and turned over, dragging most of the bedclothes with him. With a cluck of annoyance she yanked them back and settled once more to her pleasant thoughts. Emily's presence might make it difficult, but she would risk sending him a note.

She frowned as her thoughts tumbled over each other. It wouldn't be seemly to meet him here alone, and they couldn't risk anywhere public, for no one would believe they were merely friends. She smiled as she remembered their old haunt – the cave in the cliffs. It couldn't be seen from the clifftop, and in such inclement weather, there would be no walkers to spy on them . . .

Treleaven House, Cornwall, May 1786

'It's plain why you insisted upon coming here so soon after our last visit,' snapped Emily, as she faced Jonathan in the library. 'You are too predictable.'

They had been in Cornwall less than twenty-four hours, and already she was getting on his nerves. Jonathan leant against the marble mantelpiece and took another sip of brandy. He was drunk, but not drunk enough to blot out her nagging voice. It seemed this harangue had been going on for hours. 'You didn't have to come. I'm sure the delights of your dreary London drawing room hold far more interest than anything I could offer.'

'Your sarcasm is wasted on me, sir,' she retorted, fingers knotted in her lap. 'And if you think I can't see through you, you're more of a fool than I thought.'

He eyed her blearily. The brandy was at last taking effect, and its warmth was spreading through him. 'I have estate business to see to,' he said, the words slurring. 'Whatever else your warped mind might have conjured is neither here nor there. If you kept your tongue still, and used what little brain you have, you would understand that this estate keeps you in the luxury you are only too pleased to exploit.'

Her pinched face looked old in the bright shaft of sunlight that poured through the windows, and her grey eyes were hooded above the mean little mouth. 'I saw how you looked at the parson's wife,' she grated. 'It's she who brings you here, not the estate.'

Jonathan placed the delicate glass on the marble mantelpiece before he replied. It was true, he did want to see Susan again, but the estate was pressing, and although he would try, he doubted he would find time for social calls. 'I'm sure there's nothing I can say to convince you otherwise,' he said wearily. 'But logic must tell you there is a great deal to be done here. If you don't believe me, you're welcome to accompany me and Braddock when we walk the estate tomorrow.'

She rose from the couch, her skirts rustling like dead autumn leaves as she moved towards him. 'Don't take me for a fool, sir.'

'I would never presume to do so, madam.' He picked up the bottle and shot her a beguiling smile. 'Come, Emily. Loosen your stays and have a drink. You'd be surprised by how different the world is after a little brandy.' He grinned. 'You might even enjoy yourself.'

Emily stiffened. 'There isn't enough brandy in England that would change my opinion of the world – or of you.'

At that all Jonathan's past hurts and disappointments welled inside him. 'Both of us are at fault in our disastrous marriage, Emily. I apologise for any pain I've brought you over the years, and I regret that we should come to such an impasse. But if you hadn't always been so cold, so sharp, things might have been different.'

The slap on his cheek shocked him and he stared at her in bewilderment. 'What was that for?'

'All the women you've tumbled with during our marriage and the humiliation I've suffered from the gossip.' She was breathing heavily, perhaps surprised by the ferocity of her temper. 'I hate you, Jonathan, with every fibre of my being.'

Jonathan blinked, and tried to put his befuddled thoughts in order. 'The feeling is mutual, my dear,' he said. 'I have had two mistresses since our marriage, ladies of discretion, whose sweet-tempered company I've cherished over several years.' He held up his hand as she was about to interrupt. 'I like women. What man doesn't? Especially when his marriage bed is as welcoming as polar ice. I enjoy flirting, dancing and parties – but I have always maintained respect for your reputation, and that of our son.'

'That's not what I hear,' she hissed. 'I am told you have women all over London, and our son has to bear the disgrace of knowing that his father is a rake.'

'That is not true,' he roared. 'Those harpies you entertain have nothing better to do than feed your self-inflicted martyrdom. I am *not* a rake. How *dare* you suggest such a thing?'

'I shall leave now,' she said flatly. She picked up her reticule and shawl and swept towards the door. 'Our son is alone in London, and one of us should be there in case we are needed.'

Jonathan noted the barb and did not miss the light of victory in her eyes. 'Go – and good riddance,' he barked, as he poured another glass of brandy. Downing it in one he stared at the door she'd closed behind her, then flung the glass at it. 'I will *not* allow you to poison our son against me,' he bellowed.

He gathered up the brandy bottle and another glass, then

slumped into a chair by the fire. He intended to get very drunk, and forget everything.

Some time later Jonathan heard footsteps in the hall, doors slamming and voices. He peered out of the window as two carriages were drawn up to the front steps and watched blearily as his wife emerged from the house into the afternoon sunshine, issuing staccato orders to her servants as to where her luggage was to be placed. Finally she appeared satisfied, and they climbed into the smaller of the two coaches. Without a backward glance, she stepped into her own and ordered the driver to proceed. Hoofs clattered and wheels rattled as the horses trotted smartly down the drive and out of sight.

He lifted his glass in mock salute. 'Enjoy your ride,' he muttered. 'It's the only one you'll ever have – because, as sure as hell, no man will ever offer you one.' He gave a bitter laugh, gulped the drink and burst into tears.

Eventually he blew his nose and berated himself for his weakness. He hadn't cried like that since he was a child – and tears couldn't wash away the desolation. His marriage was beyond repair, and although he had little warmth in his life now that his latest mistress had married, he'd accepted that it would always be so. He would keep on the move, follow his ambitions and explore the new worlds opening every year. But how much more content he would be if he had someone by his side who loved him – someone like Susan, whose presence could light up his life.

He was pouring the last of the brandy when he caught sight of the letter from Josiah's lawyer. He had to swallow hard to force back the tears that threatened again. His uncle's death had left a huge void in his life.

The old man had seemed to find new energy after his return from Cook's first expedition and, during the ensuing years, had flung himself into an exhausting round of lectures before settling down to write a book of his experiences. Yet his weakened constitution hadn't withstood the epidemic of influenza that had recently swept the country, and he had succumbed rapidly, to die in his sleep a few weeks ago. Now it seemed Jonathan was to inherit his considerable fortune, for the old man had never married.

The room blurred as he remembered his uncle on the beach with the Aboriginal children. It was the only time he'd seen Josiah relax, and what a picture he'd made in his shirtsleeves with bare feet. A smile tugged at his lips, but his heart ached. Josiah had been like a father to him, a wise counsellor and friend. He wished he could talk to him again, share memories of the times they'd had on the *Endeavour*. Apart from Sir Joseph Banks, the men who'd given him such a thirst for adventure were dead. Cook had been murdered in the Hawaiian islands, Sydney had died on the journey home from New Holland, and now Josiah had gone.

He crumpled the letter and let it fall to the floor as loneliness and grief overwhelmed him. Josiah hadn't approved when he'd taken a mistress, but he'd understood, had remained a confidant and adviser as Jonathan had struggled through the terrible first years of his marriage and tried to be a good father to Edward. Now he had no one to turn to. No one who could understand the deep-seated longing to be unfettered from the woman he loathed, left free to follow his dreams and perhaps find true contentment. 'Oh, Susan,' he breathed. 'How I long for your comfort now. You understood more than anyone how much Josiah meant to me.'

Restlessness forced him out of the chair, and he began to pace the room. It was lined with books, each one bound in rich leather that gleamed in the spring sunshine pouring through the window. They had been collected by his father and grandfather, and soon their number would be increased by Josiah's valuable scientific journals and scholarly tomes. It was an impressive array.

He went to the window and leant against the deep-set sill. Treleaven House was a square building of elegant proportions. It sat on the crest of a gentle incline, with a backdrop of woodland and fields. The creamy stone glowed in the sun and the double line of long windows at the front looked over the gravelled driveway where water from the fountain glittered with rainbows. Manicured lawns stretched as green and smooth as a billiard table to the copse on the west, and behind the house a series of walls sheltered the gardens from the wind that came up from the sea.

From the library window, Jonathan could follow the meandering tree-lined drive to the imposing iron gates. The storm of the previous two days had moved on so the countryside and the sea sparkled as if they had been freshly laundered.

He was watching the fishing-boats trawl back and forth, accompanied by the usual swirling flock of seabirds when his thoughts returned to Susan. She was probably the only person who would understand what he was going through, and he hadn't missed the love in her eyes during their hurried conversation – but would it be fair to either of them to rekindle those feelings, knowing where it would lead?

He turned away from the window, fumbled with the tiny key and unlocked the tantalus to free the decanter of port. Perhaps if he got drunk enough the pain would ease. He picked up the pile of correspondence he'd ignored since his arrival, and slumped into a chair.

There were the usual calling cards from the local gentry and he tossed them aside with barely a glance. He would have to entertain them at some point, but now he was in no fit state to think straight or care less. There were several letters pertaining to his position as magistrate for the area, and he realised he would have to sit in court for at least a month to catch up with his duties.

Edward's headmaster had written in the politest terms, but

reading between the lines, Jonathan realised his thirteen-year-old son was fast turning into a bully and a cheat and was about to be expelled. He would have to deal with the boy. It wasn't a task he relished, for Edward was surly at the best of times and Jonathan was at a loss as to how to handle him.

He picked up the next letter, noted the cheap paper and seal, the barely decipherable scrawl. It was from the manager of one of the estate's mines. There were faults in the ceilings of the deepest shafts that lay beneath the sea. Jonathan made a mental note to go there tomorrow and see for himself. The man should have brought in an engineer – he was paid to make such decisions, but he was useless and, from the accounts, the mine was haemorrhaging money.

With a sigh of frustration he abandoned the rest and drank deeply of the port. It seemed everyone wanted a piece of him and his money, that he couldn't trust anyone to do a job properly unless he was standing over them. How much easier it was to board a ship and sail away. No wonder he rarely came down here.

As the light faded and the drink took effect, Jonathan fell asleep. It was dark when he woke and he was surprised to see that the lamps had been lit, supper had been laid on the table by the window and the shattered glass cleared from the floor. With the London servants' departure, he was left with the outside staff, and only the cook with a couple of maids to see to the house. He eyed the cold ham, beef and chicken, and decided he couldn't face it. Dragging himself out of the chair, he staggered a little before he gained his balance and headed for the door. Fresh air was what he needed.

He made ungainly progress to the front door and almost lost his footing down the steps to the gravel path. He had no idea of where he was going, but he thought he might try to find Susan. She would listen to him and not judge. She would understand.

*   *   *

Millicent Parker was tired and dispirited as she opened the side gate and began the long walk through the parkland, heading for the copse. She only had one day off a month, and had spent most of it either walking or in furious argument with her stepmother. The little cottage in Newlyn had been over-crowded as usual, and her stepmother full of gin and self-pity.

Millicent had helped with the young ones – there had been a baby each year since her father's remarriage – cooked the evening meal, done some mending and washing, and tried to tidy the house before her father came home. Len Parker was a good, quiet man who worked hard at the quarry and deserved better than his drunken sot of a wife, who did little all day but spend the housekeeping on gin. He had embraced his daughter as they passed one another on the doorstep, their silence saying much more than any words could have done.

She'd been aware of him watching her as she hurried along the cobbled street and up the steep hill to the track that would take her back to Treleaven House several miles away. He still fretted at her walking so far in the dark, but the night held no fears for her, and the paths she trod were ones she had come to know well over her fifteen years. How hard it had been to leave him, yet the weariness of the long day was taking its toll, and as she'd turned and waved to him, she'd wished only for her narrow bed.

Her day had begun before dawn but she was back on duty tomorrow, and was expected to be up and about by five thirty. As the lowliest maid in the house she had to clear the ashes and black the grates before his lordship appeared downstairs. Then there were the vast jugs of hot water to be carried upstairs, the chamber pots to be emptied and the beds made.

It was normally quiet, but when the Cadwalladers made a rare appearance it was a constant round of work, and some-times she was so tired she didn't bother to undress before she went to bed. Yet the pay was generous and the food plentiful –

and when her ladyship was visiting there were always other servants to help with the work. She had to consider herself lucky to have found such a position.

There was no moon tonight: the clouds had rolled in to blot out the stars, and a chill wind knifed up from the sea. Smothering a vast yawn, she tramped through the darkness, her hands in the pockets of her coat to ward off the cold. Yet despite the long day and the weariness that made her legs feel leaden, lightness and warmth flooded her. There was just a chance that John was waiting for her.

She smiled as she entered the ebony darkness of the copse. John Pardoe was the apprentice gardener on the estate, and they had met in the kitchen garden six months ago. He was tall and broad-shouldered, with a mop of dark hair that fell over his eyes when he wasn't wearing a cap, and a laugh that had her giggling and blushing. His twinkling eyes spoke his thoughts as he put his arm round her waist and stole a kiss.

Millicent blushed in the darkness as she remembered how pleasant it was to have his lips on hers, and his strong arms round her, pulling her close so that the whole world was shut out. He made her feel safe.

Her pleasant reverie was broken by the sound of a snapping twig and the unmistakable tread of heavy feet in the undergrowth. Her pulse quickened and she looked around eagerly. 'John?' she called softly. 'Is it you?'

Jonathan strode through the front door and shrugged off his heavy coat. He slung it on to a chair, pulled off his gloves and glanced round the hall. Where was the maid? He needed help to get these damn boots off. She didn't appear so he picked up his letters from the hall table and went into the library.

A fire was roaring in the grate, the room was filled with sunlight, and he sighed with satisfaction as he sank into the chair and stretched out his legs. Silence was golden without

Emily's nagging, and the tramp round the estate with the gamekeeper had cleared his head. He ran his fingers lightly over his temples and grimaced. He had no clear recollection of the night before, just a rather jumbled memory of darkness, moving shadows and the vague notion of a woman's voice calling to him – then nothing.

He shrugged, rose and tugged at the bell-pull. He'd had no breakfast and was ravenous after the walk. As he waited for the maid he stood in front of the fire, hands clasped behind him, toasting his backside. It was always good to come home to Cornwall, and on days like this he appreciated the clean air and sparkling sea of his home county. London was a cesspool of slums and overflowing sewers, of street cries and the rattle of coach-wheels. Even in the heart of the city one couldn't avoid the beggars and whores or the piles of steaming dung left by the horses. But on this far western coast a man could breathe, and although there was poverty and hardship, it didn't have the same stench as it did in the city.

His pleasant thoughts were interrupted by a tap on the library door. 'Come,' he called.

The little maid scuttled in and bobbed a curtsy.

'It's Millicent, isn't it?' he asked pleasantly. She was new to the household.

'Sir.' She nodded, eyes downcast.

Jonathan ordered lunch to be brought in and she scuttled out. She was like a nervous mouse, scampering back and forth. What *did* she think he was going to do to her?

He forgot about her the minute the door closed and turned to his correspondence. There were a couple of letters he'd read later, and a packet of court papers he must see to this afternoon. He tossed them aside and waited for his meal.

It arrived some minutes later, borne on a heavy silver tray by the cook, who was wheezing from the long climb up the stairs from the kitchen. Jonathan was surprised to see her, and a little alarmed at her high colour. 'You shouldn't be doing this,' he said. 'Where's Millicent?'

The tray was placed carefully on the table and the reddened face was mopped with a corner of the pristine apron that crackled like a starched sail over the sturdy bosom. 'She's indisposed, sir.'

Jonathan was about to argue that she had seemed quite well a moment before, then decided not to bother. The servants' way of thinking was beyond him. He thrust aside all thought of the domestic drama that might be unfolding downstairs and tucked into the game stew and vegetables. The cook had come up trumps once again, and the apple pie she had baked this morning was not only delicious but accompanied by a vast bowl of the thick yellow Cornish cream he could never find in London.

Sated, he returned with a cup of strong coffee to the chair by the fire and reached for his mail. Some time later he came to the last. He didn't recognise the seal but as he prised it open and read the message his eyes widened. Susan wanted to meet him tomorrow morning at the cave.

He stared into the fire, watching the flames flicker round the logs. It was as if she'd read his mind, as if she'd known he needed her. Dare he accept the invitation, knowing where it might lead? The last thing he wanted was to hurt her.

He stared out of the window, his thoughts blinding him to the glitter of the sea. Then he smiled. Of course he would see her. It couldn't hurt – not just the once.

Uluru, Australia, May 1786

The summer rains had made the long trek south more difficult than usual, for the rivers were overflowing and the earth had turned to mud. Shelter had been sought in makeshift humpies of leaves and branches, but Anabarru and her tribe had had to

keep vigilant, day and night, for the crocodiles were everywhere.

She was behind Watpipa, her four youngest children at her
side, as they looked out over the plains that surrounded the
sacred Uluru. The rain had stopped and the red desert was
carpeted with bright flowers and blossoming trees. They stood
for a moment to admire it, before moving towards the campfires that sent plumes of smoke drifting into the still air. The
great *corroboree* would begin the following day.

Watpipa was the leading Elder now, and once a campsite
had been chosen, he left with the other men to pay respect to
the guardians of Uluru. Anabarru watched with pride as
their son joined him. He was a man now, fully initiated and
due to marry her cousin Lowitja's daughter on the last day of
the gathering. He was truly a descendant of Djanay: he
already had wisdom beyond his sixteen years, and was
regarded as the rightful heir to his father's position in the
tribe.

'Anabarru, welcome.'

She smiled and embraced her favourite cousin. 'Lowitja, it
has been a long time.' They exchanged gifts of clay and shell
necklaces as they boasted about their children and grandchildren.

'It is good for the descendants of Djanay and Garnday to
come together at such an important *corroboree*,' said Lowitja,
as they sat on the ground. 'Garnday's spirit is always with me,
and she tells me in the stones that the marriage of my daughter
to your son is blessed. They will bring great wisdom to our
tribes in the troubled times ahead.'

Her amber eyes studied the frowning Anabarru. 'We will
speak, at the women's campfire gathering, of the ghost-men
who came to our sacred lands, for they will return.'

Anabarru had been unsettled by her cousin's talk of
troubled times, but the thought of the man who had so

impressed Watpipa all those years ago made her smile. 'It is good,' she murmured.

Lowitja grasped her arm, her expression serious. 'They will bring death, Anabarru,' she warned. 'Garnday has told me.'

Anabarru shivered. Lowitja had been gifted by the spirits of her ancestors and her foretelling of the future was legendary among the tribes. 'But we have met with them, talked, hunted and shared meat,' she stuttered. 'Their skin is pale and their ways are strange, but they are men such as ours.'

'They will come in great numbers and spread across the land,' said Lowitja, as she took up a handful of red earth, tossed it into the light breeze and watched it scatter. 'Like the dust on the wind they will come to every corner of our sacred lands and destroy us.'

Anabarru bit her lip. Lowitja's words frightened her, but she couldn't equate what she was saying with her experience of the white man's arrival.

Lowitja's steady gaze rested once more on her cousin. 'We must ask the Spirits to help us banish them. Their coming will bring an end to the spirituality of our people, and although this great gathering will not be the last, never again will there be so many of us.'

Anabarru looked at the milling throng that spread almost to the horizon. Tribes from every corner of the land had come as they always had, ever since the Spirit Ancestors walked the earth. Lowitja was mistaken: she must have misread the stones. Anabarru looked back at her cousin and felt a chill of premonition. In Lowitja's eyes, she saw the dark shadows of things to come – things that were far beyond her simple imagination.

Mousehole, May 1786

Susan thought they would never leave, and impatience made her sharp. She was thankful that Ernest was at the farm and

George at school or she'd have had the devil's own task. Ezra had taken an age to collect all his books after breakfast, Florence had lost her music, and Emma had insisted on writing to Algernon so the letter could be taken by coach to London that morning. Her romance with the young lieutenant had blossomed at her birthday party, and the letters she had received from him were tied with ribbon and tucked away from the prying eyes of her siblings.

The morning had dawned clear and bright, but as Susan watched Ezra and Emma walk down the path towards the school, the clouds rolled in over the sea. 'It looks like rain again,' she said to Florence, who had finally found her music and was preparing to leave. 'Take a coat and hurry up.'

Florence eyed her. 'Do you wish to get rid of me?' she asked.

Flustered by her daughter's penetrating stare, Susan began to brush the crumbs from the table and gather up the napkins. 'Of course not,' she replied. 'But you'll be late.'

'I'm never late,' Florence retorted. She finished tying her bonnet strings and put on her coat. 'You look as if you're rushing to be somewhere else.'

Her daughter's sharp eyes missed little and she was letting her emotions betray her, Susan thought. She took a deep breath and made a concerted effort to regain calm. 'It's just the weather,' she said, with a smile. 'Rain always makes me jumpy, and I think I'm going to have one of my headaches.'

Florence's demeanour softened. 'Shall I fetch you a powder before I go?'

Guilt tore through her and Susan had to avoid her daughter's eyes. She sat down. 'No, thank you. I'll rest for a while and drink some tea. I'll be better soon.' She forced another smile as she glanced at her daughter, hating herself for her duplicity.

Florence poured the tea, gathered her things and left the house. She was not a demonstrative girl so there was no kiss goodbye.

Susan's pulse was racing as she sat at the table and watched the retreating figure disappear. She had no admiration for what she was doing, but the need to see him was overwhelming and her impatience made it difficult to concentrate on anything but the rapid beat of her heart. Jonathan would come – she knew it as surely as if he'd answered her letter – for she'd heard that Emily had returned to London.

Yet her excitement was laced with dread and a small part of her mind begged for caution. She refused to acknowledge it. What her family didn't know wouldn't hurt them, and she would make certain it remained a secret. She went upstairs to finish preparing. The soft wool dress and heavy cape would be perfect.

The sun shone brightly between the scudding clouds as she strode across the clifftop and past the stone chimneys of Wheel Dragon. The salty wind stung her face as it tugged at her cape and bonnet. A feeling of youthful joy and abandonment quickened her step and she spread her arms and ran down the steep hill with a shout of happiness. It was as if she was a girl again, a young fisher-girl with few cares for the stifling world of etiquette and manners she now inhabited. She'd forgotten how joyous it was to be free.

Tramping up the next hill, she paused to catch her breath. The village was far behind her, and she could only just make out the coastline of Newlyn in the distance. The beach below was deserted, with only one small fishing-boat out on the water, sails billowing as it headed for the harbour. She was almost there.

The path they had used as children was barely discernible, and as she picked her way through the gorse and stunted, arthritic trees that clung to its sides, it was steeper than she remembered. Her boots slid and slithered, and for one heart-stopping moment she thought she would fall, but determination kept her on her feet and she was soon standing on the shingled beach. She realised she was no longer as agile or as daring as she had been – she had once raced down that path almost defiant in her confidence that she would come to no harm.

Susan waited until her pulse had returned to normal, set her cape and bonnet straight, leant into the wind and began to crunch along the pebbles. The tide was out, leaving a wide strip of damp yellow sand. Waders explored the rockpools, crabs scuttled, and seaweed marked the high-water line.

Gulls shrieked as they swooped, hovered and fought over a dead fish on the sand. Susan pulled the cape closer. It was bitterly cold for May, the wind coming in great gusts that were strong enough to make her stumble. The dark cliffs towered above her, and where they had crumbled, vast boulders reared from the shingle and formed a giant's path of stepping stones to the sea.

She lifted her skirts as she navigated the rocks, but as she was about to round the last she hesitated, suddenly aware of the risk she was about to take. She closed her eyes as her fevered thoughts swirled. What on earth did she think she was doing? Was she mad to risk everything for a moment with Jonathan? What if she had been seen? What if Ezra already suspected she was up to something? He'd looked at her strangely this morning when she'd chivvied him out of the house.

And then there were the children. Had she lied well enough to outwit them? Could she carry on doing so if things went well today? As she stood there, buffeted by the wind, she battled with her conscience. Jonathan might not come – and in a way it would be a relief if he didn't, for she was being an utter fool. She should turn back now before it was too late. Leave him in the past where he belonged.

'I didn't think you'd come.'

Her eyes flew open and he was there, not two feet away, hand outstretched to help her with the last few steps. Her heart pounded and her mouth dried at the sight of him. Reason fled as she took his hand, and as she stepped into his embrace she knew she would risk everything to be with him.

12

Mousehole, September 1786

The summer had ended as damp as it had begun, and now it was mid-September. Higgins, Ezra's manservant, had long since departed to another post nearer to London where his services could be put to better use. Mrs Pascoe had a heavy cold and had been sent home, so Susan was alone in the dining room to lay the table for the evening meal.

The day had drawn in so she had pulled the velvet curtains against the blustery night and stoked the fire. The room was pleasantly cheerful with candlelight and she hummed a little tune as she moved round the room and let her mind drift to Jonathan. Their secret meetings had ended for the winter. He would be returning to London shortly, and she would have to wait until his return in the spring.

The summer rains hadn't hindered them – in fact, they had only served to keep their secret by discouraging walkers and sightseers. Jonathan's love-making had imbued in her an energy she had thought she'd forgotten – a joy she had never before experienced. She had come alive to his touch, had given herself freely and with delight as his kisses stirred a passion within her that made her wanton. She longed for his touch and to feel their naked bodies slide over each other as they made love in the dark womb of the cave.

She paused behind one of the upholstered chairs, resting her hand on its carved back, her skin tingling with memories. The cave had become a magic grotto, with candles and blankets Jonathan had brought with him after that first day. There had been wine, too, fruit and little cakes, taken as they lay beneath the blanket and watched the sea before making love again. Her smile was wry as she adjusted the bodice of her gown. The cakes were making her corset dig into her flesh.

'When's dinner? I'm starving.'

George's demand snapped her from her reverie and she ruffled his coarse brown hair. 'When your father returns from Truro,' she said.

George hated his hair being ruffled and pulled a face. 'Why's he in Truro?' he asked, as he plumped into a chair and began to make a cat's cradle from a length of wool.

Susan watched him for a moment and sighed. His knickerbockers were torn, his shoes were grubby and his pockets bulged suspiciously. 'I have no idea,' she said. She reached into his pocket and grimaced as she pulled out an unspeakably filthy handkerchief, a collection of shells and old bits of bone, several pebbles and a half-eaten apple. 'Really, George,' she chided. 'You've ruined this jacket and it's almost new.'

George grinned and pulled a dead frog from another pocket. 'I'm going to cut him up and look at his insides,' he said, with relish.

Susan shuddered and ordered him out of the room. An enquiring mind was one thing, but even though they lived in an age of exploration and invention, George was pushing his luck. 'Wash your hands before dinner,' she called after him.

There was the thunder of his feet on the stairs, the slam of a door, and Susan shut her eyes. Reality was twice as hard to bear when Jonathan was in London, and she wondered how she would survive the winter without him.

Ezra came home just as she had thought the dinner would be ruined. She hurried him out of his wet coat and hat and led him into the dining room, where even Ernest was showing signs of impatience. 'Whatever kept you?' she asked, as he finished saying grace and began to carve the lamb.

'There were many things to discuss,' he replied vaguely. 'I lost track of the time.'

Susan served the vegetables and handed round the plates. 'I wouldn't have thought school business could take so long. You only have ten pupils.'

'It was more than school business today,' he replied. 'I had other matters to attend to, plans to make.'

She looked at him sharply. He was being deliberately evasive. What on earth had he been doing in Truro? 'That sounds mysterious,' she said lightly, in an attempt to mask her irritation. 'I hope you'll let me in on your secret – or is it so terrible you must keep it to yourself?'

Ezra began to eat his dinner, his gaze fixed on his plate. 'Not at all,' he replied, 'and you will know everything soon enough. But you shouldn't let your imagination run away with you, my dear. It isn't healthy.'

Susan eyed him, her lips forming a thin line. Ezra was beginning to annoy her – as he had quite regularly just lately. She looked away and found Florence watching her curiously. A stab of unease shot through her and she tried to concentrate on the food, which suddenly tasted of ashes. She and Jonathan had been discreet over the past four months, and she was certain they hadn't been discovered – certain she had lied well enough to cover her tracks and allay suspicion – but there was a strange atmosphere in the house tonight, and it didn't bode well.

Dinner continued with George's chatter drowning the quieter murmur of Emma and Florence, but Susan had no appetite. She noticed her husband said little, and despite the boys' lively exchanges, the tension grew, and she wished the meal could be over so she could go to her sewing room, shut the door and be left in peace to dream of Jonathan's return.

'I heard something interesting today,' said Florence, during a lulll. She paused for a moment until she was certain she had everyone's attention. 'I was down in the village and bumped into Katy Webster.' This statement was met with blank looks and she hurried to explain: 'Katy works in the kitchens at Treleaven House, and is a positive mine of gossip about the goings-on up there.'

Susan kept her hands clasped in her lap, her face expressionless as her thoughts threatened to whirl out of control.

'You shouldn't listen to gossip,' said Ezra, as he placed his napkin on the table. 'It's the devil's work.'

'Not as devilish as what's happened to Millicent Parker,' Florence retorted. 'Katy told me she'd been dismissed, bags packed and off the premises within an hour.'

'It happens,' muttered Ezra. 'Caught stealing, no doubt.'

'In the family way,' said Florence, with relish. 'She made a terrible fuss when the cook found out, screaming and crying and blaming his lordship.'

Susan felt the blood leave her face. Her thoughts were in turmoil. 'She's lying,' she managed. 'His lordship would never stoop so low.'

Florence shook her head. 'Katy said she made so much noise his lordship heard her and went into the kitchen. His face was thunderous, and he grabbed her arm and pulled her up the back stairs into his library.'

Susan wanted to run from the room, but she was frozen to the chair. She couldn't look away from her daughter, couldn't block out what she was saying: the girl's words pounded in her head like hammer blows.

'Katy crept up the back stairs and listened at the door, but she couldn't hear much past Millie's crying and his lordship's shouting. Millie eventually went back to the kitchen with her boxes and bags and, when the cook wasn't watching, she showed Katy the money his lordship had given her.' She took a breath. 'There were two guineas in that purse. Now, he wouldn't have given her *anything* if he hadn't been responsible, would he?'

Susan was trapped like a rabbit in the snare of her daughter's innocent gaze. She tore her attention from Florence and glanced at her husband, but he concentrated on the glass of port he was drinking, his expression unreadable.

She felt sick. Her world crumbled, and the haze of happiness she'd been living in all summer was ripped away to reveal her tawdry, cheap little affair for what it was. She had believed Jonathan when he'd said he loved her. Had thought she was enough for him, his prized lost love. Yet all the while he had been lying with the maid. How could she have been such a fool to risk so much for such a man?

'I don't see how any of this is our business,' said Emma, who was looking confused. 'We have only Katy's word, and you shouldn't spread gossip, Florence. It only leads to trouble.'

George fidgeted in his chair, and Ernest looked uncomfortable. This was not the sort of conversation they were used to at the dinner table.

'Poor little girl,' muttered Ezra, as he placed the glass on the table. 'Whatever the truth of the matter, we must pray that her family will take her in.' He looked up then, his eyes infinitely sad as they settled on his wife. 'Family loyalty is so important, don't you think, my dear?'

Susan could only nod. There was a lump in her throat and she could barely breathe. *He knows.* The words played loudly in her head, refusing to be silenced.

Ezra appeared not to notice her discomfort, for as he toyed with his glass his gaze ran over his children. 'Florence isn't the only one with news,' he said finally. 'Though what I have to say cannot be termed gossip. It's more a statement of fact.' He turned to Susan, his face ashen, his eyes haunted. 'You asked what I have been doing in Truro,' he began. 'I think it's time to tell you.'

Susan swallowed and a chill of foreboding feathered her spine. She knew her eyes were wide with fear, her face as pale as her husband's. She flinched as a log shifted in the fire and sent sparks up the chimney. Her nerves were taut. Would the night's revelations never end?

'I have been interviewing candidates to take over the running of the school,' he said, into the silence. 'And have secured the services of a pleasant widow.' He held up a hand as Emma tried to interrupt. 'I have also arranged with the Church Council to finish my mission here and hand over this house to my successor.'

The children began to protest, but were hushed by their father's unusually stern expression. Susan stared at him. 'Why?' she murmured.

'Because we are moving away,' he replied. He turned back to his children, who were gazing at him in confusion. 'Your uncle Gilbert and I have been corresponding regularly, and this morning I learnt that I have been asked by no less a man than Arthur Phillip to join him and the Reverend Richard Johnson in Australia.'

Florence went ashen, Emma burst into tears, Ernest was open-mouthed and George was running around the table, whooping. Susan felt numb. He was punishing her – punishing all of them for what she had done. Then a surge of rage brought her to her feet. She shoved back her chair and slammed her fist on the table. 'No!' she shouted. 'No, no, no!'

Ezra looked at her calmly. 'It's too late,' he said quietly. 'The arrangements are made.'

'It's a preposterous idea,' she stormed. 'I won't allow it. In fact, I'll fight you every inch of the way rather than put our children at risk among savages and convicts.' She was breathing heavily now, the constricting corset making her feel faint. 'This is our home and I refuse to leave it. Sail to Australia if you must, but the children and I will stay here.'

'You are my wife, and you have vowed before God to honour and obey me,' he reminded her. 'You promised in church to abide with me and remain faithful to me until death.' His gaze wavered and she felt the flush of shame heat her face, but his voice remained steady. 'Like it or not, Susan, we shall leave here at the end of next April to sail with the First Fleet in May.'

'We must discuss this further, Ezra,' she said, as she battled to remain calm.

He regarded her steadily, then nodded. 'Go to your rooms,' he ordered the children. Their protests were quashed by his tone and they trooped out, confused and uneasy at the turn of events.

'Why are you doing this?' Susan demanded. She had to be certain of his motive and the extent of his knowledge.

'You know very well,' he said, as he poured a second glass of port. His dark eyes were filled with sadness.

'How can I know anything when you do not discuss such an important decision with me before announcing it at the dinner table?' She was still angry, but fearful too.

'You are rarely here to discuss anything,' he said. 'In fact, you spend so much time with Cadwallader that I am surprised you concern yourself with us at all.'

His face was paler than usual, his eyes dark with a pain so profound she couldn't bear to look at him. 'You knew all the time, didn't you?' she whispered.

'From the day of Emma's birthday party. I saw your face when he arrived. I knew then that I would lose you.'

'Your imagination has run away with you.'

'My imagination has nothing to do with it, Susan,' he snapped, his fists clenched on the table. 'I followed you when you went running off to that cave, then sat on the top of the cliff as you met him.' His sigh was the only sound in the room. 'After that, I followed you every time you left the house.'

She was stunned. 'Why didn't you do something about it, if you were so concerned?' She was breathing hard, her thoughts running helter-skelter. 'What kind of husband are you to allow his wife to behave so and say nothing?'

'I had hoped it would fade away, that you'd come to your senses.' He grunted with disgust. 'I was afraid of losing you, hoping against hope you would come back to me when the foolishness had run its course.' His eyes were filled with loathing now. 'But you had little thought for me or for the vows we took as you cavorted through the summer.'

'That's not true,' she blustered. 'Of course I thought of you – and the children. I didn't like what I was doing, but I couldn't help it.'

'Of course you could!' His fist smashed down on the table, making the china clatter. 'You're my wife! The mother of my children! Do you have *any* idea of the harm you've done?'

She flinched as he shoved back his chair and strode to the fireplace. She had never heard him raise his voice, or seen him lose his temper, and the intensity frightened her. 'The children know nothing,' she said. 'The only harm has been to your dignity.' She knew it was a cheap taunt, and wasn't proud of it. She blinked away tears, folded her arms and turned her back.

'And my dignity is worthless?' His rage was spent, and as she turned back to him, she saw that his shoulders had slumped, his chin dipped low.

'You know it isn't,' she said, her heart aching at his hurt. 'Oh, Ezra, I'm so sorry – so very sorry.' She went to stand beside him, a hand on his shoulder, longing to comfort him. 'I was a fool. A blind, stupid fool, who thought she could recapture the romance of her youth. But I can see now that Jonathan Cadwallader was not the man I thought him, and that I have risked my marriage, which is far more precious. Punish me by all means, but not the children. They have done no wrong.'

He shrugged away her hand and turned from her. 'You don't understand.' His voice was thick with unshed tears. 'Our leaving for Australia will keep us together as a family, far away from Cadwallader and all he stands for.' He stared into the fire. 'I cannot trust you now, Susan. To remain here will only put temptation in your path.'

She reached for him again, but his almost imperceptible flinch told her it was not the right moment. 'I will prove to you that you can trust me,' she said. 'I will not betray you again.'

'Words are easy, Susan,' he said. 'Trust has to be earned.'

'Then I will earn it,' she declared. 'But please don't continue with these foolish plans to take us to a convict colony. We can begin again, here, in our home where the children will be safe.'

'The arrangements are made. We leave next spring.' His face was gaunt with sorrow and weariness. 'I will sleep in my study from now on,' he said. 'Perhaps then you will have time and space to appreciate the extent of your betrayal.'

Susan followed him up the stairs, her pleas for forgiveness ignored as he locked the study door behind him. She stood there for a long while, then turned into their bedroom. As she huddled on the window-seat in the darkness, she gave in to tears of shame and distress.

As she stared out of the window, she watched the moon emerge from behind the clouds and was chilled by its cold, impersonal gleam. A tremor of self-loathing brought acid to her throat as she remembered how it had been during the summer. There had been no love-making with Ezra – she'd either feigned sleep or had waited until he was snoring before she went to bed. Jonathan had bewitched her, had taken over her thoughts to the point at which she had become distant and careless of her husband's needs.

On looking back she knew there had been hurt in Ezra's eyes, unspoken questions on his lips and a deep sadness in his demeanour, which she had chosen to ignore. He had known all along and been in torment, unable or unwilling to speak out lest he lose her. In the stark clarity of that moonlit night, she saw how profoundly she had betrayed him.

As the tears ran down her face, she hugged her knees. Her affair had almost destroyed a man who was guilty only of loving her. 'Oh, Ezra,' she whispered. 'How could I have done this to you?'

As the lonely night wore on she realised she had to get away. Ezra's coldness would be intolerable, and the things they had said tonight would not easily be forgotten. They needed time to heal, which could only be achieved if she left Cornwall. She gnawed her lip as she tried to think where she could go.

The moon was on the wane, the sky lightening on the horizon when she moved from the window-seat to her desk. Ann lived in Bath, and with Gilbert away, involved in preparations for the First Fleet, it would be an ideal time to visit. It would seem perfectly natural to go to her sister-in-law, and not even Ezra could find fault with her reasoning. She picked up the quill and wrote a long letter to the only friend she could fully trust.

The Dunkirk *hulk, Plymouth, March 1787*

As the sun began to offer a little more warmth, the stench in the convict hulk increased and the fleas bred more swiftly. Billy looked forward to daylight and the chance to leave the stinking confines of the hold for the fresher air of the harbour. It came to something, he mused, when a man preferred twelve hours of back-breaking work to lounging on a straw pallet, but at least it released him from the bed-bugs and the groans of the sick, and kept his body strong, his mind occupied. It didn't do him much good to contemplate his life when all he had to look forward to was transportation.

It was dark in the bowels of the rotting hulk, and he lay awake, waiting for the glimmer of dawn to break through the gaps in the hull. The pier had been finished months ago and now he and the fitter prisoners had been set to building a road that would lead from the turnpike to the main harbour.

He moved his arms, feeling the muscles flex where there had once been skin and bone. Since the field marshal's visit he'd had better rations, cleaner clothes, and Mullins had laid off with the lash. It helped to have friends in high places – but he didn't boast about such things. Life was still hard, and if the others thought he was better treated than them he'd end up with a knife in his back.

He lay in the darkness and listened to Stan's laboured breathing. He'd used some of his money to pay for better food for him, but the Norfolk man was dying. He recognised the signs, for Death was a regular visitor to the prison hulks. What would happen to his woman, Bess, and the child, Billy could only guess. No doubt she would latch on to someone else: he'd seen it happen too many times. Relationships among the convicts were tenuous and had little to do with love and loyalty. It was more a clinging together for comfort and safety, and Billy had decided long ago that he was better off on his own.

Stan's chest rattled and he turned restlessly beneath the thin blanket. Billy could hear Bess trying to soothe him, and rolled over, shutting his eyes in an attempt to block it out.

Stan had been an ally ever since they had arrived in Plymouth. He had been an old hand at surviving the prison system, and although his health had suffered, he knew the tricks of survival. Despite his appearance, he was only five years older than Billy, and although they might have been friends, Billy had soon learnt that friendship was best avoided. Sooner or later death or relocation ended it.

As dawn broke, Billy and the rest of the prisoners were startled by unusual noises coming from outside. There was a stillness in the hold, and a breathless silence of anticipation and dread among the prisoners as they listened. It sounded as if a fleet of small boats was banging against the side of the ship, and they heard the tramp of many feet over their heads.

Billy sat up, pulse racing. Something was happening, and he had a feeling he knew what it was.

'On yer feet,' shouted the warder, as the hatch was flung back and daylight streamed in. 'Form an orderly line and come up four at a time.'

Billy grabbed the bundle of clothes and checked he still had the couple of coins he'd hidden in the hem of his shirt. There might not be a chance to fetch them later, and he was buggered if he was leaving anything behind for the thieving Mullins. He pulled the filthy blanket round his shoulders and turned to Stan.

He had surprisingly survived the night, and between them, Bess and Billy got him to his feet. Bess rolled up their few tattered belongings, grabbed the baby and held it close, eyes wide with fear.

'What the bloody 'ell's going on, Billy?' shouted Nell, from the other end of the hull.

'Buggered if I know,' he yelled back.

They all shuffled forward to gather at the foot of the ladder. Billy caught Nell's eye and grinned. She was a handsome lass, buxom too. She must have used her attractions to wheedle extra rations. 'Brace yourself, girl,' he shouted over the heads.

She tossed back her red curls and, hands on hips, thrust out her breasts. 'Why?' she challenged. 'You comin' to me bed at last, Bill?'

A ripple of nervous laughter ran through the mêlée. It was well known that Nell had not yet got her man, despite her determined efforts over the past few months. 'Too busy at the moment,' he retorted, as they shuffled forward. 'But the wait will be worth it.'

She laughed uproariously. 'It better be, or I've been wastin' me time.'

All conversation died as the first climbed the ladder to the deck. There were murmurs of consternation and some women were sobbing. The hulk had become familiar despite the degradation – they were used to it, had formed relationships and even given birth, though few babies survived. The unknown was far more terrifying.

Billy saw a flash of scarlet uniform and the glint of a sword. His heart began to hammer and he licked dry lips. The field marshal had said it would begin in the spring. He'd noticed the bluebells growing wild on the grassy banks by the road they'd been building, and by his reckoning it was around the end of February, or even the beginning of March. He nudged Stanley. 'Look lively, matey,' he muttered. 'Else you'll be left behind.'

'What d'you mean?' asked Bess, fearfully, as she hoisted the baby to her shoulder.

'You'll find out soon enough,' he replied. He was being unfair to her, but he didn't want his knowledge spread. Better for the fighting to break out on deck when the others discovered what was happening – there was little enough room down here as it was, and he'd seen the destruction a brawl could wreak.

It was finally their turn to climb the ladder. Billy supported Stan from behind, and once they had gained the deck, he reached down to help Bess, who was struggling to hold the bundle of clothes and the baby as she clung to the rungs.

Nell came next, grabbing his hand and almost pulling him back into the hold, such was her strength. 'Thanks, me duck,' she said cheerfully, as she arranged her filthy skirts, hoisted her bosom in the sagging blouse and tried to bring order to her matted tumble of red hair. 'Blimey, this fresh air ain't doin' my 'air no good. Look at the state of it.'

Billy shot her a grin, which she returned, but he could see the wariness in her eyes. For all her bravado, he thought, she was as frightened as everyone else.

He took it all in at a swift glance. Ranks of red-coated

soldiers, naval officers and marines lined the sides of the deck. Soberly dressed men stood off to one side with the chief gaoler, Cowdry. Two lines of prisoners were forming at either end of the deck: the young and fit stood on the right, the old and sick on the left.

'Stand still while the doctor examines you,' shouted Mullins.

Billy stiffened as the doctor listened to his chest and examined his teeth. He felt like a horse at auction and was tempted to bite the probing fingers that tasted of tobacco. But he resisted. It wouldn't be wise, with so many redcoats about.

'Over there,' said the doctor, gruffly, as he moved on to Stanley.

Billy's heart pounded as he joined the line on the right. Did that mean he was to be transported or taken to another prison? This had happened when the *Chatham* had sunk. He'd been even fitter then and sent here, to the *Dunkirk*. The sick and elderly had been taken to God knew where. Was all this talk of transportation just a ruse to get rid of men and women who were no longer useful?

He stood in an agony of uncertainty as he watched the doctor despatch Stanley to the other line. Now it was Bess's turn. After a cursory examination she was ordered to stand next to Billy.

Nell followed with a defiant flurry of her skirts and a toss of her head. She ignored the line of soldiers and took Bess's baby. 'There's pretty.' She laughed as she soothed it. 'All dressed up and nowhere to go, just like the rest of us.'

'Quiet, Nell,' he hissed. 'Give the little one back before you smother it in that bosom of yours.'

She handed it over and grinned. 'I'd like to smother you,' she murmured.

The morning dragged on and the lines of prisoners grew deeper. There were more than two hundred convicts in the

Dunkirk, and it was slow going. Billy tried to ignore Bess's sobbing and the wail of her baby, but he could understand why she was so frightened. It seemed that whatever happened to them Stanley would not be included.

It was almost mid-morning by the time every prisoner had been allocated to a line, and they stood in mute acceptance of their fate. There had been no fighting, not even a struggle, and apart from the wail of Bess's baby there was silence on the deck as the naval officer strode back and forth along the lines.

He finally came to a halt, and stood squarely in the centre of the deck, hand resting lightly on the ornate hilt of his sword. 'The prisoners on the left will be transferred to Exeter gaol. Those on the right will be transported to the penal colony of New South Wales.'

A roar of protest greeted this news, and as the soldiers and warders moved in, fists flew. Billy hauled Bess out of harm's way. Nell, it seemed, needed no such protection for she was in the thick of it, lashing out with feet and hands as if relishing the chance to get her own back on the gaolers who'd abused her.

Order was finally restored and the naval officer herded the frail convicts into the waiting boats. Bess screamed as Stanley was led away. She struggled, squirmed and kicked at the shins of the soldier who was holding her as she begged the officer not to separate them. She was not alone: other women were in the same situation and their screams were heartbreaking to hear.

'I'll be all right, Bess,' shouted Stanley, above the hubbub. 'Take care of yourself and the bairn.' He looked over his shoulder as he neared the gangway, and his eyes met Billy's in a silent plea.

Billy reluctantly dragged Bess into his arms and nodded. He would do his best to take care of her and the child until she found her feet. He owed Stan that much.

The small boats were rowed away, the heads of the pathetic

passengers bowed in defeat. No one looked back, no one spoke: they knew what awaited them in Exeter gaol.

Silence fell over the prisoners on deck, and Billy kept his arm tightly round Bess as she clung to him and her baby. She didn't have much, and it would be hard for her with the kid.

'Blimey,' breathed Nell. 'Where they takin' us now?'

'The other side of the world,' he replied. 'But you'll survive.'

She tossed her hair. 'Too right I will,' she said grimly. 'I ain't gunna let these buggers get me down.'

The naval officer was on the move again, stopping momentarily to regard a prisoner before walking on. He came to Bess, eyed her, then turned to the marine beside him. 'Take the child and arrange for it to be settled in an orphanage.'

'No!' shrieked Bess, clutching the baby to her so fiercely that it began to wail again. 'You've no right to take my baby.'

'I have every right,' he replied coldly. 'The child is too young to be a felon and I have no authorisation to carry it on board a convict ship.' He signalled to the marine.

Billy stepped forward until he was between the man and Bess. 'The child isn't weaned,' he said. 'Bess has already lost her husband, and by taking this child away you'll be responsible for its death.'

'Name?' barked the naval officer.

'Penhalligan, sir.' Billy stood tall, convinced of the justice in his argument.

'What do you know of penal laws pertaining to convict ships, Penhalligan?'

'Nothing, sir. I only know it isn't right to tear a baby from its mother's breast at the same time as separating its parents, sir.' His gaze was steady on a point beyond the man's shoulder.

The officer's laugh was a cynical bark. 'You dare speak to me of morals when the stench of your wrong-doing is clearly evident?' He wrinkled his nose and turned to the marine. 'Put this man in irons. He's a trouble-maker.'

'I'm sure Field Marshal Collinson would agree with me, sir,' said Billy, quietly, as the fetters were fitted none too gently round his ankles.

The officer's eyes bulged and his face reddened. 'Why should the field marshal care what *you* think?'

Billy tried to keep the victorious glint out of his eyes. 'He's related by marriage, sir.'

The officer strode away. A heated discussion ensued between him and Cowdry.

Billy would have loved to hear what was said, but he could make a fair guess. He felt a nudge in his ribs and looked down to see Nell grinning up at him.

'Who'd've thought it? You? Related to a toff?' She winked. 'You done well there,' she whispered. 'Showed him we ain't puttin' up with no nonsense.' She bit her lip. 'Me and you are meant to be, darling,' she added.

Billy smiled at her and put his arm round Bess, who was still clinging to the child as if her life depended on it. 'Reckon I've got enough to mind just now,' he said lightly.

She regarded him steadily. 'I can wait.'

Billy was about to reply when the naval officer strode back to him.

'She can keep it until we reach Portsmouth,' he said, looking down his nose at Bess and her infant. 'As for you, Penhalligan, you will not board the *Charlotte* today but will walk to Portsmouth in irons. By then you should have learnt to respect your betters.' With that he marched away.

Billy watched as Bess was taken to the row-boats, and cursed his sense of justice. The *Charlotte* and the *Friendship* were only minutes away as they swayed at anchor in the enormous harbour, but the iron shackles were already heavy round his ankles, the chain between them dragging on the deck as he moved. They would grow even heavier during the long walk to Portsmouth.

Mousehole, March 1787

Ann had been shocked by Susan's revelations, but had proved a true friend. She had neither condemned nor lectured, simply shown Susan the loving friendship for which she yearned.

Susan's visit to Bath had stretched to several months, but she had finally found the courage to return home. She moved round the house like a wraith, barely eating or sleeping as remorse sank deeper into her heart. She tried to be cheerful for the sake of the children, but faltered every time she saw the anguish in Ezra's eyes.

His forgiveness was the hardest thing to accept, for she knew it had been sincere, yet his Christian beliefs couldn't make him forget, and he'd moved permanently into his study. His sadness and disappointment were almost the breaking of her, for the past few months had revealed to her how much she loved him – and had proved that their marriage was worth any sacrifice: it meant far more to her than she could ever have imagined.

Life, however distressing, had to move on. It was a precious gift that should not be wasted in regret and dark memories, and although she felt hollow, she clung to the hope that one day Ezra would set aside his pain and rediscover his love for her. This new year of 1787 was to be a time of unexpected farewells as well as a time for separations and new beginnings.

As the March winds swept down from the north and threatened snow, Susan stood huddled in her fur collar on the quayside at Southampton, and watched through her tears as Emma emerged on to the deck of the great sailing ship to join her husband at the railing. Algernon had been promoted to captain and was to take up his new posting in Cape Town.

They had become engaged at the end of February, but there had been little time to celebrate for Emma had been determined not to accompany them to Australia. The wedding had been arranged in an unseemly rush to accommodate Algernon's sailing date. Now they were waving the young couple off to their new life in Africa. The agony was almost too hard for Susan to bear, for she doubted she would ever see her daughter again.

'It seems like only yesterday we were celebrating her first birthday,' said Ezra, as he blew his nose and wiped his eyes.

Susan was finding it hard to think, let alone speak, as she gazed up at her lovely daughter. She was still so young to be going so far from home and family, but Emma obviously didn't share her fears. She was smiling happily, the feathers in her hat dancing in the wind as she waved to them. The blue woollen dress suited her, Susan thought distractedly, but the fur wrap she'd been given by her mother-in-law was too sophisticated for one so young.

Ezra seemed to notice her distress, and disentangled himself from Florence's clinging hands. He reached out and patted Susan's shoulder. 'She'll be safe with him,' he said softly, 'and it won't be for ever. Soldiers are often moved about.'

'I hardly think Algernon will be posted to Australia,' she replied bitterly.

His reply was drowned in the clanging of bells and the shouts of the sailors as they swarmed up the masts and unfurled the sails. Ropes were hauled from the capstans on the dock, the anchor was out of the water and the small boats were pulling the great ship away from the quay.

George jumped up and down, waving his hat as the ship headed majestically for open water. He turned to Susan, eyes bright with excitement as he tugged at her arm. 'Will our ship be as big?' he asked. 'Will we have as many sails?'

She drew him close and kissed his forehead. At twelve he was growing fast and would soon tower over her, but she cherished this fleeting intimacy. 'I expect so.'

He pulled away and ran down the quay. She followed his

progress and caught sight of Ernest, standing far out on the end of the harbour wall. Tall and broad-shouldered, he waved in a final farewell.

Susan felt a lump rise to her throat as she watched Florence and George join him. One day soon they, too, would leave. Loneliness almost overwhelmed her and she felt as if the void she'd lived in for the past months was threatening to engulf her. She turned towards Ezra, needing the comfort of his arms and the return of the love and trust she'd once taken for granted.

But there was to be no embrace. Ezra had moved away and cut a lonely figure as he wandered down the quay towards their children. His inability to forget her betrayal had set them apart and he couldn't trust himself to remain by her side.

Portsmouth, 13 May 1787

Five of them were chained together, and with each step he took, Billy's hatred had grown. Yet it made him strong and even more determined to survive whatever lay ahead. When they reached Portsmouth he stood to attention before the same naval officer and looked at him steadily as the chains were removed from his ulcerated ankles.

The officer refused to meet his eyes, waited until the fetters were unlocked, then turned to the warder who had accompanied them on the long, tortuous walk. 'Put them in the *Charlotte*,' he ordered, 'and hurry, or we'll miss the tide.'

'What about Bess's child?' demanded Billy.

'They are both on the *Lady Penrhyn*.'

Billy felt the thrill of achievement as he watched the man retreat. The field marshal could be trusted, he thought. Perhaps this really was a chance to make good, to start again and wipe out his past misdemeanours.

His thoughts were interrupted by a rough dig in the back

from the guard. He began to walk towards the *Charlotte*, dread growing as his sharp eyes took in the extraordinary sights around him.

Portsmouth harbour was full of ships, yet the town was shuttered and deserted. Not even a dog strayed on to the cobbles. It seemed the shopkeepers and citizens didn't like the influx of so many convicts and their keepers. He grimaced as he stepped aboard the ship that would take him far from home and family to an uncertain future. They were missing a grand sight.

Some of the ships in the First Fleet had been loaded at Woolwich and Gravesend in January. The ships loaded at Plymouth had arrived at the end of March. Now they were resting at anchor in Portsmouth, ready to leave.

Susan stood with her family on the deck of the *Golden Grove* and watched the bustle of life on the quay. She had borrowed Gilbert's telescope and tried to locate Billy among the be-draggled, unkempt men who'd been made to walk from Ply-mouth, her disgust at the brutal punishment making her so angry that she wanted to lash out. They were a sorry sight, and it had been impossible to tell one man from another – they all looked half starved.

It was then she noticed the second complement of five men in chains. There was something about one that struck her as familiar. She adjusted the instrument and sobbed as she watched Billy's chains being released. He was too far away for her to call to him, and she could only watch as he was taken to the *Charlotte*. How frightened he must be, she thought, and vowed silently to do something to ease his journey and keep him strong.

She closed her eyes and tried to regain some sort of calm, for she was on the verge of tears. Saying goodbye to her mother had been the hardest part of this exile, for Maud was elderly and although Billy hadn't been told, was not in the best of health and unable to understand why Susan was leaving. Susan had held her for a moment, kissed her, then fled from the cottage. Her eldest brother's widow had promised to keep an eye on her, and the new minister would read any correspondence, and pen a reply, but Susan knew it should have been she who brought comfort to her mother's last years. It was another burden to add to the guilt she was carrying.

Jonathan had not returned to Cornwall as expected, and for that she had been grateful. It was one thing to hate him for what he'd done, but quite another to meet him face to face and put that hatred to the test – for in the deepest, most secret part of her there still flickered a tiny flame of love, which would not be extinguished.

She made a supreme effort to appear calm. It would serve little purpose to vent her feelings, for it seemed the remnants of her family were actually looking forward to the journey. She would only be isolated further if she dampened their spirits with a sour expression. This was all part of the penance she must pay for her sin.

George was almost beside himself with excitement as cannons were fired and a marching military band struck up a rousing tune on the quay. He pointed excitedly as shop shutters were raised and doors were opened for the first time since their arrival, and the citizens of Portsmouth poured on to the quay to watch the extraordinary fleet leave harbour.

Ernest had spied the pretty daughter of one of the officers and had gone to investigate, and Florence stood close to her father, her arm hooked into his, her cheek resting on his shoulder. She had always favoured Ezra, and now she rarely left his side; Susan couldn't help feeling resentful.

She turned from them and watched the great sails being hoisted and the wind billowing them. They were beautiful against the blue sky, and the sight of so many ships was breathtaking. She had always envied the fishermen, and had hung on every word when Jonathan had told her about his adventures beyond the horizon; but she was leaving her home, and her thoughts were on the house by the church, and the tiny fishing village that huddled beneath the cliffs. She would never see Cornwall again, never speak to her mother or taste the salt and smell the freshly caught herrings. She took a shuddering breath, eyes blurring with tears. She couldn't bear it.

'I know how hard this must be for you,' said Ann, as she came to stand at her side. She linked her fingers with Susan's. 'But you aren't alone.'

Susan tried to smile. 'I'm leaving so much behind,' she said, through her tears.

'We're all leaving part of us behind, Susan,' she replied softly. 'Especially those poor souls.'

Susan followed her gaze to the ships that were already ploughing through the open sea. Like her, the convicts had had no choice in the matter, so she was certainly not alone in feeling afraid for the future. 'Poor Billy,' she sobbed. 'He always hated being at sea. However will he survive?'

'The human spirit is surprisingly strong, Susan. He'll find the strength to keep going.' She squeezed Susan's fingers. 'You must try to look on this journey as an adventure.' She smiled into Susan's eyes with understanding and affection. 'Think of it as the chance to do something few others will experience. We will be making history.'

PART THREE
Convicts and Conflicts

13

Botany Bay, 20 January 1788

They had been at sea for eight months and the decks of the *Golden Grove* were crowded with passengers as they drew closer to shore. There was excited expectation in the cheerful chatter, and relief that the long journey was over.

Yet as the shoreline was revealed and the merciless sun beat down from a cloudless sky, a terrible silence fell as they took in the barren land that was to be their home. There could be no turning back, no reprieve. Even the most sanguine among them saw their dreams dashed by the sheer desolation that greeted them.

Susan gripped the railing, her gaze transfixed by the seemingly endless miles of withered trees and stinking swamps. Where were the green pastures they had been promised, the rich arable land that was waiting only for the convicts' labour to turn it into fields of golden wheat?

'It's not what we were promised,' she said. She looked up at Ezra, fear bringing tears to her eyes and a tremor to her voice. 'How on earth are we expected to survive in such a place?'

Ezra offered her no comfort. He stood stiffly by her side, face grim, eyes bleak as he surveyed the view. 'The Lord will provide,' he said, but for all his faith, even he didn't sound convinced.

'How?' she retorted, unusually blunt. 'The trees don't bear fruit, the swamps will give us fever and there's not an inch of pasture to graze animals or plough.' Her voice rose as fear threatened to get the better of her. 'We've put up with storms, sickness and weevils in our flour – for what?' she yelled. 'A swamp!'

Ezra remained unmoved by her anguish, and it was only the sight of her children's faces that silenced her. She saw her own fear reflected in them and knew she had to calm herself. 'The Lord will have His work cut out – and so will we,' she said, forcing lightness to her voice for their benefit.

'He will give us the strength to turn this wilderness into a home,' said Ezra, as Florence burst into tears. He stroked her hair absently. 'As long as we remain strong in our faith, He will guide us.'

Susan's lips were clamped in a tight line. She didn't dare voice her opinion that God wouldn't have much to do with the struggle ahead. She looked across at the convict ships. Her passage had been bad enough through the storms, but what of Billy and the others who'd been chained in the hold? How would they labour in this heat with the threat of fever and disease hanging over them as cruelly as the lash? She feared for them all. Surely no human could exist in this hell.

The ships remained at anchor in the bay for five days while Arthur Phillip and a few of his officers set off in one of the small boats to search further up the coast for a more suitable landing. Billy and the others were permitted to leave the hold, and as they emerged, blinking in the bright sunlight, they were stunned into silence. Nothing had prepared them for what they could see.

'There ain't no escape 'ere,' said Mullins, with a leer. 'Jump ship for all I care. The sharks'll get yer if the jungle don't.'

Billy stared in disbelief at the land before him. Trees smothered the parched earth as far as the eye could see. Swamps lurked with dark menace along the shoreline, the roots of the surrounding trees emerging from them like witches' fingers draped with veils of drooping weed.

Mosquitoes swarmed in clouds and the stinking, torpid silence was rent constantly by the shrieking cackle of some strange beast that seemed determined to mock them. He turned to Mullins. 'You're as much a prisoner as me,' he said quietly. 'This is the end of the line for all of us.'

Mullins spat over the side. 'Not me,' he retorted. 'I'm on the next ship out of 'ere.' His eyes were bright with malice. 'I'll be back in London 'aving a pint and a whore while you're stuck 'ere till yer bones rot.' He strode away.

Billy clenched his fists, sorely tempted to fell the bastard and beat him to a pulp. But he knew that that was what Mullins wanted. He was waiting for an excuse to clap him in irons and give him another taste of the lash. Billy concentrated on remaining calm as he watched the other ships swaying at anchor. At least he had survived the journey, even though there had been times when he thought he would go mad with fear as the holds took in water and threatened to drown them all.

He caught sight of the *Golden Grove* and his thoughts turned to Susan and her children. She had somehow managed to get him extra rations and clean clothes during the journey – but what madness had made Ezra bring his family here? They hadn't been forced, they weren't convicts, yet he'd sentenced his wife and children to death as surely as if he had put nooses round their necks.

'Oy, Billy! Over 'ere.'

He turned towards the voice. Nell was hanging over the side of the *Lady Penrhyn*, breasts jiggling as she waved. He waved back. 'How are you?' he shouted. 'And Bess?'

'I'm all right,' she yelled, 'but the kid died a coupl'a weeks ago so Bess ain't good.'

Billy felt a twinge of guilt. Perhaps he'd been wrong to insist it made the journey. As for Bess, she would have to take her chance like everyone else. He was about to reply when he received a sharp dig in his ribs. 'No talking with the women,' snapped Mullins. 'Go below, Penhalligan, and stay there until tomorrow.'

Billy looked at Nell, who was now struggling with a marine, and as they were shoved towards their separate holds she called to him, 'See you in hell, Billy.'

Arthur Phillip returned from his exploration up the coast and declared he had found the 'finest harbour in the world, in which a thousand ships-of-the-line could ride in perfect safety'. They would sail for Port Jackson on the tide.

His return hadn't come a minute too soon, for not only had fierce, spear-throwing black men been seen on the shores of Botany Bay but the first ship of the French expedition under La Pérouse had been spotted off the headland. They had beaten the French, and now it was imperative to establish the settlement of New South Wales and annex Norfolk Island so that production of flax could begin.

Lowitja had known they were coming for she'd seen them in the talking stones many moons ago. Her skills as seer and medicine-woman were respected, but her recent visions had worried her: they were of dark days and much blood, of death, magic and terror.

That morning she had woken early, more troubled than usual by her dreams, but drawn irrevocably to the headland as if the Spirits were leading her. As she watched them sailing towards the small bay her tribe called Kamay, she knew her skills had not played her false. With fear drying her throat, she gathered up her dilly bag and spears and ran to warn her uncles, Bennelong, Colebee and Pemuluwuy.

The men of the tribe gathered at the shore, shaking their spears and howling defiance as the white men brought their great sailing canoes close to land. Lowitja remained out of sight with the other women, but she remembered when these white men had come before, and knew it was the start of the dark days she'd foretold.

After the sun had risen five times it looked as if they had frightened them away, for they raised their sails again and moved further along the coast. Her uncles were elated, but Lowitja knew it was not over.

As a new day dawned, another ship arrived with different colours attached to the leafless trees that held the sails. The men rushed to the beach to scream abuse and threaten with their spears, and Lowitja watched fearfully from the trees.

A great thunder rent the air.

Lowitja and the others threw themselves to the ground.

Something flew above their heads and landed with a blast that shook the earth, lifting trees and bushes high into the sky.

She and her family huddled deep in the shelter of an overhanging bush. The visions were becoming a reality, and the end of the world was at hand.

It was some time before they dared lift their heads. The sight of two young men hacked to pieces galvanised them into flight. The fear was overwhelming, and they sought the deepest, darkest and most secret places in the bush to hide.

Lowitja cast the talking stones again and again, willing them to shed hope on their situation. But even as she fell into a trance and consulted with the Ancestor Spirits, she knew this was an enemy with whom they couldn't compete: his weapons were created by evil spirits and were no match for their spears and boomerangs.

Bennelong, her uncle, the clan's senior Elder, sent trackers up the coast to warn the Cadigal people of what was happening, and to discover where the ships had gone once they'd left the bay. On their return, he proposed that the two tribes hurry to Warang, the wider water and deeper inlets further north, to find out what manner of enemy had come to their shores.

Port Jackson, 26 January 1788

Susan and the others stood on deck as they sailed into Sydney Cove and Port Jackson. They had been terrified of the savages on the shore in Botany Bay, and although their spears hadn't touched them and they had melted back into the swamps, the passengers of the *Golden Grove* wondered fearfully what awaited them in the next cove.

Her spirits lightened as she saw the lush grass and green trees, the clear water and sheltered sandy bays of the enormous harbour. Gentle hills rose on the skyline and bright rivers wound a serpentine course through acre upon acre of forest and grassland. Perhaps it wouldn't be so bad after all, she hoped, despair pushed firmly aside.

'It'll take a fierce amount of work to clear all that before we can farm it,' muttered Ernest, as he ran his hands through his thick fair hair. His eyes narrowed at the glare of the sun on the water. 'But the land looks promising, and we'll have labour enough to help clear and plough.' He grinned at his mother. 'I can't wait to get my hands dirty and feel good solid earth under my feet.'

Susan was glad one of them appeared enthusiastic. She looked at Florence, who was clinging to Ezra's arm. She would have liked to soothe her fears, but as usual Florence had sought Ezra's reassurance. Susan tried to maintain an optimistic expression on her face. All she could do now was pray that they would come together as a family to look towards the future with hope.

Susan shared the impatience that grew among the families of the officers as the military were rowed to shore. Like her son, she was eager to feel solid ground beneath her feet – even if it was alien soil that promised nothing but hard labour.

She watched as the soldiers set up camp above the high-water line. The ring of axes and the shouts of men drifted to them from across the water as the ground was cleared and a host of white tents erected. It had the hallmarks of a military camp, with the accompanying bustle and shouted commands, and Susan wondered how she could live under canvas with no proper facilities to wash or cook.

It was late in the afternoon when she clambered down the rope-ladder to the small boat. Ezra remained stiffly formal as he helped her in, and although George and Ernest were almost bursting with excitement, she noticed that Florence clung to the side as they were rowed to shore.

The heat was almost unbearable and no matter how hard she plied her fan, the flies swarmed round her face in dark clouds. 'Thank goodness I took your advice and discarded the corsets and petticoats,' she murmured to Ann.

Her sister-in-law's face was red and her light brown curls were sticking to her cheek. 'Gilbert's years of experience in India,' she replied. 'It feels strange at first, but he tells me we will be far more comfortable without them.' They fell silent as their boat was hauled up the beach.

Susan stepped ashore and felt the ground dip and tilt beneath her feet.

Ernest pushed past his father and grabbed her arm to steady her. 'We've got sea-legs,' he said, and flashed a smile. 'Uncle Gilbert says the feeling will soon pass.'

Susan put her hand to his cheek and felt stubble. Her son was growing up, almost a man, and she loved him for the way he cherished her. If only Ezra could feel the same.

'Savages! We're all going to die!'

Susan grabbed George and Ezra grabbed Florence. Ernest grabbed his rifle.

The soldiers and marines swiftly formed a phalanx between the migrants and the handful of fierce-looking natives who were yelling and throwing spears. 'Fire above their heads,' shouted Arthur Phillip. 'No man is to be killed.'

The blacks retreated hastily, but continued to throw stones and spears and shriek abuse.

'What have you brought us to?' shouted Susan, above the thunder of gunfire. 'We're about to be massacred.'

Ezra was trying to calm Florence, who was hysterical. 'We're perfectly safe,' he yelled back. 'The army will protect us.'

Susan cowered with them behind a tree and clung to George, who seemed hell-bent on joining the soldiers. She searched wildly for Ernest, and spotted him on the far side of the clearing. Her breath was a sob as she watched him load and reload his rifle, then fire it into the air. Despite his youth he didn't appear to be afraid – in fact, he seemed to be enjoying himself, which frightened her even more.

'For God's sake, Ezra!' she yelled. 'We can't stay here! We have to protect our children.'

'They will be protected,' he said firmly, as the natives returned to the bush and the men to their work. 'We have the army, the marines and Governor Phillip to bring order. We mustn't give up now, Susan.'

She saw the light of elation in his eyes and her spirits tumbled further as tears coursed down her face. 'You see this as a chance to do God's work, don't you?' she asked.

Ezra nodded. 'The convicts are Godless and so are those poor wretched blacks. God has sent me here to do His work, Susan. I cannot and will not be turned from it.'

'Even at the expense of your children's lives?' The tears had dried, but now cold certainty clutched her heart.

'God will protect us,' he said softly. He reached out as if to touch her hand, then withdrew. 'Have faith in Him and in me, Susan. We are here for an important purpose, and it can only be fulfilled if we are strong in our resolve.'

She wanted to believe him, wanted to tell him she loved him and would follow him to the ends of the earth if only he could show her some of the old warmth. But she wasn't prepared to sacrifice her children. 'I want you to promise me the children will be sent home on the first ship,' she said. 'They can live with my family in Cornwall until your mission is complete.'

'It may be some time before the Second Fleet arrives,' he reminded her, 'and Ernest is hardly a child.' Then his expression softened and he nodded. 'If it's their wish to return when the ships come, then so be it. I give you my word.'

Billy's legs felt weak and he was finding it difficult to maintain his balance as he stepped ashore with the others from the *Charlotte*. He looked for Nell, but he soon learnt the women prisoners weren't to be brought ashore for a few days. He grinned. No doubt Governor Phillip wanted the camp fully set up before they arrived: once they were ashore the men would be fit for nothing. He hoisted his trousers, tried not to think of her soft, yielding flesh and warm breasts, and went to find his sister.

'Billy!' Susan raced towards him and threw herself into his arms. 'Oh, Billy, it's so good to see you.'

Her embrace almost knocked him over and he grinned as they clung to each other. It was good to see her too, and to feel her wiry strength instilling hope in him. He drew back and looked into her face. She was thinner than he remembered, and her eyelids were swollen from tears. He kissed her cheek, masking the fury he felt towards Ezra for bringing her here. 'We've come this far,' he said. 'We'll survive.'

Her questions were legion and he managed to skirt the less savoury aspects of his journey. Susan didn't need to know about the rats and the filth in the hold, where the men had fought over rancid food and brackish water. She didn't need to know about the sadistic Mullins and the lash that had striped his back, or the terror of water rising to reach beyond his waist so he'd had to swim to survive the battering of the ship's timbers as it rolled and plunged through the storms.

'You look so thin,' she said. 'Were you given the extra rations – and where are the clothes I sent you?'

He was suddenly aware of how he must look and smell. He stepped back from her, reddening with shame. 'Both were gratefully received,' he said stiffly, 'but the conditions meant we had only a weekly dousing of sea-water to keep us clean. Everything rotted in no time.'

Her soft hand touched his face. 'Oh, Billy, I wish—'

'I know,' he said hastily. 'But once I've found the field marshal and discovered what he has in store for me there's a chance I'll get clean clothes and soap.' He brushed away a teardrop that trembled on her lashes. 'I'm better off than many here,' he said softly. 'At least I have my family.'

'Will you be allowed to live with us?' she asked.

Billy heard the quaver in her voice and his heart twisted as he shook his head. 'I'm still a convict,' he reminded her. 'I'll sleep over there with the others.'

Later that day, as the sun was sinking behind the soft green hills, Billy stood with the other convicts as everyone gathered in the clearing. The British flag was unfurled over Sydney Cove. Shots were fired, and toasts were drunk. It was a date to be remembered, for it was the day on which the white man had come to stay in Australia.

6 February 1788

Nell had grown impatient as she and the other women had been kept aboard the *Lady Penrhyn*. Now, as she sat in one of the many small rowing-boats, the impatience had turned to fear. They were outnumbered, and the men on the shore were baying like slavering wolves.

She looked at the other women. Bess was clinging to the sailor she had latched on to. At least she had someone to look after her, Nell thought, though how long it would last, the Lord only knew. Sally and Peg were primping and preening, casting their eyes over the sailors and convicts howling on the shore, but they were whores.

She stifled her fears as she saw them reflected in the eyes of the women who had never worked the streets and taverns or given themselves willingly. Some were barely past their teens and had had a rough time on board. Nell suspected they were in for worse when they landed.

She pulled the thin shawl more firmly over her shoulders and tried to control the shivers. She had never before been truly afraid, but as the boat neared the beach she knew real terror. She was barely twenty, and as a young prostitute in the East End of London she'd known what to expect – but here, in this savage country, she was at the mercy of lawlessness and lust. What was to become of her?

Suddenly Billy was wading towards her, shoving others aside, reaching for the prow of the boat. 'Billy!' she screamed. 'Help me.'

He grabbed her as she almost fell out of the boat. 'Hurry,' he ordered. 'They're about to riot.'

Nell stumbled as he dragged her up the sand, and before he could steady her, she was grabbed by three convicts and torn away from him. 'Billy,' she shrieked as she kicked and lashed out, clawing at her attackers' eyes.

Billy waded in with his fists, and Nell continued to struggle until the men were beaten off. Then he picked her up and ran with her into the trees.

When he set her on her feet, she was trembling so hard she could barely stand, and burst into tears. 'Gawd, Bill, I ain't never been so scared in me life.' She clung to him, her confidence in tatters.

Billy held her close and tried to soothe her. 'I thank God I got to you in time. There'll be rape and murder before the day's out,' he gasped. 'Too many men, too few women and rum for all will see to that.'

They embraced in the shelter of the trees and listened to the screams and shouts. The mayhem had started. Nell was thankful for his strong arms and quick thinking. 'Billy,' she sobbed, 'I don't know what I'd've done without you.'

He helped her walk into deeper shadows. 'They're animals,' he muttered. 'Heaven knows what they might have done if . . .'

She was still shaking, and it was hard to breathe. 'They might still find us,' she whispered, her gaze darting through the trees to fix on the clearing. 'We have to hide.'

'I know. It'll be a long night, but I've rum and food stashed away, and we're free until dawn tomorrow.'

She clung to him as he went further into the bush. They reached a small clearing far from the sounds of the shore. The surroundings were strange and rather frightening, and she shot anxious glances over her shoulder. 'What about the natives?' she asked. 'They could be lurking, ready to kill us any minute.'

'I think they're more frightened than we are,' he said, as he sat her down. 'I reckon they're miles away by now.'

'Thanks, Billy. I knew you'd take care of me.' He was handsome, despite the dirt and the ragged clothes. 'I could do with a drink, and no mistake,' she said, through chattering teeth.

He unearthed the small cask he'd buried earlier that day, and they drank. The food was meagre, bread and salted meat, with a couple of apples that were past their best.

Sated and reassured, Nell drew him down beside her in the grass. His eyes were very blue as he encircled her waist with his arm. 'You and me were meant to be,' she murmured.

Billy leant over her, blotting out the sun, enclosing them in a private world she had no wish to escape. Nell gave herself willingly, for this was the man she had wanted from the moment she had first set eyes on him – the man who would protect and love her as no other had done. Her days as a whore were over.

Susan had seen Billy grab the girl from the boat. She had watched open-mouthed as they were attacked by three convicts, who seemed intent on ripping the girl from him, and sighed with relief when he had made off with her into the bush. Now she stared in horror at the scene before her.

The other women hadn't been so fortunate. They were hauled unceremoniously from the boats and raped where they fell. The convict men were reeling with rum, and fights were breaking out as several tried to take vicious possession of one woman. Some of the whores gave as good as they got, swilling rum and throwing punches – but Susan could see they were losing the battle. Some lay senseless as they were further abused.

'Why don't the soldiers do something?' she shouted, above the screams.

Ezra was shielding a terrified Florence with his body. He glanced at the retreating line of soldiers. 'There's too many,' he shouted. 'They've lost control.'

'Get Florence out of here,' she yelled, as she grabbed George and backed away from a man who had stumbled out of the mêlée and was staggering towards them. He was naked, smeared in blood and filth – his intention unmistakable.

'Touch her and you'll die,' shouted Ernest, the rifle sighted on the naked torso.

The threat had the desired effect, for the man shambled away.

Susan was almost incoherent with fear as she reached Ezra and Florence. 'Run,' she urged. 'Run for your lives.'

They broke through the cordon of soldiers who had been ordered to protect the women and children, and found shelter in their tent, which was pitched well away from the scenes of hell.

Ernest sat guard at the entrance, the rifle loaded and ready to fire at any intruder. Ezra began to pray as Florence sobbed and clung to him. George took up his father's rifle and joined his brother as Susan huddled against Ezra, desperate for comfort.

The heat was appalling beneath the canvas, and they were soon sweating and thirsty. Susan shared out the water from a bucket she'd filled earlier, and they sat in misery and stifling terror to wait for night.

As the sun went down rain pounded on the canvas. It drove the humidity to exhaustion point as it poured in rivers over the parched earth and threatened to wash them away, but the pegs and ropes held and the soldiers remained at their posts under the strict eye of Arthur Phillip.

They emerged at dawn to find the soldiers had gone. When Ezra returned from a quick inspection, he said, 'The downpour seems to have brought the bacchanalian orgy to an abrupt end. The troops are rounding up the offenders in the main clearing.'

'There's work to be done,' said Susan, as she gathered up bandages and ointments. 'The women will need attention after last night.'

'They're whores,' snapped Florence. 'They don't need your help.'

'They're humans,' Susan retorted, stung by her daughter's anger, but knowing it had been born of fear. She stroked the girl's cheek. 'They didn't ask for what happened to them yesterday, Florence,' she said softly. 'Have a little charity.'

Some kind of order had been brought to the camp, but the devastation wrought by the storm and the fighting would take longer to repair. Tents had been ripped to shreds, pottery smashed and furniture reduced to matchwood. The food stores had been broken into and empty rum kegs lay abandoned everywhere. Susan and the other women did what they could to staunch bloody wounds and set broken bones. Three women and four men had died. It was not an auspicious beginning for the new settlement.

Arthur Phillip finally put in an appearance. He was accompanied by a regimental band, and took his place on a makeshift podium where he was duly sworn in as Captain General and Governor in Chief of New South Wales.

As Gilbert read out a long, dull commission, and their new governor took the Bible and swore allegiance to the King, Susan stood with her family and searched the convict lines for sight of her brother. She found him eventually, looking decidedly the worse for wear as was the girl beside him.

Susan took in the tumble of red hair, the half-exposed breasts and brazen stance and realised what she was. With a sigh she turned away. Billy had few choices open to him and everyone needed someone, especially here.

The heat rose and the bedraggled, battered convicts shuffled and muttered as Arthur Phillip spent the next hour haranguing them on the evils of promiscuity, extolling marriage as a fit and proper state for humans. He went on to encourage them to marry at once and bring an end to scenes like the previous night's, then threatened to put a charge of buckshot into the backside of any convict found in the women's quarters after dark.

Susan glanced at her brother, who gave her a wink and a grin. That was just the sort of challenge he relished, and she could only pray he'd have more sense than to jeopardise his standing with Gilbert.

The Eora and Cadigal Camp, February 1788

The women and children had been ordered to keep well back after the terrifying strike of thunder-death from the ship. They followed at a distance as Bennelong and the other Elders

trekked to Warang and bravely faced the enemy on the beach –
but their defiance and show of strength had done no good.
The white men's terrifying thunder-sticks had roared until the
earth seemed to tremble, and they had to creep away into the
safety of the bush.

From her hiding-place, Lowitja watched the white men
pour on to the beach like termites leaving a nest, and soon
a camp of white cloth spread across the shore. Trees were cut
down while sacred stones and ancestor sites were torn away
and trampled as strange beasts were herded into enclosures by
men who were guarded by others in bright red body covers
and carried odd-looking spears.

Lowitja watched in impotent rage as the Dreaming Places of
the Eora and Cadigal people were destroyed. She was willing
to give her life to be rid of these white invaders, but Bennelong
and Pemuluwuy had counselled against it, and she had understood their wisdom. They were outnumbered and the enemy's
weapons were too powerful against spears and boomerangs.

She joined the others as, one by one, the Eora and Cadigal
people faded into the trees. They would make a united camp
and discuss strategy, but first she must ask the Spirits for
guidance.

Lowitja had earned great respect among the people of both
tribes, for not only did she have the gift of communing with the
Spirits, she was a direct descendant of the great Garnday,
the mother of her ancient tribe who had led her people
from the north to escape starvation in the lush hunting
grounds of these southerly shores of Warang. When she
stepped into the circle of Elders they were ready to listen,
for each word held the wisdom of her ancestor.

'They come with their women and children,' she said
quietly. 'They bring animals, weapons and shelter. They
are not from a wandering tribe.' She looked at each uplifted
face and carried on. 'The thunder-death is too powerful

against our weapons, so we must go to them in friendship. We must teach them the customs of our people so they learn respect for the land and our Ancestor Spirits.'

'I honour your wisdom,' said one of the Elders. 'But what if the white man does not wish to learn?'

'They have shown the great power of their weapons, but their thunder-sticks roared to the sky, not into our bodies. The Great Spirit of Garnday tells me they have no wish to kill us.'

'But they have already destroyed our sacred Dreaming Places,' shouted one of the younger men. 'How could Garnday allow that?'

Lowitja swallowed. She had seen the dark days ahead, and knew they must act now before they became reality. 'It is a warning of their power and ignorance,' she said, into the silence. 'If we are to avoid bloodshed and the destruction of our Dreaming Places we must initiate them into our ways and educate them in our spirituality.'

Pemuluwuy and Bennelong nodded, but Lowitja could see that not all of the Elders were convinced, and the knowledge chilled her. Dark clouds were gathering and, if her words went unheeded, there would come a storm so great it would sweep away their ancient customs for ever.

Lowitja realised she had to lead by example. A few days later she went alone to the white man's camp, squatted in the shadows of the surrounding trees and watched the woman as she prepared a meal. Her skin was pale, her hair glinted in the sun and she wore strange coverings that reached to her ankles. Lowitja eyed the skins on her feet, and wondered what manner of thing they were. It was all very odd, but the woman looked friendly enough, and she couldn't sit there all day.

Lowitja emerged silently from the shadows and approached her.

*   *   *

Susan had seen her lurking in the shadows, and had grasped that the child was as nervous as she. She continued to prepare the dinner, darting covert glances towards the native.

'Hello,' she said quietly, as the girl came to stand a little way off. She smiled in welcome and beckoned her nearer.

The girl hesitated, darting nervous glances around the clearing, poised to run at the slightest sound.

Susan remained where she was and they stood in silence, taking each other's measure. On closer inspection Susan saw that this was no child but a mature woman. She was small-boned and shorter than Susan, with deep welts cut into her ebony flesh that could only be tribal markings. Her hair was a tangle of rusty brown, and her eyes were dark above the broad nose and full lips. Naked but for a thin twine belt, she possessed a striking nobility.

The woman took a hesitant step towards her. 'Lowitja,' she said.

'Susan.' She smiled in encouragement and was glad she was alone, for the sight of the men would have frightened Lowitja away.

Lowitja advanced another step and reached out a tentative hand to brush Susan's skirts. She appeared to like what she felt, for she smiled, showing a row of fine white teeth.

Susan reached for the clean handkerchief she'd tucked into her waistband and held it out. 'For you,' she said. 'A present for Lowitja.'

The handkerchief was taken and examined minutely, then returned. Susan tried to make her understand she could keep it, but Lowitja seemed not to want it. They stood in the clearing unable to communicate, and at last Susan understood the frustration Jonathan had experienced with Watpipa and the northern natives. She was about to coax her to try some of the stew she was making when the woman gabbled something unintelligible and ran back into the trees.

*   *   *

As the months went by Susan became used to Lowitja appearing silently at her side. They taught each other a few words, but on the whole they got by with gestures, nods and smiles.

When Susan sat down to write to her mother and daughter, she didn't mention the hardships, the marauding crocodiles and deadly snakes, or the toil of labouring over a stove when the barometer soared beyond the hundred. She filled her letters with the wonders of the new colony and the fragile friendships the settlers had forged with the natives.

I saw my first kangaroo today. What a strange beast it is, hopping about on its big back legs, but I am assured it makes good eating, and the men often go out and hunt them for the communal pot.

The natives are beginning to understand that we are here to stay, and have made friendly advances. We have given them food, but they seem to prefer the rum, and this does not settle well with them, for their constitutions are not suited to it and they soon become senseless.

They are primitive hunters and gatherers, and do not farm, have beasts to tend or even proper shelter. We have given them tools, blankets and clothes, but they are all spurned, and Ezra is distraught at their nakedness. I find no ugliness in it, for it is natural to them and their surroundings. I wish often that I could strip and swim in the sea as they do, it's so hot here and my clothes stifle me – but of course it would shock everyone to the core, so I must continue to swelter.

Governor Phillip had hoped the natives would help in the building of the colony – and the extra hands would have been welcome – but all efforts to persuade them have failed. The black men simply refuse to labour for us, so the convicts dig, clear stones and build more permanent shelters for us.

The stealing of food, rum and livestock has become a game. Our men give chase, but the natives are too swift and rarely caught. My friend Lowitja laughs at our men's attempts to penetrate the forests that surround us, and I have to agree that they are clumsy, and that any self-respecting thief could hear them a mile off.

As for me, I am well, and spend most of my time tending the sick and my vegetable garden. Ezra has settled in to his work with Florence at his side, and the school is well attended. Ernest is already working on a government farm in preparation for when he takes up his land grant, and George is blossoming into a fine young man. He seems to have been born to this life. He is so tall now, tanned by the sun, his energy high. It is hard to keep him at his books when there are horses, fishing and mischief waiting for him outside.

Billy's work for Gilbert as quartermaster seems to be paying off. He has been given permission to pitch his tent away from the rest of the convicts, and Gilbert is full of praise for his efforts. He has fallen in love with a girl called Nell. She has boundless energy and a tough outlook, and although her manner is at times a little coarse, she will be a great asset to this new colony.

The Cadigal and Eora Camp, April 1788

The game of stealing from the whites came to an abrupt end when three young boys were killed by a fire-stick. There had already been incidences of women taken against their will, of men being lured into bad ways by the sweet dark drink that had become so desirable. Their spirituality and sacred sites were being slowly destroyed, and Mother Earth had been abused. It was time to ignore Lowitja's warnings, rid the land of the invader and restore the ancient peace.

The attacks began, and one of the young warriors speared

two men who were cutting rushes down by the water's edge at Kogerah. He was tracked with dogs for many days, caught and taken prisoner by the men in red. He was not seen again.

Several seasons later, Bennelong and Colebee were taken prisoner after they had attacked the new settlement in Parramatta, but that was only the start of their problems, for a sickness had come with the white men and the Eora and Cadigal people were dying. It was a disease that brought great fire to the body and confusion to the mind before it blistered the skin. One by one the children were taken by it, then the elderly and weak, and even some of the fittest, strongest warriors were made helpless by the fires that burned within them.

Lowitja knew it was the *galgala*, which her friend Susan called smallpox. It had come many generations before, and had not infected the settlers, but the Elders insisted it was the white men who had brought it, and it was yet another sign that they should be banished.

Susan had no magic medicine to cure the sufferers, so Lowitja returned to her stones and asked for help from the Ancestor Spirits. Despite her vast knowledge, she soon discovered she could do nothing to halt its progress, and the few who survived were left weakened, with swollen limbs and ugly scars gouged in their skin.

In less than another season the tribes had been decimated by half and Lowitja had lost three of her five children as well as her mother, her aunt and her youngest brother. The hatred for the white invader grew, and despite Lowitja's quiet counselling against violence, Pemuluwuy took over as leader of the pathetic remnants of the twenty southern tribes.

With his son Tedbury at his side, he began a campaign of guerrilla attacks that would last several years and see many more of their number dead.

14

Sydney Cove, Port Jackson, 3 June 1790

Susan paused in her work to wipe the sweat from her brow with a hand roughened by labour. The heat was appalling and the buzzing, settling cloud of flies was determined to worry the life out of her as she had scrubbed the rough table and tried to bring order to their mean wooden shack. Ezra had flatly refused to use convicts to help with the heavy work – he had said that slavery was the most evil of human sins and his family would have no part in it. Susan wished he was not so firm in his beliefs. The work was hard enough, but the conditions made it even worse. If only they had a fine house like Ann and Gilbert, she thought wistfully. At least then life would have been a little more bearable.

She dropped the scrubbing brush into the metal bucket and stepped out of the door in an effort to find relief from the heat. But the water in Sydney Cove remained flat calm, the sun blazed down from a clear sky and there wasn't a breath of wind. She found shade beneath a vast tree and sank to the ground, her bare feet peeping out from beneath her tattered skirt. Her head was spinning and her stomach growled as she lifted her thick plait of hair from the nape of her neck to cool herself.

In the first two years the harvest had failed miserably and Governor Phillip had cut everyone's weekly rations to four pounds of flour, two and a half pounds of salt pork and one and a half pounds of rice. Many of the soldiers and marines attended to their duties barefoot as their boots had fallen to pieces, and everyone's clothes were rotting.

The supply ship *Sirius* had been wrecked at Norfolk Island in February, and there had been no sign of the Second Fleet, which had been expected some months before. Now the colony, founded with such high hopes, was at starving-point.

There had been many deaths, especially among the convicts who had arrived in poor condition; Susan had tended one man who had survived a few extra days by eating grass. Theft of provisions was rife and punishable by death, yet this didn't stop the stealing. Two men had been caught only the other day, and because the government hadn't thought to include a hangman among the migrants, one had been offered a pardon on condition he took up the post. The alternative was to be shot. His first task had been to hang his co-conspirator.

Susan closed her eyes and tried to ignore the hunger and bitterness of her situation. Not only was she starving and burnt by the sun, but since the murder two years ago of a couple of convicts at Rushcutters Bay all their lives were in danger from marauding natives. They were a savage lot, with their spears and shrill war-cries, their theft of stores and killing of livestock. Why Gilbert couldn't do something about them, she didn't know. Arresting a few wasn't enough, and now it seemed the blacks were intent on either drinking themselves to death or killing them all.

She hated it here. Hated the crudity of the convict women and the lewdness of the men, the heat and the flies, the isolation from decency and the most basic morals of civilisation. But most of all she hated herself. If she'd remained faithful to Ezra they would still live in Cornwall.

She got to her feet and brushed the dust from her skirt. No amount of sewing and patching could make her clothes look more than rags. They offended her, for she'd always taken pride in being neat. If God's plan was to punish her for that vanity along with all her other sins, He'd chosen the method well.

She looked out at the party of ragged, starving convicts who were clearing trees, at the blacksmith hammering iron in his forge, and at another group of men who were hauling bricks. They were suffering even more than she was, but it was a complete shambles. If she had been in charge she would have made sure that the convicts sent here were at least skilled in farming, house-building and carpentry – but the men in London had not thought of this.

The land around the settlement was as hard as iron and bent the blades of their hoes, the timber twisted their axes, the heat oppressed, snakes lurked and giant ants bit. The natives had spurned all offers of education and British civilisation, and had refused point-blank to labour for the whites, even in exchange for food and blankets. Now they were all at the mercy of bone-idle shirkers, more used to picking pockets and selling their bodies in exchange for rum than doing a day's work. No wonder the crops had failed.

She turned away from the scene and eyed the wooden shack that had been built shortly after their arrival. It stood next to the little wooden church that the Reverend Richard Johnson had had built soon after, and had given them shelter from the heavy rain that had fallen for most of those first few months. It was a hovel.

The floor was hard-packed earth, the shuttered windows were unglazed, and in the winter months the wind whistled through every crack, driving out any heat that came from the cast-iron cooking range. The fine linen they had brought with them had mouldered in the humidity, most of the china had been broken during the voyage and Florence's piano was so out of tune it could not be played. Their furniture had rotted or been eaten by termites, and the rough wood and canvas replacements had been cobbled together by George and Ernest, who revelled in the challenges of this savage land.

She sighed. Ernest was seventeen now, and had already left

Sydney Cove. The government had given each of them a parcel of land near the recently charted Hawkesbury river, and he had set off happily almost a year ago to begin clearing and sowing. George wouldn't be far behind him, she guessed, for he was fifteen, and already making plans for his own land entitlement.

'A ship! A ship!'

The shout snatched her from her thoughts and she turned towards the water. There, making its slow way through the inlets and past the bays towards Port Jackson, was a large ship with many sails. It was flying the British colours.

Susan lifted her skirts and began to run. At last they were to be rescued. At last there would be food to eat and news from home. God had provided the miracle she and Ezra had been praying for. He hadn't deserted them after all.

She raced into the infirmary tent in search of her husband. It was stifling under the canvas, the pall of death hanging over everyone. She found him at last at the back of the tent. He was reading to an emaciated child who lay supine and dull-eyed on the mattress.

'There's a ship,' she told him. 'We are to be rescued at last.'

He didn't look up. 'Then you must go and see what it brings,' he replied.

'Come with me,' she urged, her hand resting on his shoulder.

He eased away from her touch. 'I am busy.'

Susan bit her lip. She would not let his coldness touch her, was too exhausted for tears. She left him with the child and hurried outside.

The *Lady Juliana* was a magnificent sight as she hove-to and dropped anchor. But as the settlers and convicts watched the passengers alight there was a growing murmur of unease that took on ugly overtones.

'It's a ship of whores,' breathed Billy, who had joined her at the quayside. 'And just look at them! Fat as lard and dressed for business. What do they think this is? A tea party?'

The atmosphere was ominous as the gaudily dressed women stepped off the row-boats. Their flirtatious smiles faltered as the gathering parted in silence to let them through, and they hastened their steps.

'Where's the food, then?' yelled a man.

'Yeah. We don't need fucking, we need feeding.'

The crowd surged forward. Gilbert rounded up his wife, Susan and Florence and steered them away. 'We're in for trouble,' he said. 'The captain tells me they have only enough supplies to feed the women. Governor Phillip will have to commandeer some, get the women back on board and send them to Norfolk Island. We dare not risk a riot.'

Susan looked up into his face. 'Why send such a ship if it doesn't bring supplies? Does London not know we're dying?'

Gilbert smoothed his moustache as he cast a withering glance over the new arrivals. 'In their wisdom, the government decided we need more women to bring calm and stability to the settlement – though how they think that rabble will do us any good, heaven only knows.'

Susan watched the whores' progress through the silent, belligerent crowd, and wondered if London cared a jot for what happened to any of them. It seemed they were doomed.

The Surprise, *26 June 1790*

Jack Quince lay in his own filth, chained to a dead man. He was weak and skeletal, having had no water or food for days, but he and all the others had learnt that no amount of begging would bring them sustenance. The captain of the *Surprise* seemed determined to murder them all.

He no longer scratched at the lice or felt the stinging, putrid cuts from the floggings he had received during the interminable months at sea. He no longer smelt the stench of rotting flesh or the bodily waste that churned around him in the bilge water, or was touched by the terrors of claustrophobia. He knew only that he would die if he spent another day down here in the hold, and was prepared for it.

He closed his eyes as he lay among the dead and ignored the rats that scurried back and forth, burying their snouts in the festering corpses. He was trying to remember what home had been like. Sussex was a world away – a world where the sun warmed a man's back as he harvested the wheat and tended his cattle in the vales of the South Downs. There was no starvation, no pain, and death was expected to come soberly and with dignity in old age. The hedgerows and leafy lanes, the peaceful villages with their little lime-washed cottages and thatched roofs, the beasts in the fields and the small farm he had once owned had taken on a dream-like quality.

Then there was Alice. His dry lips cracked as they parted in a smile. Alice Hobden and he had fallen in love when they were children. He thought of her rich brown hair and dark eyes, her creamy skin and throaty laugh. They had had such plans for the future before Fate had intervened and he had been falsely accused of theft.

A keening rose in his throat and was swallowed. He had known his wealthy accuser, a neighbouring landowner who had coveted his rich pastureland and was determined to get it, no matter how dishonestly. The bull had been deliberately put into the field with Jack's cows, and before he could do anything about it he had been hauled away to the Assizes.

The trial had been short, for his accuser had friends in high places and the money to bribe the judge. Jack had been thrown into a prison hulk for the first three years of his fifteen-year sentence, and it was only through the kindness of a friend that he had been able to sign over the deeds of the farm to Alice. At least it would safeguard the place from the man who had wronged him, and give Alice security for the future.

Yet he couldn't bear to see her again. He had refused to let her visit him, even when it was announced he was to be transported. He knew he had to let her go – free her from the promises they had made to one another.

The memories were too hard to bear, and he opened his eyes. Even a reality such as this was easier to deal with than the thought of Alice marrying someone else and bringing up a family in the home they had once planned to share.

He listened to the sounds around him. The scratch of vermin and the groans of the sick and dying had become as familiar as the creak of the ship's timbers. At least he no longer had to struggle to sit up, for the water no longer reached his waist as it had whenever they had entered stormy seas. That was when the claustrophobia had really hit him, for it was pitch-black down here, and as the water rose higher and the ship tossed and rolled, he had been overwhelmed by a fear so great he'd lost all control. But his screams had been ignored along with all the others. It seemed no one cared if they drowned. The owners of the ships had already been paid well, and it mattered to no one if their cargo perished.

He was about to close his eyes again and prepare for the welcome sleep of death when he noticed something. The *Surprise* was no longer sailing. She was rocking gently as if in shallow water, and he could hear the shouts of men and the creak of oars.

Jack raised himself painfully on one elbow and listened hard. A flicker of hope ignited deep within him.

Port Jackson, 26 June 1790

The ships had been sighted off the point a few weeks after the arrival and hasty departure of the *Lady Juliana*, and as the men and women of the colony gathered once more on the shore, they dared not hope that this really was the Second Fleet, and that salvation had come at last.

Billy had begged Gilbert to let him join the flotilla of small boats Governor Phillip ordered out to meet the *Neptune*; now he and five other men were rowing towards the fleet. His mouth was watering at the thought of the food she would have brought with her, for it seemed they were, at last, to be saved from starvation. Perhaps Ezra's God really did exist.

They were about to ship their oars when the call came from the governor to return to shore. He was tempted to ignore it. They were so close, almost bumping the side of the *Neptune* – but he caught Gilbert's eye and realised something was seriously wrong: the man's face was waxen.

They returned to shore, their curiosity piqued, disappointment sharp in their hollow bellies. They waited, muttering and impatient, by the makeshift dock that had been convict-built shortly after their arrival. It was small and inadequate, but the waters in the bay were deep enough for the ships to come in close.

'What's the matter?' he asked Gilbert.

Gilbert mopped his mouth with a handkerchief. He'd been sick, and there were splashes of it on his worn boots. 'I've fought campaigns all over the Empire, but I've never seen such a terrible thing,' he managed. His eyes were bloodshot as they met Billy's. 'It's a death fleet,' he gasped. 'The holds are full of the dead and dying, chained together, starved and riddled with every disease known to man.'

Billy's belly squirmed. He had experienced and survived life in the holds, and was far more interested in when the supplies would be brought ashore. 'What about the provisions?'

Gilbert's shoulders slumped. 'The supply ship, *Guardian*, foundered and was lost,' he said, voice low, stance that of a defeated man. 'The *Scarborough* and *Justinian* are carrying some supplies, but not nearly enough, with so many new arrivals.' He sighed. 'Governor Phillip has ordered them to stand off until the three convict ships are unloaded. We don't want to risk looting.'

'How many are expected?' Billy shielded his eyes against the sun's glare and watched as the five ships slowly approached the land and dropped anchor.

'One thousand and seventeen convicts, plus the crews.'

Billy swore. 'It'll make my job even more difficult. It's hard enough to keep the thieving bastards out of the stores as it is, without even more of them wanting a decent meal.'

'They'll be needing more than food,' replied Gilbert, squaring his shoulders. 'We'll have to have shelter for them and medicine. See to it, Billy, and look lively. The first are about to be brought ashore.'

Billy looked back at Gilbert, who stood on the small wooden jetty, feet firmly planted, hands clasped behind his back. He seemed determined not to show the depths of his despair and outrage, but Billy saw how his benefactor stiffened his spine as the *Surprise* dropped anchor. The irony of its name hadn't escaped either man, and Billy could tell, even from this distance, that she suffered from water seepage – and in the tropical heat of Port Jackson the stench of death, of stagnant bilge water, rotting timbers and human waste was indescribable.

He looked across at the governor and saw the same shame and disgust in Phillip's eyes as he signalled to Gilbert that they were to be the first to board the *Surprise*. With the bile rising like acid in his throat, Billy could only imagine the sight that would greet them, and when the hatch was thrown back, the stench almost knocked him over. He was about to turn away when the governor's voice rang out.

'Get these prisoners ashore immediately,' roared Phillip to the sailors, who were busy leering and cat-calling to the women on shore. 'Where are the surgeon and the commander? By God, I'll have them flogged for this dereliction of duty.'

As Billy watched, the governor stormed off the *Surprise* and headed for the *Neptune*.

'I'm going to kick backsides and the commander of the fleet's will be first,' Arthur Phillip roared.

Jack Quince felt the manacles fall away, but was too weak to get to his feet. He struggled for a moment, then relaxed as a pair of strong arms lifted him from the filth of the ship's bottom and carried him up into the fresh air. The sunlight was blinding and he buried his face in his hands, but the delicious scent of growing things was in the air and he breathed it in deeply. He could smell grass and hay, horses, dogs, sheep and cattle, and for a moment he wondered if he'd been rescued at all; perhaps death had taken him home to Sussex.

He was only partially aware of being carried ashore, and as his eyes adjusted to the light he saw rough wooden buildings, a forest of tents, a church and even a herd of cows grazing in a field. This was not Sussex, he realised, for the sun blazed too hotly from a bleached sky and the earth was the darkest blood red.

He must have fainted, for now he could feel a cool cloth on his face and soothing cream being smeared on the open wounds that covered his body. 'Here yer go,' said the female voice. 'Take a drink of this and you'll feel better.'

Jack Quince gulped the cool water, then looked up into a pair of blue eyes. 'Am I in heaven?' he said, only half joking, his voice sounding strange to him after the months of silence.

'Far from it.' The lips moved in a ghost of a smile. 'But it ain't the hell you've come from, that's for certain.'

Jack took another long drink of water and had to rest as his stomach rebelled. He knew it was important to let it settle, and he could already feel it bringing life to him. She waited until he was ready, then gave him a bowl of bread and milk. He chewed slowly, relishing the taste and feel of it in his mouth, but wincing as the hard crust caught loose teeth and scratched his rotting gums.

'My name's Jack Quince,' he said, as she was about to turn away. 'What's yours?'

'Nell,' she replied, giving him a smile of such sweetness he felt warmed. 'See you later, Jack.'

Susan couldn't believe what she was seeing. The bodies of men, women and children were being thrown overboard from the *Neptune* and the *Scarborough*. She watched the barely living emerge from the holds on their hands and knees, too weak to walk, too cowed to speak. Some died as they reached the sunlight, others merely lay on the deck waiting to be carried ashore. The marks of the lash striped flesh that was stretched over ribs and spines, and on wrists and ankles she could see the white of bone where manacles had cut deep.

'Oh, dear God,' she breathed, as the stench reached her. She covered her mouth and nose with a handkerchief.

'God won't 'elp those poor souls,' said the familiar rough voice. 'Come on, Susan, we've work to do.'

'You're right,' muttered Susan, as she fought nausea and rolled up her sleeves. 'Lead on.' She followed Billy's girl as she went along the beach towards the infirmary tents and make-shift mortuary.

The stench was appalling as the dead were piled up to await burial in the deep pit that some of the convicts were already digging – but she saw how they and the soldiers worked together to free the men and women from the holds, and rushed to help them carry those who couldn't walk, and give water to the dying. Billy was rapping out orders like a sergeant major as more tents were erected, and a hunting party was sent into the bush to look for kangaroo and wallaby, while milk was taken from the cows and goats to give to the children.

As she worked on through the day she heard that the food

had been brought ashore from the supply ships, and locked away under armed guard. There was no fighting among the settlers and convicts, only quiet desperation among the survivors of the First Fleet to save as many as possible from the Second.

Susan worked alongside the others far into the night. They had stopped only to say prayers over the mass grave Billy had helped to dig, and now she was on the point of collapse. Weak from lack of food, bowed with heat and the terrible things she was asked to do by the surgeon, she carried on willingly. At last she felt she was doing some good.

She moved from convict to convict, cleaning their wounds of maggots, giving them food and water. Her disgust for those who had perpetrated such heinous crimes against helpless men, women and children was so great she could barely contain it. In all her years she had never seen such inhumanity or degradation. It was as if God had deserted those most in need of His help.

As dawn lightened the sky, she was sent to the women's tent. The sight that greeted her was just as appalling. The women who'd sailed in the *Neptune* had fared as badly as the men. The sailors had shown little compassion for the weaker sex, for they were skin and bone, hollow-eyed and aged before their time. Most, she guessed, wouldn't last more than a few hours.

Susan filled a large bowl with hot water from the stove, picked up the last clean towel and walked to the first straw pallet. It was difficult to gauge how old the woman was, for her face was the colour of tallow, and her hair was a matted net of lice and filth. She began to wash her face and neck, noting the bruises on her arms and ribs. There was little doubt she had been beaten quite recently for they were still black.

The woman didn't open her eyes as Susan rolled her on to her side to wash her back. Neither did she react as the warm water ran over the welts the cat o' nine tails had left. Susan bit her lip. She wouldn't cry. But what had they done to this poor soul?

She rolled her back and peeled the filthy, lice-ridden rags from the wasted body. Throwing them into the corner where a pile waited to be burnt, she pulled the clean, crisp sheet over the woman and hoped she could feel comforted by it.

She was about to turn away when bony fingers grasped her wrist. 'Thank you.' It was a whisper, barely heard above the surrounding noise.

Susan looked into brown eyes that still blazed with their owner's desire to survive despite all that must have happened to her. 'I'm sorry I can't do more,' she replied, taking the hand and holding it.

'It's enough.' The ghost of a smile played on the ulcerated lips. 'At least I was one of the lucky ones.'

Susan stared down at her. 'How old are you?' she asked.

'Nineteen.' The pale eyelids fluttered and the girl fell into a deep sleep.

Susan watched her for a minute, the pity in her heart so intense she thought it would break. The girl was young enough to be her daughter, was only two years older than Ernest. She tucked the clean sheet carefully over the naked shoulders and moved away. Others needed her help, but she vowed she would return to the girl, for something about her spirit had touched her.

Billy had done all that Gilbert had asked of him and more. He had sorted out the tents, rationed the stores from the warehouse, organised the hunting party, then fetched and carried for the women and the surgeons, who had been kept busy all day and night. Now he was sitting with Gilbert and Ezra on the banks of the river, sharing a tot of rum as they watched the sunrise. It no longer seemed to matter that their social standing was at odds for the events of the day had blurred the lines.

They were simply three exhausted men trying to come to terms with what they'd witnessed.

'Two hundred and seventy-eight dead,' muttered Gilbert, 'and there will be more before this new day is over.'

'Someone must be punished,' said Ezra. 'I thought there were safeguards against such things happening.'

Gilbert took a deep draught of his rum. 'There are when the Royal Navy is in charge, but this convict fleet was in the hands of privateers. The officers' inefficiency and ignorance, and the lack of direct responsibility, meant that at sea the convicts were at the mercy of the crews. With little or no communication between those in charge of the prisoners' welfare, and crews dragooned from taverns and slums, disaster was assured.'

'I wager no one will be charged,' growled Billy. 'Convicts are of little importance to governments.'

'That's where you're wrong, William,' said Gilbert. 'I will make it my personal responsibility to call for an inquest into the treatment of these convicts on the return of the ships to England. Charges will be laid against the ships' masters and their surgeons for their heinous neglect of those in their care.'

Billy stared out beyond the harbour to the open sea. He had little doubt that Gilbert would do as he said for he was a man of his word. But he suspected there would never be a trial, and that most of the perpetrators would disappear before they were made to face justice for their wrong-doing.

15

Sydney Cove, November 1790

Ezra was struggling to write his sermon, but the words wouldn't come and his thoughts wouldn't allow him to concentrate. The rough table and bench had been placed outside the house on a knoll that overlooked the water. A breeze flapped the papers on the table and riffled through the pages of the Bible as if to remind him of his duty.

He stared out over the water, his thoughts on Susan. He had been coldly polite and almost dismissive of her, despite the strength of character she had shown during the past two and a half years of hardship. Her work with the sick and dying had been tireless, and although they had all had to suffer the terrible conditions of this new colony, she had never once faltered in her duty. He bit his lip as he remembered the many times he had caught her watching him with those sad blue eyes. She had tried so hard to make him forget, and now she was talking of leaving with the children on the next ship.

Despite his stubborn inability to forget what she had done, he knew that if she left him he would be finished. What was the point of preaching to the convicts of love and forgiveness, of the sanctity of marriage and a Christian way of life, when his own household was in turmoil? He was being unfaithful to God and the message he had been chosen to spread, and his own weakness kept them apart. He had to find the strength and courage to begin again – to have faith and trust in his wife.

He was startled from his thoughts by Gilbert's voice. 'I have surprising news, old boy.' The bench groaned and shuddered as he sat down next to Ezra and waved a letter.

The arrival of the Second Fleet and the ships that followed had brought news of the French Revolution and the return to health of King George. But it was letters from home that every colonist longed for and they had been pored over and treasured as if a little piece of England had found its way to the other side of the world.

Ezra put down the quill and leant his arms on the table, relieved to have a moment's respite from his troubles. Gilbert's moustache was finer than ever, his manner as bluff despite his loss of weight, but he had more than proved his filial loyalty over the past years and they had grown fond of one another. 'I can see you're positively bursting to tell me,' he said.

Gilbert smoothed his moustache with a finger and tried not to look too excited. 'You are now in the presence of the Earl of Glamorgan.'

Ezra stared at him. 'But that means James must be dead.'

'Quite so,' Gilbert muttered. 'Poor chap had a seizure in the middle of his speech in the House of Lords. Dead before he hit the floor.'

Trust Gilbert to be so blunt, thought Ezra, but neither of them had liked their elder brother very much. He had always been a pompous ass. He dismissed his unchristian thoughts as petty in the light of such news. 'His poor wife and daughters,' he murmured. 'It must have been a terrible shock.'

'Evidently not.' Gilbert handed him the letter. 'His wife says he'd been unwell for some time, and that he'd ignored advice to take less of the rich food and wine he was so fond of.' He sighed. 'The girls have married well, and Charlotte has been left comfortably off. But the grandchildren are all female, which means I'm next in line.'

Ezra couldn't imagine life without his brother after the past years of closeness, and his spirits plummeted. 'You'll have to return to England?'

'On the next ship.' Gilbert clamped a hand on Ezra's arm. 'Sorry to leave you like this, old chap, but it can't be avoided.' He couldn't remain serious for long and his wide smile showed the boyish enthusiasm he still possessed despite his fifty-three years. 'Ann is beside herself,' he confided, 'already making plans to redecorate the ancestral pile so she can throw lavish parties. It's a good thing there's money to accompany the earldom, or I'd be bankrupt within a year.'

Ezra smiled. 'She's a good woman,' he said, 'and she's been the making of you, Gilbert.'

Gilbert twirled his moustache as he stared out over the water, deep in thought. 'So is Susan,' he said. He turned to his brother. 'Don't you think she's earned warmer regard from you, Ezra?' he asked, softly for once.

Now it was Ezra's turn to stare at the view, for although his brother's words had echoed his own thoughts, he was still unable to extinguish the pain of her betrayal. It pierced him now, like a knife cutting deep to his heart. 'I have tried, but every time I look at her I see him.' He blinked rapidly, determined not to expose the full extent of the loneliness that rang hollow within him.

' "He that is without sin must cast the first stone." None of us is perfect, Ezra.'

' "To err is human, to forgive divine." ' He looked up at his brother. 'It's time to put into practice what I preach, isn't it?'

Gilbert nodded. 'Don't risk losing her through pride and obstinacy. Your marriage is worth more than that.' He sighed. 'Your children are growing, Ezra. Ernest left a while ago, George has just followed and Florence will marry soon. You and Susan will be on your own. Don't let bitterness destroy your final years together.' He squeezed Ezra's shoulder, then turned and walked away.

Ezra watched his brother go towards the town, shoulders squared, head high, spine straight. Gilbert would always walk as a soldier, no matter how many years passed, and he was delighted his brother had the opportunity to return home. But he would miss his company, and his uncritical advice – his bluffness and friendship.

He looked back at the sea. Gilbert was right. It was time to put the past behind them and begin again – if that was what Susan wanted. He gathered his papers together, tucked the Bible under his arm and headed for the church. He needed to pray for guidance in this most important quest.

Susan had realised quickly that Florence disapproved of her burgeoning friendship with the convict girl, and was equally shamed by Billy's choice of Nell as a partner. There was a great deal of anger in her daughter, which was understandable considering the conditions they were living in – but it didn't explain the child's hostility towards her.

She tried not to fret about it as she hoisted the covered basket over her arm and walked towards the infirmary tents. Her work with the convicts and her kinship with Billy had become a talking-point among the officers' wives in their small community, and perhaps Florence was concerned they might affect her chance of making a good marriage.

She passed the government store and waved to Billy and Nell, who were snatching a few minutes together by the wash-tubs. But then, turning, she saw an officer's wife ahead of her deliberately ignoring Florence. The sight of her daughter being snubbed by this woman made her seethe. To be ostracised because of family ties and Susan's compassion for the convicts was intolerable. She would have to offer Florence guidance on how to rise above such prejudice.

Susan hurried to catch up with her. 'Florence, ignore her,' she said, as she put an arm round her shoulders. 'She's a silly woman with nothing better to do than adopt airs and graces. Keep your dignity, and don't rise to the bait.'

'I need to speak with you,' Florence said brusquely.

Susan was stung by the contempt in her daughter's eyes. 'Whatever's wrong, my dear?' She resisted the girl's attempt to draw her away from the infirmary tent. 'Tell me.'

'You're needed at home,' said Florence, words clipped, eyes flashing with fury. 'I shouldn't have to remind you that your duty is to Papa, not the convicts.'

'How dare you speak to me like that?' snapped Susan. 'If you can't be civil, then leave me to my work.'

'You must prefer the society of convicts to that of your family.'

'Not at all.' Susan sighed. 'But you and your father are capable of looking after yourselves. Those poor souls need me.' Susan looked at her daughter, noting the bitter eyes, the narrow mouth and spiteful expression. There was something disquieting about Florence's demeanour. She wondered fleetingly if something else had given rise to her bitterness – surely it couldn't stem from the woman's snub and Susan's work with the convicts. 'You must learn to be compassionate, Florence,' she said sadly. 'We all have our cross to bear, my dear, but it's the way we carry it that determines our path in life.'

Florence frowned.

'We might not have much in the way of material comfort, but compared to others we are rich,' Susan added. 'Why don't you try to find a modicum of the Christian kindness your father and I tried to teach you, Florence?'

'I have no wish to,' she replied. 'The convicts have brought this upon themselves. They're dirty, uncouth, Godless and idle. Why should I show them anything but contempt?'

Susan lost patience. 'Because you are your father's daughter and with every word you utter you trample his beliefs into the dust.' She grasped Florence's arm and, ignoring her protests, bustled her into the women's infirmary tent and to the bed in the far corner. 'Sit down,' she ordered, 'and don't dare to move until I say you may.'

Florence glowered as she folded her arms, but she was evidently in awe of her mother's unusual stance for she had obeyed instantly.

Susan perched on the edge of the bed and took the convict girl's hand. 'I've brought you a visitor,' she said quietly. 'This is my daughter. Remember I told you about her? I'd like you to explain to her how you came to be in that ship.' Their eyes met and Susan encouraged her with a smile.

'I have no wish to listen to her,' Florence muttered. 'If only a quarter of the tales were to be believed, the convict ships carried only innocent passengers.'

Susan looked at her sternly. 'You will listen,' she said evenly, 'and you will do so with grace.'

They glared at one another.

Susan turned back to the convict girl. 'I know you find it hard to speak of what happened, but will you do this for me? Start at the beginning. Then there will be no doubt as to the truth of your story.'

The girl gripped Susan's hand as her gaze darted between mother and daughter. 'I was a maid in a big house,' she began. 'I liked it there until the master came home without his wife.' She paused. 'He was drunk one night and took advantage of me. I was very frightened, but I couldn't tell anyone because he would have had me dismissed with no hope of finding another position.'

Susan maintained her hold on the girl's fingers and watched Florence's reaction as the story unfolded. Her expression was blank, and Susan noted her cynical sneer. Her daughter seemed determined to remain aloof.

'Really, Mother,' Florence said, 'how could you be taken in by such a hackneyed tale?'

'Just listen, Florence. It will become clear soon enough,' replied Susan. She squeezed the convict girl's fingers. 'Go on, my dear. It's important you finish.'

The girl clung to Susan's hand. 'I discovered I was with child. I didn't know what to do. I had nowhere to go, and no one to turn to. I managed to hide it for a few months, but then the cook found out and gave me notice to leave.'

Her voice gathered strength. 'I told her what the master did. I wanted her to know none of it had been my fault.' She plucked at the sheet. 'He paid me two guineas to keep quiet and sent me away.'

Susan noted how Florence's gaze moved from the canvas and fixed on the girl in the bed. 'What happened then?' she asked.

'I went home, but my father had been killed in the quarry and my stepmother refused to take me in. Most of the money was stolen. No one would hire me in my condition, and I had to live on the streets, begging for scraps and sleeping in doorways. I could have sold myself, but I had to hold on to the little pride I had left.'

The girl's brown eyes regarded Florence steadily. 'But pride doesn't fill your belly when you haven't eaten for days, and I began to steal food. I was caught with a loaf of bread and thrown into prison. My baby was born too soon and died. For that I'm grateful. It meant she didn't have to suffer.'

Susan saw Florence's rigid posture relax, and knew she had begun to understand. There was even a glimmer of compassion in her eyes that made Susan want to hug her – but the girl was still speaking.

'I was put on the *Neptune* with the other women. We were used by the sailors, then beaten and starved. When we docked somewhere in the tropics, and the men from the slave ship boarded the *Neptune*, it was worse.' She closed her eyes, tears seeping through the lashes and down her pale cheeks.

Susan stroked her hair soothingly. 'It's all over, my dear.

You're safe now. Just concentrate on getting your strength back.' She looked at Florence, knowing the question that was burning in her mind.

Florence sat forward in her chair. 'What's your name?' Her voice was small in the silence.

The girl opened her eyes. 'Millicent Parker.'

Susan realised that Florence was stunned by the girl's revelation, but her daughter's demeanour made plain that this was not the time to discuss it. They walked home in silence. She had been harsh with Florence, but it had been a salutary lesson, and she hoped some good would come of it.

She wondered if she and Florence would ever be close. Their relationship had started badly: when she had been born, Susan had still been grieving for little Thomas. Florence had screamed when she had tried to hold her, stiffened in her arms and pushed her away. It was as if she had known Susan hadn't wanted another baby so soon. Perhaps that was why she had turned instinctively to her father.

Susan tamped down her meandering, troubled thoughts. She would probably never understand completely. She turned her thoughts to Millicent – another troubled girl, who was innocent of blame. It had come as a terrible shock to discover who she was and the part Jonathan had played in her downfall. The man she had loved with such passion had betrayed them both.

Ezra was waiting by the door when they returned home. Susan noticed that he barely acknowledged Florence's warm greeting, and her face crumpled in disappointment. Poor Florence. She was too old to worship her father. It was time for her to find a husband.

Ezra stepped forward and held out his hand. 'Susan,' he began, his voice low but laced with urgency, 'will you walk with me for a while?'

Susan paused in untying her bonnet ribbons. Her gaze was steady as she searched his face for some sign of his thoughts. Ezra rarely sought her company, these days, and his sudden invitation worried her. 'I was about to prepare supper,' she said, with unusual hesitancy.

'Florence can do that,' he replied, with the carelessness of a man who knew his daughter would do his bidding without question. 'Come, Susan. I wish to talk to you.'

Susan retied the ribbons and tucked her hand into the crook of his arm. 'This sounds serious,' she said, in an attempt to make light of her anxiety.

He remained silent as they walked away from the house and down the knoll to the water's edge. The trees there were slender eucalyptus, with pale green leaves and silver bark. Their shade was dappled as it fell on the bank and lush reeds where the black swans had their nests and the white ibis strutted. 'This is my favourite walk at the end of the day,' he said.

'It's very pleasant,' she replied, her thoughts in a whirl. Was Ezra about to send her home to England? Had he decided their marriage was indeed a sham? Or was this an attempt at reconciliation? She prayed it was the latter: she had waited so long for things to be right between them.

They reached the bend in the river and now the house was out of sight. Susan was tempted to glance over her shoulder for she could have sworn she felt Florence's eyes on them. Resisting the urge, she tried to pretend that this was a normal, everyday occurrence, that walking alongside the river at the end of the day was something she and her husband did regularly. How lovely if that were true, she thought sadly.

She shot a sideways glance at his face, wondering at the reason for this unusual closeness. He'd aged, she saw. The black hair was liberally streaked with grey, the nose had drooped and deep lines were etched round his eyes and mouth. He worked too hard, cared too much for the people in his charge. Yet the way he carried himself showed his strength of character, and his belief in his mission. How could she ever have doubted she loved him?

Ezra came to a standstill and took her hands. 'Susan, there are many things I wish to say to you, but first I have some news that may affect us all.'

His expression was serious. This didn't bode well. 'What is it, my dear?' she asked, with a calm that hid her inner turmoil.

Ezra told her of his brother's death and Gilbert's imminent departure for England, and she sighed with relief that was tinged with sadness. She would miss Ann for they had become as close as sisters over the past few years.

'I promised when we arrived that I would send the children home if that was what they wished. It's time to fulfil that promise, Susan.'

So it wasn't to be a reconciliation. She swallowed her disappointment, drew her hands from his and clasped them at her waist. 'The boys are happy here, but Florence would be better suited to life in England. She has never settled and it's a tough life for a young girl – not one I would have chosen for her.'

Ezra nodded thoughtfully. 'Gilbert and Ann could certainly offer her more suitable surroundings and a better chance of marrying well. I'll speak to her later.' He reached once more for her hands and clasped them tightly. 'And you, Susan? Do you wish to return to England?'

She had a sudden vision of Cornwall, of soft rain and green grass, of gentle rolling hills, wide beaches and craggy cliffs, of creatures that didn't sting or bite, were not deadly poisonous, of clean clothes and soft beds, polite society away from this convict outpost where savages threatened their lives. She remembered stone churches, choirs singing by candlelight at evensong, and the deep peace of Sunday mornings in the company of her family.

She looked back at him, ready to accept, but something in his expression made her hesitate, and she found she couldn't speak the words that would free her from this awful place – not while there was hope for her marriage. 'My place is with you,' she murmured. 'Wherever that may be.'

His dark eyes held hers, and his fingers tightened. 'Susan,' he began, 'I ask for your forgiveness.' He shook his head to silence her protest. 'Please, let me finish.' He took a deep breath. 'I have wronged you through my own weakness. I have sought to punish you with coldness when it was clear you didn't deserve it.' He fell to his knees before her, eyes burning with entreaty. 'Will you forgive this weak and lonely man who adores you? Will you be my wife again?'

She saw the love and hope in his face and joined him on her knees. Taking his anxious face in her hands, she looked deep into his dark eyes, and ran her thumbs down his cheeks. Then she kissed his lips and tried to convey that she loved him, that there was nothing to forgive, that she had always been his wife and would remain by his side until death parted them.

A long while later they returned, arm in arm, to the house. Florence was busy in the kitchen, the smell of kangaroo stew in the air as the mosquitoes whined and night fell. Her expression was sour as Ezra greeted her cheerfully. 'Your mother and I have reached a closer understanding, and we wanted you to be the first to know.'

'Congratulations,' she said stiffly.

Susan noticed her lack of enthusiasm and was puzzled. Surely she should be pleased at their reconciliation.

Ezra carried on, evidently unaware of his daughter's tension in the light of his happiness. 'We have also agreed to add several more rooms to our little home, and to employ a maid.' He beamed. 'But we have other news that is even more exciting.' He hugged Susan, and they smiled into each other's eyes before he went on to tell Florence about Gilbert. 'I promised your mother I would give you children a chance to return home, should you wish it. It has taken rather longer than expected because of the delay in the arrival of the Second Fleet, and although I'm assured the boys won't wish to leave, I mean to keep that promise.' He paused. 'Florence, my dear, do you wish to return home with Ann and Gilbert?'

Susan watched differing expressions flit across her daughter's face as she digested the impact of Ezra's offer. The same memories and longings were no doubt sweeping through her as they had through Susan, but would she accept? Susan was torn between wanting the best for Florence and the knowledge that if she left, she would probably never see her daughter again. It was an impossible choice.

Florence rose from the table and went to Ezra. 'My place is with you,' she said, unwittingly echoing Susan's words.

Susan was stunned. 'But you'd have all the advantages of life with Ann and Gilbert!' she cried. 'You'd live in luxury, mix with the highest in society and have your choice of the most eligible young men.' She struggled to control herself. 'Florence,' she said, 'you haven't thought it through.'

'I have no wish to be paraded on the marriage market like prize livestock,' she retorted.

Susan grasped her hands, willing her to see sense. 'Florence, you have always hated being here. I thought you'd leap at the chance to return home.'

Florence drew back and turned to Ezra. 'A year ago I would have done,' she said, 'but I believe my life will be put to better purpose here.' She smiled. 'I have decided to dedicate my life to God, and what better place than here to do His work?'

'Don't be ridiculous,' snapped Susan. 'You're far too young to make such a sweeping declaration without thinking long and hard about what it might mean for your future.'

'Not at all,' Florence retorted. 'God has spoken to me and shown me where I am most needed.'

Susan could hardly believe what she had heard. She was about to protest but her daughter went on, 'His message must be passed to the Godless and wanton souls who live in this place – and with your help, Father, I mean to bring them the light of His love.'

Susan was speechless. She was shocked by how swiftly Florence had turned down the opportunity to escape when it had been clear to everyone that she hated life here. Whence this sudden missionary zeal? The girl had shown little sign of it before now.

She looked to Ezra for guidance, silently urging him to make Florence see sense. But his joyful expression told her the battle was already lost.

PART FOUR

Changes of Fortune

16

The Hawkesbury River, February 1791

The heat danced in waves across the land, blurring the horizon, drowning the trees in shimmering, shifting light. Black swans drifted regally on the waters of the Hawkesbury river, and the chatter of brightly coloured parrots was punctuated by the mournful caw of crows and the raucous laughter of kookaburras.

A warm breeze sifted through the acres of wheat, making it sway in ripples of gold beneath a clear, dazzlingly blue sky. Ernest worked beside his sixteen-year-old brother as they swung their scythes and gathered the wheat into sheaves. The sweat stung his eyes and soaked his shirt, his hands were calloused, the nails ingrained with dirt, but he'd never felt so invigorated, and couldn't help grinning at George as they reaped their first harvest. Contrary to all expectations, it looked as if they had tamed this wild, unforgiving land and had achieved success where others had failed.

They reached the end of the field and paused in the shade of the remaining stand of eucalyptus. Ernest eased his aching muscles and tugged his sodden shirt out of his trousers, leaving the tail to flap in the breeze. He watched George do the same, for neither worked bare-chested any more: they had suffered from sunburn and lost days of labour. Each wore a broad-brimmed hat, loosely woven linen trousers and sturdy boots; their hair had been left to grow beyond their shoulders.

Ernest pulled a rueful face. So much for the smart young men about town they had once aspired to become – they had more in common now with the convict labourers in Port Jackson. But he had to admit the clothes were practical and far cooler than those they had brought from England, and as they were living on the edge of civilisation, it didn't matter that they were unkempt.

In fact, he thought, as he took a long drink of cool water from a tin mug, he liked not having to shave and be trussed up in stiff collars and tight jackets. It gave him a sense of freedom that he had never known in Cornwall. Looking back on his childhood, he was reminded of the strictures of society and the numbing boredom of living in such a small community. England and all it represented had taken on a dream-like quality during the past three years, and now it was difficult to believe any reality other than the sheer grandeur of this new country.

He stared out over the land they had cleared and marvelled at what boys of sixteen and eighteen could achieve. This was good, fertile land with promise. A man could make his fortune here if he was willing to work – and George's stamina, despite his youth, matched his own.

Ernest turned away eventually and threw himself down into the tough grass beside his younger brother. The slender trees gave a pleasant shade, and the grass was cool at his back. He stretched out, hands behind his head, long legs crossed at the ankles. 'I could eat a horse,' he said, through a vast yawn.

George dug in the saddle-bag. 'Here's the last of the duck and some bread, and there's a flagon of cold ale.' He apportioned it and they munched as they looked out over their fields, which swept almost to the distant mountains.

The governor had granted land to every free man and woman, and as neither their parents nor their sister wished to farm theirs, the boys had taken it on with their own. For every hundred acres they cleared they would receive a further hundred. There were still three more fields to harvest, but

Ernest was undaunted and already planning the next season's ploughing.

'It's time I found a wife,' he said, as he grimaced at the sourness of the ale. 'At least I'd be fed properly.'

George laughed. 'No woman would have you,' he said cheerfully. 'Besides,' he added, 'what woman in her right mind would want to come and live in that?'

They looked across the field to the rough wooden shack Ernest had erected when he had arrived to take up his land grant. Unlike the governor's fine house, which had been brought complete with glass windows and oak doors on board ship and assembled within weeks, their home had been hewn from the surrounding trees, the chimney made from the large stones they had cleared from the land. The remains of a canvas sail formed a roof and the floor was hard-packed earth. It had one room, no windows and a piece of sacking as the door. The furniture consisted of wood and canvas beds, chairs and a roughly hewn table with legs of differing lengths.

'You're right,' said Ernest. 'We'll have to improve it and we should ask Mother to teach us to cook. It may be years before any woman will want to live with either of us.' He got to his feet and dusted off his clothes. 'Come on, let's finish this field, then walk the acreage down-river and plan what to do with it.'

They worked in silent concentration until the field was harvested, then stood and admired the neat sheaves that glowed in the last golden rays of the sun. Ernest pushed back his hat and mopped his brow; his fair hair was dark with sweat and clung to his scalp. 'A good day's work,' he murmured.

'Not bad,' said George. 'It beats playing croquet with giggling girls.'

'Oh, I don't know,' Ernest mused. 'I used to be quite good at croquet.'

George dug him in the ribs. 'Good at putting your arms

round the girls and whispering in their ears,' he teased. 'Come on, I'll race you to the water.'

Ernest chased after him and they plunged into the cool, fast-flowing river, yelling and splashing, their weariness forgotten in the sheer joy of knowing they had achieved much through their labour. Their muscled backs and strong arms gleamed as they washed away the sweat and filth, then wallowed in the shallows. They eventually waded out and began to stroll further down-river to examine the parcel of land that Gilbert and Ann had given them.

It was good and fertile, as all the land was around this great river. Heavily timbered, it would take a great deal of clearing, but the promise of good crops and excellent grazing for cattle was enough to spur a man on.

'We still haven't thought of a name for this place,' said Ernest.

'Mmm.' George's hands were deep in his pockets. 'I suppose we should,' he said. 'Have you any ideas?'

'I thought of calling it Mousehole, but so few people know how to pronounce it the Cornish way – Muzzle – that it would defeat the objective.' He walked on for a few moments in silence. 'What about Hawks Head Farm?'

George nodded, dark hair glinting almost blue in the sun. 'Sounds good to me. Hardly Cornish, though.'

'I know, but Cornwall's another life now, isn't it? We have to embrace this new country and as we're on the Hawkesbury river it seemed appropriate.'

'Hawks Head Farm it is, then. I'll make a sign tomorrow.'

They walked along the river and slowly paced out the acreage that would soon come to them. 'It's a pity the convicts aren't allowed to work for us,' said George. 'We'd get things done twice as quickly.'

'You're right. We need them on the land, and I'm sure we aren't the only ones willing to pay them a wage.'

'Something has to be done,' agreed George, as he surveyed the acres of scrub and thick tangle of trees they would soon have to clear. 'The colony's growing all the time and there isn't enough food.'

It was a keenly argued dilemma, but one with little chance of being solved without a radical change in the colony's laws. They fell to discussing their plans for the following day.

Then they froze.

'What was that?'

Ernest listened hard, alert for danger. The Cadigal and Eora people had so far caused them no trouble, but they had known they were watched and followed – had heard stories of other farmers being speared as the settlers moved further inland and up the coast. It was probably only a matter of time before they met the same fate, and he cursed his carelessness at having left their rifles in the shack.

George nodded towards the primitive fishing-tackle and dug-out canoes, then caught movement in the grass further up the riverbank. He pointed and mouthed, 'Over there.'

They approached the spot until they could see what lay hidden in the long grass.

The girl was as black as night, and as naked as Eve. Ernest guessed she was about sixteen, and she lay in the long grass, burrowing deeply into the meagre shelter, the tears flowing as she watched them approach. A terrible keening came from her slender throat as her eyes pleaded with them not to harm her.

'Looks like she's had the smallpox,' Ernest muttered, as he noted the swollen knees and elbows, the pocked skin and the weakness of her movement, 'which would explain why she couldn't run away when she heard us. The poor girl's terrified.'

'But she's not alone,' replied George. 'There were two canoes down there, with the fishing-tackle.' He looked around warily. 'We must be careful.'

'We can't leave her here,' retorted Ernest. 'She's in pain and unable to fend for herself. Her friends who were fishing with her are probably miles away by now.' He squatted beside her and noted how she shrank from him when he raised his hand to comfort her. She was slender, the swelling of her joints making her limbs appear even more fragile. 'Don't be frightened,' he said softly, as if to a small child. 'We shall not hurt you.'

Her amber eyes glistened with tears as she curled into a tight ball like a cornered animal.

Ernest peeled off his shirt. It had dried since his swim, and it was the only thing he had to warm her now that the sun was almost lost behind the hills. 'We should take her to the house,' he murmured, 'but that would only frighten her even more.'

'*Baa-do*,' she whimpered. '*Baa-do.*'

'What is she saying?'

'I don't know,' replied Ernest. 'But we need to light a fire so we can cook the fish she's caught and keep her warm.'

George hurried back to their shack and soon returned with the rifles, an armful of firewood and a tinder-box. Ernest had already prepared a fire-pit, surrounding the shallow hole with rocks he had gathered from the water's edge. Striking the flint against the metal, he coaxed the spark into a flame until it began to devour the dry kindling. With the three large fish skewered on a stick, he placed them over the fire.

As George tended the fish, Ernest went on talking to the girl, trying to calm her fears. Little by little she began to relax. '*Baa-do*,' she whispered again. '*Baa-do.*' At his frown of puzzlement, she stuck out her tongue and ran it over her cracked lips.

Comprehension brought him to his feet. He hurried down to the river and filled his hat with water. Returning to the girl, he helped her to sit and she drank greedily. 'Water,' he explained.

The shadow of a smile flitted across her face. '*Baa-do*,' she said. '*Watta.*'

The sun had disappeared by the time they'd eaten the fish. The brothers collected more kindling and put it close by so that she could replenish the fire during the night, and filled a pot with fresh water so she wouldn't be thirsty. Then they tipped their hats in farewell and turned towards home.

Lowitja emerged from the surrounding scrub. She had been watching from the trees as the young men approached her daughter, and had been poised to spear them should they harm her. She had kept up the vigil as they fed her and gave her water, and realised they were as kind as the woman at the big camp. There was nothing to fear.

She waited until the moon was high, then helped her daughter into the canoe at the river's edge. When she was settled, she approached the strange shelter the boys slept in. She placed the shirt on the ground with some fishing-tackle and a large woven reed bag with three fine fish in it. They would find her gift when they woke, and know that their kindness to her daughter was accepted as a token of friendship.

Port Jackson, April 1791

Billy took great pleasure in knowing that his nemesis, Arthur Mullins, hadn't been given permission to return to England. He was still a bully, his brutality stoked by the quantities of rum he imbibed, but he was stuck here like the rest of them, and Billy's spirits soared to know that Mullins hated every minute. His bullying and perverted pleasure in flogging had made him a loathed figure among the convicts, and Billy was amazed that someone hadn't done away with him long ago.

It was an hour past dawn, and as Billy strode along the dirt road towards the warehouse, he noticed that Mullins was already gathering together his work party of convicts. He unlocked the warehouse and turned in the doorway. Mullins was watching him, bleary eyes full of hatred. Billy smiled and tipped his hat, knowing how Mullins resented his position in the colony and that he could no longer touch him because he was under direct orders from the governor.

The guard clambered out of the straw to greet him as he entered the warehouse, and Billy made a note to have him replaced for night duty. It was no good having someone watching the place who couldn't keep his eyes open, and he was damned if he'd leave the comfort of Nell's arms to sit here all night himself.

He looked round the warehouse and inhaled the delicious, dusty aroma of tea and grain. It was well stocked now that the farms were harvesting their crops, and the arrival of whaling ships and merchantmen had increased the store of much-needed oil and paraffin, flax, soap, rum and shoe leather.

Billy admired the sacks, crates and barrels, then looked at the sturdy walls and tin roof. He'd insisted that the old warehouse was pulled down – it was so dilapidated it wouldn't have stood up to a mouse – and had given strict instructions on how to build this one. He was pleased with the outcome, but the morning ritual still had to be observed.

Vermin, animal and human, had a way of depleting the stores, and although he set traps for the possums and bush rats, he also had to check that there had been no attempt to break through the wooden walls, or burrow beneath them. He knew all the tricks, and checked every item on his inventory as he moved round his kingdom. Guards could be bribed to turn a blind eye; they could also be light-fingered, replacing rum in the barrels with water, and flour in the sacks with soil. He trusted no one.

Eventually satisfied, he made a cup of tea on the camp-stove, ate the biscuits Nell had made the night before, and prepared for the morning rush. The new manager of the government farms was due this morning, and Billy was look-ing forward to meeting him. A convict, like himself, Jack Quince had survived the unspeakable degradation of the *Surprise*. By all accounts he was a proper farmer and knew more about beasts and crops than most people here – although Ernie and George were making a good fist of it out on the Hawkesbury; despite their youth, theirs had become a model farm.

He settled himself comfortably behind the big desk, which gave him an excellent view of what went on outside, and opened the large red book. The cooks would want flour, the laundresses soap, and the weavers flax. Then the cobbler would come for leather and nails, the work-party leaders for tools, and the officers' wives for needles and thread. Each item had to be noted down and signed for, although Billy was self-taught, and his writing resembled a spider's crawl across the page, it gave him no end of satisfaction to know it didn't matter as long as it was legible and everything added up.

He was carefully writing down the number of aprons that had been taken for the women working the looms when he heard Mullins's voice out in the street. He left the account book and sauntered to the door.

Mullins's target was a scrawny man of average height, brown hair streaked with a flash of white above the brow. Dressed in the convict uniform of loose linen trousers and shirt that only served to make him look thinner, he leant heavily on a walking-stick as he stood before Mullins. He didn't flinch as Mullins shouted in his face, merely stood like a patient mule and waited for the other man to finish.

Whoever the man was, Billy admired him – not many could have survived the stench of Mullins's breath without batting an eyelid or dropping in a dead faint. He leant on the door jamb, hands in his pockets, enjoying the entertainment.

Quite a crowd had gathered, he noticed, and even some of

the blacks had crept out of the shadows to watch. They hated Mullins too: he had kidnapped one of their girls and kept her tied to his bed for days before the authorities heard of it and rescued her.

His amusement died when Mullins shoved the man in the chest. But it seemed he was stronger than he looked, for he rapidly regained his balance. Mullins pushed him again, harder this time, making him stumble.

Billy edged from the doorway and took his hands out of his pockets.

Mullins waited for the man to regain his balance, then kicked away the walking-stick.

Billy stepped into the street, his hands clenched and itching to punch the rum-sodden face to a pulp.

The man stumbled as he tried to remain standing on his one good leg. Mullins kicked out again, and his heavy boot connected hard with the shin. His victim cried out and fell to the ground.

As Mullins took three paces back, sized up the target and swung his boot again Billy was already on the move. He caught Mullins with a satisfying right hook. The man swayed, his expression baffled, then hit the ground like a felled tree.

There was a roar of approval from the bystanders, and Billy was almost tempted to take a bow. Turning from Mullins, he helped the other man get painfully to his feet, and was surprised to see that he was much younger than he had thought. He handed him the walking-stick. 'Are you hurt?'

The other man shook his head. 'I'll be all right once I've got my breath back.' He gave Billy a wan smile as he held out his hand. 'Jack Quince. Thank you.'

'Billy Penhalligan. I've been expecting you.' They shook hands, and Jack cast a worried glance at the poleaxed Mullins, who was now being prodded and jeered at by the little crowd. 'Don't worry about him,' Billy said, as he rubbed his sore knuckles. 'I've been waiting to do that for years, and there isn't a man here who won't thank me for it.'

They burst out laughing. 'Well, Jack Quince, I've a nip of rum in the warehouse, and it would be a shame to let it go to waste.'

They spent the morning getting to know each other, and Billy soon discovered that he and the Sussex man had much in common. They were both thirty-four, shared the same sense of humour and quick wit. They also possessed a dogged determination to make the best of things until they received their pardons and became free men. Ties to England had been irrevocably severed, but each knew this could be a land of opportunity for the adventurous and hard-working. With Billy's organisational skills and Jack's knowledge of the land, they could have the best farm in the colony, given half a chance.

By the end of that morning they knew they had made a friendship that would last a lifetime.

17

Port Jackson, September 1791

Billy and Jack had been summoned to Gilbert's office and, having heard of his imminent departure, wondered what was in store for them.

'Who will take over as judge advocate?' asked Jack, as he limped down the broad, dusty road avoiding the bullock carts, horse dung and drunken Aborigines who lay supine where they had fallen. He was still thin, and the walking-stick was a permanent fixture.

Billy dug his hands into the pockets of his trousers, and slowed his pace to match Jack's. His friend had still not fully recovered from his experience on the *Surprise*, and found it difficult to exert himself for any length of time. 'I don't know, but we won't be granted the same privileges of extra rations and sleeping quarters apart from the other convicts.' He laughed. 'But as we're the only ones who can run the government stores and farms efficiently, we'll manage.'

'I'll miss him,' mumbled Jack, as he ran his hand through the shock of white in his hair.

Billy was philosophical. 'So will I, but we'll make the best of it.'

They were shown into Gilbert's office by a junior officer, and their spirits fell. Gilbert glared at them over his spectacles from behind his vast desk. The two friends exchanged a glance. Neither could think what they might have done to anger him.

'I expect you've heard the rumours. Nothing remains secret in this place for long.' Gilbert sat back in his chair, took off his spectacles and began to polish them with a handkerchief. He didn't wait for a reply. 'I would have left months ago if my replacement had arrived on time, but as it is, I am forced to remain here until the end of the month,' he rumbled. 'Before I go I have several important decisions to take.' He peered at them from beneath his bushy brows.

Billy sensed the tension in Jack and heard the scrape of his boots on the wooden floor as he eased his bad hip. 'I'll be sorry to see you go, sir,' he said quickly, 'and so will Jack. You've been good to us.'

'Hmph. That's as may be.' The gimlet eyes fixed on Jack, who was leaning heavily on his walking-stick. 'Jack Quince, you were convicted for stealing the use of a bull and sentenced to fifteen years' hard labour.'

Jack's sharp intake of breath was loud, and Billy saw that his friend had turned even paler than usual. Surely they weren't to be dismissed.

Gilbert went on: 'I have read the court details with unease, and noted the contribution you have made in the colony since your arrival. Your experience of farming has proved invaluable and your conduct has been admirable.' He paused as if aware he held centre stage. 'I therefore grant you a conditional pardon, and thirty acres of land in Parramatta.'

Jack swayed and almost fainted with shock. The walking-stick clattered, unheeded, to the floor. 'Does that mean I'm free?' he asked.

'Not entirely,' admitted Gilbert. 'You must remain in the colony until the original term of your sentence is completed, but you may work your own land and employ others to help you, on the understanding that you will sell any surplus stock or harvest to the government stores.'

Jack slumped into a nearby chair, his face in his hands, his words of thanks barely audible as he struggled to regain his composure.

Billy's spirits rose. He could hardly keep still as he waited to discover what Gilbert had in store for him.

'William Penhalligan,' intoned the upright old soldier, 'you are a scallywag.' His face broke into a smile at Billy's startled expression, and his tone held the warmth of affection. 'But you have proved a reliable and willing master of stores. I feel justified in setting a thief to catch a thief, as you so aptly put it five years ago, and therefore I am granting you, too, a conditional pardon and thirty acres at Parramatta.'

Billy was smiling widely as he thanked him, overwhelmed to have the chance at last to prove his worth. He grabbed Jack, hauled him out of the chair and pulled him to his chest in a bear-hug. 'We've done it, Jack. Now we can do all the things we planned.'

Jack's ashen face flooded with colour. 'We'll have the best farm in Australia,' he averred. 'And now I can write to Alice.'

Billy's smile faltered as Jack's words reminded him he'd forgotten something important. He turned back to Gilbert. 'I have a woman, sir,' he stuttered, 'and there's a child on the way. Is there any chance of a pardon for her too?'

Gilbert pursed his lips and twiddled his moustache. 'Ah,' he intoned, 'the lovely Nell Appleby.' He riffled through his papers and sat in silence as he frowned over Nell's documents.

Billy was in an agony of uncertainty as he tried to read the other man's expression and glean a hint of his thoughts – but the old soldier continued to shuffle papers. Billy was at bursting-point when he spoke again.

'The child, of course, will be a free citizen, but Nell is not due for release for another two years. As she is not your dependant, I cannot grant her a pardon. I'll have all the convicts after me if word gets out that I've favoured your application – and Nell's not a quiet little thing, is she?'

Billy's euphoria was dimmed at the thought of starting his new life without Nell. Her warmth and sensuality had chased away his loneliness, and her humour in adversity and bound-less energy had somehow reaffirmed his own lust for life. He stared at Gilbert in dumb despair.

There was a glint of humour in Gilbert's eyes. 'Of course, if you were to marry her . . .'

There was a moment while Billy digested his words. He and Nell rubbed along well, and he supposed he loved her in his own careless way. But marriage hadn't been thought of, let alone discussed – not even when she had told him she was pregnant.

Gilbert gave a discreet cough and Billy realised he was waiting for an answer. He cleared his throat and ran his sweating palms down his trousers. There was a decision to be made, and as he didn't want to lose Nell and the child . . . 'I'd be happy to marry her, sir,' he said, with rather more dash than he felt.

Gilbert leant back in his chair, eyes crinkling in merriment. 'I'm sure my brother will be delighted to perform the cere-mony, and once that's done I'll have the papers drawn up for Nell's conditional pardon.'

He rose from behind the desk and marched round it to shake both men's hands and give them their precious docu-ments. 'Good luck to both of you,' he said heartily. 'Australia will be a great colony one day, and it is men such as you who will pave the way for generations to come. God speed.'

Nell was spinning flax when Billy crashed into the vast barn and shouted her name above the racket of the weavers' looms. She pushed her hair out of her eyes and laughed with relief. Something good must have happened at the meeting he'd been so anxious about. Ignoring the woman in charge, who was hard-faced with a sharp tongue, she dropped the cleft stick that held the raw flax and ran towards him. 'What is it, Billy?'

He grabbed her by the waist, swung her round until her skirts flew out, and kissed her until she was breathless. 'Will you marry me, Nell?' he roared.

All work stopped and there was silence in the vast barn as the other women waited for her answer. Those had been words she'd thought she'd never hear, and her joy threatened to bring her to uncharacteristic tears. 'Yes!' she squealed. 'Yes, Billy! Yes!' She threw her arms round his neck and kissed him, almost toppling them both to the floor.

'Men aren't allowed in the women's shed,' said a steely voice behind her. 'Your behaviour is inappropriate. I shall report both of you.'

Nell was about to protest roundly, but Billy intervened. 'I've just been granted a conditional pardon, and no longer have to obey your rules,' he said quietly. 'Once we're married, that will also apply to Nell. I suggest you get back to your work and mind your own business.'

A round of applause and a roar of approval came from the other women as she looked askance at the two convicts. Then she pulled herself to her full height and, chin high, turned on her heel and marched back to her table from which she tried without success to restore order.

'That's told 'er,' said Nell, and tossed her head. Then she turned to Billy, hardly daring to believe it was all true. 'Tell me again,' she said, as the looms clacked and the women's voices rose in discussion of the morning's events.

Billy drew her outside and explained what Gilbert had done, and when she could believe at last that it wasn't a dream she stepped into the circle of his arms, knowing she had come home.

Susan and Ezra were delighted with the news, and refused to let Florence spoil the arrangements with her scornful sniping at the bride's lack of pedigree and her condition.

Billy borrowed a suit from Ezra, which was a little tight across the shoulders and had seen better days, and Jack managed to put together an outfit that befitted the best man. They were determined not to wear convict clothes for the ceremony.

Susan had only a day to alter her best dress to fit the buxom Nell, but she sewed through the night and even found time to decorate her Sunday bonnet with a few ribbons to match. Millicent Parker, who had moved into the new extension of their little shack, baked an enormous cake for the occasion.

The ceremony took place early in the morning. Dressed in another woman's clothes, and carrying a bouquet of bright yellow wattle, Nell stood proudly beside Billy as they exchanged their vows and Ezra pronounced them man and wife.

Susan and Millicent cried, Ezra and Jack looked happy, and Florence scowled. Gilbert made a speech, beaming with pleasure at the part he had played in bringing about the day's celebration. He declared they were a handsome couple, and he had every confidence that they would make a success of their future together.

After a splendid tea, Susan leant into Ezra's embrace as they all gathered on the front lawn and watched the newly-weds prepare to depart. Her little brother had come good, and was about to embark on his biggest adventure yet. She decided to write a long letter to her mother so she could share in the joy of the occasion and know her son had turned his back on the old ways.

With their conditional pardons tucked carefully among their meagre belongings, Nell, Billy and Jack climbed into the overloaded wagon. Because of Nell's land grant, they had ninety acres between them, and the governor had given them a couple of goats, a cow, a sow that was about to deliver piglets, chickens and enough supplies to see them through several months. Sacks of seed lay in the back of the wagon with kegs of rum to pay the convict labourers they would soon employ, and all the tools they would need to build a home, clear the land and plant their first crop.

Billy put his arm round Nell. 'Are you ready, my girl?'

'You bet your bum I am,' she said, and kissed his neck.

He winked at Jack and flicked the whip above the horses' ears. It was time to head west and start their new lives.

'What a lovely day,' said Susan, as the cloud of dust settled and the wagon disappeared. She put her arm round Millicent's waist and gave her a hug. 'The cake was delicious,' she said. 'You are a clever girl.'

Millicent blushed. 'It was nothing,' she murmured.

'There's no need to be modest with me, Millie. You're a good cook, and you know it.'

'It was a lovely wedding and I'm so happy for them.'

Susan eyed her fondly. Millicent was still too thin and her hair hadn't yet recovered from the drastic cut she'd had to inflict to rid it of lice, but there was colour in her cheeks and her complexion was clearing. 'You're part of our family now,' she said softly, 'and you will be included in everything we do.'

'How touching,' snapped Florence. 'When can we expect another convict to join us? After all, we have three – what's one more?'

Susan turned to her daughter, furious at her discourtesy. 'Billy is my brother,' she said. 'He's served his time and earned his pardon, just as Nell has. You will apologise, Florence.'

'I'll do no such thing. And I hardly think we should discuss such things before a convict maid.' She shot Millicent a venomous glare.

Susan stayed Millicent's flight by catching her hand. 'There's no convict maid here, Florence, only Millie.' She smiled in an attempt to cajole her out of her ill-temper.

'Come,' she coaxed. 'Don't spoil the day. Just be happy for us all.'

Florence was having none of it. 'How do you expect me to be happy when you fill our home with convicts?'

Susan was determined not to continue the argument. 'Millie has come to live here as a member of the family, not as a maid, and her convict status matters not a jot to me or to your father.' With that, she swept Millicent across the lawn to where the remnants of the wedding party lay scattered on trestle tables.

'I'm sorry, Susan. I didn't mean to cause trouble between you and Florence.'

'It's not your fault. Florence and I have had our differences for a long time, and although it pains me to say so, there are times when she exasperates me beyond reason.'

She looked at the tables and decided they could wait awhile. She sank on to a bench, opened her fan and encouraged Millicent to join her. 'It's too hot to work now.'

Millicent sat beside her, looking troubled. Susan studied the neat little profile with its dimpled cheek and delicate nose, the ragged brown hair that now reached almost to her collar. Millicent must have been pretty before she was put through the horrors of transportation. No wonder Jonathan had been tempted.

The thought chilled her and she turned away to stare out over the water. She must not think of him or of what he had done to them both. She must think only of Millicent and try to right the wrong. She watched the black swans float regally on the tide, and wished that her life was as uncomplicated as theirs.

'I meant what I told you,' she said, some time later. 'Ezra and I love to have you with us. We do not regard you as either a servant or a convict.'

'Thank you,' replied Millicent. Her big dark eyes regarded Susan. 'Are we friends, then?' she asked.

'I'm too old to be your sister, and wouldn't expect you to see me as your mother but, yes, we are friends. Good friends.'

The dimple in Millicent's cheek flashed. 'I never had a friend before,' she said.

Susan stood up and pulled Millicent to her feet. 'Well, you've got one now. Let's see if Gilbert's left any of that wine.'

18

Sydney Cove, October 1792

Millicent had been living with Susan and Ezra for more than a year. Her room was at the side of the newly refurbished and much enlarged house, with views down the hill towards the rapidly growing Sydney Town. There was an iron bedstead covered with a patchwork quilt she and Susan had worked on during the rainy season, a nightstand, chair and pretty curtains at the window. It was all far removed from the austere servants' quarters in Cornwall, and the stifling, cramped cottage in Newlyn, and she felt settled and happy.

As she regarded her reflection in the hand-mirror Susan had lent her she saw she had blossomed. It was her twenty-first birthday and her brown hair was now as glossy as the chestnuts she had collected as a child on autumn mornings in England, and her eyes were no longer shadowed from past experience. In fact, she was almost pretty – which surprised her, for she'd never thought of herself in that way, especially after . . .

She bit her lip, then wondered if she was pretty enough to catch a certain young man's eye today. He had been invited, but that was no guarantee, for he rarely came into Sydney Town now – yet the possibility of seeing him again made her breathless. She put down the mirror and stared through the newly glazed window. 'He probably doesn't remember me,' she murmured.

She turned away and finished dressing, her fingers clumsy as she tied the lacing of her bodice and smoothed the skirt she had finished sewing the previous evening. The material had come on the ships with the officers and men of the newly formed New South Wales Corps, and Susan had shared it with her.

With a last glance in the mirror, she left her bedroom and hurried into the kitchen where she was greeted by the sight of several naked Aboriginal children in the doorway. 'Cheeky little devils,' she said, and smiled, 'but it's hard to resist those big brown eyes.' She turned to Susan. 'Can I give them some of those buns?'

'It's what they've been waiting for,' Susan replied. 'They've been under my feet all day. I wish Lowitja would keep them out of the house, but she seems to think I don't mind running her nursery when she goes walkabout.'

Millicent gave each child two buns and shooed them out. 'We'd better not put anything on the table,' she said. 'They'll eat the lot, given a chance.'

'Ezra encourages them.' Susan took more buns out of the oven and tipped them on to a wire mesh to cool. 'But, then, so do I.' She smiled as she caught sight of Millicent's new outfit, and left a dusting of flour on her forehead as she brushed her hair off her damp face. 'Don't you look a picture? That shade of soft green suits you, Millie. We must buy more.'

Millicent put her arms round Susan and gave her a hug. 'You've done more than enough,' she said. 'Thank you for being so kind.'

'Kindness has nothing to do with it,' said Susan as she hugged her back, then began to roll pastry. 'We're friends, remember? I'm entitled to give you a present now and then.'

Millicent found an apron and covered her precious dress before she began to ice the buns. When it was done, she went outside to where the table had been placed to catch the breeze that drifted up from the river. She smiled when she saw that the children were now hiding beneath the tablecloth, and pretended to give chase when they scampered off shrieking with laughter.

As she stood in the shadows at the edge of the encroaching bush, she blessed her good fortune. The memory of England had faded, and out of the dark days had come the sunshine and warmth of knowing she was loved, that her future was secure here with Susan and Ezra.

She heard Susan move about the kitchen, her heels tapping on the newly laid wooden floor. Despite the years between them, they had grown close as they'd worked side by side at the infirmary and in the house. The long evenings they passed in sewing while Ezra read to them, or they discussed the day's events had underlined that closeness, yet Millicent suspected her friend harboured troubles she was determined to keep to herself. It had soon become apparent that there was conflict between Susan and her daughter, but the reason was never revealed, and that intrigued her.

Millicent folded the linen napkins, another purchase from the ships bringing the soldiers, and placed them on the table. Florence didn't approve of her living in the house. She was an unpleasant girl, always quick to find fault, with that holier-than-thou expression and acid tongue, and Millicent had been relieved when she had moved out. But she knew Susan had been hurt by it and longed for rapport with her daughter.

But the girl seemed determined to cut her mother out of her life, refusing to offer solace, even when news of Maud's death had come. She had moved first into the Johnsons' house, then into a tiny cottage that stood in the shadows of the stone walls being laid by the convicts that would soon become the new church that the Reverend Richard Johnson had planned for so long. She had immersed herself in good works and rarely came to visit, but when she did she made a point of talking only to her father.

Millicent sighed as she finished placing the cutlery on the table and stepped back to see if she'd forgotten anything. Poor

Ezra had tried to make peace between the women he loved, but to no avail. Florence hated her mother, and there seemed no way to change that. She stared at the water, so pretty in the sunshine, and wondered what could have caused such a rift. Then she shrugged. It was none of her business, and everyone had secrets – even her.

Ezra came home from his parochial duties looking tired and drawn, but his smile was warm as he kissed Susan and gave Millicent a fatherly hug. Their birthday gift to her was a beautiful shawl, embroidered with the finest silks. It had the longest, softest fringe, which rippled as she moved, and Millicent was so overwhelmed by their generosity that she could barely speak.

George arrived at full tilt on a horse and came to a halt outside the picket fence in a cloud of dust. At almost eighteen he was tall and powerfully built, his energy astounding. He threw himself to the ground, and almost broke Millicent's ribs as he hugged her and handed her a mangled bunch of wild-flowers. She blushed and tried to thank him, but he was already moving chairs and getting in his mother's way so she went into the house and put them in water.

'Is anyone at home? I picked up Ezra's mail on me way. Another ship's come in.' Nell bustled through the front door with seven-month-old Amy on her hip and an enormous carpet-bag slung over her arm. Like her mother, the little girl was resplendent in a frothy scarlet dress. Her fine red hair had been brushed into a cock's-comb, and her lively blue eyes almost disappeared into plump cheeks as she gave a toothless grin.

'Don't she look a treat?' Nell exclaimed, as she put the mail on the table and handed the baby to Susan. 'Got the material off the ship. 'Ad to fight fer it, mind. It were popular. 'Ope you like it.'

Millicent received the bolt of fabric. 'It's lovely,' she lied, as she tried to think what on earth she could do with such a garish red. But she liked Nell, despite her taste, and admired her cheerful, robust character. 'Where's Billy?'

'I left the men on the farm, so I could 'ave a bit of female chat,' she said. 'Tea parties ain't really to their likin' and there's still plenty of clearing to do.' Bloody trees are everywhere.'

'You're very brave to come all this way on your own,' said Millicent, who was terrified of the bush and the lonely miles of emptiness that lay beyond the town.

Nell shrugged. 'Working the streets of London teaches a girl a trick or two, and I wanted to catch up with me old friends and take care of some business.' She reached into the carpetbag. 'I'd like to see some man try their luck when I've got this to 'and,' she said, and pulled out a rifle.

Millicent looked at the weapon and swallowed. 'Do you know how to use it?' she asked timidly.

'I do – and I won't be afraid to prove it neither.'

George joined them as they moved out of the house into the garden and sat at the table. Tea was poured, and Ezra read the more interesting snatches of news from his letters.

At last, after almost a year of silence, there had been news of Emma, who was now the proud mother of three and living in the middle of what she called the 'veld'. Algernon had been promoted and was now in charge of a full company. They had taken advantage of their pioneering life and built a large, sprawling adobe house, which was surrounded by acres of good grazing. They had several servants. Most of their neighbours were Dutch Boers. Although there had been some trouble with marauding blacks, it was mostly further out in the wilderness.

'She sounds content,' said Susan, 'but I worry about her.'

'If she's anything like her mother, she'll be fine,' said Ezra, with a smile. He picked up another letter and scanned it.

'Good heavens!' he exclaimed. 'Gilbert and Ann are expecting a child!'

'Let's hope it's a boy,' muttered Susan, 'or you're next in line.'

Ezra put the letter down. 'I hadn't thought of that.' He frowned. 'But Gilbert's sturdy and will probably see me out. It's more likely Ernest who will inherit the title.'

'God forbid,' spluttered George, as he choked on his tea.

'Language, George,' Ezra chided mildly.

'We're getting carried away,' said Susan, as she poured more tea and passed George a napkin so he could wipe his chin. 'Ann is bound to have a boy. She wouldn't dare provide Gilbert with a daughter.'

They all laughed, and soon the conversation turned to the four companies of the New South Wales Corps who had recently arrived.

The commanding officer of the marines, who'd accompanied Governor Phillip to Australia to protect the inhabitants from the natives and keep order, had flatly refused to allow his men to act as overseers or guards. Filling such positions from the ranks of the convicts had proved unworkable, and Phillip had been forced to beg the British government to raise a special regiment.

The first of the corps had arrived some months previously to take up their posts, and it was generally agreed that the government must have scraped the bottom of the barrel to find recruits. Most of the privates had come from a military prison, and the calibre of the officers was questionable. There had already been several incidences of brutality towards the natives, drunkenness, theft and whore-mongering, which didn't bode well for the future of the colony.

Millicent listened as the debate flew back and forth, but she couldn't concentrate for she was constantly looking towards the gate.

'Waiting for someone special?' murmured Nell, as she leant towards Millicent, revealing even more of her cleavage. She dug her in the ribs and winked. 'Wouldn't be a certain young man you've had an eye on for a while, would it?'

Millicent blushed. 'Don't be silly.' She giggled.

Nell raised an eyebrow, eyes twinkling. 'I ain't daft. A person could cook a meal on the heat coming off your face.'

Millicent was saved from having to reply by a shout, but as she turned with the others to greet the new arrival the blush deepened. Ernest was coming across the lawn. At nineteen he was already weathered by the sun, his shoulders and arms honed by the labour in the fields. His fair hair needed cutting, and although he had made an effort with his clothes today, Millicent could see they were in danger of falling apart. Her heart thudded painfully as she stood to greet him.

'Happy birthday,' he said shyly, as he leant down to kiss her cheek and blushed furiously.

Millicent could hardly breathe as his lips brushed her jaw. It was as if she had been struck by a bolt of lightning.

He seemed to feel it too, for he pulled away as if he had been stung. In an effort to cover his embarrassment, he shoved something into her arms. 'I didn't know what you'd like, so I bought you this.'

Millicent looked at the second bolt of scarlet material and couldn't help but smile as she thanked him. She now had enough of this stuff to make an entire wardrobe, and even though scarlet wasn't her favourite colour, she would probably be wearing it for the next ten years.

The tea party progressed with conversation flowing as Amy was passed from lap to lap. Millicent and Ernest exchanged shy glances, painfully aware that Nell's knowing eyes missed nothing.

As the sun sank behind the trees and the mosquitoes set up their whine, Nell wrapped the sleeping Amy in a shawl and popped her into a specially adapted saddle-bag with the mail for Billy and Jack. 'Gawd knows what them men've been up to for the four days I been away. Time I was going.' With a shout of farewell, she rode off on her horse in a cloud of dust.

'Billy's a lucky man,' remarked Susan.

'We should take our leave too,' said George, slapping his hat against his thigh and causing a miniature dust storm. 'It's a long ride home to Hawks Head.'

Ernest glanced at the sky, then at Millicent. 'You go ahead,' he said quietly. 'I'll follow later.'

George's face creased into a grin and he nudged his father. 'Ernie's courting,' he said, in a stage-whisper.

Ernest cuffed his brother's ear. 'Go home, pest. And get on with some work instead of loitering around the docks. Whaling ships might be infinitely more interesting to you than farming, but there's a field needs clearing and a barn to raise.'

Millicent watched this exchange and hoped against hope that Ernest wished to spend time with her. As George cantered away on his horse, she realised that Susan and Ezra had gone into the house. She and Ernest were alone.

'Would you like to walk?' asked Ernest, hat in hand, eyes on his boots.

Millicent nodded. Her pulse was so rapid she couldn't speak. She placed her hand on his proffered arm, felt the warmth of his skin beneath his shirt and wondered how deeply you could blush before you exploded.

'Let's go down the hill and into the town. I don't often have the chance, and I can see there have been many changes. What do you say, Millie? Would you like that?'

Millicent was disappointed, but she didn't want to put him off so she nodded again. She didn't like it down there. The soldiers and marines were a rough, drunken lot and fights were always breaking out in the narrow cobbled streets and alleyways. She took a deep breath and berated herself silently. The horrors of the convict ship were far behind her and Ernest would see that she came to no harm. With her hand tucked into the crook of his arm, they strolled away from the house.

Her fears suppressed, she suddenly realised her senses had never been so acute. She could smell the heat of the day in the earth, and the scent of eucalyptus mingled with the wood-smoke of many chimneys. She could feel the warmth of the evening, and the sinewy strength of Ernest's arm, see the stars twinkling high above her in the soft velvet of the sky, hear the saw of crickets and the chatter of parrots as they returned to their roosts. She had never been happier.

They had almost reached the broad dirt road that ran towards the centre of town when Ernest halted. 'Millicent,' he said, in a rush, 'I don't want to see the town. In fact, I don't even want to walk.'

She tried not to look crestfallen. 'We'd better go back, then,' she said wistfully. 'It's late, and your mother will wonder where I am.'

'She knows exactly where you are,' he said distractedly, his gaze never quite settling on her face. 'I spoke to her before we left.'

'Oh.'

He still seemed distracted. Then he took a deep breath and looked at her. 'Millicent,' he said firmly, 'would you mind if I courted you?' He swallowed and his Adam's apple bobbed.

Millicent felt light-headed, and could scarcely breathe. 'I certainly wouldn't object,' she said, trying not to giggle at how stiff and awkward they were being with each other.

His eyes were dark as they looked down at her. 'Do you mean it?'

She was blushing furiously as she dared to gently prod him. 'Of course I do.'

'Would you object awfully if I kissed you?'

She could see that he was blushing too, which made her love

him even more. 'Not awfully,' she murmured, lifting her face towards him.

She was crushed to his chest and his lips claimed hers. Millicent was swept away in a whirlwind of emotion as she kissed him back. The dream she'd once thought impossible had come true. Ernest had noticed her.

Nell knew she could have stayed with Susan for as long as she liked, but she'd missed Billy these past four days, and now that she had concluded her business and visited her friends, she was eager to be home.

Outside the town, she changed out of her new clothes and put on the loose-fitting, faded dress and broad-brimmed hat she wore every day. She packed the dress and delicate shoes she had worn at the party into the other saddle-bag, shoved her feet into her old boots, checked that the rifle was loaded and climbed back into the saddle. The carpet-bag with the rifle hung from the pommel, within easy reach should she come across trouble on the way.

Nell rode through the night, stopping only to feed Amy and to ease her aching backside. She had never ridden a horse before she and Billy had married, and although she had been wary at first, she'd been surprised at how easy she found it.

Dawn had lightened the sky as she crested the last hill, and she halted the horse, climbed down and took the sleepy child from her saddle-bag cocoon. With Amy in her arms, she looked over the land they had been granted a year ago and felt at peace. It was beautiful in the pearly dawn. Great swathes of trees emerged from the clinging mists of night, and the Parramatta river gleamed like a sheet of grey silk amid the cleared fields and rolling green pastures.

Despite the hours of back-breaking work, and the isolation and dangers of living there, she had no desire to return to city life or England. As a child of the workhouse she had never known a family and had learnt to be tough and independent early in life. Now, as she regarded the place that was her first real home, she knew that the many years of labour still to come would be worth it.

Her gaze drifted to the tiny two-roomed wooden house that had replaced the tent. It had been finished a month ago and tendrils of smoke were emerging from the stone chimney while the fresh paint on the shutters glinted in the shadows. How cosy and safe it looked, with its sloping roof and deep veranda, the sturdy stilts set deep in the rich black earth that would nurture their crops and provide good grass for the animals.

Looking further down the river, she saw the smoke coming from Jack's chimney. His house was even smaller than theirs. Back from the river and almost hidden by the trees, a sprawling shack housed the convicts they were now permitted to employ. The five men were still clothed and fed from government stores, but their wages were paid in rum – a dangerous commodity, which had to be rationed to one evening each week so that no work was lost and they could sleep it off on Sunday. But their labour had been invaluable in clearing the trees and ploughing the fields, in building the houses and putting up fences, and she knew they couldn't have achieved so much without them.

Further back, she could see smoke from the native camp, drifting up through the trees. They had proved friendly enough, and sometimes even helped about the place in exchange for baccy and rum – but, as with the convicts, the rum was carefully rationed. She chuckled as she thought of the women who came to the house to stand, stare and push a mop about the floor. There was no way she could get her tongue round their real names so she called them Daisy, Pearl and Gladys. They were useless at housework, and only came to play with Amy or see what they could find in her cupboards, but they were the only female company she had, and in an effort to educate them, she'd taught them every swear word she knew. Poor old Billy, he'd been shocked to the core when Daisy called him a 'bluddy bugga', after he'd told her off for filching flour.

Nell emerged from her daydream and her breath caught as the wings of a flock of white cockatoos blushed pink as they flew across the rising sun. The beauty of this place, the silence, space and sheer grandeur never failed to touch her. How her life had changed – how fortunate she was to have been given the chance to start again with the man she loved. 'Look, Amy,' she whispered, as she held the child up to watch the splendour of another dawn, 'that's Moonrakers, and all of it is yours.'

Amy reached out chubby arms and gurgled as a darting flock of chattering budgerigars swooped past.

Nell smiled, content as she planted a kiss in the child's fiery hair. 'And do you know why we called it Moonrakers?' she murmured. 'We were sitting out one night, just after we'd arrived, and your father saw the moon's reflection in the river.' She hitched the child up to a more comfortable position. 'The old story goes that a group of smugglers were caught on the moors by the Revenue men, and when they was asked what they were doing, one took a stick and dragged it across the water. "Why," he says, "we be raking the moon for its gold."' Nell chuckled. 'The Revenue men thought them fools and let them be, and the smugglers kept their booty.'

Amy regarded her solemnly, and Nell realised it was nearly time to feed her. 'Let's go home,' she murmured.

Billy slammed through the screen door and stood on the veranda waiting for her. As she rode into the clearing in front of the house he ran down the steps and swung her out of the saddle. Her hat fell off and her hair tumbled round her shoulders and down her back as he kissed her.

'I've missed you,' he said, moments later, as he took Amy

from her arms, 'but you must have ridden all night to get here so quickly.'

Nell grinned. He was handsome, her Billy, so brown from the sun, so broad of chest and strong of arm that she could have stayed in his embrace all day. 'You said you'd 'ave a surprise for me,' she reminded him, as she pulled away and looked around. 'What is it?'

'I'll tell you soon enough,' he said mysteriously, then grimaced. 'Go in and see to Amy while I look to the horse,' he said, handing over the child.

'I'll leave my surprises until later then,' she retorted, as she smothered her impatience and gave him the mail. He looked at her quizzically and she grinned. Two could play at that game. Billy was always teasing her, but she enjoyed it, and the surprise would be all the better for waiting. As long as it was a nice one – but Billy seemed excited so she had little doubt that it would be.

She went inside, her boots rapping on the sweet-smelling wooden floor as she crossed the big main room and checked what was cooking in the pot on the range. The stove stood within the chimney breast on one side of the room that was the heart of the house. Sparsely furnished with home-made table and chairs, it was where plans were made, ideas exchanged and games of cards played after a long day's labour. There were no curtains, no carpets, nothing feminine or frilly to feed Nell's love of colour and girlish softness, yet she wouldn't have changed a thing.

Satisfied that Billy had prepared something edible, she resisted the temptation to taste the porridge and hurried outside to wash and change Amy, then use the malodorous earth closet. Returning to the house, she went into the bedroom, fed the baby and put her down to sleep between the pillows on the big brass bed Billy had exchanged for a half-keg of rum in Sydney Town. After a short attempt to get a brush through her tangled curls, she gave up. How much easier it would be to cut it all off – and she was sorely tempted to do so – but Billy loved her hair and he'd be furious if she snipped off so much as an inch. With a sigh, she put down the brush and went back into the main room.

As usual Jack had arrived for breakfast, and was sitting at the table, an empty bowl in front of him as he read his letters. Billy was next to him and Nell saw the look of conspiracy that shot between them when she walked into the room. She decided to ignore them. They would soon give up their game and tell her what was going on, but now she needed to eat.

The porridge was delicious, if a little lumpy, the goat's milk added sweetness and Nell ate hungrily. It was some time before she was ready to tell them the startling news of Gilbert and Ann's imminent parenthood.

Billy and Jack stared open-mouthed, then roared with laughter, slapped each other on the back, and toasted Gilbert with a cup of rum.

Nell eyed them wearily. Anyone would think the man had done something clever, she thought, as she continued with her breakfast. Making babies was easy, and her sympathies lay with Ann: it was giving birth that was the hard part.

Silence fell, until Billy said quietly, 'I brokered a deal on another ninety acres yesterday.'

Nell dropped her spoon with a clatter. 'How? We haven't any money.'

'I had three kegs of rum and that's currency enough when a man's thirst becomes too much and he no longer wishes to work his land.'

Now it was clear. 'You bought Alfie Dawson's land grant,' she said. 'What about his wife and daughter?'

'The daughter's gone back to town, and his wife's thirst for rum matches Alfie's.' He eyed her warily. 'I also bought the few cows he hadn't already sold,' he added, 'so it was a real bargain.'

Nell knew her disapproval showed in her eyes.

'I'll see them right,' he added hurriedly, aware of the danger in rousing Nell's temper. 'He'll work the land and tend the cows for me when he's capable, and I'll pay him in rum like I do the convicts.'

'Pay a drunk with liquor? Very sensible.' She folded her arms tightly beneath her bosom and glared at him.

Billy gave her his most mischievous smile. 'Come on, Nell, you know it makes sense. And when have I ever let you down?'

She would have liked to count the times, but as she couldn't think of any, she kept her mouth shut. She thought instead of the beautiful acreage further up the river. It was good grazing land, and Jack had often spoken of it with longing; now it seemed they owned it. What a fool Alfie was to abandon the one chance he had had to better himself for a few tots of rum.

Nell sighed and the anger left her. She could understand why he had done it, for he'd come from the rookeries of London. His idea of work was to pick pockets and steal from shopkeepers. The grant of land on his conditional pardon must have been a burden to him and his trollop of a wife.

'Well? Aren't you pleased?'

Billy was looking worried, and well he might. They had more than enough land to handle, too few workers and too little time to look after it properly. She wasn't about to let him off the hook – not yet. 'What's the point of all that grazing land when we only have a few scraggy old cows?'

'That's the other surprise,' said Jack, as he set aside his letters. 'We are about to become sheep farmers.'

'We can't afford to buy sheep and, anyway, there aren't enough in the colony to go round, especially with the blacks running off with them for their cooking fires.'

'They won't be coming from the colony,' Jack explained. 'They'll be coming from South Africa.'

Nell discovered her mouth was open and shut it. She looked from Jack to Billy and recognised the excitement in their eyes. They reminded her of a couple of naughty children. 'You'd better tell me what you two have been up to,' she said, trying hard to remain stern.

Billy leant back in his chair and stuffed tobacco into his pipe as Jack began to speak. 'I've been talking to John Macarthur.' He must have seen this meant nothing to her and went on to explain: 'He's an officer with the New South Wales Corps, and he's taken up two hundred and fifty acres further up the Parramatta river. He's an intelligent man, even though his manner is too blunt for some. He thinks this land is ripe for producing the best wool in the world.'

'What does a soldier know about farming?' Nell was not convinced.

'Enough to see that this colony has a natural wealth in its land. He reckons the merino sheep is ideal for this grazing, and that we could produce wool to compete with the quality and price of wool from Spain and Germany, if enough convicts were released from government work and allowed to help us.'

'It won't happen,' she said. 'The government still has to feed and clothe most people here because few are self-sufficient – it can't afford to lose any more labourers.'

'They wouldn't have to if free settlers were encouraged to come,' he said quietly.

Nell stilled. The idea was preposterous. This was a convict colony, run by the government and the military: what right-minded free settler would want to live here? She looked from Jack to Billy, saw the excitement in their faces and realised they might indeed have something. She let her mind explore the possibilities as she reached for Billy's clay pipe and took a puff.

'So,' she began, some moments later, 'you think that if we

follow Macarthur's advice and take up merino sheep farming, we'll be able to compete with the best?'

Both men nodded.

'From our profits, we'll buy more land and more sheep, and grow rich, which will encourage free settlers to come over here and do the same?'

'Not only that, but we can sell the meat and lanoline to the government stores. The government will no longer have to support us or pay for our convict labour, and the economy of the colony will flourish. Everyone wins.' Jack could barely contain his enthusiasm and he rocked back and forth on his chair, making the legs creak.

Nell returned the pipe to Billy. 'Very clever,' she said. 'But Macarthur will set up in competition with us. He already has more land, and can afford to buy many more sheep.'

'The land is big enough to withstand any amount of competition,' said Jack, 'and although we can't afford as many sheep as Macarthur, we can certainly buy enough to set us up.'

'How?' she said bluntly. 'A few kegs of rum won't be enough to make our fortune.'

Jack picked up the stack of letters from the table, and Nell thought she saw a glimmer of regret in his eyes as he looked back at her. 'Alice is going to sell the farm,' he said. 'She'll use most of the money to transport three merino rams and thirty breeding ewes from South Africa to Port Jackson.'

Nell could only stare at him. They had worked it all out, and she could see that this plan had been in the making for months. It made her news seem tame, and she was miffed they hadn't consulted her. 'When will she arrive?' she asked.

'Probably by the middle of next year – perhaps later. It depends on how quickly she sells the farm and can get passage to South Africa.' There was a tremor in his voice and the suspicion of a tear in his eye. 'I can't believe I'm going to see her again after all this time, Nell. It's a miracle she still wants me.'

'She'd be stupid if she didn't,' retorted Nell. 'You're a good man, Jack. Any woman would want you.' She eyed Billy and decided it was time to get round to her own news. 'Under the circumstances it'll be good to have Alice here,' she said lightly. 'Let's hope she comes sooner rather than later.'

Billy lifted his head. 'Why?'

Nell grinned with delight. 'Ann's not the only one with a sprog on the way. Amy's brother or sister will arrive in March.'

Billy was out of his chair, pulling her to her feet before she could catch her breath. He kissed her long and hard.

They were so taken up with each other that they didn't notice Jack tuck his precious letters into his pocket and quietly leave the house.

Lowitja settled the youngest children beneath the pelts and sang to them until they fell asleep. Leaving them under the watchful eye of her grandmother, she left the camp and, with her stabbing spear for protection, began the long trek through the bush to the special cave. She no longer felt safe, walking alone at night, for many women had been taken by the white men who had stolen the land.

Her thoughts were troubled as she reached the mouth of the cave set high above the water-line overlooking the fast-flowing river. Although she had made friends with Susan and her family, and some of the other white people could be trusted, she could not dismiss a growing sense of danger. Her people were changing slowly, the old ways set aside for the sweet dark drink that made them act like fools and left them senseless. The spirituality of the dwindling tribes was being lost, the original unity shattered as opinion divided them. Some women had even gone willingly to the white men's shacks to live with them, while others gave their bodies in return for rum and fancy clothes.

She stood at the mouth of the cave and watched the Moon

Goddess high in the sky as she thought of Anabarru. She had followed the ancient way and been cleansed so that she could rejoin her husband and tribe, but this strict law had not been followed here. The women who had gone to live with the white men had kept their children, and would never again be accepted at the campfires. Those children, whose lighter skins set them apart from both black and white, would never be initiated in the ancient ways or be accepted in the white man's world. They were destined to wander a lonely path for the rest of their lives.

Her sigh was deep as she sank to the floor and took the precious stones from her dilly bag. Holding them, she intoned the special prayers to her ancestor Garnday, and waited for her to reply before casting them to the floor. What she saw made her shiver.

A great darkness was coming – and it took the form of a white man in a red coat. This devil would bring slaughter to her people, would take them to the edge of extinction in the attempt to obliterate the ancient spiritual ways. She closed her eyes and began to pray. Never before had she needed Garnday's wisdom so urgently.

19

Sydney Cove, February 1793

'Will you go into town and give Ezra this note?' said Susan, as she handed it over and returned to packing a small basket with the things she would need for her visit to the convict infirmary. 'He is probably with Florence so I'd try there first.'

Millicent reluctantly put the note into her pocket. Eleven ships had entered Port Jackson some months ago, and now Sydney Town was full of soldiers and sailors who were as coarse and drunken as the Irish convicts they had transported. It was certainly no place for a timid girl. 'Is it really important?' she asked.

Susan stopped what she was doing and put her hand on Millicent's shoulder. 'I wouldn't have asked if it wasn't,' she said softly. 'I need Ezra to administer the last rites to Mrs O'Neil. She's been calling for a priest, and I suspect she won't last through the night.'

'But she's one of those Irish Catholics,' Millicent stammered. 'She doesn't like Ezra, or anything he stands for.'

'I know,' replied Susan, and mopped her brow. It was sweltering in the house as the summer dragged on. 'Why on earth the British government sent the Irish to our staunchly Protestant shores I have no idea.' She smiled, although there was an uncharacteristic impatience in her stance. 'But here they are, with more arriving on every ship and no priest to care for them or understand their superstitions. Mrs O'Neil is dying. She wants to hear the last rites. As Richard Johnson is at the mission house, Ezra will have to read them.'

'Very well,' Millicent murmured, 'but it'll be dark soon,' she added, as she glanced out of the window. Sunset came with little warning – as swift as a blown-out candle.

Susan's patience must have been thinning for her tone was unusually sharp. 'The sooner the message is delivered, the sooner you'll be home.' Her expression softened immediately and she put an arm round Millicent's waist. 'You really must try to be brave. I can't always be with you.'

Millicent knew Susan was right, but that didn't make her any bolder. She still flinched at loud noises, and shied away from social gatherings unless they involved the family. The sight of a group of men, however sober and respectable, made her quail. 'I'll try.'

'Good girl,' said Susan, briskly. 'And when I get back we can put the final touches to your wedding dress.' She kissed Millicent's cheek and hurried out of the door.

The thought of Ernest gave Millicent a modicum of courage and she felt the familiar warmth as she remembered his proposal. He had been a regular visitor over the past five months, and had proposed just before Christmas, on the day she had finally received her full pardon, going down on one knee when they were alone in the moonlight.

She smiled as she looked at the ring he had bought from a passing sailor. The gold band with its diamond chip was so precious, and promised a wonderful future. Her gaze drifted to the dress hanging in a muslin sheet awaiting the final bit of embroidery. The wedding was to be in a month's time, and then she and Ernest would travel to Hawks Head Farm and begin their new life in the house he was having built for her.

Millicent realised she was daydreaming and took off her apron to reveal the faded grey dress she always wore when she was working in the house. She liked grey. It made her invisible when she had to go out.

She stood in the doorway and watched until Susan was out

of sight. With trembling fingers she tied the ribbons of her plain bonnet, put on her light cloak, and stepped outside. The sun was low in the sky, but the heat was a haze over the landscape, smothering her with its intensity. It was all so different from a Cornish February, when the sky became leaden, the sea lashed the shore, and roaring fires took the chill from the house. She took a deep breath and began to walk.

The noise from the town drifted up to her, and as she drew nearer she was surprised at how busy everyone seemed to be. The looms in the women's factory clacked and rattled, the smith's hammer clanged in the forge, and a gang of chained convicts broke rocks to the shout of the overseer and the crack of the whip.

Women convicts in bright yellow dresses were labouring in the open-air laundry, their raucous laughter at odds with their situation as they scrubbed and manhandled heavy blankets and uniforms in clouds of steam. The harbour was alive with the sound of repairs to the eleven ships that had arrived three months ago, the cloying heat made worse by the acrid smoke billowing from burning tar barrels.

Millicent scuttled along in the shadows of the store verandas, her eyes fixed on the ground. Yet she was all too aware of the group of sailors roaring encouragement as they gave a drunken Aborigine more rum and made him dance, of the soldiers who lounged outside the grog shops and the swaggering officers who rode their fine horses with dangerous indifference along the newly laid road. She was sweating beneath the cloak, but she would rather that than take it off. There wasn't far to go now, but the high walls of the unfinished church still seemed a long way off.

She turned off the main thoroughfare with relief and entered the relatively peaceful grounds of the church. Convicts were working on the wooden scaffolding high above the ground as others laboured with hammers, nails and chisels under the watchful eyes of their overseers. To a man, they were dressed in the baggy shirts and trousers marked with black arrows that denoted their status, but at least they had been spared chains.

Millicent's nerves were stretched to breaking-point as she hurried past their watchful eyes towards the large area behind the church. Susan had asked her to come – how could she have refused?

The broad sweep of land behind the church had been cleared some time ago and where once there had been only scrub and trees there stood a large but plainly built house surrounded by pleasant, flower-filled gardens. This was the home of the Reverend Richard Johnson and his wife, and in the corner of this lush garden, set apart by a picket fence and in the shadows of the rising church, was the much smaller cottage where Florence lived.

Millicent opened the gate and walked up the neat path that divided the tiny lawn, noting that Florence did not share Mary Johnson's love of flower-beds and pots of blooms on the porch. She climbed the scrubbed steps, saw the pristine curtains at the windows and rapped on the door.

Florence opened it. 'What do you want?'

Millicent would have liked a drink of water, to sit down and recover from her ordeal, but knew better than to ask. 'I must speak to your father,' she said, as she glanced over Florence's shoulder into the gloom of the house, hoping he was there.

Florence clasped her hands and stood squarely in the doorway, making it plain that Millicent was not to be invited in. 'He's not here.'

'Do you know where he is?' Millicent was edgy. The sun was fast disappearing and she wanted to get home.

'I am not my father's keeper,' returned Florence, with a smugness that would have made a less nervous person than Millicent want to slap her.

'It's urgent,' said Millicent, in desperation. 'Your mother needs him at the convict infirmary.' She handed Florence the note.

Florence glanced at it and bristled. 'My father has better things to do than attend heathen Catholics,' she said coldly. Her hand was already on the door, and she took a step back.

Millicent didn't stop to think. She moved forward, placed her own hand on the door and pushed it back. 'She needs him to read the last rites for Mrs O'Neil,' she said, in a rush. 'The poor woman won't live much longer, and she'll go easier knowing the right prayers have been said.'

'My father is not a Catholic priest,' Florence said icily, 'and I'm sure Mother's intimate knowledge of the criminal classes will see her through without his help.'

'Why do you hate her so?'

'That is none of your business,' snapped Florence, once more pushing at the door.

Millicent stood firm. 'It is when she's been so good to me,' she said. 'She and your father have treated me like a daughter, and I don't like to see them hurt.'

Something shifted in Florence's eyes. 'You are not their daughter, and never will be,' she snapped.

'I'm no threat to you,' Millicent said, stung by the knowledge that what Florence had said was true. 'Why are you always so unpleasant?'

'Because you're nothing but a common convict and you dare to think you can take my place in my parents' affections.' Her face was flushed and her eyes unnaturally bright. 'You might think you've fallen on your feet and wheedled your way into our family, but I know the real reason you were taken in and it had nothing to do with Christian duty or even pity.'

Millicent could almost feel the waves of jealousy coming from the other girl, which frightened her. 'What do you mean?' she stammered.

Florence advanced, eyes gleaming with malice. 'You and my mother have more in common than you know,' she snarled. 'Because of that she's tried to ease her conscience by looking after you.'

Millicent had no idea what Florence was talking about, and wondered if she was unhinged. 'I don't understand,' she said.

'Why should you?' Florence sneered. 'You're only a servant, and therefore not privy to family secrets.' She came closer and Millicent took another step back. 'But as you seem determined to poke your nose into my family's business, let me enlighten you,' she said.

Millicent suddenly didn't want to hear any more, but she was transfixed by the other girl's malice, and could only stare in bewilderment into that angry face.

'My mother lay with Jonathan Cadwallader at the same time he was servicing you.'

'I don't believe you,' whispered Millicent.

'My father knew. I heard him accuse my mother – and she admitted it. That was why we came to this God-forsaken place. To get away from Cadwallader.'

Millicent's eyes widened, her thoughts in turmoil.

'So, you see, she took you in to assuage her own guilt. It had nothing to do with love and friendship,' she finished.

Millicent took a shuddering breath and the tears streamed down her face. She couldn't bear to look at Florence – couldn't bear to be near her. She turned and ran down the steps, flung open the gate and, without looking back, headed for home.

Moonrakers, February 1793

Nell had milked the two cows and three goats before she realised that the niggling pain in her back was worse. She rose from the stool and lifted the heavy buckets, determined not to panic. If the baby was coming, there was nothing she could do about it but get back to the homestead and prepare herself. That it was early was worrying, but Amy's birth had been trouble-free and she didn't anticipate any problems now.

She grimaced as the buckets weighed her down and the pain moved from her back to her groin. There was no mistake. This one was in a hurry to be born so she had better get on with it. She struggled through the screen door, placed the buckets beside the sink and covered them with muslin to protect the milk from flies.

She rested until the pain eased, watching the sleeping Amy, who lay in the rough wooden cot Billy had made from local timber. The child was her joy, but at this moment Nell was glad she was sleeping, for she couldn't cope with giving birth and looking after an inquisitive, hungry Amy.

'Where's Billy?' she muttered, as she put water on the stove to boil and gathered clean strips of linen, a bundle of towels and a sharp knife. 'Why do men always disappear just when you want them?' She made her way to the bedroom, stripping off her clothes as she went and leaving them where they fell.

She rested for a moment, leaning on the brass bed-head, sweat beading her forehead as another vice-like pain tore through her. Billy had been in and out of the house every day for the past few months, getting under her feet until she had told him to leave her be. It seemed he had taken her at her word, for as she peered through the window there was no sign of him.

Neither could she see Daisy, Gladys or Pearl. Nell blinked away tears and chided herself for being soft. This was no time to be fretting for another woman's company. Or for wishing she was not alone and that they were closer to civilisation – and it was *not* the time to give in to weakness. She was having a baby, which she had done before and would no doubt do again. The black women managed on their own in the bush, and she was damned if she couldn't do it too.

Having stripped the bed of its linen, she covered it with an old, but clean blanket and went to fetch the hot water. With everything set she climbed on to the bed and tried to ignore the silence of the great emptiness beyond the window. The pains were more frequent now, and her waters had broken. It would soon be time to push.

Sydney Town, February 1793

Millicent ran blindly through the churchyard and out into the darkening street. Florence's words were ringing in her head, the images they conjured flashing before her with a terrible clarity as her racing feet took her further from the church. She could see her baby dying in her arms, her tiny body buried within the confines of the grey prison walls where the sun never shone and no flowers grew. She could see Jonathan Cadwallader, hear his rage as she had faced him on that last day – and couldn't believe Susan had betrayed Ezra by loving him. It was a web, a tangled web, and she was caught in the middle.

She was so distraught she had no sense of direction, no idea that she had strayed far from her destination. Tears blinded her as she ran and ran, trying to stifle the sobs that racked her. Susan had taken her in out of pity, as a sop to her own guilt at betraying Ezra. Her friendship was a lie.

Millicent's head felt as if it was bursting and she tore at the ribbons of her bonnet, letting her hair tumble as she tossed it away. Her breath was tight in her chest, her throat constricted as she turned a corner and ran full tilt into a pair of hands that clutched her.

Moonrakers, February 1793

Billy was restless. He had been out since dawn to oversee the building of the sheep pens and drenching ponds and had grown impatient at the slowness of the convicts who were supposed to be helping him. It was at times like this that he wondered if perhaps he had made a mistake in partnering Jack in this crazy idea. The land was a harsh task-master, the tools and hired help worse than useless, and it was frustrating that everything had to take so long.

He took off the wide-brimmed hat and mopped his brow. Despite the sunset, the heat was stifling, dancing in waves on the horizon, bringing the noisome flies and the sibilant hiss of a million insects. The land stretched as far as the eye could see – empty, isolated, as primitive now as when it was first created. It was all so far removed from England, and in that restless moment he wished he was back there, riding across the moors, hiding from the Revenue men, drinking in the taverns as he brokered deals for the smugglers.

The memories haunted him as he stared into the past. He had always had money in his pockets and fine clothes on his back, had relished the excitement and danger of his life, the notoriety it had earned him. Now he was a dirt farmer, poorer than a church mouse, with a wife, a child and another on the way. His clothes were little more than rags and his home was a wooden shack in the middle of nowhere. He had never wanted to be a farmer.

In despair he looked at his hands. The skin was darkened by the sun, the nails were broken and encrusted with dirt, the calluses rough on the palms. In that moment he realised they had been honestly earned. He might be poor, but he could hold up his head in pride for the land that had been cleared, for the health and well-being of his little family and the promise of greater things to come. This land was tough and raw but it could be tamed. An honest man could make his mark here by honest labour, could forge the pioneer trails for the generations to come, and show the world that this convict colony was peopled by men and women who were not afraid to make the most of what they had been given.

His spirits rose and he whistled to his horse. Life was good and it would be better. It was time to go back to Nell and tell her he loved her.

The house was quiet as he pushed through the screen door and left it to slam behind him. Amy was asleep beneath the fly-net in her cot, her thumb plugged firmly into her rosebud mouth. 'Nell?' he called softly.

'In here.'

Billy chortled and threw his hat on to a nearby chair. If Nell was in the bedroom she might fancy an afternoon romp. He opened the door and froze.

Nell was propped up in bed, her glorious hair spilling round her face and over her luscious breasts. She grinned as she took in his stunned expression. 'No good standing about there, Bill,' she said, eyes sparkling. 'I could do with a rum and no mistake.'

Billy moved towards her as if in a trance. His stupefied gaze rested on his wife and travelled slowly down to the bundles in her arms. 'There's two,' he breathed.

Nell laughed. 'Don't I know it! Little wretches couldn't wait, and no sooner was one out than the other was halfway there.' She held up the babies to him, and Billy saw that one had hair the colour of autumn leaves while the other's was as gold as the Australian sun. 'This is William, and this is Sarah.'

Billy took them and stared at them in wonder. They were perfect and beautiful, and the love he felt was so overwhelming he wanted to cry.

Nell slid off the bed, kissed Billy's cheek and then, still naked, left the room.

'Where are you going?' he asked.

'To get that rum and cook some supper,' she replied. 'Me throat's as parched as a parrot's cage and I'm hungry.'

Billy stared at her retreating figure in admiration. All the fine clothes and money in the world couldn't buy a woman as precious as Nell. He was a very lucky man.

The Rocks, Sydney Town, February 1793

'Well, well, what have we here?' The voice was the familiar upper-class drawl of England.

Millicent froze. Her face was pressed against the rough fabric of an army officer's jacket, and she could scarcely breathe in his determined grip. 'Please, sir,' she sobbed, 'let me pass. I have to go home.'

'What do you think, men? Shall we let her go, or do you fancy some sport?'

'Sport, I say. Looks lively enough, if a bit scrawny.'

Millicent's heart was racing and her mouth was dry as they closed in a tight, menacing circle round her. There were at least six in that dark, unfamiliar alley that stank of piss and filth, and she could smell the drink on their breath. She searched wildly for other pedestrians, a grog shop, lights from a house – anything that might save her. As her eyes adjusted to the gloom she saw a watching figure in the shadows. 'Please help me,' she cried. 'Please. Don't let them . . .'

The figure shifted and she saw the army boots and the gleam of his smile as he remained a spectator. She knew then that she would have to fight for her life.

She kicked out with her boots, and began to squirm, but her captor's arms tightened as he roared with laughter. 'We've caught ourselves a real little cat,' he spluttered. 'She'd scratch my eyes out if I wasn't careful.'

'Please, sir,' she begged, gazing up into the reddened face and bloodshot eyes. 'I'm not that kind of girl. Let me go home.'

'Not until we've had our sport,' drawled a new voice.

Millicent struggled again as the officer who had been lounging against the wall in the darker shadows stepped forward. Her heart hammered and she thought she would faint when she recognised him.

'As senior officer I'll have her first,' he said. 'Hand her over, Baines.'

She was numb with terror as she was thrust into his arms. This couldn't be happening. It wasn't possible. But the grip on the neck of her dress confirmed it was all too real, and as the faded cotton was rent from neck to waist she began to plead. 'Don't,' she screamed. 'Please don't.'

The officer held her arms tightly as he flung her round to face the others, showing them her naked breasts. He ignored her kicks against his booted shins as if they were nothing.

Millicent was swept from one pair of rough, clawing hands to another as they laughed and spun her round within their circle. At each turn another shred of clothing was ripped away until she was naked but for her boots. Her screams were almost drowned in their shouts of laughter and ribald remarks.

'Quieten her,' growled the senior officer, 'or we'll have the troopers on us.'

A hand was clapped over Millicent's mouth and she was bundled into the darkest part of the narrow alleyway. She kicked as she wriggled, squirmed and tried to claw their faces, but they were too strong, too drunk and aroused to notice when her nails ripped flesh and her boots caught a glancing blow. She was thrown to the ground, the wind knocked from her lungs as her face hit the dirt.

'Hold her down,' panted the senior officer, as he knelt between her legs and unbuttoned his trousers. 'And keep her quiet, for God's sake.'

'Got just the thing,' giggled one of the others.

Millicent was face down and spreadeagled. Heavy knees and hands pinned her to the rough ground as a man grasped a handful of her hair and yanked her head back so far she thought her neck would break.

She fought for breath as the giggling young officer knelt before her, his trousers unbuttoned, eyes wild with excitement.

The hand in her hair yanked harder, and as she opened her mouth to scream, he rammed thick, pulsating flesh down her throat.

Millicent gagged and retched. She had to get rid of the *thing* in her mouth so that she could breathe. Her teeth closed round it.

The sharp point of a knife nicked her neck. 'Bite me and I'll cut your throat.'

She couldn't breathe as she fought nausea and pain, but then the torture began in earnest. As the senior officer violated her, the agony was so overwhelming she thought she would die and longed for oblivion. But as the excited men encouraged each other, and she felt the chill of the blade on her throat, she knew she was not to be given such merciful release.

She couldn't move, couldn't escape the double attack, and as the senior officer finished, and the giggling youth withdrew, others took their places.

Millicent sought refuge inside herself, so deep she no longer felt pain or humiliation, no longer cared what they did to her. All emotion died and it was as if she floated outside her human frame, a mere spectator. Yet a tiny glimmer of reason remained, and she etched their faces in her memory. They would pay for this.

20

Sydney Town, February 1793

Susan had been kept at the infirmary for longer than she had expected, and as she hurried home through the darkness she wondered what had happened to Ezra. There had been no sign of him, and Mrs O'Neil had died in fear of endless purgatory, whatever that was. It was too bad, she thought crossly. Ezra couldn't ignore his Catholic parishioners because their beliefs differed from his – and it was unlike him not to come when she had sent a message.

As she went down the hill she saw lamplight streaming through the open doors and windows, and a trickle of smoke drifting from the chimney. At least Millicent had returned safely, she thought. The girl was still far too nervous, and she had felt guilty about sending her to find Ezra, but what else could she have done? She pushed open the gate, her mouth watering at the smell of dinner cooking. She hadn't eaten for hours and was bone weary.

'Where have you been?' said Ezra, as he turned from taking the meat out of the oven. 'I was about to come looking for you.'

Susan put her basket on the table. 'You know where I've been,' she snapped, 'and poor little Eily O'Neil died in terror of eternal damnation because you wouldn't stir yourself to tend her.'

He looked at her in shock. 'I have no idea what you're talking about,' he gasped. 'Please explain.'

Susan told him about the note she had sent with Millicent, and when he denied having received it, she was about to argue with him when she realised the house was too quiet – that the scene before her was out of kilter. 'Where *is* Millie?' she asked.

'I thought she was with you.'

'She should be home by now. I sent her to Florence hours ago.' She hurried through the house calling Millicent's name, panic rising as she found every room empty. 'Millie.' She stood in the corridor and put her trembling fingers to her mouth. 'Oh, dear God, what have I done? I should never have sent you to town. Please be safe.'

'Susan?' Ezra emerged from the kitchen, his face creased with worry.

She clutched him. 'We have to look for her! She's always so terrified of the dark, and she's out there alone. Something must have happened to her – she didn't want to go! It's all my fault.'

Ezra took her hands and stilled her. 'She will have decided to stay with Florence until morning,' he murmured.

Susan wanted to believe him, but they both knew the idea was preposterous. She pulled away from him and grabbed a shawl, then went back into the kitchen for a lantern. She had lit the wick and replaced the glass when she heard something. She stood still.

'What is it?' asked Ezra.

Susan put a finger to her lips to silence him. There it was again – and this time she recognised it.

She raced to the door and almost fell down the steps in her haste to reach the huddled figure in the shadows. 'Millie?' she breathed, her voice trembling with dread. 'Millie, is that you?'

The sobs continued and the figure curled into a tighter ball of misery.

Susan signalled to Ezra to stay in the house. The girl was distraught, and although Millicent adored him, she had the feeling that whatever was wrong with her would be best dealt with without his male presence. She approached the huddled figure, uncertain of what to do and dreading what she might find.

'Millie? What's the matter?'

The sobbing figure cowered further into the shadows as Susan touched her shoulder. 'Don't look, don't look,' she sobbed. 'I don't want you to see. I don't want Ezra to see.'

Susan glanced over her shoulder and saw Ezra hovering in the doorway. She waved him away. 'He's in the house. Come, you can't stay out here, and whatever's frightened you is over now. You're home, safe.' She drew the girl into her arms.

Millicent clung to her, sobs racking her skinny frame as she broke into incoherent speech.

Susan tried to calm her, but as her hands ran over the slender shoulders she realised with horror that they were naked. It was almost impossible to see anything in the deep shadows, but her exploring fingers discovered that the cotton dress was in shreds, the petticoats and cloak gone. She held the girl tightly, rocking her until the sobs died away.

As she sat there in the warm stillness of night, her pulse raced as suspicion grew and dread returned. As the moon appeared from behind the clouds there could be no doubt as to what had happened to Millicent.

She looked at the face that was streaked with blood and tears, and saw the scratches and bruises on her arms and neck. There were smears of blood and filth on her legs and on the remains of her dress, and bald patches on her head where someone had yanked out her hair.

Something cold settled round her heart. Whoever had done this would be punished. She would make sure of it – and when they were hanging from a gibbet, she would spit in their faces.

'Why did they do it, Susan?' whispered Millicent. 'Why me? Am I so wicked?'

An overwhelming sadness engulfed her. If only she could take on Millicent's burden of pain and despair – if only the hurt could be eased by the love she felt for the poor girl. 'It's the men who did this that are wicked,' she replied.

'But why, Susan?' She began to sob again, her words coming thick and fast as she tore at her arms with what was left of her fingernails. 'I don't encourage them – I've *never* encouraged them – but they seek me out because they can see I'm dirty, disgusting, filthy.'

Susan quickly stilled the hands and held them before Millicent could do herself any more damage. The girl's plight swept away her belief in a kind, caring God. Through no fault of her own, Millicent had been a victim of men since she was fifteen. How *dare* God be so cruel as to give her a glimpse of security and happiness, then rip it away?

Ezra had been unable to sleep, and as dawn lightened the sky, he left the house. He was as distressed as Susan over what had happened to Millicent, and his steadfast faith had been shaken to its foundations.

His fury and anguish must have shown in his face as Florence opened the door for her welcoming smile faltered as he strode past her into the parlour. He waited for her to join him.

'Florence,' he began, the name ringing out in the tiny room, 'are you aware of the terrible damage your spiteful tongue has caused?' He didn't wait for a reply, but related the events of the previous night. He didn't mince his words or leave out any of the details, just spoke in a monotone that couldn't have failed to chill the hardest heart.

Florence stared at him in horror as she sank into a chair. 'I can hardly take in what you're saying,' she murmured. 'Poor Millicent.'

Ezra heard the insincerity in her voice. 'Poor indeed,' he snapped. 'The child was frightened of shadows. How on earth she survived such an ordeal I'll never know.'

'I don't see why you're so cross with me, Papa,' she said softly, tears welling. 'It's hardly my fault she got lost in the Rocks.'

His fury was so great he could hardly contain it. 'What have you to tell me, Florence? What was it you said to Millicent that made her so upset she couldn't find her way home?'

'I didn't see her yesterday,' she said, 'and I'm mortified to think you suspect me of collusion in this tragedy.'

'She didn't come to you with a note from Mother?' Ezra towered over her, aching with grief at her wanton denial.

'If she had I would have given it to you,' she replied, her eyes not quite meeting his as she clasped her hands in her lap.

'Really?' he said coldly. 'Then how do you explain this?' He saw her blanch as she looked at the letter he had found as soon as he had walked into the room. It was crumpled and stained with soot, but still legible.

'She must have called while I was out,' she blustered.

'I think not,' he replied, as he smoothed the paper and folded it carefully before putting it into his pocket. 'She would hardly have discarded the letter in the fireplace.' He regarded her sadly. 'Besides,' he went on, 'Mary Johnson was sewing by her parlour window last evening and saw her arrive.'

The silence in the room was disturbed only by a ticking clock as they looked at each other. He felt no compassion for her distress, just a profound sadness that his daughter could lie so easily.

'Mary saw you come out on to the porch, and was concerned that you appeared to be haranguing her. She was about to intervene when Millicent ran off in clear distress, but by the time she'd gathered her wits and followed her, she was nowhere to be seen.' The sadness of the situation was almost overwhelming him. 'What did you say to her, Florence?'

She stared at him and Ezra could see that she was trying to think of a way out. She resorted to tears.

'It's too late for that,' he said. 'Dry your eyes, Florence, and have the courage to admit your part in this heinous episode.'

Florence seemed to shrivel. 'I'm sorry, Papa,' she whispered. 'It was a silly argument.' She raised her tear-filled eyes in mute appeal. 'I would never wish such a terrible thing to happen to anyone – least of all to poor Millicent.'

He was unmoved by her false show of contrition. 'An argument over nothing would not have led to Millicent's rape,' he retorted. 'But you evidently have no intention of telling me the truth.' He held up his hand to silence her denial. 'The authorities have been informed and there will be a trial. You will be called as a witness to the events leading up to Millicent's ordeal, and you will be under oath. For once, Florence, you *will* speak the truth.'

Florence mopped her eyes. 'Yes, Papa.'

Her false humility sickened him. Ezra's voice was low, but cracked with emotion as he said, 'My heart is heavy, Florence. Something must be lacking in me that has made me fail as a father.'

'Never,' she interrupted.

He ignored her. 'I will pray for guidance, and when God sees fit to show me the way, I will speak with you again.' He picked up his hat. 'Until that day, you are not welcome in my house or my company.'

Florence threw herself at him, flinging her arms round his waist. 'Papa,' she gasped, the tears coursing down her face and soaking his shirt, 'you can't do this. I love you.'

He remained stiff and unyielding in her embrace as she wept, pleaded and clawed at his coat. Then, tired of her tears, he grasped her arms and held her away from him. His voice was rough as he looked down at her. 'You say you love me, that you have been chosen to help me in my ministry, but real love is born of humility and compassion for others. It is selfless and all-encompassing, bringing joy to both giver and receiver.'

Florence was clearly confused. 'Papa?'

'You have tainted that word and all it stands for,' he said sadly. 'Please do not use it again.' He turned on his heel and left the house, slamming the door behind him.

Millicent soaked for what seemed like hours in a tub in front of the range after the doctor had been. She had urged Susan to replenish the scalding water many times as she sat and scrubbed away the stench of the beasts who had attacked her. Yet no matter how hard she tried, she couldn't get the feel of them off her skin, couldn't rid her head of their voices, their wild eyes and the things they had done.

The doctor had been kind; his examination thankfully brief and impersonal. Susan had finally coaxed her out of the tub and into a clean nightshift, and now she was tucked up in bed in her room. The shutters were locked against the sun of this new day, and she had wedged a chair beneath the door handle so no one could enter without her permission. She lay curled up on the bed and listened to the sounds beyond the door. They were distant, as if from another time and another world, and she no longer connected them with the people who lived there.

She closed her eyes and was tormented by the memory of what had happened, opened them and was assaulted by the evidence in the dark bruises and livid scratches that covered her. There was no escape – nowhere to hide. From the roots of her hair to the tip of her toes she bore their marks – and as she drew her knees to her chest and made herself as small as possible, she wished she could disappear.

Her mind drifted to Ernest, and she knew without doubt that his loving arms had held her for the last time, that his sweet smile would be given to another. She felt as if her heart was breaking: their plans had been shattered and life would never be the same. He would not want her now – and why should he? She was used and dirty, not fit to be his wife – not fit for anyone.

There was a gentle tap on the door, and she was startled from her woeful thoughts by Susan's voice. 'Millie? May I come in?'

She lay there for a moment, unwilling to move, afraid of what might be on the other side of that door. She didn't want to see anyone or talk to them, didn't want to face whatever came next in this catalogue of horror. But Susan was persistent, so she climbed off the bed and took away the chair, then returned to hide beneath the sheet.

The bed dipped as Susan sat beside her. 'The senior law officer is here,' she said. 'He needs you to tell him what happened so that he can bring charges.'

Tears rolled down Millicent's face. Would the agony never end? How much longer would it be before her tenuous hold on reality disintegrated? Where would she find the strength to see this through?

Susan's hand was soft on her arm, her voice soothing and encouraging. 'I cannot begin to imagine what you're suffering, Millie, but you must stay strong a while longer.' She held her close. 'You've become my dearest friend,' she murmured, 'and if I could do this for you, then I would.'

Millicent looked at her as she moved from the embrace, and saw compassion, as well as the pain that her friend was enduring. Florence had lied, she saw through the fog of pain. Susan really did care about her, had not taken her in out of pity. 'You'll stay with me?'

'Of course. And when it's over you can sleep, and I'll make sure no one disturbs you.'

Millicent dredged up the last of her courage for the interview, and nodded. She knew she would have to dig even deeper if she was to win the real fight that lay ahead.

Tahiti, February 1793

Tahamma's wife stood on the shore and watched as he and the other men left for their fishing trip. They would be gone at least three days, for the black pearls they sought could only be found on the outer reef. She remained there until they were specks on the horizon. It would be lonely without him, for Tahamma was a big man, and she already missed his powerful, jovial presence.

She smiled as she watched her children play in the sand with her mother. Her son and daughter had the pale skin of their father, the little boy bearing the teardrops of red on his shoulder, which had always fascinated her. He had just learnt to walk and was tottering towards her with a shell in his tiny hand. She scooped him up and kissed him – but he was not one for cuddles and wriggled furiously until she set him down.

Her attention was caught by shouts from further down the beach. A ship was unloading and the other women were hurrying to see what the sailors had to barter. Leaving the children with her mother, she ran to join them.

The ship had dropped anchor in the next bay, and the seamen had set up tables of delicious things to exchange for pearls and perfumed oils, sandalwood and exotic birds. She looked at the tiny mirrors and saw how the light dazzled from the jewelled frames. She fingered the ribbons and the delicate cloth, touched the beads, bracelets and pretty combs. She would have loved to own them – but she had nothing to barter until Tahamma returned, and the missionaries had stopped women offering themselves.

She was about to leave when her eye was caught by something glinting in the sunlight. Moving closer, she plucked it from the box of beads, and knew she had to have it. The dagger was sheathed in an ornately tooled silver casing. Its handle was encrusted with beautiful stones that shot ruby, sapphire and emerald fire in the sunlight. The blade was broad, tapering and very sharp – ideal for opening oyster shells. She held it up to the sun, twisting it this way and that to admire its beauty.

'A dagger fit for a maharajah,' said the man watching her from the other side of the table. 'Tooled in the palaces of India by the finest craftsmen, and yours for only a handful of black pearls.'

She understood most of what he was telling her, for the sailors and merchants were frequent visitors. 'I no pearl,' she replied, voice sad, eyes full of longing as she gazed at the beautiful thing in her hand.

He took it from her and set it back on his stall. 'No pearls, no dagger.'

She bit her lip, her attention pinned on the lovely thing she wanted so badly. It would make a wonderful gift for Tahamma. Surely no other man on Tahiti could own such a treasure?

'If you ain't no pearls,' said the man, 'what else you got?'

She was tempted to offer herself – but the lessons of the missionary kept her silent. In the old days she would happily have exchanged her favours for the lovely thing. But the threat of everlasting hell-fire and the anger of the missionary's God were powerful deterrents. Then a thought struck her and she realised that perhaps she might have something he would take in exchange for the dagger. 'You keep for while? I come back. Plenty good thing.'

At his nod she was running towards her hut as fast as she could. She had to be quick – she didn't want him to give it to someone else, and it was so beautiful, so desirable it was bound to be taken soon. She was out of breath as she tore into the hut and threw aside the sleeping mats. Digging into the sand she had recently smoothed, she found the tin box and pulled it out, hands shaking with excitement as she opened the lid.

The pocket watch glinted dully as she took off the scrap of

material that protected it. She held it up and wondered if the man would deem it valuable enough to exchange for the dagger. There was a dent in one side that surely made it worthless, and it didn't shine and glitter – it had only one jewel and served no useful purpose.

It had been hidden away for years, and she had almost forgotten it, for Tahamma had shown it to her only once, just before their marriage ceremony. She remembered him opening it, showing her the pictures inside and the little key. He had told her some story about the man, but she hadn't been listening for her mind was on their forthcoming marriage. Now she couldn't even remember how to open it.

She turned it over in her hand, aware that she had to make a swift decision if the dagger was not to be sold to someone else. The thought of it, and the pleasure that would light up Tahamma's face, made up her mind. She folded the watch in the cloth, then ran back to the beach.

The dagger was still there, and she breathed a sigh of relief as she held out the cloth-wrapped watch.

'What you got fer me, then?' the trader asked, as he began to unwrap her offering.

She edged towards the table and reached for the dagger. She had to hold it. Had to slide the blade from the sheath, watch the sun sparkle on the jewelled handle and know it was soon to be hers.

'Very nice,' he muttered, as he looked more closely at the pocket watch. He took something from his pocket, wedged it into his eye-socket and took a closer look. With trembling fingers he removed it again and turned the watch over in his hand.

'Plenty good?' she asked. He seemed pleased with what she'd brought, but was it enough?

He pulled a face as he twisted something on the side of the watch and the casing sprang open. 'It's got a bit o' damage, but . . .' He gazed down at the two portraits with studied indifference.

She clasped the dagger to her chest. 'I keep?'

He watched her race away, let out the breath he had been holding, and found he was trembling. The dagger was worthless, a tawdry bit of tin and coloured glass cobbled together in the back-streets of India, but this thing was worth a fortune. It was gold, the diamond was flawless, and it was the most exquisite piece of English workmanship he had ever seen.

His fingers were clumsy as he opened the casing and looked once more at the signed miniatures, which added to its value. The sweat soaked his shirt as excitement took hold. This was his chance of a lifetime to make a fortune. He knew just the person to sell it to, and a ship was leaving for the Americas today.

21

Sydney Cove, March 1793

Ernest stood at the door and pleaded with Millicent to open it. The day before he had received the message from his mother and had ridden through the night to be there. 'Millie, please talk to me. At least let me see you so that I know you're safe.'

'She's been in her room ever since it happened,' murmured Susan, 'and refuses to communicate with anyone but me – and even then not easily.' She put her hand on his arm. 'I'm sorry, my dear.'

He was close to tears, frustration and anger making coherent thought almost impossible. 'I must see her,' he rasped. 'She must understand that none of this has made any difference to us.' He turned back to the door and put his lips close to it. 'I love you, Millie,' he called, 'and I want to marry you. Please, dearest, come out.'

The door remained bolted and he could hear no sound from the other side. He turned away in despair and flung his arms round Susan's waist as he burst into tears. 'What can I do, Mother?'

Susan held him as she had when he was a boy. She smoothed his hair and kissed his brow, her own sadness clear in the timbre of her voice. 'I don't know,' she admitted, 'but you might try a note under the door.'

He rushed into the kitchen. 'Where's your notepaper?' When he was settled at the table he began to write. He poured out his love for her, wrote of his hopes for the future and promised to help in any way he could if only she would let him see her. When it was done, he folded the paper and pushed it under the door.

He waited outside her room, watching the piece of paper – but it remained where he had left it, untouched and unread. As night fell, he sat on the floor, determined to remain there for as long as it was necessary to do so.

'Ernest, wake up and have some breakfast.'

He opened his eyes and found he was lying on the floor, his mother standing over him with a plate of fried eggs. Furious that he had fallen asleep, he glanced towards the door. The letter was still there.

He staggered to his feet and took the plate. 'Millie,' he called, through the keyhole, 'I've some food for you. You must be hungry, my sweetheart. Please eat.'

A rustle at his feet made him look down. A slip of paper had been shoved beneath the door. He almost dropped the plate in his eagerness to retrieve it.

'Ernest, please go away. I do not wish to speak to you or to anyone else. Stop banging on the door and shouting. It's making me feel ill.'

Ernest stared at the note and handed it to his mother. 'I don't know what else to do,' he murmured, the tears welling again.

Susan put an arm round him and steered him into the kitchen. 'Leave her to me,' she said softly. 'Eat your breakfast and go back to Hawks Head. She'll come round eventually, and I'll send a message to you when she's ready.'

Ernest had little appetite for breakfast, but he ate what he could, and after one last attempt to talk to Millicent, he headed for the Hawkesbury river.

Port Jackson, April 1793

Jack Quince had ridden into town for supplies and to collect any letters that might have come from the many ships that now visited the port. Nell had given him a long shopping list, and it had taken him an age to collect everything, but as he was prepared to remain in town for at least another week, it didn't matter.

The recent arrival of the twins had Billy strutting about the place like a cockerel as he fussed over Nell and the children, and Jack had become inured to his habit of ceasing work well before sunset. He couldn't help but envy their domestic bliss, and was glad of the chance to escape for a while. Their happiness only reinforced his longing for Alice's arrival.

Having accomplished all he had set out to do today, he loaded the wagon and drove once more to the bustling quayside to find out if there was any news. He had made the short trip every morning since his arrival, for Alice had written to him from the Cape several months ago. She had warned there might be a delay in finding passage, but she was hopeful of getting on to the *Lady Elizabeth*. His impatience to have her at his side was making him fret, and he was beginning to think something might have happened to her.

As he steered the horse through the streets he glanced towards the house on the low hill where Ezra and Susan Collinson lived. He had heard about Millicent, and although he had been shocked by what had happened to her, he thought it inappropriate to call on them. He wasn't family, and he had suffered enough cruelty in his life without taking on someone else's grief. Billy's terse account of his own visit had told him all he needed to know.

Not wanting to risk the contents of the wagon to an opportunistic thief, he bought a meat pie from a street vendor and ate it sitting on the buckboard as he watched the bustle down by the quay. There were several American whaling ships at anchor, as well as a couple of merchantmen – Sydney Town had become a popular stopping-off point and trade was brisk. The starvation years were over, and the place was beginning to take on the appearance of a permanent settlement.

Then he caught sight of the boys in the chain gang. They had been assigned to clear the rocks the convict men had dug out of the earth, and to barrow them to the landfill for the new wharves. As he watched them he realised that no matter how much was achieved in the colony, it would never rise above its convict status as long as children were chained and forced into slavery.

'Watch what yer doing, yer idle piece of Irish shite,' yelled the overseer.

Jack flinched as the vicious whip Benson carried flicked over the boy's thin shoulders. He clenched his fists, longing to snatch it from him and beat the living daylights out of the man. Mullins might have drunk himself to death, but his evil lived on in the vicious Benson, who was a ticket-of-leave convict, with no skills to make a living, only the sadistic temperament endemic among such overseers.

He watched as the youngster struggled with a large rock from a pile that must have seemed never-ending, the shackles on his ankles hampering every step. The overseer's curses told Jack that he must have arrived on the *Queen*, a ship loaded with Irish Catholics, the majority children who had been caught up in the unrest in Ireland. There was mutiny in that young face, each insult and abuse another spur to his determination not to be cowed, but Jack knew from experience that the boy dared not complain or fight back for it would earn him a flogging.

He shivered as the old memories flooded in. There were fearsome punishments for those who fought the system, and youth was no protection. Those small boys could be hauled before a magistrate for the most minor offence, made to withstand fifty lashes of the cat – or, if the overseer was particularly cruel, subjected to a thousand cuts and thrown into solitary confinement where an offender was made to wear the heavy, smothering hood that everyone dreaded.

The lad had learnt an important lesson in not retaliating, for the unflogged could still believe in a future, but the flogged, who couldn't straighten after receiving the lash, surrendered to a despair that made them long for death.

Unable to watch any more, Jack flicked the reins and urged the horse into a fast walk. Punishment had become a way of life for those poor children, just as it had for him during the terrible voyage on the *Surprise*. Designed to deter, it merely degraded and stoked the fires of rebellion. The governor was a fool if he ignored the simmering resentment of the Irish convicts: their hatred of the English meant that sooner or later they would take revenge on those who had enslaved them.

Appetite gone, Jack took a long drink from the bottle of straw-coloured ale that the Americans brought in. It wasn't a patch on the dark, bitter ale of Sussex, but it took away the sourness in his mouth, slaked his thirst in the debilitating heat and didn't make his head buzz. He eased his hip on the unforgiving wooden seat and stretched out his leg as he brought the horse to a standstill on the quayside. It still pained him, even after all these years, but he had come to accept it as the price he'd had to pay for his freedom.

He sat in the sunshine, his broad-brimmed hat shading his face as he squinted into the glare and watched it dazzle on the water. The sea still held terrors for him, bringing nightmares of being chained up in the flooded bowels of the convict trans-port ship that woke him in a cold sweat, gasping for breath. Today it appeared benign, and he could even see a certain cruel beauty in it – but the memories would remain.

'Ship coming in!'

Jack looked out to the point and saw the flag being raised on the headland, but no sails. Climbing down from the buckboard, he led the horse along the cobbles to a better vantage-point. His pulse was racing but he tried to remain calm. There had been many bitter disappointments over the past days, and he dared not hope that Alice might finally be arriving.

He spied an elderly mariner sitting on a capstan and noted the fine telescope he was holding. 'Can you see her yet?' he asked, as he moved closer.

'She be a fine ship,' muttered the gnarled old seaman. 'Broad of beam and riding deep in the water. Reckon she be loaded with cargo.'

Jack sidled closer. He could see the sails now, but no matter how hard he squinted into the glare he couldn't make out what manner of ship she was. 'Can you tell her name?'

For a moment faded blue eyes regarded him, then the man returned to his telescope. 'She be flying British colours,' he mumbled. He twisted the sights on the telescope. 'Don't look to be a whaler or a merchantman, and she be escorted by two others.'

Jack could barely contain his impatience. He was itching to snatch away the glass and look for himself, but his innate sense of propriety stopped him. 'But can you see her name?'

It seemed an age before he replied. 'They be takin' her to t'other dock,' he muttered. 'She must be important.'

Jack clamped his lips together in frustration. The old boy seemed determined to keep him in suspense.

The telescope was lowered and the faded eyes were almost lost in the wrinkles of his tanned face as he grinned. 'She be the *Elizabeth*,' he said. 'The *Lady Elizabeth*.'

Jack's crippled hip hampered his speed as he raced across the cobbles and grabbed the reins. 'I'm coming, Alice,' he shouted, as he climbed awkwardly into the wagon, and set the startled horse into a shambling trot.

There was quite a gathering on the dockside, but he forced horse and wagon through the crowd, heedless of their complaints. He stood on the buckboard, scanning the ship for Alice, hope soaring.

The passengers were crowding the decks, waving and calling to those on the quay, but there was no sign of the familiar little figure and beloved face. The frustration and anxiety grew, and the minute the gangplank was lowered he left the horse and wagon and elbowed his way through the mêlée.

'Alice,' he called, his gaze darting from one face to another, desperate for a glimpse of fair hair and blue eyes. 'Alice, where are you? It's Jack.'

There was no answering call, merely amused smiles and murmurings of advice from the milling passengers and crew. Jack tore off his hat and shoved his way through until he had searched the *Lady Elizabeth* from stem to stern. 'Alice,' he shouted, 'where are you?'

'Are you Jack Quince,' said a voice at his shoulder.

Jack whirled to face the man. 'Yes,' he said, 'and I'm looking for Alice Hobden.'

The captain stroked his neat beard. 'I think everyone in the colony knows that.' He laughed. 'But I'm afraid she isn't on board.'

His spirits plummeted. 'But she said . . .'

The older man nodded. 'Miss Hobden was indeed to sail with me,' he said, 'but she has been delayed in the Cape.'

Jack felt the chill of dread. 'Why? What's happened? She hasn't changed her mind, has she?' Despair sharpened his tone.

'Not at all,' said the captain, as he reached into his pocket and pulled out a letter. 'She asked me to give you this,' he said, 'but before you read it, I must assure you that she is expected to recover and is determined to join you as soon as possible.'

'Recover?' Jack stared at him in confusion.

The captain patted his shoulder. 'I'll leave you to read your letter. Come and find me when you're ready. I have your sheep in the hold.'

Jack hardly heard what he was saying as he broke the seal and opened Alice's letter.

My dear Jack,

   Please try not to worry. The doctor says it isn't typhoid but malaria, and that I should be well enough to travel within months. I must have contracted this disease when, despite the netting I bought, I was bitten by mosquitoes. Cape Town is hot and crowded, but luckily I have enough money to pay for a room and treatment, so my recovery is assured.

   I am sorry to cause you anxiety, my dear, and I hope your concern will be tempered by the safe arrival of our sheep. It wasn't possible to keep them here, and the captain was very understanding, and promised he would keep an eye on them. They are good stock, and it was hard to barter a fair price, but I think you will agree that they make excellent breeders.

   I think of you every day as I wait to join you, and try to picture Moonrakers as you have described it, imagining you there. It won't be long now before we are together again. Take heart, my love. We have waited so long that a few more months will fly past. Look after yourself and our sheep, and I will let you know as soon as I have arranged passage.

   My love, as always,
   Alice

Jack's eyes were blurred with tears as he folded the letter and put it into his pocket. It was all too brief, giving him little detail of her illness, but Alice had never been one for words. He stared into the distance, his thoughts churning. If only there was a way to reach her – but Cape Town was so far away, and the letter months out of date. She might already be on her way.

He stood there in an agony of indecision. He was unable to leave the colony, and had no money to pay for passage. Then there were the sheep. He couldn't leave them in the hold, and there was nowhere to keep them in Sydney Town. 'Oh, Alice,' he breathed, 'what am I going to do?'

'I suggest you tend your sheep,' muttered the captain, when Jack approached him again. 'Miss Hobden knew you would wish to go to her, and asked me to persuade you otherwise.' His smile was kind. 'She's right, Mr Quince. She is being well looked after, and is in the finest place to recover, with an English nurse to care for her. Her greatest wish is for you to tend the sheep and wait for her. I suggest you do so.'

Jack knew he had no other option, and his sigh was filled with anguish. 'Where are they?'

The captain took him below, and as Jack herded them from the pens and steered them down the gangway on to the quay, he saw that they were indeed high-quality stock. Alice had done them proud. With a wave to the captain, he set off on the long trek back to Moonrakers.

The journey would be slow, kept to the pace of the slowest animal, but as he led the horse and wagon and chivvied the sheep before him, he felt his spirits rise. Alice and he shared a dream of owning the best flock of merinos in Australia. Their wool would make their fortune, and as Alice recovered in Cape Town, he would nurture the beasts as if they were their children.

Hawks Head Farm, May 1793

The men were asleep when the warriors crept closer to the shack. They didn't see the dark shadows move round the outside, or the flicker of the fire-sticks they carried. They slept on as the fire-sticks brushed against the brittle grass, and flames licked at the parched wooden walls and the roof.

Lowitja's uncle Pemuluwuy and his son Tedbury melted into the darkness and joined the others who were already leading the cattle and horses through the trees. They numbered only seven, for the great tribes that had once roamed this southern quarter were no more, their people dead, lured away by white man's rum or simply too afraid to remain there now that the Dreaming Places were destroyed.

Pemuluwuy's hatred for the invader spurred him on, and although he found it difficult to understand the complacency of many of his people, he knew someone had to fight for their right to live on the land entrusted to them by the Great Spirit.

As they moved swiftly and silently through the darkness, Pemuluwuy's mind was already on the next raid. The lands were being taken over, the animals chased from their natural feeding grounds. The remnants of the many tribes who had once lived there were being pushed into areas that offered poor hunting and brackish water.

He should have taken more notice when Lowitja had read the stones and communed with the Great Spirits, for she had seen the exodus of their people into the harsh interior. They were indeed on the edge of extinction, and it seemed that no matter how many farms he burnt and how many cattle and horses he stole, he couldn't halt the white tide that was destroying his people, the essence of their way of life and spirituality.

Ernest moved restlessly against the lumpy pillow. The knowledge of what had happened to Millicent filled his dreams, and the anguish he felt at her adamant refusal to see him or talk to him meant he was in constant turmoil. Tonight the dreams were entwined with the scent of smoke and the crackle of burning timbers. When he opened his eyes he realised it was no dream. 'George!' he shouted. 'We're on fire!'

The brothers leapt from their beds, grabbed their rifles and ran outside in their underwear. They were met by the convicts who had been assigned to them and were standing about watching the conflagration.

The lovely new house was well alight, the convict tents blazing – they had all been lucky to escape – but of the arsonists there was no sign. 'Oh, no,' breathed George, 'they've torched the barn as well.'

'Quick! We must save the harvest.' Ernest threw a bucket at his brother, then grabbed anything that might hold water and tossed it to the convicts. 'Move!' he yelled.

Startled into action, they ran to the river, filled the buckets and tore back to the barn – the house was no longer important but the barn held their future.

The smoke choked them, stung their eyes and made it hard to breathe, but the fire had to be extinguished, the harvest rescued, or the past year's labour would have been for nothing. The convicts worked as hard as the brothers, for they had realised that this was their livelihood too: none wished to return to Sydney Town and the cut of the lash.

The flames spread as they feasted on the sun-bleached wood and climbed to the tar-pitched roof. The brothers and their convicts hauled water and ran until their lungs felt as if they would burst and their muscles grew leaden. It had become a battle against time and the ravenous element that was devouring their livelihood. Pain and exhaustion were shrugged off and they moved in mechanical symmetry from river to barn.

'It's no good,' gasped George, as he threw yet another pail of water on to the inferno. 'There are too few of us and it takes too long to carry the water here from the river.'

'We must,' shouted Ernest, above the roar of the inferno. 'We'll beat it yet.'

The flames leapt higher as the ravening beast fed on the roof and pushed through the disintegrating timbers to the wheat that lay inside. A gust of wind sent sparks into the night sky and a tentacle of flame stretched from the house to snake through the grass. It divided, then divided again, tracking rivers through the grass until it was a delta of fire.

'Look out!' George shoved Ernest out of the way as a sheet of flame shot from a gum tree and threatened to engulf him.

Ernest, half-blinded by smoke, seared by heat and exhausted from his labours, hit the ground, his ankle twisting beneath him. He rose swiftly, biting down on the pain as he swerved to avoid the advancing flames and the burning tree.

The chain of men broke as the inferno advanced and cans of kerosene exploded. Ernest knew the fight was lost. 'Get into the river,' he shouted, as he hobbled down towards the water. 'Save yourselves!'

The water was warm, as if the strength of the fire had heated it. Ernest and George waded in and sank up to their necks to soak away the dirt and weariness, and to ease their trembling muscles. They were joined by the convicts, whose faces were blackened by smoke and streaked with sweat. There was nothing anyone could do but watch as the barn began to creak and sway under the onslaught.

They heard the crack of timbers, the groan of heavy beams, the roar and crackle of the fire, and were smothered by the thick smoke that swirled, eddied and carried the sparks that would ignite more fires.

The walls of the barn seemed to hesitate for a moment, but then, as the roof caved in, they crashed, showering sparks into the night sky to mingle with the stars.

Birds flew in alarm from the trees as kangaroos, wallabies and shambling wombats made for the safety of the riverbank and beyond. Lizards scuttled away and possums carried their young on their backs as they leapt out of burning branches and sought refuge upstream.

The flames moved on, spreading, dancing, devouring everything in their path.

When the sun lightened the sky and filtered through the pall of smoke that still hung thick in the air, Ernest and his brother left their makeshift night shelter and, with their convict helpers, waded back across the river. They stood in silence as they regarded the horror of the scene before them.

The new house was a charred ruin, the barn and tents were no more. The earth was charred black and tendrils of smoke still twisted in the morning breeze. The three cows and the bull were gone, there was no sign of the two horses, and every tool they possessed had been burnt with the barn.

'At least we won't have to clear that plot of land,' said Ernest, as they regarded the charred remains of the stand of trees. 'And there's enough ash on the soil to make it fertile.'

George was pale, his fists knotted so tightly that his knuckles showed white through the tanned skin. 'I'm going to find the bastards that did this and kill every last one of them,' he muttered.

'That won't help,' Ernest said quietly. 'They're long gone.'

'But we've lost everything, Ernie. We're marooned here, and who's to say the blacks won't come back for us now we're unprotected?'

'They would have speared us last night if that was their intention,' murmured Ernest, as the reality of their situation dawned on him. Millicent would be in court in three days' time and he had vowed to be there. Now it would be impossible, for Sydney Town was at least two days' hard riding, and it would take many more to walk.

22

Sydney Town Courthouse, 1 May 1793

The military court was in session, and the new chief justice was resplendent in his dress uniform, epaulettes glittering in the shafts of light that flooded through the windows.

Susan regarded him thoughtfully. He was an imposing man, much like Gilbert, with a flaring moustache and beetling brows. But there the similarity ended, for Susan knew that Major Hawkins was known to be biased when it came to judgments concerning convicts. It was generally agreed in Sydney Town that he considered most of them irredeemable. Hanging and flogging were his answer to most misdemeanours – or he would simply banish miscreants to the convict settlement of Norfolk Island, where they could live out their wretched lives in a hell-hole that offered no escape.

Susan glanced round the room and felt glad that he had ordered a closed court today. It had been decided that this trial was a military matter, and therefore would be kept within the confines of military jurisdiction. The accusation of rape against six officers of the New South Wales Corps made it so, and she thanked God that millicent was to be spared the usual hordes of spectators who made it their business and entertainment to come to the court sessions.

She felt the chill of apprehension as she glanced at the dock and the men waiting there. Their demeanour varied from defiant to terrified – but one stood out in particular, not only because his face was all too familiar but because he showed no shame for his crime and was leaning nonchalantly against the wooden partition as if he were waiting for a stage-coach.

The judge had noticed his lack of respect. 'Stand to attention,' he roared, 'or I'll have you in contempt of court.'

Susan watched the officer sigh and obey the command, but she noticed the insolence in his careless salute and knew it wouldn't serve him well in the judge's eyes. With a nervous glance over her shoulder, she scanned the room. Thankfully there was no sign of the one man she dreaded seeing, which went some way towards calming her.

The room was almost silent but for the rustle of paper and the low murmur of the officers representing the accused and the accuser. Susan could not see Millicent's face, which was masked by the black veil she had sewn to her hat brim, but she could feel the tension in the girl, and eased her arm round her waist to bolster her courage.

She watched Hawkins shuffle the papers before him and reach for the gavel. He would be impatient for the case to be under way, for Major Grose, the newly elected governor, was holding a party that afternoon, and there was nothing Hawkins liked better than to bait his old rival. The competition between them for the illustrious post had been bitterly fought, and Hawkins had never forgiven Arthur Phillip for choosing over himself the man he considered very ordinary.

Hawkins slammed down the gavel and called for order.

Millicent had known that today would come eventually, and although she and Susan had pleaded for her absence, the judge had refused. The rest of the family had been firmly denied entrance to the courtroom and for that she was grateful. It would be hard enough as it was, and the last thing she had wanted was for them to bear witness to the depths of her shame.

She huddled against Susan, clutching her arm as the charges were listed and her statement was read out. It was as if those terrible things had happened to someone else – as if once again she'd left her mortal body and was watching from afar.

The doctor took the oath and gave his evidence clearly, describing her injuries in laymen's terms so all could understand what had happened to her.

The veil was smothering, and the sweat ran down her face to soak her dress as the heat rose in the courtroom and intimate details were revealed. She had no more tears to cry, just the cold, almost impersonal acceptance that her fate had been sealed and she could do nothing further in her quest for justice.

'The prosecution calls Florence Collinson to the witness box.'

Millicent braced herself for what was to come. She didn't trust Florence. Would she tell the truth and reveal Susan's secret for all to hear, or would she resort to her usual lies? It was difficult to tell, but for Susan's sake she hoped it would be the latter, and guessed that Florence would find it easier to bend the truth. She had already alienated her father, and the revelation of Susan's affair would only drive a wider breach between them, tearing the family apart.

'The witness is absent, m'lud,' intoned the bailiff, as he returned from the side room alone. 'It appears she does not wish to testify.' He put a note on the judge's desk.

Hawkins grunted as he read it and set it aside. 'She will be held in contempt,' he growled. 'See to it after today's proceedings, bailiff.'

Millicent breathed a sigh of relief.

Susan stiffened beside her. 'That girl is beyond redemption,' she hissed. 'How *dare* she defy the court?'

Millicent grasped her fingers. At least Susan would be spared humiliation. Yet Florence's absence shouldn't have surprised either of them. She was not the sort of girl to admit the part she had played in the events of that awful night, and although she expected only the highest moral fortitude in others, she herself was sadly lacking in it.

Mary Johnson, the minister's wife, gave her evidence in a clear, concise fashion, stating that she had seen Millicent and Florence in conversation that evening, and had witnessed Millicent's distress as she ran off. The defence lawyer had no questions, and she was thanked and dismissed.

One by one the accused took the oath and presented the court with their story. Millicent listened in growing disbelief as each brought forth a witness who swore on the Bible that the accused had been nowhere near the alley that night.

The loyalty stood firm: the testimonies were unshaken by the probing questions of the prosecution lawyers. There had been a card game they had all attended until the early hours and the landlord of the tavern testified to their presence.

Millicent's spirits plummeted. They had thought of everything. It was her word against theirs. The suit she had brought so bravely was being torn apart.

'Miss Millicent Parker.'

'Be brave,' murmured Susan, as she helped her to her feet. 'The truth will out. Justice will be done.'

Millicent peered through her veil at the judge. Her legs were trembling so that she could barely stand. Her moment had come – and she dreaded it.

'You may remain where you are, my dear,' Hawkins intoned, with brisk kindliness. 'Will you please point to the men you say are guilty of this heinous act? Are they in court?'

Clutching the railing in front of her, Millicent forced herself to look at the accused. She took a deep breath, reminding herself that she was safe here. She wouldn't even have to see them after today. 'Yes, my lord,' she whispered. 'That's them there.' She pointed to the six defendants.

'You must speak up,' the judge said, as he peered over his spectacles. 'The court must be able to hear your testimony.'

She took a deep breath, determined to be strong. 'It's them,' she said clearly, as she pointed again. 'Those six men over there.'

'Thank you, my dear. Now, will you be so kind as to indicate which of these men incited the attack upon your person?'

Millicent pointed at the smirking, arrogant young senior officer, who seemed to find the occasion little more than a passing amusement. 'Him,' she said firmly. 'Him on the end.'

'To save you further distress I will not ask you to take the witness stand, but will demand an oath from you that the details in your statement are true before God.'

Millicent was so relieved she almost fainted, but the ordeal was nearly over and with superhuman effort, she remained upright. The bailiff handed her a Bible, and she took it firmly. 'I swear before God and on this Bible that my statement is true,' she said, into the silent court.

'I object most strongly.'

The voice came from the back of the court, and everyone turned, startled by the interruption. The sound of boot-heels rang on the flagstone floor as the man strode into the centre of the room. 'This trial is a travesty of justice, and your main witness is a proven liar.'

Millicent froze. She was aware of Susan's clutching hands, of her sharp intake of breath and the tremor that ran through her – but all coherent thought was swept away and she could only stare at him in speechless horror.

'I will not have these interruptions in my court,' snapped Hawkins, as he banged the gavel ferociously. 'Who are you, sir? And what business do you have here?'

'I am Jonathan Cadwallader, Earl of Kernow here to defend my family's good name along with that of my son, Edward.' He indicated the protagonist in the line of defendants.

'I apologise for my earlier rudeness, my lord,' said Hawkins, meek in the presence of an Englishman whose reputation as a powerful and wealthy member of the aristocracy was well known around the world. 'If you would be so kind as to enter the witness box, my bailiff will take your oath.'

Susan stared at Jonathan, mouth open, eyes wide in disbelief as his voice rang through the courthouse. It was hard to take in what she was seeing. How had he managed to arrive so secretly – and with such devastating timing?

She glanced towards his cur of a son, saw the smirk deepen and wondered if he had known his father would come to his rescue. But Jonathan Cadwallader hadn't been in Australia at the time of the attack – and she would have known if he was, for he was an unmistakable presence.

'Please tell the court why you felt compelled to appear today,' said Hawkins. 'I was not aware that you were in the country.'

'I arrived on the *Lady Elizabeth* from Cape Town,' he replied, 'and have been the guest of the governor over the past few days.'

He looked across the room and Susan saw his eyes widen in surprise, but she gained little satisfaction from his almost imperceptible hesitation: Jonathan had always been self-assured and his momentary lapse would be swiftly overcome.

Jonathan turned his attention back to the judge. 'My shock at discovering my son's predicament was further endorsed by the identity of his accuser, my lord. I realised justice had to be done – and swiftly.'

Susan battled to control herself as she watched him in the witness box, and tried to comfort a devastated Millicent. She knew he would lie through his teeth to save his whelp so Millicent had an even tougher fight ahead of her now.

Jonathan stood tall as he began his testimony, his voice ringing with the arrogance of an accomplished public speaker. 'The girl who accuses my son and his fellow officers of this heinous crime once worked as a maid on my Cornish estates. She was walking out with one of my gardeners at the time and was soon with child.' His cold gaze flitted past Susan to settle on Millicent.

Susan felt her shrink from it and pulled her to her side.

'When she was confronted with her condition she threw accusations at me. A man in my position would never contemplate such a liaison, and of course I dismissed her,' he continued, in the hushed silence. 'It was then that I discovered her theft of two guineas.'

Susan was startled by Millicent's reaction. The girl leapt to her feet. 'That's not true,' she shouted. 'You gave me that money 'cos you raped me.'

He seemed unperturbed by her interruption, merely raising an eyebrow as he turned to the judge. 'You see, my lord,' he intoned, with a world-weary air, 'the girl has cried rape before. How can any of us believe such a liar when she is also a proven thief?'

'I'm not!' she shouted.

Susan saw the tears of frustration and tried to coax her to sit down, but Millicent shrugged her away.

Jonathan drew a sheaf of papers from the leather case he carried. 'But you were convicted as a thief at Truro Assizes and transported here.'

Susan saw the slump in Millicent's shoulders as she sank back on to the hard wooden bench, and knew she had neither the wit nor the strength to fight any more. But her own anger at the injustice was all-consuming, and she rose from the bench. Millicent had given in, but she was damned if she would.

'She stole bread to keep from starving,' she stated loudly, as she marched into the centre of the room and stood defiantly before the judge. 'Hardly a crime worthy of transportation – let alone the abuse and ill-treatment she suffered on the transport ship. Millicent has been granted a full pardon – it is why she has the legal right to bring this suit. You *cannot* and *must not* let her unfortunate past overshadow the crime that will be punished here today.'

She was fully aware that she had the court in thrall, and her rage gave her the strength and courage to look Jonathan in the eye. 'Edward Cadwallader and his friends raped Millicent without pity or thought for the consequences. She identified each and every man – has the doctor's evidence to prove what they did to her. She overcame her shame and natural timidity to appear here today. It is *they* who are on trial, not Millicent.'

'I will have silence in my court,' yelled Hawkins, as he grew red in the face and crashed the gavel on the desk.

'And I will have justice!' cried Susan. 'Those men are guilty of the most wicked crime, and I will *not* allow you to be overawed by *him*.' She stabbed an accusing finger at Jonathan. 'He might be an earl but he's still capable of lying.'

'Sit down or I'll have you in contempt of court,' roared Hawkins.

'Not until I see that justice is served,' retorted Susan. She was breathing hard, her audacity making her strong. All the years of careful manners and tightly reined emotion had been swept away to reveal the tough little fisher-girl she really was – ready for battle, ready to defend her weaker friend regardless of the consequences.

They glared at one another in the ensuing silence and everyone seemed to be holding their breath. Susan refused to be cowed by the judge, even though she knew that her outburst might hinder Millicent's chances of winning in this trial. But if Jonathan wanted to play dirty, so could she.

Jonathan brought the stalemate to an end. 'If you'll excuse me, my lord,' he said gravely, 'the court should understand this woman's reason for her vindictive attack on me and my son.'

Susan glared at him, waiting to see what devious ploy he had ready to fight back.

Jonathan avoided her eyes. His gaze drifted to a point beyond her shoulder, his expression inscrutable. 'Hell hath no fury like a woman scorned, my lord,' he said, into the stillness. 'And Susan Collinson has chosen the perfect opportunity for revenge.'

She experienced a twinge of unease as she saw how he stood so tall and composed in the witness box. 'Revenge?' she snapped. 'Why should I seek revenge?'

He ignored her. 'Mrs Collinson and I were once neighbours in England, my lord, and although I don't wish to appear ungentlemanly, her advances towards me became somewhat embarrassing.'

'How dare you blacken my character?' Colour burnt her face as she clenched her fists.

He ignored her and smiled at the judge as if acknowledging that they were both men of the world. 'She offered herself to me in the most blatant manner, my lord, and when I rejected her, she swore vengeance.' He looked at his enthralled audience in the courtroom. 'Today is proof of that.'

'You lie.' Susan strode over to the witness box, prepared to spit in his eye and punch his aristocratic nose.

'One more step towards the witness and I will throw you into the lock-up,' snarled Hawkins.

'He's a perjurer,' she yelled. 'He's making this up to clear his son's name. Don't listen to him!'

'The lock-up awaits, Mrs Collinson,' warned the judge, eyes snapping. 'I suggest you hold your tongue.'

Susan clenched her teeth and folded her arms. She was seething, her frustration almost too great to control.

Hawkins adjusted his wig and turned to Jonathan. 'That is a serious accusation, my lord, and I would respectfully remind you that you are under oath.' He glanced at Susan, who was still standing in front of him. 'Mrs Collinson is a respected citizen, the wife of our esteemed minister. Her work among the convicts is testimony to her good character.' His stern gaze returned to Jonathan. 'Do you have proof to the contrary?'

Jonathan avoided her glare as he pulled a sheet of paper from the leather case and handed it to the judge. 'This is one of her letters, sir. You will see it is an invitation to join her in a tryst.'

Susan stifled a groan and held on to the nearest table for support. His betrayal had struck at her core, leaving her as winded as if he had punched her in the stomach. 'How could you?' she rasped. 'How could you twist everything to your advantage like this?'

He showed no reaction.

'Look at me, you bastard.' The rage had returned. 'Look me in the eye and tell your lies.'

He reddened, but his back remained stiff.

'I know why you're doing this,' she hissed, as again she approached the witness stand. 'You're protecting your son, and your family's reputation. But I never thought you could stoop so low – never suspected you capable of such dark betrayal.'

'Sit down!' Hawkins banged the gavel, his face puce with fury.

Susan could see the nervous tic in Jonathan's cheek and knew her accusation had struck home – but she also knew she was beaten. She lifted her chin and went back to Millicent, who was wide-eyed with admiration. She sat down with a thud and fought to control her rage.

Hawkins read the letter and handed it back. 'You have proved to me that both witnesses are unreliable, their evidence tainted by their past unfortunate involvement with your good self and your family.'

Susan's fists tightened. Her nerves were taut and she had to force herself to remain seated as the judge turned his attention to the rest of the court.

'There is the doctor's evidence of a gruesome attack upon Millicent Parker, but as the accused seem to have been elsewhere that night, their guilt cannot be established.'

There was a long pause. Susan and Millicent braced themselves for the verdict.

Hawkins glanced at his pocket watch and gathered up the papers. 'I declare the charges unfound. Case dismissed.'

Jonathan watched as Susan put her arm round the girl and virtually carried her through the back door to a waiting buggy. He felt sick with regret. He had had no intention of blackening Susan's character today, and had brought the letter in case he needed a last resort. The evidence against Millicent would have been enough, but Susan had brought about her own character assassination by flying into a rage and disrupting the court.

It had shocked him to see her, even though he had made enquiries and had known she would be in court to support the maid. She had been magnificent, he acknowledged, and a lesser man would have wilted beneath that awesome temper. Susan had clearly lost none of her fighting spirit, and despite her years as a respectable matron, she still possessed the fire and energy of the fisher-girl with whom he had fallen in love all those years before.

He began to stuff the papers back into the leather document case, the knowledge of what he had done making his head pound and his stomach clench. He'd been too harsh in shredding the girl's suit, and now he'd made a lifelong enemy of the one woman he had ever loved. If only she hadn't interfered – but there was no salvation in wishing a deed undone. The enmity between them could never be vanquished now.

He looked at the letter, then crammed it into the case with the other papers. He had taken a gamble in using it, and it was fortunate Susan had not demanded to read it, for the original had long since been destroyed and he had penned it himself last night.

The gamble had paid off, and although he felt guilty for what he'd done, Susan had left him with no choice. The family name and reputation had to be protected, and if that meant perjuring himself, so be it. But the loss of Susan as lover and friend was harder to bear, a price too high for what had been achieved today.

'Thank you, Father,' said Edward, stiffly. 'I knew I could rely on you.'

Jonathan collected his things and turned reluctantly to his son. He looked into the steady blue eyes and the smirking face and loathed what he saw. 'We will talk,' he said quietly, as the others crowded round to thank him before they left to celebrate their release with their lying witnesses. 'But not here.' He looked at the clock on the wall. 'Come to my lodgings in an hour.'

Edward looked less cocky now as he eyed his father. 'I have other plans,' he muttered.

'Change them.'

'Yes, sir.' The salute was executed with mocking disrespect before he turned to his friends.

Jonathan's expression was grim as he faced the unpalatable truth. The boy had been ruined by his mother's indulgence and believed he could get away with anything. He was certainly in for a nasty shock. He watched in disgust as the flask of brandy was passed round and they set off to carouse in the town. He would have flogged the lot of them until they were incapable of walking anywhere.

He waited until they had gone and he could no longer hear them before he strode out of the courthouse. The sun glared into his eyes, the heat washing over him as he stood on the step and gazed out into the street. Apart from a youth lurking on the corner and a drunken Aboriginal sleeping in the gutter, there was no one about.

He sighed with relief. Today was fraught enough, and his guilt at having betrayed Susan and the girl too strong for him to face either of them yet. But he would, he vowed, for justice had not been done, and he needed to assuage his sense of loss by letting them know that he planned his own kind of justice.

The track from the Hawkesbury River, 1 May 1793

Ernest had been walking for three days and as he tramped barefoot through the bush, he realised he must look ridiculous in his long combinations. He could not imagine how he would get to his parents' house without being seen. But the thought of Millicent, of the ordeal she must be going through at this moment, spurred him on. He had made a promise to himself that he would be there when she discovered she needed him, and he was determined to keep it. Millicent was his love, and when all this was over he would take her back to Hawks Head Farm and keep her safe.

He grimaced as he thought of the charred remains of their new homestead and the devastation the fire had wrought on the harvest. The work had been knocked back at least a year and they would have to begin again – but the government stores would supply more tools and seed, and a house could be easily built and furnished. Times would be even tougher for a while, and some might expect them to walk away from it – but he and George were made of stern stuff, and no matter how hard life became in the following years, it would all be worthwhile if Millicent was at his side.

The heat was less ferocious in the bush, the light filtering through the trees as the insects clicked and the birds' sharp cries filled the air. Ernest kept walking, stopping only at the river to drink, wash away the sweat and ease his swollen ankle. By nightfall he should begin to see the lights of Sydney Town.

Sydney Town Courthouse, 1 May 1793

Ezra had been waiting with the horse and carriage in an alley at the back of the courthouse. His hands were restless as he held the reins, his thoughts tumbling over each other as he tried to imagine what was happening inside. His faith had been sorely tested in the past weeks and he had found it hard to believe that a loving God could permit such an atrocity against an innocent young woman.

Then there was Florence. The depths of his despair were evident in the slump of his shoulders and the lines in his face. He was an old man whose beliefs had been shattered with the structure of his family. He had failed his daughter, his wife, Millicent – and there seemed little chance of redemption. All he had wanted was a close, loving family and the certainty of God's blessings, but his dreams had been destroyed.

He was snapped out of his gloom by the door opening. One look at Susan's face told him everything, and as he climbed down to help his wife with Millicent he cried out silently to God to have pity on them all.

Government House, 1 May 1793

Jonathan strode down the road towards the cottage he had leased in the grounds of Government House. It was clean and comfortably furnished and the broad veranda at the front was pleasantly cool in the heat of the day. But the best thing about it was the anonymity it had offered during the past few days when it had been so important to remain out of sight so that his court appearance would have the maximum effect.

He tossed his hat, cane and briefcase on to a day-bed in the parlour and ordered his manservant to bring some tea outside. Having changed into more comfortable attire, he returned to the veranda and sat in an easy chair.

Governor Grose had invited him to this afternoon's party to meet the so-called great and good of the colony, but he preferred not to make polite conversation to people he neither knew nor cared for. There were more pressing things to see to. He had not come all this way merely to dig his wretch of a son out of a hole. Once the interview with Edward was over, he would be free to bring his plans to fruition.

He sipped the tea and gazed with little interest at the gathering on the far western lawn. He could see the fluttering of colourful dresses and parasols, the striking red of uniforms, the glint of brass buttons and gold epaulettes. Servants bustled about carrying trays and several dogs were racing around getting in everyone's way. He smiled for the first time that day. They reminded him of Banks's damned greyhounds.

The memory of that journey took his thoughts back to Susan. He would never forget the expression on her face when he had produced that bogus letter, and would certainly never forgive himself for bringing her so much pain. She deserved better than that from him after all they'd been to each other, and he was determined to make it up to her.

He stared into the distance at the kaleidoscope of colour that shifted and swirled on the far lawns. As for Millicent, he had thought her long dead – had even had reports of her demise from her slut of a stepmother. He had been shocked to discover the identity of his son's accuser, and the circumstances that had led her here.

'Father?'

He was startled from his thoughts. 'You're early.'

'I have an appointment with my commanding officer at four,' Edward retorted. He threw himself into a chair and stretched out his legs.

Jonathan watched him. At twenty, the boy was tall, handsome and looked well in his uniform, but his mouth was petulant, like his mother's, his eyes and posture arrogant. 'I regret not having been a proper father to you, Edward,' he said, as he put down the cup of tea on the table between them. 'If I had been given the opportunity for some say in your upbringing, we might have become friends and avoided this day's terrible events.'

'You were never at home long enough to be a father,' Edward said, as he sprang from the chair. 'And if you are about to embark on a lecture, I will take my leave and rejoin my friends at the tavern.'

'You will sit down until I give you permission to go,' said Jonathan, and stood up to face his son.

'I'm not a child any longer but a lieutenant in the British Army.' Edward's eyes flashed and his fists were rigid at his sides as a pulse worked in his jaw.

'You are a liar, a thief and a rapist,' said Jonathan, flatly. 'And if I didn't have the family name to protect, I'd have seen you horsewhipped and left to rot in prison.'

'So speaks the loving father,' sneered Edward.

Jonathan knew the boy was trying to provoke him, but he would not retaliate, even though his hand itched to slap the supercilious face. 'Your mother was your downfall,' he said tersely. 'She drove me away with her evil tongue and deprived me of knowing you as a son. She spoilt you, gave in to your demands and turned you into an unpleasant, immoral wastrel.'

'My mother was a saint,' his son hissed, face red with anger. 'She not only had to shoulder the burden of running the estate and looking after me while you gallivanted across the world, she also had your endless love-affairs to contend with, and the gossip they caused. She was shunned by society and lived in disgrace because of your reputation. No wonder she died of a broken heart.'

'Broken heart?' He snorted. 'She didn't have one to break.'

'I will take my leave,' Edward replied coldly. 'It seems we have nothing more to say to each other.'

Jonathan grasped his arm. 'You'll leave when I permit it,' he barked. He took little satisfaction from his son's frozen stance and ghastly pallor. 'I have spoken with your commanding officer. We agree that you and your friends have brought nothing but disgrace to your regiment and, regardless of the outcome today, it would not be fitting for any of you to remain in Sydney Town.'

Edward's eyes narrowed. 'What have you done?'

Jonathan shrugged. '*I* have done little,' he said. 'Your own actions have earned you demotion and five years' transfer to the Brisbane river district where your exposure to the fleshpots will be curtailed.'

'Brisbane river? There's nothing but marauding blacks and jungle up there.' He licked his lips as he ran his fingers nervously through his dark hair. 'We'll refuse to go,' he said. 'The case was thrown out – we've committed no crime.'

'We both know that that isn't true,' said Jonathan, with bitterness, 'and I have lodged a full statement with a lawyer. If you return to Sydney Town before the five years are up, or make contact with either woman again, that statement will be handed to the courts.'

'You wouldn't dare.' Edward's eyes blazed. 'You'd be charged with perjury.'

Jonathan relaxed, but his smile didn't reach his eyes. 'I was always a gambling man, Edward, but this time the odds are with me. For all your bullying ways, you are a coward. I'll take my chance.'

Edward's frustration was clear in the clenching of his fists and the rapid pulse beating below the teardrop stain on his temple. After a long, hard stare, he turned and stormed off the veranda.

Jonathan watched him leave, regret at the loss of his son and the years they might have spent together lying heavily on his heart. Edward might have been a fine young man if things had been different.

He looked across the lawn, deep in thought. His journey to Australia was to have been one of reconciliation, an opportunity to put the past behind them so that they might become acquainted with one another now that Emily was dead – but that had been before he had reached these shores and discovered Edward hurtling towards damnation.

Jonathan fretted for his son's future. Edward needed a strong influence to keep him on the straight and narrow, but Jonathan knew he was not the man to provide it – not after today. It was clear that Edward had to be reined in before he committed further atrocities, and the years in the wilderness of Brisbane river should go some way towards that. But it was with a heavy heart that Jonathan decided the only real solution was to find his son a wife.

Sydney Cove, 1 May 1793

Millicent had looked for Ernest as the buggy turned the corner. She had come to regret her treatment of him, knowing she had been unjust and hurtful. Now she wanted to see him again, to feel as she once had and know that his promises had been given with a true heart. But there had been no sign of him and Millicent had to accept that she had destroyed the only good thing in her life. Not that it mattered: the Millicent who had once loved him so dearly no longer existed.

She sat next to Susan as Ezra coaxed the horse into a trot. She could hear her friend's soft voice, but her words were meaningless. She was aware of colour, noise and movement outside the confines of the hooded buggy, but saw nothing. It was as if she existed in a void where nothing was real: all emotion had been spent and the Millicent she had once been was a hollow shell.

Susan and Ezra helped her down from the buggy and she went with them into the house. She let them fuss about her as they took her hat and veil, and set a cup of hot milk before her. Their soft talk drifted over her, and although she knew in some distant part of her mind that they were trying to make things better, she wished only for silence and solitude.

As night fell and she was finally alone in her room, she sat down at the little desk and began to write a letter to Susan. Her hand was uneven, the grammar and spelling that of a child, for she'd had little education, but it was something that had to be done if she was ever to find peace, and she left nothing out.

When it was finished, she propped the letter against the lamp and placed her precious engagement ring beside it. In her nightdress, she went to stand at the window and look down upon the town. They were out there somewhere. She could almost sense their presence in the dark shadows and hear their voices, and she trembled as she stared down at the twinkling lights. They would find her again – would seek her out and exact their revenge. Not for them the prison of memories, but the freedom to do as they pleased in the knowledge that lies and injustice would protect them.

Millicent gathered up the unfinished wedding dress and put it on. The material whispered as it settled over her shoulders and drifted to the floor. It was in the softest cream, the tiny ribbon rosettes stitched on to the bodice and gathered into a posy at the waist. She couldn't reach the laces at the back, but that didn't matter.

She stared at her reflection for a long time in the mirror, then moved silently through the house. The stool was on the porch. She picked it up and drifted into the garden.

A strange calm descended as she gazed at the starlit sky and the reflection of the moon on the water, and watched the patterns of the shifting leaves in the trees. Her feet were wet with dew, the hem of her precious dress soaked. But she scarcely noticed as she fetched a rope from Ezra's shed and climbed on to the stool she had placed beneath the stoutest tree.

When all was ready she took one last, longing look at the little house she had once called home and stepped into eternity.

Sydney Town, 3 May 1793

Ernest reached the outskirts two days after the trial. He had hoped he could catch a ride on a passing wagon, but he had met no one on that lonely track, and it had taken him five days to walk the distance. Following a circuitous route to avoid being seen in his tattered, filthy underwear, he arrived at the little house that overlooked the river just after dawn.

It was ominously quiet, the doors and windows shut, the screens firmly closed against the weak sunlight of a storm-laden sky. He climbed the two wooden steps to the new veranda. The front door was unlocked as usual, and he went inside.

Stillness greeted him, and with it a strange, almost sweet smell he could not identify. He stood in the kitchen and looked at the unwashed plates on the table, the pots and pans in the sink. His mother would not usually leave the house like this – something was wrong. Fear dried his mouth and his pulse raced as his imagination conjured disaster. He went from room to room in search of reassurance. But the silence mocked him, and when it had been proved to him that no one was at home, he gathered up some boots, a shirt and a pair of trousers his mother had left in her sewing room. He had to find Millicent.

His hair still wet from a hasty wash, he snatched up bread and cheese and hurried outside. He hesitated, unsure where to start his search. Millicent must be with his parents, but where would they have gone so early on a Saturday morning? After a moment's thought, he hurried down the hill towards the town. His father was more than likely at the church, preparing for tomorrow's services.

The sun was hidden behind a thick layer of cloud, and the wind was chill, blowing off the sea. As Ernest threaded his way through the bustling crowds at the wharves and narrow alleyways, he felt the first spots of rain. Harder and swifter they fell until he was drenched, his shirt sticking to him like a second skin, trousers clinging to his legs. But he hardly noticed the discomfort as he made for the church. He had to find the girl he loved and know she was safe.

The walls of the church rose before him, the dark red bricks glistening in the rain. He was about to push through the heavy oak door when something caught his eye. He peered through the deluge, and saw a little group of people huddled under umbrellas on the far side of the boundary fence in the graveyard for executed convicts and suicides, banished for ever to remain outside hallowed ground.

He shivered and was about to turn away when he realised there was something familiar about one of the mourners. His heart thudded so painfully against his ribs that he could barely breathe as he waded through the puddles. His hands were numb with cold as he fumbled with the latch on the gate, but his eyes remained fixed on the woman's face.

'Mother?' It was a whisper, drowned in the rain, muffled by the thunder that rolled overhead.

Susan came to him and took his hands. Her face was luminous with grief, her eyes dark with torment. 'Ernest,' she murmured, 'my precious boy. I'm so sorry – so, so sorry. We sent a messenger to warn you, but you must have missed him.'

Ernest looked over her head, searching for Millicent. His gaze fell on his father, and as he noted the lines of sorrow on his face he knew he wouldn't find her. He stepped away from his mother and approached the grave.

The hole seemed very deep, and was already filling with water. The coffin lay there with only rain-splattered roses for company. He fell to his knees in the mud, his tears mingling with the rain as he tried to understand what had happened. 'Millicent?' he sobbed. 'Millie, why? I love you, I'll always love you – don't leave me. Please don't leave me.'

'She's already gone, my darling,' murmured Susan, as she knelt beside him and put her arm round his shoulders. 'She couldn't stay any longer.'

The Reverend Johnson cleared his throat and resumed the service as his wife sheltered mother and son with her umbrella. Ezra stood grey-faced and blank-eyed beside the grave, his faith shattered, and his grief so unbearable that he had nothing left with which to comfort his wife and son.

23

Sydney Town, August 1793

During the three months after Millicent's funeral, the atmosphere in the house showed no improvement. Ernest was still seething with rage against the Cadwalladers – and against the justice that had betrayed his innocent bride. Ezra was a wraith-like presence, his silent, inward battle against his loss of faith in God all too evident from the anguish in his face. George had returned to Hawks Head within hours of his arrival on the day of the funeral, unable to stand the gloom and the silence.

Susan stared out over the water that lay like a sheet of green glass in the bay. She was in turmoil, for she had been forced to face many unpalatable truths. Now she wondered if her family would ever recover from the lies and deceit that had plagued it and brought it almost to the point of no return.

With a trembling sigh she remembered how Ernest had demanded to be told every detail of the court case that had led to Millicent's suicide. Ezra already knew, she had told him as soon as they had been alone that awful night – but as she had dredged up every ounce of courage to explain to her son about the *billet-doux* she had sent Jonathan all those years ago, she had seen again the hurt in Ezra's eyes.

She had loathed what she was doing, but the subject was unavoidable: that note to her lover had been the turning-point in the trial, and would doubtless fan the gossip. It was better that he should hear it from her, even if such a revelation destroyed the remnants of her family unity. The contempt in

Ernest's eyes had been bitter punishment, and she knew he would find it hard to forgive her.

Now she had no more tears. Her husband was as drained and dispirited as she, and her son avoided her. The battle to rescue her family and bring them together again would be long and hard – she had no illusions about that – but battle she would, for although they did not know it, they needed her now more than ever.

She stared, dry-eyed, at the far bank as her fingers sought and found the piece of paper in her apron pocket. Millicent's final letter had added to her burden and threatened to shatter her resolve. The girl had proved far from the innocent victim Ernest believed in, and she would never destroy that illusion. She thanked God that she had found the missive, for she could only imagine the harm it would have done if Ezra or Ernest had got hold of it.

She pulled it from the pocket. She would read it one last time, then commit it to the fire where it belonged. The scrawl was hard to decipher, the grammar questionable, but the message was clear and could still make her feel sick with bitterness. Susan's hand shook as she smoothed the creases. After a swift glance to make sure no one was watching, she began to read.

Can I still call you friend, Susan?

Or did you take me in out of some kind of warped sense of responsibility once you realised who I was? Florence told me about your affair with his lordship. I didn't want to believe you could betray Ezra, but it explains why Florence is so bitter, and why you took me in.

But I have a confession. I have lied not only to you but to others.

Me and John Pardoe were lovers. We found his lordship, dead drunk, sprawled under a tree, and John carried him back to the house. When I found out I was with child, John

*Pardoe refused to stand by me. He left shortly after for a
position on an estate in Devon. I knew I would be dismissed
once my condition was discovered, and that my stepmother
would never take me in. I did a terrible thing, Susan. I
accused his lordship, gambling he would have no memory of
the night we found him. I had little understanding of his
sense of honour and I'm not proud of what I did. But I had
to have money to see me through. His lordship gave me the
two guineas out of kindness and I cannot understand why he
said in court that I stole it. I don't want to believe Florence's
story about you and him, because she's one for twisting the
truth. But I fear this time she is not. I wish you could have
been honest with me, Susan, for I found great comfort and
happiness with you and Ezra. You gave me a home, with
love and warmth, and I thank you.*

Please forgive me for the lies I have told as I forgive you.

*I will be gone by the time you read this. Tell Ernest I love
him, and that I'm sorry, but I can't face this world any longer.*

Millicent

Despite the warmth of the day Susan shivered. She began to
shred the letter. The web of lies had ensnared them all, and
flawed her judgement. She took a deep, trembling breath as
she crushed the paper in her fist. Florence was far away, in the
north with a group of missionaries. How she wished she could
talk to her – to explain and try to heal the breach between
them. How she wished she could tell Jonathan she was sorry
she had doubted his honour – she had believed Florence's
gossip and Millicent's lies and condemned him out of hand.

She shielded her eyes from the glare of the water, determined not to cry. Nothing could excuse his blackening of her
name, his deliberate destruction of the love they had shared
and the consequences of his actions for her husband and sons.
She could never forgive him that.

The sadness weighed on her spirits. Millicent's single lie had brought her to Australia and into their lives. 'Secrets and lies,' she muttered. 'How tightly they bind – how insidious their evil.'

In the following days she moved about the house, performing her tasks as if she were sleep-walking. The house was so silent, so filled with sadness and memories that it was almost unbearable. There had been no visitors, not even Reverend Johnson, and none of them had ventured far from the house although the gossip must have died down by now. At the end of yet another long day she knew it could not go on.

Ernest was outside chopping wood with a furious energy that did little to quell the anger that still burnt so fiercely within him. Ezra was on the veranda, the Bible on his lap, his vacant gaze reaching beyond the garden to who knew where?

'We cannot go on like this,' she said, as she emerged from the house and closed the screen door behind her. 'It is time to take stock and make changes.'

Ernest rammed the axe-head deep into a log and wiped the sweat from his face with his shirt-sleeve. 'There's been change enough,' he muttered, his gaze sliding away from her as usual.

Susan looked to her husband for support, but he was lost in his own world. 'Ernest, you have a farm to rebuild, and you owe it not only to your brother but to yourself to get on with it.'

Ernest took a long drink of water and wrestled the axe from the log. 'George can manage without me.'

Susan's patience snapped. 'He cannot.' She stepped down from the veranda and stood in front of her son, heedless of the flying chips of wood and the dangerous blade. 'You're not the only one grieving, Ernest, and it's time you realised how deeply this has affected your father.'

Ernest glanced at Ezra and carried on chopping wood. 'It's rather late for you to consider him in all this,' he snarled.

'Your father forgave me a long time ago, Ernest,' she told him, 'and I will not let you take out your anger on me. He needs us both. Fighting among ourselves helps no one.'

His shoulders slumped and his chin dropped to his chest. Then he plunged the axe into the log and straightened. 'I know,' he said. 'But what can I do?'

Susan wondered how loving someone could hurt so much. It was an ache that never left her, but a burden she would gladly carry if by doing so she could alleviate his suffering. 'He needs to leave here,' she said quietly. 'We all do.'

Ernest raised his head, eyes bright with unshed tears. 'But where could we go?'

'To Hawks Head Farm,' she said.

'There's nothing there.'

'There's nothing here, either.'

The silence stretched as Ernest gazed at her. 'Father's too old to start again, and it's rough country out there, not fit for a woman.'

'I've survived this place,' she replied. 'We had nothing in those first years but a tent and straw pallets. It did me no harm.' She saw the flicker of understanding in his eyes, took a step towards him and rested her hand on his muscular arm. 'Your father's finished here,' she said quietly. 'The Church no longer provides the solace he needs and neither does prayer. His faith in God has been shattered, Ernest, and he's lost in a wilderness I cannot enter.' She glanced over her shoulder at her silent, blank-eyed husband. 'I fear for his sanity, Ernest. I must get him away.'

'But Hawks Head Farm is no place for you both,' he protested. 'The blacks are likely to strike again, and there's nothing left after the fire. Not even a house.'

'You know as well as I that the government stores will provide what we need,' she said fiercely. 'Why are you so reluctant to return?'

His eyes said it all.

'We must learn to take each day at a time,' she said softly. Her heart was heavy as she looked into her son's face. 'The plans you had made must be forgotten, but that doesn't mean Millicent won't remain alive in your memory.' She swallowed the lump in her throat, determined to instil hope in her boy, even though her words brought her bitterness. 'She will always be with us in spirit,' she managed.

'But . . .'

'No excuses,' she said briskly, to hide the wave of emotion that threatened to overcome her. 'We will go to the government stores today and arrange to collect everything we will need for the next six months. You had better make a list.'

She turned from him and went to Ezra. He hadn't moved from his chair, and was still staring into space. She kissed his lined forehead and stroked back the thinning grey hair. 'I'll look after you,' she murmured.

His dark eyes remained focused on some distant point and she had no idea whether or not he was aware of her presence. With a sigh she went into the house. There was much to do if they were to leave soon and there was nothing like hard work to stop her thinking.

Over the next two weeks there was a subtle change in Ernest. His step seemed lighter, and his eyes less dull as he ordered supplies, new stock and seed. If only she could have said the same for Ezra, Susan thought sadly, as she took a moment to catch her breath. He remained a silent, lonely figure in the veranda chair, lost in thought, heedless of the bustle around him. She could only pray that leaving for Hawks Head Farm would give him the chance to recover, to see life differently and rediscover the faith that was so vital to him.

'Mother!'

Susan spun round and, for the first time in months, her face split into a joyous smile as she saw the handsome young man jump down from his prancing horse. 'George!' She hurried down the steps to be gathered into his sturdy arms and swung off her feet until she was breathless with laughter. George had not shed his youthful enthusiasm even though he was almost nineteen. 'Put me down,' she gasped. 'It isn't seemly to treat your mother so.'

George set her on her feet but kept hold of her hands. 'How is everyone?' he asked, with unaccustomed solemnity.

She gave him a brief account, then hugged him close. How tall he had grown, she thought, how sturdy and strong after his years on the farm. And how handsome, with that rich brown hair, the moustache and his laughing eyes. No wonder he was the toast of Sydney Town's female population when he came in from the bush. 'It's so good to see you,' she said. 'Your father will be delighted.'

'Where's Ernie?'

'Gone into town for the last of the supplies.' Susan smiled up at him. 'We're all coming out to Hawks Head,' she explained. 'It will be a fresh start, and your brother is looking forward to the challenge.'

George smoothed his moustache and grinned. 'We've been working like dogs for the past three months,' he said, 'and the house is almost finished. It's about time we had some decent cooking – I'm fading away!'

She laughed as she noted the broad chest and shoulders.

George laughed too, then came to the reason for his visit. 'I've some news that might cheer Father,' he said, as he reached into an inside pocket of his coat. 'The Reverend Johnson asked me to give him this.'

Susan read the note. It was an invitation to go to the Johnsons' house to meet Governor Grose and discuss founding a mission on the Hawkesbury river. Richard Johnson must have second sight, she thought. How could he have known they were planning to move there?

She glanced at her husband, who seemed unaware of what

was happening around him. This might be the answer, the chance to begin again with a new challenge. But would he take it? 'You can see how he is,' she said to George, her spirits tumbling. 'I don't know if he has the energy, or even the belief any more, for such a thing.'

George kissed her cheek. 'Never fear, Mother,' he said. 'I'll soon have him champing at the bit.'

Susan watched him stride across the lawn with the rolling gait of a man who spent much time on horseback, and couldn't help but compare father and son as they sat together. George was tall like his father, but there the likeness ended, for where Ezra was gaunt and defeated, George glowed with energy, and a lust for life that radiated into her own soul.

How good it was to have him here, she thought, with a smile. His presence had given her heart, and would no doubt stir his father to life. The atmosphere had already lightened and at last she could look forward to the future.

Lowitja had become a regular visitor to Susan's house, bringing her youngest children with her grandchildren to play on the grass and eat the delicious food that was always offered. She knew they were safe with this white woman, and although she still found it difficult to communicate with her, she had learnt enough of her strange tongue to get by.

She stood now, alone in the shadow of the trees, watching the activity in the yard. She recognised the signs and knew that Susan and her family would soon be leaving. Lowitja watched as her friend bustled in and out of the house, and was glad she had found her spirit again, for she had seen the sadness that had weighed heavily and made her steps slow after the girl had swung from the tree.

Lowitja squatted in the cool shade, remembering the night many moons ago when she had come this way as she had returned from hunting. She had heard footsteps and the swish of grass as someone moved through the darkness – and had frozen in fear. When she saw who was walking through the grass as the Moon Goddess rode towards the west wind, she had crept into the deeper shadows to watch, curious as to what the white girl was doing.

Lowitja remembered hearing the thick vine creak against the branch, and the strange silence as it tightened round the pale throat. She had waited to see what manner of strange game this was before she emerged slowly from the shadows. As she had stood before the lifeless figure, she tried to make sense of it for it was beyond her understanding. She had turned and hurried back to the camp, troubled.

Now she turned back to the activity in the yard, and watched as Susan waved to her husband and sons and watched them walk down the hill towards the town. She waited until they were out of sight, then left her hiding-place: she was still in awe of the white men, even though they had done her no harm.

'Susan,' she said softly, as she approached.

Susan's face was alight with welcome.

'Susan alonga men,' she began. 'Susan alonga away.'

Susan nodded. 'Yes,' she replied. 'We are leaving for the Hawkesbury tomorrow. Ezra has agreed to found a mission on the river, and we will live with our sons on their farm.'

Lowitja understood little of this, only that she had been right about their imminent departure, but she, too, had news – it was the reason for her being there. 'Lowitja alonga Meeaan-jin.' She pointed north. 'Alonga me Meeaan-jin,' she said again, for emphasis. 'No white man alonga Meeaan-jin – good for Lowitja peoples.'

Susan frowned as her tongue stumbled on the strange word. 'Meeaan-jin? I've never heard of such a place. Where is it?'

Lowitja again pointed north, her skinny finger prodding the air as she tried to make herself understood. 'Turrbal people. Meeaan-jin. Big rivvu. Plenty good hunting.'

'You must mean Brisbane,' Susan muttered.

Lowitja stamped her foot, not realising Brisbane was the white man's name for Meeaan-jin. 'Meeaan-jin,' she shouted.

Susan grinned. 'It doesn't matter,' she said. 'We're both leaving here and will probably never meet again. But it will be safer for you and your family away from this place, and I'm glad for that.'

She took Lowitja's hand. 'I will miss you and your children. Go safely, Lowitja.'

Lowitja understood the sentiment even if she didn't understand the words. She grasped the white woman's hand and smiled. 'Go in the protection of the Ancient Spirits.' The time-honoured blessing was given in her own tongue, but she had little doubt that Susan would understand.

They stood in silence for a moment, then Lowitja stepped away and, without a backward glance, headed for the bush encampment. The tribe would leave tomorrow at first light, and there was much to do. The Ancient Spirits had to be appeased, and Garnday blessed for her great wisdom in such troubled times, for it was she who had come to Lowitja in a dream, and told her they must leave their sacred Dreaming Place, and go to the lands of the Turrbal, and the Honey-bee Dreaming.

Tahiti, August 1793

Tahamma stared at his wife, then down at the dagger she had given him. He had been away from the island for five months, and although the pearl diving had been successful, he was glad to be home. Her welcoming gift was pretty, but the blade was tarnished and the coloured glass was already coming loose from the handle. 'What did you barter for it?' he asked.

Solanni's happy expression clouded. 'You don't like it?'

Tahamma replaced the knife into the sheaf and felt its lack of weight. 'It will fall apart if I use it to gut fish or prise open the oysters,' he replied. His gaze was steady on her face, and he saw that she would not look him in the eye – which worried him. 'How did you come by it?'

'I had it from one of the beach traders,' she muttered. She picked up their youngest child and fussed with his hair.

Tahamma eyed her, the dark suspicion growing stronger. In two strides he was across the hut and digging in the sand. The tin box was still there and he felt a momentary easing of anxiety. But when he opened it, it was empty. He turned back to Solanni. 'Where is the watch?' His voice was dangerously calm.

Solanni licked her lips. 'I – I . . .' She fell silent.

He grasped her chin and forced her to look at him. 'You exchanged it for the knife.' The words were clipped, the anger tightly reined.

She nodded, as a tear trickled down her cheek. 'But the knife is useful,' she blurted out. 'That old thing was always in the box, and you never did anything with it. I didn't think you would care.'

'Of course I do!' he yelled. He threw the empty box into the corner of the hut. 'It was not yours to give away.' He suddenly realised he had frightened his children and made them cry with his ranting, and tempered his tone. 'My mother's dying wish was for me to keep it,' he said, his voice low and angry. 'My aunt was killed for it – and you give it away for a useless piece of tin.'

Solanni looked up at him dumbly, tears rolling down her face.

'That watch was all I had to remind me of my dead mother and the man who fathered me. My aunt took a sacred oath to protect it for me and I promised the sacred spirit of my mother to keep it for our children, and their children, and future generations of our blood.'

'I'm sorry, Tahamma,' she sobbed. 'I didn't understand.'

He looked at her with disgust. 'I explained before our

marriage, but you didn't care enough for my family tradition to listen.' He tossed the dagger into the sand. 'You will leave our hut,' he said coldly.

'But where will I go?' There was panic in her eyes as she reached out him. 'Please, husband, don't banish me.'

Tahamma stood tall and straight, unmoved by her pleading. 'You have your sisters and your parents. They will take you in,' he said. 'I will tell you when I have forgiven you.'

He made no move to help her as she gathered up her few belongings and led the children out into the sunlight. It would take him a long time to forgive her, and even then he would not forget how she had betrayed everything he held sacred. The loss of his one link to his dead mother and the breaking of his holy oath had left him almost numb with pain.

Sydney Cove, August 1793

Susan watched Lowitja disappear into the bush, and returned with a sigh to the house for a shawl. Ezra and the boys had gone into town for their final meeting with Richard Johnson, and for the first time in months she was alone. The cool of the dwindling day was welcome after the stifling heat, and the lure of the shore was too great to ignore. She would walk for a while, gather her thoughts and say goodbye to the place that had brought her both solace and sadness.

The beach was deserted, the sand unmarked by footprints, and as Susan stood on the grassy dune, she understood with startling clarity what the white man had done to Lowitja and her people. This ancient place had been untouched and unspoilt since time began – until the First Fleet had arrived. Now the silence was shattered not by birdsong and tribal chants but by the ringing of axes and hammers, the crack of the lash and gunshots. Death and destruction had come to this southern paradise. No wonder Lowitja was leaving.

It was with trepidation that she stepped on to the sand, and as she made her way along the beach, she looked behind her. Her footprints marked her passage, but they would be washed away by the tide, and soon there would be no sign that she had come this way. The thought pleased her. She lifted the hem of her dress and walked faster, revelling in the breeze coming off the water, and the freedom to be alone but not lonely.

She breathed in the clean, salty air as she watched a flock of brightly coloured parrots screeching and squabbling in the yellow wattle trees that drooped over the shore. She smiled at their antics, then clapped her hands and laughed as they rose in a thunder of beating wings and flew away. Now she could hear the soft warble of the magpies and what Lowitja called the *kurrawongs*, their music far sweeter than the songbirds she had heard in Cornwall.

She continued her walk, her thoughts turning over the events of the past months as the heady scents of wattle and eucalyptus filled her senses. The light had returned to Ezra's eyes now that he was reassured his God had not deserted him but needed him to run His mission. She had the Reverend Johnson to thank for that – and George, for he had cajoled his father from his stupor and made him see how much they loved and needed him.

Susan smiled as she thought of his new enthusiasm for the future. It would be lonely out on the Hawkesbury river with no other women to talk to, but the company of Ezra and her sons would more than compensate for that.

She sighed as she thought of Florence. There had been no word from her since she had left for the northern mission. She could only hope the girl would one day return to her family so that the healing process could begin, and a new understanding be forged.

She dabbed her forehead with a handkerchief. Despite the breeze, her pace had made her hot. At forty-one she had no business to walk at such speed, let alone on a deserted beach – but old habits died hard, and she wouldn't have thought twice about it if she had been in Cornwall. She grimaced. She was getting too old for the upheaval and change ahead. Life had never promised to be so hard – not even when she had been working on the quay at Mousehole – and the struggle to survive here had taken its toll. She was tired beyond exhaustion and the thought of beginning again made her want to weep.

She was about to turn for home when she saw him. He was standing on the dune watching her, and as their eyes met, he left his horse and came, uncertainly, towards her.

She froze, heart pounding, heat rising in her face as she waited.

'Susan?'

She hit him. A stinging blow to his cheek that left the marks of her fingers on his flesh.

Jonathan's eyes darkened, but he didn't flinch.

Susan hit him again. 'Damn you, Jonathan! Damn you for blackening me in court. For lying, cheating and laying bare our most intimate secrets.' She was crying now, the sobs racking her body as she pummelled his chest. 'You destroyed everything.'

He stood before her as if hewn from stone.

'I'll never forgive you for what you've done,' she sobbed. 'Never.'

When her rage was spent he took her fists and held them still. 'I deserve any punishment you mete out,' he said softly, 'but don't deny me your forgiveness, Susan. I couldn't live without it.'

'Then why did you do such a thing?' She raised her chin and looked into his face. 'I had to explain to Ezra and my sons about the letter. Do you know what harm that did?'

'I can imagine.'

She pulled away from him. 'You couldn't begin to imagine

anything,' she snapped. 'And if you truly regretted your actions, why did you not come to apologise and explain?'

'I tried,' he said, 'but you were never alone until now. I knew how hurt you must be, and believe me, Susan, I share your pain.'

She looked into his eyes and saw the hurt. She chose to ignore it. 'Words are cheap. You could have written.'

'You're right,' he said. 'But a letter is impersonal. I needed to speak to you, to look into your eyes and tell you how much I regret hurting you.' He stood before her, a silhouette against a pink-streaked sky. 'Please forgive me, my love.'

The rage died as swiftly as it had come, and as she looked into his face and tried to speak, she found she could no longer find words to express her confusion. There were wings of grey in his dark hair, and lines on his face, but they only enhanced his handsomeness. The longing in his face was tearing her apart, yet she had vowed never to trust him again, never to be swayed by the love she still felt for him.

Jonathan seemed to understand, for after a brief hesitation, he captured her hands again and held them to his chest – but tenderly now, as if they were the most precious, fragile burdens to be cherished. 'I have loved you for as long as I can remember,' he began. 'I have carried the memory of you all over the world, and it has brought solace and peace to me in the darkest hours. I bitterly regret the hurt I've caused. Please say you'll forgive me.'

His entreaty reached into her soul and she knew she was lost. 'Of course I do,' she breathed. 'Oh, Jonathan, my dearest love, how did we come to this?'

'I don't know, my sweet, but it seems Fate is determined to keep us apart.'

Susan drew back from him, her sadness making it difficult to speak. 'You are not the only one who should beg forgiveness,' she began. She saw him frown and rushed on to tell him about Millicent's letter. 'I misjudged you,' she finished. 'I should have known better than to believe the gossip.'

He still held her hands as he gazed into her eyes. 'Your perceived sin is so much less than mine that there's nothing to forgive.'

'I should never have doubted you.'

He shook his head. 'I realised you would have heard the rumours, and although it hurt not to hear from you again, I understood why.' He drew her hands to his lips, his kiss as light as the touch of a butterfly wing. 'Oh, Susan, if only things could have been different. What fools we've been.'

'Foolish, maybe,' she murmured. 'But what joys we shared.'

'They will live with me always.'

They stood in silence, and as Susan looked into the eyes that still had the power to mesmerise, and at the mouth she longed to kiss just once more, she knew she had never stopped loving him – that a part of her would always be his.

'You are still beautiful,' he murmured, as he caressed her cheek and ran his hands over her hair. 'Your eyes remind me of the wild seas of Cornwall, and your hair still holds the gold of ripened wheat. How I wish we could have those days again.'

She blushed, which she hadn't done in years. 'This place ages women,' she said quietly, 'and I know there are lines on my face and silver in my hair.' She was drawn to him by the invisible ties that bound them, and realised that if she didn't pull away now she would be lost. 'It is late,' she said, and stepped back. 'I must go.'

'Not yet,' he urged. 'There are so many things I have to tell you, so much we both need to say before you leave.'

'You know about the Hawkesbury?'

'Sydney is a small town. News travels fast.'

Susan tried to smile, but her heart was heavy as she told him of their plans for the future.

'Why not return to Cornwall?'

She was startled by the question. 'It has never occurred to any of us,' she admitted. 'George and Ernest are settled here, and Florence needs to know she can reach us . . .'

Her words faded and coherent thought fled as he bent his head and kissed her. She leant into his embrace and kissed him back as the familiar hunger returned and the longing grew almost unbearable. The need to lie with him, to feel his hands and mouth on her skin – to know the bliss of loving and being loved was almost too much for her.

'No,' she gasped. 'No.' She pushed him away and stood trembling before him. 'We mustn't, Jonathan.'

His smile was sad. 'I know,' he murmured, 'but how could I resist when I still love you so?'

'We have to be strong,' she said, hands trembling as she smoothed the creases from her dress. 'Ezra has forgiven me, and although he doesn't know the full extent of my betrayal, I am determined to be a good wife to him.' She looked up at him. 'I have loved you for as long as I can remember, but my love for Ezra is founded on something far more solid – and after what happened in Cornwall, I will not betray him again.'

Jonathan frowned. 'Ezra knew of our love before the trial?'

Susan nodded and gave him a brief glimpse into her life since their affair. 'But he didn't know everything,' she said finally, her voice breaking. 'I couldn't tell him everything. It would have destroyed him – us – and everything I've worked so hard to achieve over these past years.'

His expression was concerned and questioning. 'What do you mean?' he asked quietly.

The tears were running down her cheeks as she looked up at him. She had to tell him – needed to tell him. The secret she'd kept for so long must be revealed to the only person she could trust not to betray her. 'There was a baby,' she whispered. 'Our baby.'

'Our baby?' His face was drained of colour. 'You had our baby?'

She nodded, unable to speak, blinded by tears.

He gathered her into his arms and held her until the sobs petered out. 'Oh, my love,' he whispered, 'I never knew – never suspected . . .' He was silent for a long while. 'If only you had confided in me at the time . . . I could have . . . What happened to it?' he asked.

She buried her face in his coat, unwilling to witness his pain. 'She's gone, Jonathan, for ever.'

His arms tightened round her, his groan piercing her. 'Poor baby. Poor Susan,' he said. 'I can't bear to think of you going through such an ordeal alone.'

She was bereft of strength, washed out by the tears, the pain, the memories of those times. Eventually she pulled herself out of his embrace and took his handkerchief.

'I wasn't alone,' she said, as she dried the tears. 'My friend Ann cared for me. I went straight back to Ezra after . . . after . . .' She took a deep breath. 'I tried to carry on as if nothing had happened – but my arms were so empty.' Fresh tears assailed her and she was gathered up once more and held close.

'And you've kept this to yourself for years,' he murmured, as he caressed her hair. 'You're so brave, so much stronger than I. How can I ever make it up to you – to her?' His kisses feathered her brow as the sun sank behind the hills, and their tears mingled as they mourned their lost happiness and their lost child.

Time passed and the sun sank further towards the horizon. Eventually she withdrew from his embrace, blew her nose, dabbed her eyes and took a deep breath. 'I'm glad I've told you at last,' she said quietly, 'but the telling was as painful as keeping it to myself, and I'm sorry to cause you such hurt.'

He cleared his throat. 'You must tell me where she's buried,' he said, 'and I will make sure her grave is tended.'

She shook her head. 'Better to leave her to God,' she murmured, as she watched the sky flame with the dying sun.

'As you wish,' he replied sadly. 'She must know her parents loved her. Flowers comfort only the living.' He reached into his pocket and found his cigar case. With a cigar lit, he seemed to gather his strength and once more stood tall and straight. Only his eyes betrayed his pain.

'I, too, am leaving Sydney,' he said. 'I shall go north to the Endeavour river, to find Watpipa and his people.'

Susan took his lead. 'I hope you find them in better condition than the poor souls here,' she murmured. 'I envy your freedom to travel and explore this wild place.'

'Then come with me,' he said, as he threw away the half-smoked cigar and took her hands. 'It will be the adventure we talked about in Cornwall.' His face was alight with hope as he clasped her hands to his breast. 'Marry me, Susan. Leave Ezra and live with me as my wife until you are free to do so.'

'I wish I could come with you,' she sighed, 'and I wish so very much that we could finally be married, for I know we would have been happy together.' She tried to draw away from him, but his grip had tightened, making her a prisoner. 'But I'm not free,' she said. 'I will never be free. And I've hurt Ezra enough.'

'But I love you, Susan. I always have loved you.'

'I know,' she whispered, as she touched the beloved cheek and felt his kiss on her palm. 'And I have always loved you, too. But it's too late.'

She caressed his cheek, and ran her fingers over the tear-drop stain on his temple, so familiar and beloved. With a soft kiss she drew back from him for the last time. Tears blinded her as she began to run back down the beach.

'Goodbye, my love,' she whispered into the wind.

If you enjoyed Lands Beyond the Sea,
read on for the first chapter of the sequel,
A Kingdom for the Brave, *coming soon . . .*

TAMARA McKINLEY

A Kingdom for the Brave

PROLOGUE

Brisbane River, 1795

Dawn had yet to lighten the sky, but the group of eight horsemen was already on the move. Edward Cadwallader looked up. The moon remained behind the thick layer of cloud. It was a perfect night for killing.

They made little sound in the stillness of the outback scrub, for the horses' hoofs and jingling harness had been wrapped in hessian, and the men knew better than to talk or smoke. It was a familiar routine – but Edward felt the excitement he always experienced in these last few moments before an attack. It was sexual and empowering, and the images of what was to come enhanced his impatience to begin.

His gaze trawled his surroundings. The escarpment rose on either side, rearing up in jagged peaks from the scrublands. Dark boulders and stands of trees offered deeper shadows, and the horse beneath him twitched as something skittered through the undergrowth. Edward's hands were firm on the reins, but he, too, was tense, for their destination was close, and a single sound might give them away.

He glanced behind him at the men who followed him willingly on these night forays, and acknowledged his grizzled sergeant's grin with one of his own. He and Willy Baines had joined the New South Wales Corps at the same time, and had shared an army prison cell before that. The older man had stood with him in the dock during the rape trial, and had helped him celebrate their victory – they knew each other's thoughts and understood each other's blood-lust, and although the divide was great between them, Edward looked upon the other man as his closest friend.

He glanced briefly at the other six men before he turned to peer into the darkness ahead, his night-sight keen after two hours in the saddle. They were good men and could be trusted to keep their mouths shut when they returned to Sydney. Dispersals were not something to discuss in public, even though they were becoming ever more frequent, and it was common knowledge that the blacks were being forced off the much-needed land. The less the public knew about the military methods of clearing them out, the better – and, after all, who cared?

The Hawkesbury had already been cleansed, and although the renegade Pemuluwuy was still on the loose, Edward was convinced that it would be just a matter of weeks before he and his son were rounded up and shot. Now, Edward's task was to clear the last of the Turrbal from the Brisbane river.

These were exciting times, and Edward was at the heart of them. During his years of exile in the wilderness, he had learnt much, and had discovered how thrilling it was to hunt down the black men. His reputation and the high regard in which his men held him had filtered down to the authorities in Sydney Town. Despite his questionable record, he had been promoted to major, responsible for ridding this area of the black vermin with an assurance from the general that his banishment would be shortened by two years. Life was good, and he was looking forward to returning to Sydney so that he could begin to make his fortune and build a house that would be the envy of every man.

Thoughts of having a white woman once more heightened his excitement. The gins stank and often fought like cats – but he liked a challenge, and although he had found the black velvet exotic, he preferred the scent of white flesh.

He brought his thoughts back to the job in hand. There would be time enough to think about women after it was done. For now he would need all his wits if they were to avoid an ambush. The blacks might be ignorant savages, but this was their territory and they knew it far better than any soldier, no matter how well trained.

The patrol advanced silently through the scrub, alert for hidden warriors in the dark shadows. As the sky began to lighten to a storm-laden grey the tension mounted. This was the most dangerous part of their journey for they were within a mile of the camp.

Edward drew his horse to a halt and swung from the saddle. He waited for the others to join him. 'You know what to do?' His voice was barely a whisper.

They nodded. It had been planned in great detail several days before, and they knew they would have free rein with any women they captured.

'Prime your muskets,' ordered Edward, 'and remember, there are to be no survivors.'

'What about the piccaninnies and gins?'

Edward eyed the newest recruit – a thin, bright-eyed young trooper, with a dishonourable service record and a penchant for native women. His expression was grim, his eyes cold as he reinforced his authority. 'Gins breed, and piccaninnies grow up to breed. I don't care what you do, or how you do it, but I want nothing left alive after tonight,' he hissed. He glared at the trooper, gratified to see fear spark in his eyes.

The youth nodded, and his pale face flushed.

Edward turned back to Baines. 'We'll do a recce first,' he murmured, 'just to make sure they're still there.'

Baines scratched the stubble on his chin. None of the men had washed or shaved in four days: a native's nose could pick up the scent of soap and pomade a mile off. 'They should be,' he murmured. 'They've been coming here for centuries, according to my spies.'

Edward grinned. 'You and your spies, Willy. How do you persuade the myalls to tell you so much?'

Willy shook his head as they moved away from the others. 'They may look black to us, and I'm damned if I can tell one from another, but tribal differences linger, and for a flagon of rum or a bit of baccy, the right man will tell all he knows.'

Edward put his hand on the other man's shoulder. 'They're all a mystery to me, Willy, and the only good myall is a dead one. Come on. Let's go and see what we've got.' They left the others priming their muskets and made their way carefully through the last of the undergrowth to the water's edge. The river was shallow and meandering, the reeds and overhanging trees giving perfect cover on this moonless night. The two men lay on their bellies, their heads just above the long grass as they regarded the sleeping encampment.

The young single men, who made up most of the warriors, were sleeping in a rough, protective phalanx round the women, children and elderly. Most slept on the ground, but there were three or four gunyahs – grass and eucalypt shelters – in which the Elders rested. Dogs stirred and scratched, and wisps of smoke rose from cooled campfires as old men hawked phlegm and babies whimpered. Edward smiled as his blue eyes took in the sight before him. The Turrbal had no idea of what was to come.

Lowitja stirred from sleep and instinctively tightened her hold on her five-year-old grandson. Something had penetrated her dreams, and as she opened her eyes she heard the mournful cry of a curlew. It was the call of the Spirits, the sharp, haunting note of souls in torment, a warning of danger.

Mandawuy struggled in her tight embrace and would have cried out if she hadn't put her hand over his mouth. 'Quiet,' she ordered, with the soft firmness he had learnt to obey instantly. He sat, silent and unafraid, as his grandmother's amber eyes became unfocused and she stared beyond the encampment. What could she see? he wondered. Were there spirits in the clearing? Could she hear their voices – and if so, what were they telling her?

Lowitja listened to the cry of the curlews. There were many more now. It was as if the spirits of the dead were gathering, their voices coming together in a wail of distress that pierced her heart. Then, from out of the grey of a new dawn, she saw ghostly shapes twist among the trees. She knew who they were and why they had come.

Edward and Willy melted back into the deeper shadows and returned to the waiting men. They would have to hurry, for the camp was stirring. Edward could see that the hammers of the carbines were cocked, and the faces of his men were alert with anticipation. The fun was about to begin.

'Mount up,' he hissed, as he caught the reins of his horse and swung into the saddle. 'Walk.'

The line moved forward in practised precision until the men were almost in sight of the camp. Edward nudged his horse in front as they came once again to a halt. The excitement was almost tangible as he raised his sword and the first rays of the sun caught the blade in a blinding flash. He held it there, anticipating the moment, relishing the suspense.

'Charge!'

As one they kicked their mounts into a gallop. The animals strained their necks, nostrils distended, ears flat to their heads as the men who rode them whooped, yelled and urged them on to greater speed.

Lowitja was mesmerised by the appearance of the Spirit People. In all her thirty years she had never seen them so clearly, and at first she thought that the distant thunder was born of a sudden summer storm. She drew back from the visions, her hands automatically tightening on Mandawuy as she noticed how the dogs' hackles were rising, and the birds cried with sharp alarm as they flew in a storm of beating wings from the trees.

As the thunder grew the rest of the clan were shocked from sleep. Babies and small children cried as their mothers snatched them up. Warriors grabbed spears and clubs, and the elderly froze as the dogs began to bark with furious intent.

The thunder drew nearer until the air was full of it and the earth beneath her began to tremble. Lowitja's fear brought her to her feet. Now she understood why the Spirits had come to her, why they had warned her. She had to save Mandawuy. She forced every ounce of strength she possessed into her trembling legs and arms, grabbed her grandson and began to run.

Thorns snatched, branches whipped, roots threatened to trip her as she raced through the bush. The thunder of horses' hoofs and the shattering crack of gunfire ripped through the air behind her, but she didn't look back, didn't stop running.

Mandawuy made no sound as he clung to her, arms and legs twined round her neck and waist, his tears of terror hot on her skin as the screams, shouts and gunfire echoed in the clearing.

Lowitja's heart was pounding, her chest ached, her legs and arms grew leaden as she wove through the bush with her son's only living child to uncertain safety. But still she ran.

They crashed through the flimsy gunyahs and scattered the smouldering fires into a blizzard of scarlet embers. The first volley of lead shot had flung men, women and children into bloody heaps upon the ground where they were trampled by the charging horses. As screams rent the air, and the more agile began to run, the sport was on.

The dogs scattered as women clutched children and men scrabbled for their spears and *nullas*. The elderly tried to crawl away, or sat with their hands over their heads in a pathetic attempt to ward off the swords. Small children stood in frozen terror as the horses bore down to trample them into the dark red earth. Some of the younger, fitter men tried to defend their fleeing families, but they had no time to throw their spears or wield their *nullas* before they were hacked to pieces.

Edward's blood-lust was up as he wheeled his horse in a tight circle and fired his second shot into an old woman cowering by the remains of the fire. He reloaded swiftly as he watched her collapse into the flames. He would waste no more lead on her – she would be dead soon enough.

He loaded and reloaded until the barrel was too hot to touch. When he could fire no more, he used the carbine as a club, wielding it left and right to smash skulls and break necks, to stun and bring down those who couldn't run fast enough, and finish them off with his sword. His horse was lathered, its eyes rolling as gunyahs caught fire and smoke filled the clearing. The air was filled with the sweet stench of burning flesh and eucalyptus, the smoke thick and black, making eyes water and throats close.

Two of his men had dismounted and were chasing a couple of women who had fled into the trees. Willy was making short work of some children and the others were occupied with cutting down three warriors who had raised their spears in defiance.

Edward wheeled his horse in tight circles as he chased two youths and brought them down with a single slash of his sword. The blade was red with their blood, his uniform splattered, the flanks of his horse sticky. But he wasn't finished yet – his lust was not satisfied, and his eyes sought out another victim.

The girl was on the far edge of the clearing. She had almost reached the trees – but her progress was slow, for she had already felt the cut of a sabre. He could see the bloody gash on her shoulder, the black flesh gaping like an obscene pink mouth.

He kicked the horse into a gallop and raised his sword. 'She's mine, Willy,' he yelled, as his friend had also spied her.

She glanced over her shoulder, eyes wide with terror.

Edward raced past her and blocked her escape.

The girl froze.

Edward beheaded her with one blow and, without a second thought, raced back to the clearing to see what the others had left for him.

Lowitja remained hidden in the sheltering branches of the tree, high above the forest floor. She clung to Mandawuy and kept him quiet by suckling him as the carnage raged in the distance. She trembled as she heard running feet below her, the crack of guns, the terrible screams of the dying – and shed silent tears as she smelt burning flesh. She could only imagine the horror of what was happening to her people – could only pray to the Great Spirit that some would survive this day.

Yet the silence when it came was even more terrifying. It weighed heavily on the air, laden with a darkness that, to Lowitja, seemed endless. She waited through the night, her body trembling with the effort of keeping Mandawuy in her arms and her perch secure on the high branch. She dared not fall asleep.

The sun was a thin pale line on the horizon when she clambered down from the tree with the precious child on her back. With his little hand clasped in her own, she was poised for flight as she headed cautiously back to the clearing. She feared what she would see, dreaded the knowledge she would have to face. Yet the Ancestor Spirits were calling to her, leading her to the killing fields so that she could witness what the white man had done and pass on that knowledge.

She stood on the edge of the clearing, not yet brave enough to enter this place of death. The camp was silent and still – and in that silence she could hear the whispers of long-dead warriors who had come to fetch the people of the Eora and Turrbal and take them to the Spirit World. Wreaths of smoke drifted upward in the windless dawn and hung in shifting, ghostlike trails over the scattered cooking pots, mangled bodies and broken spears.

Lowitja stood with her grandson and shivered. No one had been spared – not even the smallest child. She could hear the hum of flies, and see the dark clouds hovering above the shattered bodies that lay trampled into the ground. They already bore the marks of the scavenger crows, and the dingoes that had come in the night to fight over the fresh carrion. Soon the goanna would come, with its sharp teeth and claws, to finish off the rotting flesh, and the insects and grubs would make short work of the rest.

Lowitja regarded the killing place and knew her people were gone. The prophecy of the Spirit Dreams and the throwing stones had been fulfilled. She would never return to this place, but would move further west towards Uluru. It was a long, dangerous journey for a lone woman – but Uluru was her spiritual home, and she would rather die trying to get there than remain here among the white savages.

She picked up her grandson and kissed him. He was the last of the full-blood Eora – the final link between her, Anabarru and the great ancestor Garnday. He must be guarded well.

17|8|07 لا ١-3-14